THE IMMORTALITY TRIALS

Madison Nicole

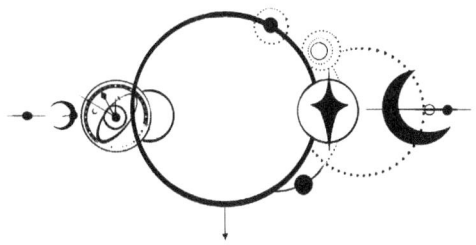

For my sister,
who was the first to call me a writer

&

For those who are afraid of the darkness that prowls within,
I see you.
I hear you.
I am you.

If you are interested in listening along to the playlist I used while writing this book feel free to find it here:

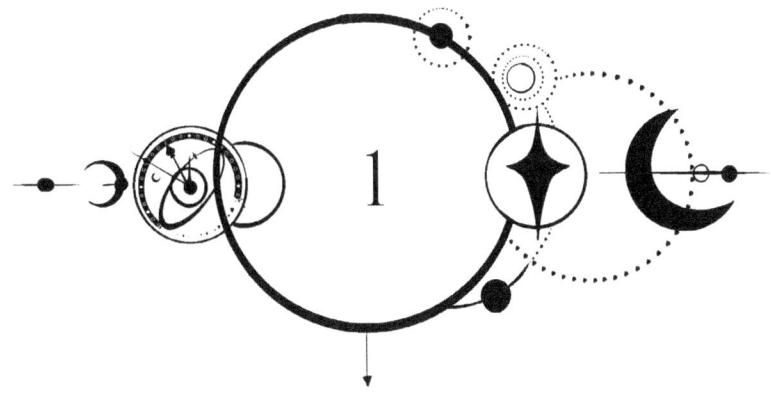

Greer

A nother round of tequila shots, sweetheart," the man slurred.

He wasn't the first man who'd thrown out pet names while I worked my tables, and he certainly wouldn't be the last.

His half-lidded eyes raked over my body from where he was sprawled across in the corner like he owned the place. The man looked human, but that didn't mean anything. Looks could be deceiving and, human or not, this large man with pale skin, a receding hairline, and an asymmetrical handlebar mustache ate me up with his eyes. It made me want to claw them out with my long black fingernails until my hands were bloody.

He was already drunk, along with the rest of his companions. All of them were impeccably dressed in dark, expensive suits and they were throwing money around, clearly celebrating something.

"Top shelf only," another one of them bellowed.

"Absolutely, coming right up," I said with a flash of teeth through my dark red lipstick and a swish of my long wine-colored ponytail.

More alcohol means more money.
More alcohol.
More money.
I silently chanted in my head.
Ugh.

I ran over to the sleek black countertop where my bartender, Arlo, was already lining up the limes and clear liquid. He was a dragalúme, which meant his senses were heightened and he moved with precision and grace. Not to mention, his skin was covered in iridescent scales that reflected the candles and smoky lights of the lounge.

His snow-white hair was pulled back in a low bun, so his high cheekbones and dusty white eyelashes were on full display. He wore black head to toe, with a dress shirt buttoned all the way to his throat and a pair of slacks that hit right at the ankle. The whole staff was required to wear all black at The Shadow Lounge—part of the allure, I supposed.

It was once said the dragalúme could reflect light in a way that made them nearly invisible. Light benders, according to the old texts. And apparently, they were skilled in espionage as well. At one point, they were coveted operatives by the old kingdoms and their skills deeply sought after, but that was long ago.

When I had asked Arlo if he could bend light after our shift one day—with a few shots making my head fuzzy and my speech bold—he snickered and said it was only rumor. He claimed that the only thing his kind did now with their "abilities" was eavesdrop on other people's business and work more efficiently than others while looking beautiful. I knew we would be good friends after that.

Arlo gave me an apologetic smile through pale lips as he glanced over at the table of rowdy men. There were eight males in total filling up the deep green velvet couches in the corner. It was a slow night since it was a Thursday, and they were by far the loudest and rudest ones here.

A few pairs of people were milling around, but everyone else was engaging in quiet conversations on their dark velvet chairs or snuggled into alcoves, sipping leisurely on their drinks. These men had come to get plastered, and honestly, who the hell gets this hammered on a Thursday?

Usually on Thursdays I got let go early, but not tonight. Tonight, I would be here until the very last one of them had left, and by the looks of it, it didn't seem like they would be going anywhere any time soon.

I quickly collected the shots through a few pouty sighs.

"Greer… play nice," Arlo teased as he deftly filled other glasses with amber colored liquid, his bone white fingers were covered in gems that created a kaleidoscope of colors on the bar top as he worked.

Arlo knew I could take care of myself, but I'd come in with an attitude at the start of my shift and I was having a hard time snuffing it out. Attitudes didn't equal tips … and I wanted the tips. Especially from these annoying males.

"I'm always nice," I replied with a wicked grin and a wink.

I was fine to deal with annoying and disgusting males. Most of the time. But tonight, I just wanted to go home. I wanted to sleep. And I really wanted them to leave and never hear the term sweetheart *ever* again.

I easily navigated through the dimly lit lounge and black glass tables. The lounge was supposed to feel dark, moody, and sensual with the mix of candles, sparkling black crystal chandeliers, and expensive cocktails. This evening, I was fitting right in with the dark and moody part.

My thigh-high black velvet boots clacked along the black marble floor as I made my way over to the table of boisterous males.

"Eight tequila shots, top shelf…" I said through a smile, trying not to look like I was grimacing. One of the men, who looked to be about mid-twenties, wrapped his slightly green fingers around my wrist as I was setting down the liquor.

Ew.

"You should take a shot with us." He smirked, showing off his rows of pointed teeth. His hair was as black as his eyes and his dark navy suit almost looked like it had been painted on by how tight it wrapped around his body.

I always showed up to my shifts in a black long sleeve for this precise reason. Males liked to get handsy.

Tonight, I had chosen a leather bodysuit that circled my throat, with mesh paneling running along my ribs to my hips, fishnets, and black satin shorts. My usual array of constellation piercings studded my ears, and glittering rings accompanied my pale hands—a girl needed a little sparkle to add to the drama.

The sleeves of my bodysuit connected to my middle finger for the exact reason that I could not tolerate drunken males touching my bare skin with their greedy fingertips and hungry eyes.

Truly disgusting.

It was something that the other servers had warned me about early on and I experienced relatively regularly, especially since I was human. I might as well have been wearing a glaring red sign on my forehead that said, "Please try to take advantage of me because I am weak and vulnerable." Except I wasn't. I could damn well hold my own, even if society liked to pretend otherwise.

And why any male was inclined to touch *anyone* without their consent was beyond me … It took everything in me not to spit in his face with the darkness surrounding my mood tonight. I was practically looking for a fight at this point, but I tried to rein it in.

Rage pulsed through my veins while I grabbed the man's fingers and pried them away from my arm.

"Unfortunately, I can't drink on the job, boys," I said with a wink and a swish of my hips as I easily maneuvered out of his reach. The other men snickered, and the male hungrily followed me with his dark eyes.

"Maybe another time then, *human*," he said, his tongue flickering over his lips.

Go fuck yourself.

"If you're lucky," I called over my shoulder while flipping my hair. More snickering and laughter followed.

The males stayed for three more hours, finally stumbling out around 1:00 a.m., being the last ones to go home. There was a constant stream of shots, cocktails, and bottles of champagne throughout the evening.

But at least they had tipped generously.

I don't know what you all were celebrating, but I am glad to take your money.

Arlo and I were the last ones here as I counted the bills and rounded up the last pieces of glassware.

"Arlo, go home. I'll finish cleaning and lock up," I said.

Arlo raised one of his snow-white eyebrows and pursed his lips. "You sure?" he asked, tipping his head slightly, the small chain on his earring brushing his sharp cheekbone.

"Yeah, go home to your husband … I'll see you tomorrow," I said with a genuine smile for a genuine friend.

I didn't know how old Arlo was. Could be thirty or 300. All specialized species lived far past the average age of a human and had the aging process to match.

"And this is why you're my favorite, dear," Arlo said, quickly finishing up the glassware and kissing me on the cheek light as a feather. "Be careful going home. Can you please text me when you make it?" he said, stopping at the heavy black metal door.

"Of course," I said, turning my back to him and wiping down the tables. I heard the metal door groan as Arlo cheerily said good-night, and then it slammed shut.

I sat down on one of the plush velvet loungers and unzipped my boots and wiggled my toes. I closed my eyes and fell back on the soft cushions for a moment to relax. My feet ached and my eyes felt heavy.

Maybe I would ask Leah to cover my shift tomorrow. I had made plenty tonight, and I was exhausted. I could curl up with a bottle of wine and see if Lux wanted to watch some terrible Netflix rom com.

Maybe a night off would help my sour mood.

It wasn't anything in particular that was weighing heavy on me … just the fact that I was twenty-four and felt like I didn't know what the hell I was doing with my life. But, you know, it was a casual identity crisis. Not a full-blown anxiety attack … yet.

I sighed and wondered if other people felt like this. Like life was simply passing them by and they were a bystander, not an active participant. I shook off the dramatics and told myself that I didn't need to have it all figured out. It was fine. *I* was fine.

"Are you seriously sleeping?" a deep voice sounded from the direction of the doorway.

"I'm taking a second to breathe because I had to deal with eight testosterone-charged hooligans for over four hours this evening … and I'm exhausted from my internal pity party," I said, not bothering to open my eyes. I knew that voice like I knew my own. It was my best friend Luxton, but to me he was Lux.

He was fairly familiar with my pity parties. They had been happening quite frequently lately. Lux always listened and offered support; it was one of the many things that I absolutely adored about him. He didn't shove answers down my throat, just a steady presence of love and empathy.

I felt a shift in the lounger as he sat right next to my head. The heavy weight of him caused my head to dip. I squinted up at him.

"You didn't have to wait for me," I said.

I knew I should have texted him earlier, but those males had kept me busy most of the night. Usually, we walked home together when I worked late. It wasn't that I couldn't handle myself; it was just you didn't know what sort of things might be lurking in the shadows and Lux worried after my pretty human head.

The Shadow Lounge was on the upper west side of Odessa, the Republic's capital city. Which was normally pretty safe, considering this was where a lot of the money was in the city. The higher up you were in the city, the more money swirled and danced around the streets. The upper west side was home to many bars, clubs, restaurants, trendy Instagram spots, and all kinds of expensive entertainment.

We lived right on the outskirts of the upper west side, so ideally it should be fine. Except sometimes I took shortcuts through alleys, snaking through the city to get home faster, which really didn't guarantee safety the way the well-lit streets of the city did. And *one time* I had had a run in and some male pulled a knife out on me.

I kept a switchblade on me at all times, because where I grew up you weren't caught empty-handed. But he'd landed a deep gash on my forearm and Lux had freaked out. In all fairness, as soon as that motherfucker had seen me charge him with my own weapon, he scampered away—but not before I nailed him with a slash on his chest.

But I was a human woman, a relatively easy target by society's standards, so it wasn't like Lux's worries were unfounded. *It just is what it is.*

Either way, I could take care of myself, but it was nice for him to worry. To care.

And of course he cared—Lux and I were roommates and best friends. The luxurious penthouse apartment we shared was courtesy of his dead parents, who, if you asked him, he had mixed emotions about them being gone. It may seem weird, but they weren't close, in fact, they had very different ideologies, the main one being that Lux's focus should have been on continuing their magic line with another shifter.

They had many heated arguments about Lux's pansexuality and his choice to not have children, and when they had died in a helicopter accident a few years ago, their entire multibillion-dollar tech company went to their son. They had wanted to keep their magic bloodline perfect for their shifter magic, and having a son who didn't care about any of that at all, was really just not in their plan for their shifter legacy.

Lux had immediately hired someone to take over and moved to be a silent partner, but he still would never need to work a day in his life if he didn't want to. He mostly worked high-end consulting jobs nowadays and worked to give money back to those who had also suffered from toxic relationships and had their sexuality used against them.

Even though his parents treated him poorly, their deaths were still hard to deal with. He had bought a whole building where rent was basically non-existent for those who needed a safe place to stay, and then had sheepishly asked me to move in with him so he wouldn't be alone in the large penthouse that occupied the top floor by himself. Not only was this a truly spectacular deal for me, but I would do anything for him. We had met in college and immediately bonded over margaritas and tacos.

I had a flash of memory of the first time we went out together. He was wearing a shirt with *LQBTQIA+* written across it and I had a shirt with a pride flag. We both laughed and immediately bonded, since it was literally painted on our chests what we stood for. I smiled at the memory and how we had fallen into one of those soul-deep friendships that seem to only come around once in a lifetime. We had many memories around frozen margs and tequila shots.

He never seemed to bat an eye at the fact that I didn't have a lick of magic or that I would only live to be maybe a hundred. He once told me that society and their cultural standards could go fuck themselves and I think that was really when I knew that no matter what, we would be tied together forever.

When I first moved in, Lux told me I wouldn't need to get a job if I didn't want to, and I had scoffed at that. I loved living with Lux, but I sure as hell wasn't going to let him fund the rest of my life.

After graduating from college with a degree in engineering, I realized I didn't know what I was supposed to do with that. I had chosen engineering because I grew up poor. My mom told me it would be a way to save us if I could get a nice job, and at the time I believed her. Except there was no way for my job to save her anymore.

I winced, thinking about the places I had lived in growing up. We would go from crappy motels, to dirty apartments, "friends" couches, our car, to finally a steadier place in the RV park. My mom had been so excited when we finally had a place of our own in that park. It was where I learned how to wield my switchblade, hot-wire a car, and live off practically nothing.

Sometimes it felt like a faraway dream, considering where I was at now.

And some days my life now felt like a dream.

My mind was a strange place sometimes.

I remember thinking that everything would be magically fixed once I graduated with a degree. As if becoming an engineer would be the saving grace of my mother's life and eliminate my own guilt and shame about the things we did to survive that hung around my head like a cartoon rain cloud.

So now I was stuck with a degree I didn't particularly like or care for, that reminded me of my dead mother.

I had worked odd jobs trying to figure out what I was supposed to do with my life until the Shadow Lounge became a full-time gig, and anything else I looked at had shit pay, even if the hours were better. And I liked the people. Arlo was the owner and the bartender, and he made me feel less alone. He made me feel seen and heard in a way so many didn't because I was human.

But I was only twenty-four years old, for gods' sake … I had plenty of time to figure my life out, right? My impending identity crisis came in waves, and right now was just a particularly low point.

In the meantime, I got to live with my best friend in a nice ass penthouse that I would probably never *ever* be able to afford in a million years.

So, what if my housing and lifestyle peaked in my twenties? It would be fine. *I* was fine.

"Yes, I did. We don't need you getting into knife fights regularly. I would hate to bail your ass out of jail … again," he said gently, chuckling and pulling me back to the conversations as I had drifted deeper into my sour thoughts that had perturbed me this evening.

But Lux was good at that. He made me feel safe. And he did bail me out the one time I had started a bar fight in college.

I cracked a smile, remembering how some drunk idiot had tried to start a fight with Lux by taking a swing at him. Except Lux hadn't been looking, and the dumbass's face met my fist first, before he could land his punch on Lux. No one messed with my best friend.

He started to untangle the ends of my ponytail with his callused dark brown hands, and I gazed lovingly up at him. Lux was breathtakingly handsome. His thick black hair was in braids today, reaching down his back and tied loosely with a piece of black fabric. His gold eyes were bright and framed with dark, thick lashes. His bone structure made everyone swoon as his sculpted cheekbones matched his perfectly sculpted cupid's bow and studded nose.

He was broad and muscular, with tattoos swirling around most of his six-two dark brown body. He wore the tattoos like an accessory, changing them some days or keeping some for years. The advantage to being a shapeshifter meant that he could manipulate any part of his body on a whim. But he kept this image pretty consistently as his own.

However, shifters long ago were punished for shifting into other's identities. It was the Republic's way of keeping them in check. Everyone was required to have a way to be easily ID'd that matched who they were in the Republic's system.

So, this was the version of Lux I had always known. Bright eyes, dark skin, handsome as sin ... Everyone always tried to put us together, but in reality, there was absolutely zero romantic interest from either party. It was easy for them to assume I was *his* arm candy, since not very many of the wealthy and powerful toted around humans as more than playthings.

But our love was one of family, not romance or lust.

"Can you snap your fingers and have this place cleaned up and us on the couch at home?" I whined, shutting my eyes and turning to bury my face into his thigh.

He laughed darkly and replied, "I'm not a witch or a teleporter, but maybe we should find some and befriend them to help you next time."

Groaning, I sat up and rolled through my neck. I could do this. Taking a deep breath, I looked at Lux and said, "Okay, fifteen minutes. Feel free to time me." I winked before I vaulted up and started racing around the room without my boots, quickly trying to clean up the mess that all our patrons had made this evening.

"Done," I shouted, panting slightly. Sweat dripped down my brow and I rapidly wiped it away with the back of my sleeve.

Lux gave me an amused smile and uncrossed his jean-clad legs, smoothed out his white shirt and adjusted the lapels on his camel-colored coat and stood up.

"Fourteen minutes and fifty-eight seconds. Not the best, but Arlo will love you all the same." He snickered. "Let's go."

I swiftly zipped up my boots and grabbed my purse, then shrugged on my red faux fur coat and shut off the lights. I walked through the heavy metal door and locked it tight.

"Let's go home," I said. I looped my arm through his and laid my head on his shoulder as we walked through the quiet city streets bathed in moonlight.

☾

Odessa was quiet tonight. The city seemed to be sleeping.

Which made sense, because it was very late and most people had normal jobs that consisted of doing the same thing over and over again at their nine-to-five.

I leaned heavily into Lux, letting my exhaustion spill out as we walked through the cold streets of the city. I let his arm steady me and guide me through the familiar path home.

We passed huge glass skyscrapers, over the top coffee shops, designer retail stores, and steel office buildings. It was like a glamorous mix of what constituted as trendy and hip for the wealthy of the city. What they could boast about to their friends and claim was the newest and upcoming *thing*.

The streetlights cast a soft glow upon the empty streets, creating an ethereal glow along the black pavement as we weaved through the city. It might have been a little bit creepy or scary, but with Lux by my side it seemed like any other night. I let my mind get distracted by thoughts of the larger Republic.

Odessa was the biggest city and the only one I had been to. There were four other major cities and then suburbs surrounding them with mountains, deserts, and dense forests weaving between the terrains, for anyone who was interested in not living in a place that seemed to bustle with noise and energy from the millions of people packed into an urban concrete jungle.

I liked being surrounded by all the noise. Even if it wasn't always kind to me, it made the noise in my head less loud at least.

The world had been divided once upon a time by kingdoms that fought, pillaged, and plundered for pieces of land, resources, and control. It was thousands of years ago, and it was supposedly because there had been gods and goddesses who had walked the earth and created races, which inevitably led to an insane amount of chaos as all the races collided and battled for the top-dog spot.

I didn't necessarily believe that the world had been created because some gods had decided it would be fun to decorate the earth with random beings. But apparently peace had happened, and then slowly they had moved to a modern, progressive world. Except sometimes it didn't feel all that progressive. The history we had learned in school was full of holes and barely touched upon, as if the teachers themselves were unsure about the origin story of our world.

And there was the mystery of the Eastern Hemisphere. The Republic was the entirety of the Western Hemisphere, and we didn't know jack shit about the Eastern Hemisphere. It might as well have been a different world. People didn't go there from here and people from there didn't come here. It was practically unheard of. The most we got told in school was that it was a rural, traditional land that didn't embrace the technological age, and to keep peace we, the Republic, respected their wishes by not speaking about them and not bothering them with our people and vice versa.

I didn't often think of the world in a big picture, because I was usually too preoccupied with my own bubble, trying to stay afloat and navigate my own mess. The old kingdoms, gods, and goddesses seemed wholly unimportant, and almost blatantly like a legend or a myth, because it had nothing to do with what was happening right now.

Plus, it got brushed over. People didn't concern themselves with what happened thousands of years ago; there was too much going on now to worry about how we all came to be.

But tonight, my mood was making me feel contemplative about myself, the city, and the world.

"You're making your thinking face," Lux said, glancing down at me, his gold eyes twinkling, and his little nose stud shined in the yellow streetlights.

"Oh, just trying to figure out the secrets of our world…" I said casually, snuggling closer to him as my breath came out in little clouds. I often said things like this and Lux played along.

"Mmmm, find anything useful yet?" he said as we rounded a corner and our building loomed ahead of us.

"Nope, still a giant question mark on how life really started, but really, what did I expect? Can't solve everything in one night, right?" I said, dripping sarcasm.

"That's my girl. Go big or go home," he said as we reached our building.

"Tonight, let's go home," I said, smiling as we walked in and I left the thoughts of the world at the door.

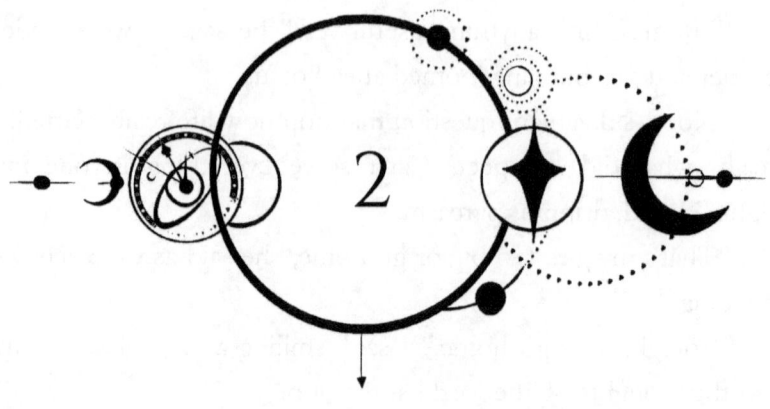

Greer

I think I'm gonna ask Leah to cover my shift tomorrow. Do you want to get drunk and watch something sexy?" I called to Lux from our kitchen.

I was starving after my shift, and Lux's assistant always had our fridge stocked with goodies.

Lux had grown up with everything at his fingertips. He was comfortable with the wealth around him and the large kitchen filled with the most up-to-date stainless steel appliances, long white marble countertops, and huge crystal chandelier overlooking an island practically the size of a full-size bed.

I, on the other hand, had to slam down the anxiety that would creep up through my spine when I thought about it too much. My mom had to work day and night to provide for us, and it never looked like this. It often looked like bologna sandwiches and whatever canned goods we had around. It was never fully stocked fridges or modern-day appliances.

She had been just eighteen when she had me. I didn't know who my dad was, which was fine by me. He abandoned my mom, and so did her family, for that matter.

She did the best she could with what she had. And I loved her for that, but I still would have liked to have had her around more. I was left with neighbors a lot or by myself. As a kid I didn't get it, but as an adult, I now understood the sacrifices she had to make for our survival.

I fought hard to get a full ride scholarship in order to go to college, only to have addiction slither its way into my mom's life and cause such immense depression and loss that she turned to suicide. I can vividly remember getting the call while out with Lux, drinking cheap vodka at some dumb house party. He held me the whole night as I sobbed, and then I terrorized through our apartment, destroying everything in my path. When the numbness settled over me, he held my hand through the small funeral and pretty much through the rest of my life.

At the time it felt like the right thing to do, to finish my engineering degree. To get a normal job. To do what my mother had pushed me to do. But when I walked across the graduation stage, all I felt was emptiness and apathy. I had been living my life for someone else and I didn't want to do that anymore.

Therefore, I tried not to dwell on the fact that all this was temporary and that one day I would need to move out and find my own way. Which I didn't know exactly what that would be. Thankfully, that day wasn't coming any time soon.

I had pendulum-swung from one extreme to another, and sometimes I got whiplash when I replayed my life in my head, which was happening way too much of late.

For now, Lux's dead parents, his consulting jobs, and my waitressing gig were funding my life, and that would just have to do.

"Maybe I have plans for tomorrow…" Lux said from across the penthouse.

I cursed quietly underneath my breath. I really needed to try being more present. I kept getting suckered into my dark thoughts and zoning out in our conversations.

He had already plopped down on the black leather couch that was about the size of two king-size beds and was nestled right in the middle of the space, along with a large circular glass coffee table. A sizable TV was directly across from the couch and underneath it a glass fireplace kept a steady heat. Windows lined the entire wall, which allowed for a beautiful view of the city. We were on the twenty-fifth floor, so we had the whole skyline to ourselves.

The view was incredible. It showed off the modern buildings that screamed the upper west side, and you could see some of the older districts where the buildings had more character and more heart in their bones. They had stone, ornate carvings, old wood doors, and a personality that couldn't be replicated with glass and steel.

That's where the best food was and the bustling markets that smelled of every kind of cuisine you could think of mixed together. It highlighted the vibrant cultures that had been smashed together here. Sometimes, I wondered if it would feel different living in a place like that, opposed to the clean lines and uppity energy of this side of the city. If it would be more welcoming to someone like me, human and uncomfortable with the clear markers of wealth that practically screamed at me every time I walked down a street.

But it had its perks, Lux being the biggest one of them.

I padded over to the living space, which had two steps leading down into a large nook covered with plush white carpet. Half-eaten pad thai occupied my plate as I sat on the opposite side of the couch and raised one brow at Lux's sprawled out form.

"You don't have plans," I said through a mouthful of noodles.

Lux scrunched up his face at me. "I always thought we could be more than friends, you know, until I saw how you eat."

I laughed out loud and shoved an obnoxious amount of food in my mouth, exaggerating my chewing and making a loud *mmmm-mmm*.

His eyes lit up as he doubled over laughing at the sight of noodles half in and half out of my mouth.

"Okay, please stop," he said, making a dramatic gesture to cover his eyes with his hand.

Sighing, I set my plate down and grabbed a cream-colored blanket and wrapped it around myself.

"As much as I love you, the sexual chemistry just isn't there for me…" I said with a wink.

Lux halfheartedly rolled his eyes and directed his attention to something on his phone.

It's no wonder people wanted to shove us together. I should have wanted us to be together, but Lux had always been more like a brother. Romance with him creeped me out. Plus, we were practically family, and we'd had a conversation a long time ago about what we were to one another. Neither one of us had any family anymore, so we would always have each other.

Not looking away from his phone, Lux said, "We could watch the opening ceremony of the Immortality Trials tomorrow."

I scoffed. "Yeah, right. No thanks…"

Lux widened his eyes and feigned shock, even though neither one of us had any interest in watching that shit show.

The Immortality Trials had started long ago, after peace had been restored to the world. It was supposedly the *reason* peace had happened. A parting gift from the gods and goddesses of old as they left their earthly playthings and went to wherever they went.

With so many species and powers trying to live harmoniously, humans had apparently been made to sit at the bottom of the food chain to serve the other races. Not only were we without powers, but we also had no chance of immortality or living past a hundred or so years. Almost every other species lived at least over 200 years.

And for some reason, everyone and their mom had it in their head that the best thing you could do with your life was to live forever. Immortality meant that you were somebody. It was the ultimate power move. A way for the world to fall at your feet and to never want for anything ever again.

Immortality had been declared a luxury long ago, which basically meant the rich and the powerful could "buy immortality," and the poor and powerless began and ended life working themselves into the ground.

You could be gifted with immortality if you had contributed enough to society, won academic accolades, furthered science, were an elected official, blah, blah, blah. Basically, you could apply for an immortality application if you believed you deserved it for free. But interestingly enough, human's applications never seemed to be approved.

Wonder why...

Or you could buy it for a hefty price. Like a *really* astronomical price.

Some people would never be able to have that luxury. Thus, the Immortality Trials had been created as an equalizer between the races. Every year in January, the Trials would begin and last through a chunk of the year. You had to fill out the application and pay a large dollar buy in, or you could find someone rich to sponsor your application. A lot of wealthy elites thought it was fun to offer money and bargains to people to enter the Trials, purely for their own entertainment. Specifically, humans who were their playthings or looking for a way out of whatever situation society had shoved them into.

They would have parties like it was fucking fantasy football, instead of people risking their lives.

Yuck.

Once you applied, you filled out a blood contract, which bound you to the Trials until you either lost or won. Except humans *never* won. We were without power, influence, and wealth. So even though it was supposed to even the playing fields in a fair and unbiased way, it did nothing of the sort. Those with natural brute strength, speed, and magic power beyond comprehension won. Basically, the less human you were … the better.

And humans were targeted in the Trials, because it was an easy way to guarantee one less contestant that would beat you. Humans were injured or killed, and nobody seemed to give two shits about it.

The Trials were supposed to be a show of good faith and equality, but more often than not, the people who won were not people that should have been given the gift of immortality anyways, in my opinion.

If you ranked in the top one hundred, you would get some wealth, power, and years added to your life cycle, but I had only heard of a couple of humans barely squeaking into the top one hundred out of the thousands that entered. In addition, the winner got more "power, influence, and riches," which was vague as hell, but the past winners went on to become celebrities, government officials, island owners, party goers, etc. They would have a say in politics, war if they wanted … and the world was at their beck and call.

Some used their power for good and others used it as an excuse to drink and fuck their way through life with little regard to others.

I had never told Lux this, but my mom had thought about doing the Trials when I was younger. I heard her on the phone with someone, talking about entering and trying to figure out how to cover the fee, as if it would save us. She was in a bind with someone she owed money to and needed a way out. It was a potential for a new and better life.

Except that it wasn't.

It was just a lie.

She would have lost. Humans didn't win. And I would have been left alone even more so. I had no idea why she thought she would be different.

But the official Trial committee did a damn good job spreading propaganda about how honorable and glorious it was to compete in the Trials. They had duped most of society into believing it was for the love of the people, equality, honor, and glory.

Yeah, right.

The Trials were rather straightforward. There were five rounds to eliminate contestants as they worked their way to the winner.

For the first round, each contestant got the photo and identification of one other contestant. They had to capture their designated contestant and bring them to the trial office located in the heart of the city. You needed to be in the first 1000 people to turn in your hostage to move on to the next round. There was a sixty-day time limit, but they almost always got to 1000 people within a few weeks.

It was a giant messed up game of Assassin, which I'd played when I was younger. Like we actually played it in our school gym class. The Trials had an odd way of becoming games and jokes when you were younger and you didn't realize what they actually were. Pretty fucked up, if you ask me. And if you lost … well, you lost a sixth of your life cycle or you owed one-sixth of your life cycle to the government. It was indentured servitude, and they owned your ass so they could make you do whatever work they needed done.

The second trial was about physical strength. Usually some sort of race or physical feat. The first 750 to survive or finish would move on. Those who didn't would owe a third of their life cycle or pay in servitude. This was where any nymph, animalia, or really anyone with enhanced physical abilities really shined, and anyone without was an easy target for violence, death, or failure.

The third was an escape room. It was supposed to be about your intelligence. Your ability to think quickly, efficiently, and effectively. They whittled this round to the top 500 and losing cost you half of your life. Poof, gone. Or working for them.

How they took away and gave life was beyond me. I didn't understand it all, and it was never information that seemed to be shared.

The fourth was always a surprise. A mix of the previous three … and the pool got smaller and the stakes higher. This was where most humans were eliminated if the previous rounds hadn't taken them out. It was a free-for-all. Contestants would most likely die or get severely injured. You entered the trial to win at all costs, because losing would demand a heavy price. So the fourth round left...

250 contestants.

Two-thirds of some people's lives gone to death or servitude.

The final round was a maze. A race to finish first. The top one hundred received accolades, the rest gave up five-sixths of their lives. Which for others maybe wasn't that much. Humans lived considerably less than every other race and species that walked the earth. For others, it may mean they still had hundreds of years left.

If you were a shifter like Lux, you would have over 600 years in your regular life easily, so if you lost in the top round, you would still live to be a hundred. But if you were human and you had already lived past the age of twenty, it was an actual death sentence. You were quite literally fighting for your life.

The rules were plain and simple. Win at any cost. Killing was discouraged but not punishable in the games. Deaths happened and sometimes one of the contestants would go absolutely rogue with lust for power and prestige and wipe out a good chunk of the contestants just for fun.

Bottom line, the Trials were disgusting. It was a whole bravado show of the government and society to show they wanted everyone to have an equal chance for immortality, even though that was a bunch of bullshit. A human had never won the Trials and never would. How could we win against races who had more life to bargain with and more power to win with? It felt like a giant oxymoron.

In my opinion, the Trials enforced the stereotypes already in place by society and preyed on the poor, weak, and uneducated since it promised wealth, glory, and life even though few achieve it. It was all televised, and the elite *loved* to show off their watch parties like it was the academy awards or something.

Participation was voluntary, but I couldn't help but notice it seemed like a lot of humans who participated didn't feel like they had much of a choice. The patrons of the lounge would often circulate rumors of how the weak little humans ate up the opportunity to compete if it meant they could get a little extra money from the social elite. The best gossip always came from the customers at the lounge, where they thought no one was listening. The other species who entered seemed to take it as a hobby, or fun piece of entertainment for the year, that could maybe result in prestige and power.

I remember specifically one year they interviewed a guy who looked like he was half bear, an animalia, and he said he had been dared by his friends to enter, so he did. Animalia usually had over 450 years easily.

A dare.

Seriously?

I would be lucky if I made it to a hundred without keeling over to the many ailments that seemed to plague human bodies specifically. It seemed like every other race had a natural immunity to diseases, viruses, and infections.

No wonder we were easy targets.

"Gods, it's two in the morning. I've got a ten o'clock meeting, so I'll see you tomorrow night?" Lux said, interrupting my spiraling thoughts about the Trials.

I really needed to start meditation or something, because this zoning out was getting out of control.

"Night, Lux," I said, nodding and waving him off as he headed to bed.

I quickly texted Leah, asking if she could cover my shift tomorrow, and then decided to turn on a cheesy Netflix movie. Snuggling into my blanket and grabbing a large fluffy gray pillow, I let myself settle in and drift off to sleep, leaving thoughts of the Trials behind.

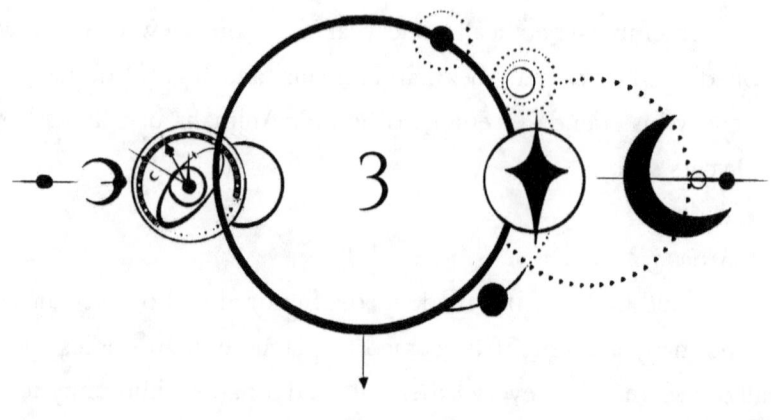

Greer

"Table eight is ready," Arlo said, garnishing four drinks with mint before working his way back down to the bar, where a customer was already asking for another.

Bottles of different colored liquor lined the back wall and were quickly being drained by the crowd as drink after drink slid across the shiny black countertop.

I didn't even have a chance to say thank you before I scooped up the drinks and weaved my way throughout the lounge, making mental notes of who needed a new drink, who needed to be tabbed out, and who probably needed to start on some water.

There were people just standing around as every plush seat, booth, high-top table, and bar seat were occupied. I was glad I got my shift covered last night, because I knew the day after the Immortality Trials opening ceremony things would be crazy. Everyone was out drinking and making bets, or at least speculating about who would win or bragging about a contestant they knew or were sponsoring.

The ceremony was more of an announcement; the real pomp and circumstance would start later. This was just the beginning of the insanity that would be the Trials.

The Shadow Lounge had premium cocktails and served the upper echelon of the city, so it was no surprise that people of all shapes, colors, powers, etc. congregated here to make boisterous claims about who would win and who would lose.

Even though the whole concept made me sick, I would happily take some of their money. Especially the ones who felt the need to comment on my skintight black sleeveless jumpsuit and strappy heels. It was almost like my own coat of armor, with a black leather vest and a silver belt wrapping around my torso and fingerless mesh gloves snaking their way up to my biceps.

I had turned up the charm and the allure tonight to really sucker these people into dropping some serious coin, and for the most part, it was working quite well for me. People loved it when the pretty human girl served them and fulfilled their every desire. I might as well make money off the stereotype and oppressive generalizations while I could. Because if I got their money, then who was really the winner here?

We were slammed almost all night until about 1:00 a.m., an hour before close.

There was an attractive young male loitering near the bar who I kept passing on my way back and forth across the lounge floor. He looked like he might be some sort of faerie, with pointed ears and slightly pointed fangs, but it was hard to tell since faeries could easily conceal their iridescent wings. From the way his hair glittered a deep violet to match his eyes, I at least knew he wasn't human.

Hmmm, haven't been with a faerie in a while.

He was hot.

I was hot.

And horny.

Yes, please.

I smiled and thanked some of my tables for their generous tips, making a note to go check this guy out.

I could feel his eyes tracking my movement as he casually sipped on his old fashion. His slightly purple skin was flawless, just like his impeccable navy suit with a white turtleneck peeking out underneath.

Classy.

I breezed past him and headed behind the bar to check in on Arlo, only to have him wave me away as he poured drinks for a couple seated at the opposite end. I worked my way over to the man and ran my fingers through my long wine-colored hair, which was falling in soft waves tonight, laying the trap.

"Can I get you anything else this evening, sir?" I asked, batting my eyelashes and smiling as I leaned in a little closer.

His full lips framed almost too white teeth and those slightly pointed fangs. "Ah, well, I suppose I'll take another one of these," he said, gesturing to his drink and leaning in a little bit closer as well. "But I would love to know your name. It's not often you get waited on by a beautiful human woman." He winked, his dark violet eyes sparkling with arousal.

Heat curled in my belly. *Easy.*

Even though people seemed to need to point out that I was human. All the time.

Didn't mean I couldn't let him help get me off, you know?

It had been a while since I'd hooked up with anyone, and honestly, it would be nice to let off some steam with this handsome guy. Plus, I was a sucker for faerie wings.

"Greer," I said, carefully pouring his drink. I slid it over to him and cocked my head to the side so he would have a full view of my blue-rimmed green eyes, long lashes, and dark red lipstick.

"What a lovely name, for a lovely human woman," he said as he took a drink and maintained eye contact.

"A name for a name. Why don't you tell me yours?" I said casually, running my eyes up and down his body.

"Riddley," he said a little deeper.

Mmmmm, yum.

I eyed the last two tables I had, to make sure they were still happy and taken care of. The couple in the corner booth seemed to be more interested in sticking their tongue down each other's throats than their drinks, and the table full of females seemed to be in a deep conversation about something that had all their brows furrowed.

"Well, Riddley, what's a handsome male like you doing at this lounge all by yourself?" I said, setting my elbow on the bar and gently resting my chin on my hand.

"Just looking for a good drink and maybe even better company." He leaned back into the dark leather bar stool, smirking with those wonderful lips.

"I get off in about thirty minutes … I could help you with the company part," I said in a husky voice. This man was gorgeous and looked like he would be perfect for what I needed this evening.

"Thirty minutes…" he said and gently took my hand away from my chin with long fingers and kissed my knuckles.

What a gentleman.

I gave him a smile and a wink and went off to take care of my two tables. Honestly, I deserved some fun tonight and Riddley seemed like the perfect fit.

☾

"What an extraordinary place you live in," Riddley said as we stepped off the elevator straight into the foyer of the penthouse.

It was always amusing to watch people walk into Lux's and I's place for the first time, because the shock and awe on their face was pretty much how I felt every day I lived here. Not that I shared that with anyone, but it was nice to see I wasn't alone in feeling like this place was over-the-top, draped in luxury.

"Thank you," I said and walked over to the kitchen, setting my coat and purse on the counter and then heading to the wine cellar encased in glass that filled the side of the space. I stepped in and quickly grabbed my favorite cab and placed it on the counter.

"Do you like red?" I asked as Riddley perched himself on one of the black barstools.

His eyes were taking in all the details of our place, from the ginormous kitchen to the all-glass walls, the infinity pool and balcony, the living space to the large dining table that could seat twenty people. Then his gaze flashed toward the hall that led to Lux and I's bedrooms. He seemed a bit dazed and overwhelmed.

How I feel literally every single day living here myself, buddy.

"I do, yes..." he said, pulling his eyes back to me and glancing quickly over to the glass wine cellar.

I grabbed two wine glasses, popped open the bottle, and generously poured a glass for both of us. I handed Riddley the glass and smiled.

"Cheers," I said, gently clinking my glass to his. On the way here, he had said he was an accountant at a firm not far from the Shadow Lounge. He seemed harmless enough to take home, but interesting enough to have a good night.

His teeth flashed in a smile before he took a few sips of the wine.

"Do you want to come sit in the living room?" I asked, nodding over to the couch and slowly walking toward it.

"Sure," he said, making clumsy movements toward the couch.

Is he nervous? Cute.

But his movements became a bit more rigid and stiff as he sat down on the opposite end of the couch to me.

Weird.

He straightened his spine as I gave him a quizzical look, and he settled back into a more casual position with his legs crossed and his glass of wine on the glass coffee table. He spread his arms along the back of the couch and swept his purple eyes—no longer filled with heat but something else—along the length of the penthouse.

"Do you live alone, Greer?" he asked, trying to sound casual.

Red. Flag.

I set my glass down and uncrossed my legs. "I don't … I have a roommate," I said, purposefully keeping it vague. People knew Lux by his full name, and it wouldn't be the first time someone had tried to get close to me to get close to him. Or tried to take advantage of the fact that I was a human, seemingly innocent and helpless.

I shuddered, thinking of the time I had brought someone to our place and after we had slept together, I caught them rifling through Lux's room. I had to call the police after Lux scared the living daylights out of them and he got a restraining order in place.

Lux did a lot to protect our privacy, but sometimes things slipped through the cracks, including my sexual escapades. But, hey, things happen, you know?

Usually, my meter for bullshit was pretty good, though, and I hadn't gotten weird vibes at the lounge. Additionally, I didn't know where Lux was tonight. He'd said something about having a date with a lion animalia or something.

"Oh," he said, raising his brow and trying to keep his face calm, but it seemed like anxious energy was buzzing off him now. "I would love to meet them."

This guy was definitely giving off weird vibes now.

"He isn't here right now…" I said with a bit of an edge. "Riddley, why are *you* here?" I didn't play games, and this was starting to feel creepy really fast.

I cursed myself for slipping my switchblade into my purse on the way here since I didn't want him to feel it on my body if we started taking off each other's clothes. It was a weird thing to try and explain without seeming a little bit crazy. It had happened before and let's just say the male ran out of here with his tail tucked between his legs.

Literally.

I tried to hold a neutral expression as I was silently trying not to jump to the worst conclusions possible.

He swallowed hard and shifted in his seat like he was about to get up. I raised an eyebrow at him and dared him to make another move with my gaze.

He started to laugh then. It bubbled out and then erupted in a deep throaty cackle where he threw his head back and grabbed his stomach.

Red flag. Red flag. Red flag.

My eyes flashed to my phone in a moment of fear, and I shot off the SOS code Lux and I had established years ago in college if either of us needed help. And with the way he was laughing, I felt like I would need his help. ASAP.

Greer: *Pineapple.*

He would track my location and get here as quickly as he could. Probably in some animal form—hopefully something with claws, fangs, and speed.

"Surely you know, Greer? I got your picture." He stood and a small bottle of clear liquid appeared in his hand.

My picture? What the fuck?

My phone buzzed and Lux's reply showed bright.

Lux: On my way.

I just had to stall this guy. The bottle was winding its way through his fingertips, like some sort of magician asking you to pick a card. I didn't know what was in the bottle, but I sure as hell wasn't going to find out. I quickly stood, the glass coffee table separating us by only six feet.

"What the hell are you talking about? What picture?" I said, nearly snarling at him. My heart was beating fast now. *I can't believe I let this guy into my home.*

Fuck. Fuck. Fuck.

Who the hell was he?

"Playing hard to get, I see. Well, don't worry, as a human you were doomed for a short life anyway. I can't imagine who you had to sleep with in order to get this monstrosity of a place, but at least you'll live in a bit of luxury through your last days. But I don't see why someone like you would enter the Trials, seeing as you've got a nice set up here. Trouble in paradise?" He sneered at the last part.

I was going to kill this guy. And what in the actual hell was he talking about?

He slowly started winding his way around the table as I did the same. I was trapped between the couch and the coffee table. I glanced over at the kitchen and the knife set sitting on the counter. If I could run toward it, at least I would have a weapon to defend myself. Riddley followed my gaze to the knife set.

"Really, dear, there's no need for violence here. Just come with me peacefully and I won't even make you drink my potion," he said, revealing all of his teeth in what felt like a feral grin.

Godsdamnit.

"I don't know what you're talking about, but I will go absolutely *nowhere* with your slimy ass." I spit out the last word and grabbed one of the fluffy pillows next to me and flung it at his face. He laughed and swatted it away, but it gave me just enough of a distraction to vault off the couch and land in a crouch and run over to the kitchen.

But Riddley was already there, standing in front of the knife set. His grin and eyes were malicious as he gazed down at all five-four of me and made a grab for my neck. I tried to duck away, but his long fingers started to close around my throat before I had a chance to escape.

"Let … me … go," I choked out as his hand started to squeeze tighter around my neck. My airway was screaming for it to stop as I thrashed around, trying to release myself. Black dots started to appear in front of my eyes and my vision started to go hazy. I dug my nails into his hands until I drew blood, but he seemed unfazed.

"Now, now, dear. Open your mouth and swallow this so there will be no more fighting," he said as he uncorked the small bottle with his free hand and brought it to my lips, which I was trying to firmly keep shut, even though all I wanted to do was scream. My body begged for air and I refused.

Fear was curling through my belly and my breath was huffing out my nose in rapid succession.

Is this how I die? Trying to bang some dude who turned out to be a serial killer? The universe has a fucked up sense of humor.

Where the hell is Lux?

Riddley tried to pry open my lips while simultaneously holding the small vial of liquid. He almost had just enough space to dribble the liquid through when the elevator door dinged open.

Riddley glanced over, anger taking over his face, and he released my throat to have me fall in a heap to the ground gulping in air. Stars danced in front of my eyes. I gasped on the floor, trying to get my vision in check.

"Lux…" I choked out.

There was a huge white tiger stalking his way toward us, claws clicking on the marble floor. Lux was indeed one for drama. I would have laughed if my trachea wasn't crushed.

Riddley didn't seem so confident anymore. Lux released a roar and charged toward Riddley with long white fangs bared. His eyes, always the same gold, were filled with pure malice as he knocked Riddley's ass to the floor.

Gasping for air, he tried to claw and wriggle his way out from underneath Lux's massive paws, but Lux kept putting pressure on his chest. I scrambled for the vial of clear liquid that had half spilled on the floor. Still catching my breath and recovering from the chokehold, I yanked open Riddley's mouth and poured the remaining contents into his throat.

"Take your own medicine, bitch," I choked out.

Riddley tried to sputter and spit it out, but Lux's other paw came to rest on his face, and he wriggled and screamed until his muffling became silent and his body stilled.

I slumped back against the island and gazed at Riddley's now unconscious body. Well, this night hadn't exactly turned out as planned. All I had wanted was to bang some hottie ... Was that really too much to ask?

Lux transformed back into himself and crouched in front of me, his eyes scanning my body and lingering on the bruise that would have already started forming around my throat. He gently took the vial from me and sniffed it.

"This is a sleeping potion. A pretty strong one from the smell…"

He grimaced as he placed it on top of the counter.

"Greer…" He gently pulled me to my feet and wrapped his arms around me. I stood in silence while he held me. He pulled away and again let his gaze linger on the fingerprints already making a mark on my throat. "Are you okay? What happened?" he asked, worry taking over his golden eyes. His strong hands grounded me as my head spun a little from the last ten minutes.

"I don't know," I said, in a bit of shock. I glanced down at Riddley and wondered what the hell he had meant by the trial and my photo.

And what exactly would we do with his now unconscious body?

☾

Lux had called the police on his way over and two officers were now occupying our apartment. Along with Riddley, who was still fast asleep and now laid across the large couch with his hands and feet bound by two of my scarves.

One of them was a tall woman with horns poking through her blond hair and a petite brown snout sitting right above her thin lips. Her feet ended in hooves and were bare, allowing her uniform to fall around her blond-covered fawn legs.

The man accompanying her was short and portly, with reddish orange scales covering his head and hands. His eyes were more like slits and his nose was flat against his face. Both were pleasant enough and made several calls while Lux told them what I had told him moments before they had arrived.

The shock wore off a little, and I studied Riddley's face.

Did I know him?

Was I supposed to?

"This man is a part of the Immortality Trials," the woman said to me. I squinted at her nametag and saw her name was Officer Jayda Hammond.

"Officer, I'm not sure what that has to do with this situation…" I said, not really understanding how that explained why this man was here.

In my home.

Trying to drag me away.

"Well, Greer Roberts, so are you…"

I looked at her, wondering if this was a joke. I glanced at the other officer, who by the look of his name tag was Officer Briggs Raymond. I looked at Lux incredulously.

Then I started laughing. More like cackling, as it came out harsh and hysterical. It was their turn to look at me like I was losing my mind. I wiped away a tear that had escaped my eyes and shook my head.

"No, I'm not," I stated matter-of-factly, staring into the officer's eyes. Not sure why she would lie about this, but it was funny in a not funny sort of way.

"Yes, you are," she said with a bit of pity in her eyes. "And Riddley here had you for the first round. Seeing as this is official Trial business, we can't interfere. You would need to contact the Lord of Trials or Ambassador Kyra."

"I'm sorry, ma'am, but there isn't anything we can do here," Officer Raymond said with a flick of annoyance in his eyes, as if I was putting on a whole show just to waste his time.

I glared at them both and then looked at Lux, who was already typing away at his phone and excusing himself to make a call. Lux had tons of contacts. He was a prominent name in the city, after all. He would help me get to the bottom of this. Love welled up inside me at how aggressively he rushed to support me.

"Great. Thank you. You can leave now, then," I said, ushering them toward the elevator and giving them a curt wave on their way out.

I groaned in frustration. Obviously, there was some sort of mistake. I hadn't entered the games. Maybe someone who looked like me and also had a similar name had entered. Whatever the mix up was, I wasn't about to let them get away with it.

Lux walked back into the room and scowled over to where Riddley was still sleeping peacefully.

"I just contacted the Lord of Trials and Ambassador Kyra. We have a meeting at the office space I have downtown tomorrow," he stated casually, like we weren't meeting with two huge immortal public figures on such short notice.

The immortals in the city didn't often conspire with us lesser beings, A.K.A. humans. They would deal with Lux because it was basically expected at some time, he would accept immortality because of his power, wealth, and parents.

In fact, Ambassador Kyra had been a past winner of the Immortality Trials. Not that it mattered, but that was the power of winning. He now held a political position and acted as an emissary of sorts between the contestants and the rulers of the game. He had power, wealth, and influence. Exactly what the Immortality

Trials promised and what they banked on the population desiring enough to risk their lives.

Why anyone would want that position was beyond me. He loved the trial so much he just couldn't stay away? Why didn't he offer aid to the people who entered the game as a way to escape poverty and violence? Specifically, the humans who could barely face magic without walking away broken, traumatized, or dead.

Whatever.

He was a powerful warlock as well, blessed with fire magic before the trial and then blessed with explosive magic after that. He could level the whole city if he wanted, but obviously that was illegal.

All magic had rules and regulations. Even Lux's shifter magic had specific laws. He was never allowed to present as anyone besides himself or the punishment would be swift and harsh. He would be stripped of his shifter magic wholly, which would be the equivalent of losing an arm. The typical punishments included magic being taken away, your life cycle being cut, imprisonment, or government servitude. The greater the crime … well, the harsher the deliverance of justice.

They basically made you human.

What a lovely way for society to reinforce that being human was the actual worst thing that could possibly happen to you.

"Good. I want to get this mess sorted out as soon as possible," I said, giving him a half-smile. "Only you could get both those men in a room … on such short notice … on a Sunday," I said, chuckling slightly.

"I'm sorry I wasn't here sooner, G," Lux said with guilt and pain in his eyes as he rubbed his callused hands down my arms

"It's okay. You didn't know … I didn't know …" I said, wrapping my arms around his muscled torso and burying my head into his strong chest. "I just wanted to have sex with some hot male." I pouted slightly.

He laughed at that and rolled his eyes.

"Only you, G," he said affectionately, as if he didn't go out looking for a hookup on the regular. Because we both did—no shame in that.

"I have needs, and ones that are much more satisfying if someone else fulfills them," I said, slightly annoyed. He laughed again and his megawatt smile warmed my heart. "But now I just want to get some sleep and figure this out tomorrow."

I gave him another quick squeeze and wiggled my way out of his arms. "Thanks for setting the meeting up … What time?" I said, wrapping my arms around myself.

"Ten. And I'll take care of this," he said, gesturing to Riddley with furrowed brows.

"Okay, goodnight," I said and started heading toward my bedroom.

I didn't ask what that meant. Sometimes I just didn't ask questions, because Lux could get away with things that I simply couldn't. The power of being a social elite. I was thankful that he never expected me to be anything besides what I was. But sometimes I wondered how long I could keep myself closed in this little world that was just Lux and me.

In college, the discrepancy between our worlds wasn't nearly as obvious. The playing field was more level. Everyone was just living in their little college bubble. And when our bubble burst because of grief, trauma, and anger, we built our own, even though we both had come from two different worlds.

I knew there were parts of his life I wasn't included in. He offered but I simply refused. I didn't want to get involved in things that clearly were not designed for me. The sight of a young, outspoken human would be met with disdain and disgust. It would be suspicious and weird to have a human woman as more than a plaything for the elite. People already struggled to understand how we were just friends, let alone why Lux had a human woman living with him out of the kindness of his heart or the basis of a soul-deep friendship. It would not compute for those who thought humans were bottom feeders.

And I liked my privacy. It was exhausting sometimes to think of all the things Lux had to do to run his company, even as a silent partner, and fight for the things he cared about. I just couldn't imagine doing it all with him. So I was pretty content with the way things were.

Plus, it wasn't like we went around explaining how not great Lux's parents were, considering many remembered them as wonderful people. We didn't say how we bonded in our freshman orientation class and how we both just understood each other. No judgment. No ego. We made each other feel seen and heard in a way that other people just didn't understand. There were pieces of our hearts and souls that other people would run away from, but we simply accepted that from one another.

It was rare and beautiful. I was so thankful to have him.

So I couldn't imagine many would be understanding about any of that, considering most people didn't concern themselves with any type of social justice or inequality work in the social elite, because once you became immortal, you were untouchable. You could get away with too much and you would give too little to those who needed it.

And they didn't mingle with humans very often. Or ever.

Especially when they all aimed for the same things. Immortality. Power. Money. And I didn't want that. I just wanted to live a happy, content life where I wasn't scraping by.

I had that with Lux … except at some point I wanted, or rather needed, to find something deeper.

Ugh.

I really needed to stomp out this restlessness and stop being so angry at society for who and what I was. Tonight just wasn't that night, though. I wasn't going to drag up all my demons today. I had dealt with a real life one who spouted lies and nonsense under the ruse of trying to sleep with me.

Honestly, I had no energy to push myself toward self-healing at the moment.

Sighing, I couldn't help but feel lighter knowing that after tomorrow this would be just a funny story we would joke about and nothing more.

I could start all that self-healing next week, anyways.

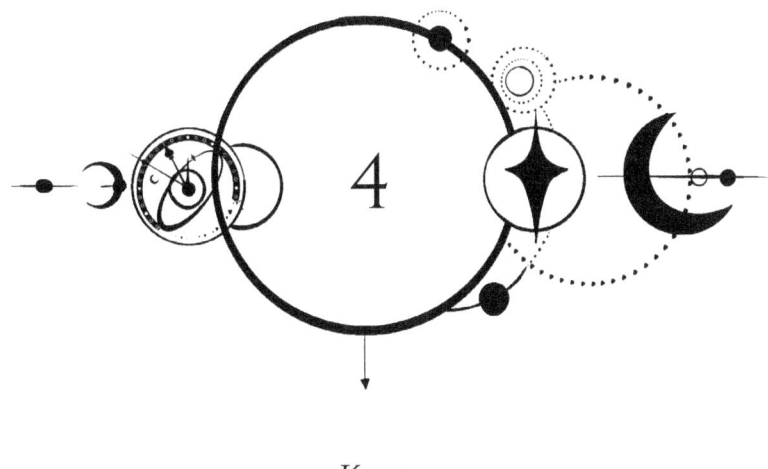

Kyra

I t wasn't every day you got a call from Luxton Gilmore request-
ing an "emergency meeting." Not that I had been doing much
of anything anyways, but it had been an interesting turn of
events from the usual Saturday night of drinking scotch and
sifting through some paperwork.

The Immortality Trials had just started, which meant my usual
philanthropic and humanitarian efforts would be delegated to my
staff and I would need to focus on being the face of the Trials, at
least for a few weeks. It was truly my least favorite time of the year,
not that anyone knew that.

I had accepted the Ambassador position because I thought I
could help people, make a difference, but in reality I just got
slapped with a fuck-ton of red tape and was barely kept in the
know of what was going on with the Trials. I was a nice symbol for
them to use and lean on, since I was the perfect picture of a contestant who'd tried to use the status for good instead of pleasure
and chaos. Not that those things didn't call to me from time to time
... It just felt like there was always something more I could do, even

if I was just a figurehead and a handsome face for the whole damn thing.

It was exhausting. It made me feel like I was living under a microscope, portrayed as the idol for the Eastern Hemisphere, since few knew of or had met anyone from that side of the world. I put on a good front, though, steering questions away from my past and my home. The relations between the east and west were nonexistent, so I didn't necessarily blame people for asking questions, but it had never been my choice to share it. I should have been able to keep my secret since it's not like anything about my power or my life would give any indication that I wasn't from the Western Hemisphere. The information had been leaked. I had a pretty damn good guess who was responsible and there wasn't anything I could do about it. But the constant questions about my home had to be avoided. I didn't have a choice.

It was truly a miracle I had been semi-accepted here after that piece of information got out, but winning the Trials had basically forced people to see me and speak to me, even if they did so with trepidation. If only they knew the reality behind who I was, they might run screaming in the other direction.

I tried not to dwell on it too much, because it was out of my control, like so many other things in my life. I continued to do what I could and make a difference with the time I had. I wanted our world to be better. I knew it could be—I just didn't exactly know how to do it. Because change was slow, and people were stubborn, and bigotry existed *everywhere*.

But I put up with it in order to try and genuinely help others. Most of the time I was doing something good, except when the Trials first started and ended. I was duty bound to the whole thing.

I had lived through the Trials once, and the only reason I could stomach being the face of it year after year was knowing that at least I could help keep people safe before, during, and after the Trials, which I was sure was why I was called to this meeting as well as the Lord of Trials.

It was a bit of a shock that Edward Harrington was even here. He must have gotten a call from the rich and powerful shifter as well. Edward was a dwarf that ruled the games. His physical strength was legendary as a dwarf, but his cunning mind was one hundred percent of his own volition. It was no wonder he had been elected as Lord of Trials some hundred years ago, after he had won several Nobel Prizes and been awarded immortality.

The whole concept of immortality was bizarre, to say the least. It was earned and rewarded to those society deemed worthy, even though for the most part that excluded humans. So many of the City's elite, which were a lot of immortals, didn't want anything to do with humans. They would never achieve the same things other races could, and therefore were repeatedly picked on and targeted. It wasn't okay, at all, but it was hard to control when those with immortality were pretty much above the rules.

Which was just another point of society that was really messed up. Sometimes it overwhelmed me with the change that needed to happen. I had all this power and time, but little control to change culture. I had to remind myself I was in a position to make a difference.

And I would.

I was.

It just took a long damn time.

I looked back over to Edward, who was scowling. His long white hair was in a single braid running down his back, and he'd donned his Lord of Trials robes, which consisted of black robes, several multicolored cords, and a silver stole. It looked more like he was attending a graduation than running a huge glorified survivor game.

His half-moon glasses perched on his long, crooked nose and his ice-blue eyes gazed forward, giving nothing away. He was all wrinkles and business. The room Luxton's assistant had guided us to was a conference room with a view of the city and a large black table running through the center with about fifteen chairs circling around it. Currently, the Trial Lord was at the head of the table and I was sitting to the right of him. We had been offered drinks and food, which he politely declined. I gladly accepted a cappuccino and a croissant.

He had given me a curt nod upon entering and seemed pretty set on ignoring me until this meeting started.

The bastard had never liked me. He couldn't control me very well. And it seemed like his politeness toward me only extended when other people were around. I was the handsome winner when it was convenient for him, but I was useless if I wouldn't bend to his every barking order.

We both had been about fifteen minutes early. I checked the dark metal Rolex on my right hand. It was almost 10:00 a.m. on the dot.

Suddenly, the glass door we came in through opened to reveal Luxton himself and a very curvy, short, red-haired human next to him. At least she looked human. She could be something else; you never really knew until you asked or the information was voluntarily given.

She had bright green eyes and was dressed for what looked like battle. Black leather leggings hugged her muscular thighs and gave way to knee-high black boots. She had a tight black turtleneck that had cut outs on her shoulders. Her curtain of red hair was pulled away from her pale white face in a slicked back low ponytail, revealing bright red lipstick and a collection of studs and hoops around her ears. She had a long white coat folded over her arms and a black satchel slung over one shoulder.

She looked like someone who didn't take shit from anyone. I couldn't help but be intrigued and wonder who this woman was and how I could go about getting to know her a little better. The fire that settled beneath my skin hummed at the thought of peeling back the layers of armor she had so carefully woven around herself for this meeting.

"Thank you both for coming today. I appreciate you being here," Lux said with an easy smile. He was dressed a bit less harshly in an olive-green long sleeve and gray slacks that gave way to fine black leather shoes. This woman was ready for blood, while Lux was ready for appeasement and mediation.

Edward smiled, showing off his yellowing and crooked teeth. "Of course, Mr. Gilmore. It's not often we hear from you, so I assumed it was urgent."

He glanced over at the woman who sat next to Luxton with a stiff spine and bright eyes raking over him as if trying to weigh his strength.

"It's good to see you, Lux. What can we help you with?" I said with a casual smile.

Lux and I went way back. We'd met at a charity gala a few years back and ended up sneaking away with a bottle of whiskey in an effort to ditch the event that was more for the rich to boast their donations than it was to help the cause. We periodically would meet up to drink, play pool, plan events, and sometimes get into trouble.

I had dressed a bit more casually in a long sleeve dark gray shirt and black jeans with brown leather boots. Considering it was Sunday and I was *the* Ambassador Kyra, it didn't feel like what I wore to meet an old friend mattered.

Lux's eyes seemed to soften as he glanced over at the woman at his side. They seemed very familiar, and I wondered why he had never talked about her before. Or if they were together.

She couldn't be more than twenty-five, but then again, Lux was around the same age.

I won immortality about five years ago, making my current age thirty years old, which was around when they had told me my aging would stop. The whole procedure and concept was off-putting … Nothing a stiff drink and a run couldn't push away when it was too heavy to think about.

"My name is Greer Roberts, and for some odd reason someone from the Immortality Trials tried to kidnap me last night, claiming that he had my photo and my ID credentials, in order to pass the first trial." She slid two folders over to me and Edward as she spoke.

I opened mine to find the photo she was talking about and a copy of the information each contestant was provided to complete the first trial.

"It's nice to meet you, Greer." I meant it. "I mean … this looks like you and matches your name." I continued, not quite understanding where this was going. I wondered why she had entered the Trials. It was a death sentence for humans, which her file confirmed was her race. And no matter what aura of strength she was giving off in her all black ensemble, it wouldn't be a match for the other powers that would ripple through the Trials.

The thought made me queasy. I wondered idly again how Lux knew her, and considered how most would think it odd that he was so close to a human and advocating for her. But Lux had never been traditional; the work he had done around the city was often thought of as eccentric and unnecessary, but I knew it was absolutely essential to achieve a better society for all. He was an advocate for all sorts of marginalized communities, and it was one of the reasons we had clicked so well. He was a good man with integrity and spirit.

It seemed like Greer was obviously a special person to him.

I pulled my attention to the next piece of paper in the file, which was a police report filed last night for a kidnapping charge. A large red stamp that read "Immortality Trials" was plastered on top of it.

"Except I didn't sign up for the games," Greer said, carefully monitoring the reaction of myself and Edward. She didn't look like she was kidding. Her mouth was set in a hard line and her jaw was clenched with narrowed eyes.

"Miss Roberts, we do not make mistakes at the games. We use a blood contract," Edward said politely, trying not to look annoyed. I could already tell he'd taken one look at her and immediately thought her less than because she was a pretty human woman.

Asshole.

"I pulled the blood sample that was assigned to the contestant Greer Roberts and compared it to the real Greer here," Lux said evenly. "And it was a match."

"See, I think you are mistaken, *my dear*," Edward said while folding his hands over the file. He had a look of pity that seemed to fuel her anger and irritation. A muscle feathered over Greer's jawline as he drew out *my dear*.

Good gods, what was it with old men and saying creepy shit like that?

I didn't know Greer Roberts that well, but she didn't seem like someone who would roll over underneath the dwarf's patronizing words. I sat up a little straighter and gazed at the file, realizing things just got much more interesting.

"Except on the date and time of the contract, I have proof that I was with Lux," she said through gritted teeth, clearly trying to rein in her anger.

"We have proof that she wasn't there to sign the contract. I assume an impostor, most likely a shifter, was there to sign it," Lux said calmly, leveling his stare into the Trial Lord. "Even though it's illegal … a shifter can mask himself as someone else down to their blood type if they know it. It's labor intensive and forbidden, but not impossible."

He would know. He was from a long line of powerful shifters. They were told the rules very early on, just like everyone else who had specialized powers learned the limits society placed on us very quickly.

It didn't mean they weren't broken, but many were good at hiding their transgressions. Especially if you had influence; it wasn't hard to scrub your sins from being permanently stained on your record if you were an immortal or someone of power.

"And why would someone do that, Mr. Gilmore?" Edward said nonchalantly, flicking an annoying gaze over to Greer.

Man, he was really working himself up to be chewed out by her.

I could feel her tension flowing off her in waves. I tried not to think of how it slightly turned me on. This human woman was going toe to toe with the Trial Lord. I couldn't help but be *very* intrigued.

"We don't know," Greer interrupted anyway, dragging the conversation back to include her. "But I want my name taken out of the Trials and I want you all to get to the bottom of this. *Now.*"

"Miss Roberts, a blood contract cannot be broken except with the price of death, and unless you can catch and prove that there was an impostor, you must go through the Trial or simply lose, which would mean you would be punished just like everyone else.

Either your life cycle or signing up for government servitude will welcome you," he stated matter-of-factly, eyes hardening.

"But I didn't consent to be in this. I shouldn't be punished for your lack of security in the application process!" she hissed, standing up and leaning over the table. She pointed to the file. "I am human, in case you didn't already realize, and it's nearly fucking impossible for me to compete in the Trials, because unlike all of you in this room, I don't have a built-in advantage. So I want my name taken off the list *immediately* and you to clean up this mess." Her voice was made of steel as she practically barred her teeth at Edward and shoved one pale finger at him.

I struggled not to laugh and bit my lip. Not because what she said was funny at all, but I'm sure Edward wasn't used to anyone speaking to him like that, especially a human. Honestly, the bastard needed to be knocked down off his high horse.

"Unfortunately, without the presence of this impostor, there isn't much we can do with the blood magic. We need undeniable proof. However, we will look into your case if you file it officially and do our best to get to the bottom of this. Until then, you will suffer the punishment if you lose. I suggest you do your best to clear the first trial, as you have sixty days to do so or until the thousandth person turns in their designated contestant. Mr. Gilmore, I assume will be your liaison and representative ... I think you've snarled at me enough today, Miss Roberts. Good day," Edward said, dismissing her.

He swiftly got up and moved past a boiling Greer and a very annoyed Lux to the doorway. For a dwarf standing at a little under three feet, he sure had a way of looking down his nose at people twice his size.

"G, we will work on him," Lux said irritably, rubbing his hands across his face after the door had slammed shut.

"WHAT THE FUCK IS HIS PROBLEM?" Greer roared as she looked around the room for something to throw or destroy—I'm not really sure. She had a lot of anger pulsing off her.

"You!" She pointed that accusatory finger at me, and I lifted my brows, feeling a bit perplexed at this near-feral woman in front of me. I had been a silent observer to most of this, trying to wrap my head around what was going on, and it seemed like that was absolutely the wrong thing for me to do to gain favor with Greer.

"You literally said *nothing* while he was here. Aren't you supposed to be some big humanitarian man or some bullshit? Aren't you supposed to help the people who get suckered into this scam of a trial?" she yelled at me. Her eyes were bright with fury. She stormed out of the room, huffing and stomping away in those sky-high boots. "I need some air," she said, not giving me even a chance to respond. She came in like a whirlwind and left just as fast.

Her anger in itself was enough reason for me to believe her claims were true. Nobody could fake anger and hostility like that. Her feelings were justified … just maybe not justified exactly at me. I smiled to myself; people didn't often talk to me like that either. It wasn't nice exactly, but it sort of was. She didn't sneer at me or walk on eggshells around us. Greer just existed exactly as herself and unapologetically demanded that other people follow the same rules.

It didn't dim my desire to get to know her in the least bit. In fact, it made me even more interested in understanding what exactly was happening here.

Clearing my throat, I looked over to where Lux had laid his head down on the table.

"I won't apologize for her behavior. You would be upset too if you had been signed up for the Trials under a falsehood, not to mention she was nearly choked to death last night. Plus, you did just sit there," he mumbled into the table.

I pressed my lips together and leaned closer to the table to inspect the file Greer had given us.

"They choked her?" I said, a kernel of anger blooming in my belly. The Trials incited violence like no other. It was something I had brought up multiple times, but I usually got ignored or was reminded I had also been violent when I won the Trials. It didn't mean I liked it. Or was proud of it. I did what I had to do to survive the damn thing.

Bastards. All of them.

Lux looked up at me with a smirk as I realized I had mumbled that thought out loud.

"No need for apologies. I should apologize for not stepping in. Edward has a stick up his ass anyway, and whatever's going on here … we will get to the bottom of it. Soon," I said, patting one of Lux's hands reassuringly. "Greer seems…" I was trying to think of what I was trying to say. Nice? Not exactly. Stunning? Felt a little inappropriate. Passionate? Seemed a bit invalidating to her feelings around this situation.

"Intense?" I landed on, saying it almost like a question.

Lux lifted his head, snorting, his gold eyes dancing with amusement. "You have no idea."

I didn't exactly know what that meant, but I didn't have much time to dwell on it.

"All right, Ky, let's do some digging … I'm gonna make a call first. I appreciate you helping on this," Lux said sincerely as he dug out his phone and started typing away and then stood up to chat with someone on the other end.

I pulled out my phone to do the same and wondered who the hell had it out for the intense and lovely Greer Roberts, and how in the gods' names they had slipped through and duped the blood contract.

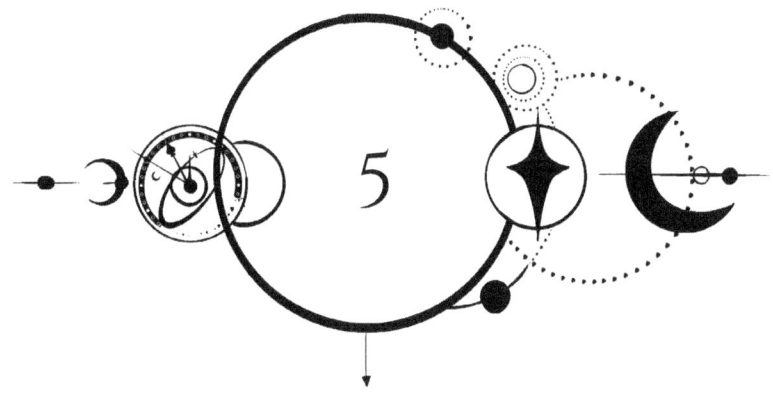

5

Kyra

S
o you and Greer seem close..." I said, looking at Lux typing something on his phone.

I wanted to know more about her, and it had been about thirty minutes since she had stormed off. I wondered if he would go after her, or maybe I should try and speak to her since clearly some of her rage was directed at me and I did feel like she was right. I should have said more than just sitting in awe of her like a dumbass.

"We are," Lux said, flashing a smile at me and tilting his head to the side. His gold eyes were sparkling with amusement again, like he was holding on to some secret. Or maybe he just enjoyed making me spell out what I was getting at.

"If there's something you'd like to know, Ky, you can just ask, you know."

He leaned back in his seat and set his phone down, as if challenging me to actually speak my mind. Damn it all to hell if I wasn't going to fall for the trap he was setting.

"I just am curious, considering I don't think you've ever mentioned her when we've hung out together, and you're going to great lengths to advocate for her here," I said, leveling my scarlet eyes at him, sending a challenge right back.

He chuckled then and relaxed his shoulders. "She's my best friend and my roommate," he said casually.

I looked at him expectantly, as if he would just offer up more information, but he wasn't doing anything of the sorts. He just continued to smirk at me.

"Damnit, Lux, just tell me about her. Who is she to you, and why have you hidden her away?" I said, running my hands through my black hair that often liked to fall into my eyes.

He laughed loudly then, throwing his head back and wiping a nonexistent tear from his eyes in mockery.

"See, was that so hard?" he said, smiling with his whole expression.

"Yes, it was…" I grumbled. "But seriously, why haven't I seen her before if she's your best friend *and* roommate? Seems like someone you might have brought around to some of the events we've attended together." *And I would have remembered her*, I thought.

It wasn't often someone had wine-colored hair, and her bright green eyes seemed not human. I would have noticed someone with that sort of internal fire that radiated confidence and strength. She was stunning, to say the least, and had an energy that demanded to be noticed.

Lux was really enjoying me squirm here, with his snarky grin as I got lost in the image of Greer, but then his expression softened.

"We met in college. We've been best friends practically since the day we met. Do you ever just meet someone and know immediately that you're supposed to be connected? That was us…"

I looked at him quizzically. I had never experienced that with someone. It sounded like they were romantically involved, to say the least.

"You're together, then, I assume?" I tried not to ooze disappointment. I just had never seen anyone like Greer before. People often talked to me like I was some sort of god, an Eastern mystery, or avoided me all together. Or a mix of all three.

It was refreshing to have someone similar to Lux, who seemed to treat me like a person. Even if she had screamed at me. She commanded what she needed and wanted. And I respected the hell out of that.

Lux's eyes widened and he laughed loudly again. "Absolutely not."

I tried not to give a sigh of relief. I didn't realize I had been holding my breath waiting for the answer to my question.

"Greer and I have never, and never will be, romantically involved. Our friendship is more like a chosen family. We both have gone through a lot of things that other people just don't seem to understand or it scares them. I honestly don't know what I would do without her," he said lovingly.

I had a pang of envy. I had never had a friend or family member like that. I was an only child, and there were many reasons it was difficult to let people get close to me.

People's reaction to me ranged from hateful to worship. It was one of the many reasons I kept to myself. Plus, I had things I couldn't allow myself to share. We all had demons of sorts, and mine could not be announced to the general public.

"Why haven't you brought her around?" I said, still trying to piece together the enigma that was Greer.

"I don't bring her around for a few reasons. One being that you know as well as I do that as a human, she would be treated like a lesser being or just like my pretty plaything. I would go to bat for her with every single asshole who treated her that way, but she decided a long time ago that she didn't want to use her energy fighting her way through the social elite. And I've respected that. And by doing so, I have fiercely protected her privacy. People have used her before to get to me and I don't want that to happen again. She's the last person I ever want to get hurt because of me and who I am. She deserves better than that. All humans do," Lux said seriously.

I knew what he meant. The immortals and elite of the city were exclusive and dismissive of anyone they thought to be lesser beings. Humans especially. But they liked them as playthings, especially during the Trials.

They often lured them into the Trials with the promise of something extraordinary, whether they won or lost. But then they would go back on their end of the deal. It wasn't illegal but it should be. It was wrong and too many fell victim to it. It was often covered up, but I kept tabs on that sort of thing. It was something that I was actively trying to work against. So far I wasn't making a ton of headway.

"I get that. But c'mon, Lux … Don't you think you can trust me? I'd like to think I'm not like the rest of those assholes," I said, realizing that maybe he didn't.

Maybe he thought I was exactly the rest of them, and that hurt. I was a lot of things, but someone who discriminated against others based off things out of their control was not one of them. I knew what it felt like to be on the shitty end of that stick, and I would never want to make anyone else feel that way.

I could see Lux and I getting close, but I just didn't allow things like that to happen very easily. But for some reason, adding Greer into the equation made it seem a bit more possible. Like I wanted to be a part of the special energy they created together.

Because it was something I had never experienced.

Something that was one of a kind.

Something that seemed like it had immense power in itself. Like their friendship had the ability to create waves in the lives around them.

At least that was what I told myself, and not that I wanted to know what Greer would taste like. Like fire itself, but with a mouthwatering aftertaste. I tried not to dwell too much on it.

"Ky, I know you aren't like the rest of them. But Greer is the single most important person in my life. I protect her when I can. Even with someone like you. And maybe I had a good reason, since you seem to be very interested in her now," he said, teasing, but I could see the protectiveness in his eyes.

If I messed up with Greer, I messed up with Lux. I didn't take that lightly.

"I feel like I should apologize to her. I didn't mean to seem disengaged … I think I was a bit overwhelmed by the way she went head-to-head with Edward. And this situation is strange, to say the least. I've never heard of anything like this happening before, but I believe you and Greer," I said, glancing back at the file on the desk.

I had a bad feeling about this. These types of things didn't just happen.

"I'm worried someone did this to get to me," Lux said quietly. I could see the anger and guilt in his eyes. "It's one of the many reasons I protect her identity. I don't want bad things to happen to her because of me … She's suffered enough already."

I got up and walked over to where he was sitting and placed a reassuring hand on his shoulder, wondering idly what he meant by her suffering.

"We will catch whoever is doing this. You can't control what other people do. I know without knowing the specifics that you do everything you can to protect her. Hell, I didn't know she existed, so I don't know how other people would either. We will catch the asshole who did this … Now, tell me where she went so I can go ask for her forgiveness for not saying anything earlier and being a passive asshole," I said, smiling crookedly at Lux. His shoulders seemed to relax a little.

"She probably is up on the roof," he said, smiling back, but it didn't reach his eyes.

I turned to walk away. Lux grabbed my hand with his tattooed dark brown one.

"She might be tough on the outside, but on the inside she's scared. And so am I. She has some things she's been going through recently that have been weighing heavy on her. So just try and give her the benefit of the doubt," he said seriously.

I wondered what exactly was happening with Greer but didn't ask.

"Okay, Lux," I said, giving his hand a reassuring squeeze before I let go.

"And thanks, Ky … this means a lot to me. To us," Lux said, pinning me with his gold eyes. A swirl of emotions went through them, but his expression was serious.

"Wish me luck," I said as I walked out of the room to find Greer.

"Good luck," Lux said, chuckling. "Hopefully she doesn't tear you apart…"

I smiled, thinking I might actually like that, coming from Greer Roberts.

☾

I found her standing on the roof, just like Lux had said.

It was close to midday, so the sun was high in the sky and the rays bounced off her hair, making it look like a living fire. Her back was to me and she had pulled on her white coat. I flickered my hands and small fire orbs surrounded her. She looked over her shoulder at me.

"Ambassador…" she said, flashing her teeth. But it was less venomous than before. Now she seemed tired. Exhausted by her own anger. "Cool party trick." She nodded to the orbs.

"Thank you. And please, for gods' sake, call me Ky," I said, offering my most charming smile as I walked up to stand beside her as she leaned against the metal railing.

"I used to dream about what it meant to live in the city," she said suddenly, as if she was far away in her memories. I glanced over and noticed the sharp lines of her jaw and arched eyebrows. On closer inspection, I realized her eyes were actually navy blue on the outside, and the green seemed to fade from dark to light from the outside. Her cheeks were flushed from the cold. A sad smile seemed to dance on her lips.

I had a random thought of tracing my finger along the shell of her ear and quickly squashed it, thinking that would absolutely not go over well coming from someone she'd just met and screamed at. Plus, it felt super inappropriate and creepy.

I hardly felt the cold with the fire in my veins, but I waved my fingers and gave a little more heat to my orbs.

I waited for her to continue. Standing next to her, even in her tall heeled boots, I easily towered over her. But she didn't feel small or weak. She felt strong and maybe a little sad. She smelled like vanilla with a little bit of spice and it made me want to lean in close and inhale her.

"I thought that the bright lights, tall buildings, and diversity of people made for a colorful dream. Like a movie that always had a happy ending … Until I realized I never belonged in that movie. I was always destined to watch from the outside. And now I've been thrust into the dark side of that dream. A nightmare for those who don't have a choice or a way to leave," she said wistfully and drummed her long black fingernails on the railing.

I didn't know what to say.

She wasn't wrong. This was a nightmare. One that was going to be extremely difficult to wake up from.

"I'm sorry this happened to you and I'm sorry I played a passive part back there. I believe you. Lux is a friend… And I should have had your back better in there," I said, wondering if my words would mean much of anything to her.

Greer turned to me fully at that point, with one hip leaning against the railing. Her eyebrows lifted in surprise.

"I appreciate that. I didn't mean to pin it all on you. I feel a bit out of control with all of this … You know, it's funny you say Lux is a friend, and he's never mentioned you, *Ambassador*," she said, smirking and drawing out Ambassador.

I had never detested that title more than I did at this exact moment.

"Well, he's certainly never mentioned you, Greer Roberts. I would have remembered," I said, taking a step closer to her.

She smiled wickedly at that. I really couldn't tell if I should be slightly scared or excited. I was a bit of both.

"Well, he has his reasons," she said, softening a little bit when talking about Lux. There was that pang of jealousy again of having a best friend who would move mountains for you. What was that like exactly?

"Greer," I said, moving to place my hand over her drumming fingers. She stilled as I lightly brushed her fingertips, sending a bit of heat through them.

Her eyes darkened, and she looked at my hand but didn't move away.

I opened my mouth to say something and suddenly the door to the roof groaned open and Lux appeared, scowling.

Greer moved her hand away and tucked it into her coat pocket.

"How long are you going to stand up here freezing your ass off?" he said from the other side of the roof.

"The Ambassador generously shared his fire, so it's fine, but I'm ready to go when you are." She walked over and he wrapped an arm around her in a comforting and familiar gesture.

"Ky," I said, correcting her, and she just smirked with her full red lips.

"*Ky*, you coming?" Lux said, smiling down at Greer and then looking up at me.

"No, I'm gonna make a call. Besides, the cold doesn't do much to me," I said, crossing my arms.

"Okay, I'll text you later," he said, turning and tucking Greer in close.

She looked over her shoulder and gave me a smile. "See you later…" she said, wiggling her fingers.

I turned my back as the metal groaned shut.

Yes, Greer Roberts, I would make it a point to see you later.

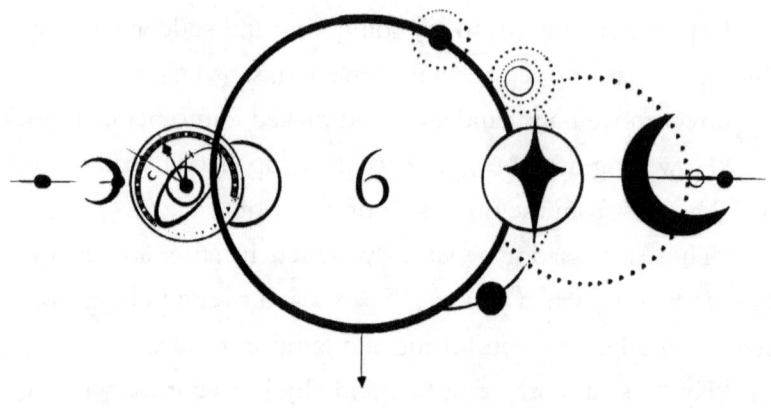

Greer

I had never met a blood witch before. If we're being honest, I didn't even know there were witches or warlocks who special-ized in blood magic. I guess I had never really needed a reason to seek one out before. Seemed a bit eerie, not that I was judging. But it seemed intense.

Lux had made a few calls after the meeting we had with the Tri-al Lord and the *Ambassador*. Now we were meeting with a blood witch a week and a half later. I didn't know who drove me more to anger, the hoity toity dwarf or the passive Ambassador.

But I suppose that wasn't exactly fair. *Ky* had come and apolo-gized to me later. It felt like we had a weird moment on the rooftop when he put his hand over mine and I felt the warmth of his fire magic. It felt oddly intimate. I wasn't entirely sure if I liked it or not.

How convenient that I didn't know Ambassador Kyra and Lux were apparently good friends. But I guess when you were as rich and powerful as Lux you, accumulated powerful friends. I had asked Lux about it after the meeting and he said they would link up at parties or charity galas. I asked him why he had never told me, and he laughed and reminded me I often had no interest in knowing about those events, which wasn't untrue. I always assumed Lux had a terrible time at those events because everyone there was most likely awful. But I didn't like that Kyra had brought it up on the roof. I didn't like surprises.

And I was Lux's best friend … How dare he have other friends I didn't know about? I knew that was a wildly insecure thought before it had fully formed, but I was feeling vulnerable right now and that had just been a little cherry on top.

I did remember Kyra's win of the Trials, vaguely, since it was only a few years ago. He was the first warlock from the Eastern Hemisphere to ever win. Most of the time, the winners were species of brute forces or champions of the elite and wealth with lots of training and money … not cunning attractive young men who came from the other unknown side of the world. I had always wondered how that worked out for him. The paparazzi splattered that information across all media outlets and everyone had been hungry for more information. I imagined that hadn't been easy for him.

People were assholes about a lot of things. The west never spoke of the east except in vague terms. So I was sure he would have gotten berated with invasive questions. His magic and features resembled other people from the west even if his specific magic had felt oddly intimate the other day when his hand had touched mine.

I knew there were some people who didn't think he should have been allowed to enter the Trials because he wasn't from the Western Hemisphere. The way they talked about him sometimes ranged from weird awe and fascination to straight up suspicion and fear. People were so close minded.

I should have probably been kinder. We were more alike than I thought, which Lux had reminded me of later. Not that we had the exact same life experience, but people seemed to be turned off by things we couldn't control about our identities.

I had just been so angry and wound up by Edward's patronizing tone. I had told Lux a long time ago not to fight my battles for me, so he had let me defend myself, but sometimes I wished Lux would just tiger out and rip people's throats out. *Sometimes*, I wanted to wake up and choose violence, but that would have literally helped nothing. I wanted to be effective, not just right.

Even though I wanted to be right too.

My thoughts drifted back to Ambassador Kyra Valequay. He was really good looking, with dark black hair that was cut short on the sides and faded up toward longer strands up top. His deep set scarlet eyes looked like rubies and showed the fire and explosive power within. The man was definitely built, standing easily over six feet tall, with slightly olive skin and a jawline that would make most people faint or boil in jealousy. He filled out his casual clothes nicely with defined biceps and decently broad shoulders.

When I first walked into the conference room, I had to check my features not to turn to anything flirty. Gods forbid a woman be sexual and powerful at the same time, you know.

Kyra's power wasn't just in his body but in his head. It was rumored he could charm many politicians and leaders to donate to his causes. But that could easily be because people didn't say no to Immortality Trials winners, especially those who wanted positions of power.

Many people who won would scurry off to party their way through all types of nightlife, enjoying their newfound wealth and power. Very few actually took an interest in doing something good for humanity, even though they had the power to. I winced, thinking that I definitely had been a little too harsh the other night, screaming at him and then acting all aloof on the rooftop. But, honestly, my life was on the line and I needed these *people* to take this seriously. Lux had told me afterward that he was a good guy. He had done a lot for the communities in the city and he'd said he was usually the first one to offer Lux support in any of his philanthropic efforts.

I had grumbled that I was sorry and I would play nice next time. Lux had just lifted one eyebrow at me and smirked. Sometimes I just wasn't nice. I was allowed to be bitchy sometimes. *Especially* about this.

I made a mental note to look more into Kyra and paw through some interviews on how he won, why he entered in the Trials, why he had left the Eastern Hemisphere and what the hell he was doing now, besides irritating me slightly and giving my belly weird butterflies with his nice warm hands.

But now was not the time to think about the *Ambassador.*

The blood witch was here. She had black skin with eyes the color of fire. Tattoos of silver stars danced around her temples and her hands. She looked like she couldn't have been much older than me, but her eyes held depths and knowledge that made her look older and wiser.

She had a tall and muscular frame, and her head was shaved, so her pink hair just made a dusting over her scalp. She was one of the most beautiful and striking women I had ever seen. Clearly, Lux thought so too, because he had a lazy smile on his face and his eyes seemed a bit unfocused. It really looked like he was trying not to drool as the witch hunched over our dining room table, reading the contract and information we had gathered about the blood contract with the games. Lux was such a flirt sometimes ... but I couldn't blame him with her.

"Well, it's very thorough…" she said with a voice like silk.

Her name was Nova Zemen, and she apparently was the most sought-after blood witch in the city. I had no idea what other ways blood magic was used besides contracts, and I felt like I probably didn't want to know how else it could be wielded, because genuinely it scared me a little.

"I don't think there's a way out of this," she said carefully, meeting my eyes across the long black table. Her gaze was intense but not unwelcome. She felt like the kind of person who would go to the ends of the earth for those important to her. And I could respect that.

"Not unless you can get the impostor to confess with their blood. Blood magic demands payment for a broken contract, which would mean your life. And I am assuming you do not want to forfeit your life. So the only option is to find the impostor before the first trial ends, or play in the Trials until the impostor is found." She furrowed her pink brows, matching her hair, and her flame eyes danced as she spoke.

It looked like she was mentally working through all possibilities of how this could happen and where a loophole could be.

"I just don't understand. Why would someone enter me in? Who has it out for me that I would have to pay with either my death or some part of my life cycle?" I said, suddenly feeling more scared than I initially thought.

This no longer felt like a joke or a dream. This shit felt *very* real.

"Greer, I'm sorry. I can't imagine how unsettling this is," Nova said with empathy in her voice.

I was fucked. There wasn't a way for me to get out of this unless the person was captured and prosecuted, but that could take weeks or months or even *years*. How did you catch someone who could masquerade as anyone they wanted?

Lux came to stand behind me and set his hands on my shoulders, squeezing slightly.

"We will get to the bottom of this, G. Whoever it is will pay for what they did," he growled slightly, sliding into something more animalistic. Another swell of love blossomed in my chest. Lux was the best family a girl could ask for.

His phone dinged, and he pulled it out of his pocket and furrowed his brow.

"It's from Ky. He said he has some news and to call him. This is good, G. I'll be right back," he said as he strolled over to the kitchen to make the call, with his long, lean frame in casual ripped jeans and some random band tee.

I wondered when our Ambassador would come back into the picture.

He had said he believed me, but he hadn't exactly detailed out how he was going to help. I guess I never really gave him a chance. I sighed and rubbed my eyes. He could be a true ally in this. I should make a better effort.

I let my thoughts wander and tried to get my breathing in check as I stared out at the skyline and my head started spiraling. Just a few weeks ago I had been happily living my human life, thinking I would get at least ninety years of life and now the best possibility is that I would lose maybe twenty years of my life or dedicate that to the government. Well, maybe not happily exactly. I still was trying to figure out how to live my life outside of Lux supporting me. But it certainly had been less complicated and deadly than this.

I had checked the stats of the Trials this morning; about 550 people had already moved to the next trial, and it had only been a week and a half. Nova gave me a look of understanding and turned back toward the paper.

"You could … technically offer a counter contract," she said carefully, her star-covered black hands flipping through the file. She chewed on her bottom lip and scowled at the pieces of paper.

"A counter contract?" I said, weighing the words in my mouth. For some reason, this did not feel like a better option. My stomach started to drop.

"Blood magic is fickle and powerful. The reason the games committee uses it so things like this don't happen. They use it as a ruse to make everyone feel like there is no coercion or political play going on with the Trials, even though that's bullshit," Nova said with an edge.

Well, she didn't like the Trials and she scored some mega points in my book for seeing it for what it really was.

"They should have never been allowed to use blood magic for this. Someone long ago showed them how, and now they weaponize it against the contestants. A counter contract would be a conditional clause that you would have to sign in blood and would need to be agreed on by both parties, but the cost would be high. It would have to be higher than the original agreed upon terms."

"What could I bargain for with more than my own life? Like a giant amount of money?" I asked, a bit dazed.

Was I really going to have to put a monetary value on my life? That felt … not great.

Nova scanned my face, which I'm sure reflected how I felt.

"It's an option … one I don't think they will take, but it's worth a shot. Especially since you seem to have some assets at your disposal," she said with a sarcastic grin, scanning the giant penthouse I currently lived in.

But that I had no part in paying for.

Ugh. I myself had little to my name.

Great.

"I'll talk to Lux…" I said, flinching because it sounded like he was my keeper or something.

Nova gave me a sympathetic smile, as if she somehow knew I felt like I was on borrowed time and generosity with Lux.

Not that he ever made me feel that way. We had talked about this before and he would always reassure me in his usual kindhearted way that he loved me, and he was happy to share this with his family, A.K.A. me. It was just something that would sneak up in times of vulnerability and emotional rawness. Right now, I pretty much was stuck in the emotional despair dumpster fire that was currently my life.

Not to mention, I hadn't showered and had basically lived in leggings and oversized hoodies, my hair permanently fixed in a bun on the top of my head, for several days. And I think the last meal I had was a glass of red wine and chocolates. Which was not a meal. At all.

Fuck, I needed to get it together. No wonder I was wallowing hard in this pity party.

My nerves felt like they were running rampant through my body and if I moved too quickly or did too much, they would rip me apart. I was pretty sure if you looked up "hot mess" in the dictionary, it would be a picture of me right now.

Good gods.

"Ky is coming over," Lux said seriously, walking back into the room and taking the seat next to me on the opposite side of Nova.

"What? Why?" I asked incredulously.

How was it that the Ambassador had copious amounts of time for Lux? How close were they really? Why the hell did I not know about him before a week ago?!

And why did I look like this when he was coming over?

My thoughts zinged off in a million different directions and I tried not to think too hard as to why it mattered what I was wearing for Kyra to come over.

I told myself it didn't matter. It didn't matter what I looked like right now, because Kyra was just a friend of Lux's.

Ugh.

These emotional snarky responses of mine were really getting out of control.

I breathed a minute to clear my head and looked up at Lux's expectant eyes. He could always see right through my toughness, and in this case he was giving me a minute to prepare for what he was going to say.

"There's been a new development in your case," Lux said through a tight jaw.

"And?" Nova said, now clearly invested in what was going on here. Why, I wasn't exactly sure. I tabled that for another conversation.

"Edward has put an official team on it..." Lux said slowly.

"That's good, right?" I said excitedly.

Why did he look like he had just been sucker punched in the gut?

"Yeah, except only for optics. Kyra said the paperwork got shuffled through and there are no resources and money being put behind it. Because he doesn't want backlash on the Trials. So for you it looks like there's an investigation and for the rest of the world it looks like nothing," he said, his voice changing from defeat to annoyance to being really pissed off.

"Fucking asshole," I swore angrily.

Nova laughed outright at that, and I think that's when I decided we would indeed be good friends.

"We will see what Ky has to say. But we're going to have to take some of this into our hands," Lux said, narrowing his eyes.

I swallowed and gazed out toward the city. I wasn't ready to have some of my life taken. I didn't want to sacrifice any of my life cycle. I didn't want to pay in government servitude. I didn't want any of this. My life felt like it had barely started.

My thoughts suddenly flashed to my mom, which they often did when I was struggling emotionally. I would not be forced into a corner the way she had. The world had been cruel to her. No one had been there to help her when she needed it.

I wasn't there when she needed it.

And by sheer dumb luck, I met Lux and we became inseparable. Then tragedy had struck his family as well, even though his parents were hurtful to their only son.

Part of me wanted to feel sorry for myself. I wanted to throw a rager of a pity party and say that I caused hurt to people around me and myself. As if my presence was a curse inviting tragedy into my life and those around me.

Except I was angry.

Because it wasn't my fault. Or my mom's. Or Lux's. It was everything else.

And it had started with these damn Trials.

"I just need to win," I said, finding some resolve in my voice. Straightening my spine, I looked into Lux's confused eyes.

"What?" he asked.

"I need a plan. I need to play. And I need to get to the next trial," I said a bit louder and stronger. Well, maybe not win, but I needed time.

"G, this is your life ... We will find a way out of this," Lux pleaded.

I looked into my best friend's face and realized he really believed it. There was no way his power, money, or influence could get me out of this. At least not immediately. There was no way out until we caught this impostor, and right now we had no leads and we had no time. And until we did, I would play.

I had to buy myself some time.

I would no longer sit idly by, waiting for the rest of my life to unfold.

I needed to do something.

I needed a plan.

I needed to *win*.

I used that anger to fuel my energy and sizzle beneath my skin and exude confidence.

"Nova," I said, locking eyes with the witch, who was carefully observing us with flame-infused eyes. "Tell me about this counter contract."

"It will come at a great cost," she said carefully, weighing her words. The stars on her temples seemed to wink with every word.

"Okay," I said, lifting my chin.

"Okay," she said, nodding, a small smile tugging on her lips.

A ding sounded as the elevator door opened to Ambassador Kyra and a woman in uniform by his side.

"Later," I said to Nova. She nodded in reply.

Lux looked like he was at a loss for words. "We need to talk about this more, Greer," Lux said seriously.

For the first time in a long time, I felt like I knew what I was supposed to do. What I needed to do. Somehow, the prospect of losing some of my life cycle, or more, made me feel motivated and free.

I smiled a little wildly at him. "Okay," I said.

Let the Trials begin.

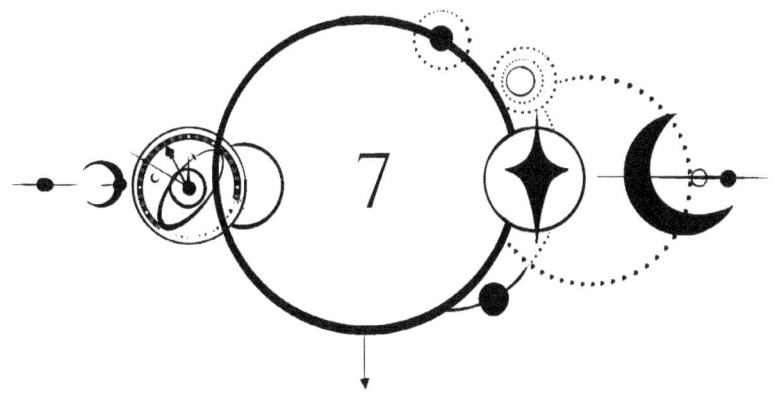

Kyra

I felt like I had interrupted something when I walked in with Special Agent Waverly Banks. Edward couldn't be bothered to show up even though this was a large-scale Immortality Trial issue, and as the Trial Lord, he should be a little more sensitive to all that was happening.

But he had said he was more than happy to have me be a liaison and work with the Federation of Extraordinary Cases, or FEC for short, even though no one else from the Trials had been notified about this. And no resources had been given to Greer's case except, well, me.

It made my blood boil that he was so dismissive. Edward was a regular on my shit list, and honestly, this just kept him securely locked in on my list for years to come.

The penthouse was massive, clearly taking up every inch of the twenty-fifth floor. Sleek white marble, gray, black, and white furnishings decorated the apartments. Lots of windows lined one side of the living area and large interesting crystal shapes created soft lighting around the space.

A worried Lux and a wickedly smiling Greer sat on one side of a long black table and a beautiful witch with stars dotting her black skin and eyes of flame sat on the other end. Papers had been strewn about on the table, as well as a few drinks and takeout containers.

I stole a glance at Greer, and even though her smile was broad, she looked like she had been sulking a bit. I wondered if she was doing all right with everything going on. Which honestly was stupid, because of course she wasn't doing all right. This whole thing was a giant mess, and she was paying the cost.

Clearing my throat, I made my way over to the table, since nobody seemed to be in a hurry to get up.

Lux's golden eyes met mine and gave a tired smile that didn't reach his eyes.

"Ambassador Kyra, this is Nova Zemen, a witch specializing in blood magic. Nova Zemen, this is Ambassador Kyra. He's helping us figure out this shit show," Lux said, nodding to each of them and working hard to keep irritation out of his voice. Clearly whatever they had been discussing before we came in had been a bit intense.

Nodding, I sat down in the chair across from Lux and gestured for Agent Waverly to sit next to me.

"This is Special Agent Waverly Banks. She has been assigned to the case and will be leading the formal investigation. The Immortality Trial Conglomerate has placed their *full support* behind this investigation but at this time wants to keep it relatively quiet as to avoid, er, complications." I was trying to remember the message I had gotten from Edward himself about how they were handling the publicity of this particular "hiccup," as he had called it.

Nova snorted and Greer's smile had disappeared into a full-blown frown and eye roll at what I said. Lux seemed relatively unaffected.

I had nearly thrown my phone against the wall at Edward's message as if the Trials didn't already screw with people's lives and now this. Edward was toeing a dangerous line here with Greer Roberts, especially since Lux was involved.

I hadn't realized how close Greer and Lux were until Lux had explained it to me the other night and now I could see it clearly.

I could feel it. And it was hard not to be envious of their strong bond.

Lux had given a few more details since we last chatted in person at the meeting with Edward. He said neither one of them had any family, so when Lux's parents died in the crash, he asked her to move in.

I tried not to ask too many questions to show how deeply interested I was in Greer, but I wanted to know more. She was the first person in a long time who made me feel something in my chest. I wanted to understand what that meant, and I wanted to understand *her*.

The more I learned, the more obvious it was that Lux and she were like brother and sister, nearly inseparable. In some ways, that clearly helped her case and in others it royally screwed the Immortality Trials Conglomerate, because Lux was powerful, rich, and influential.

But it was about time the ITC got checked. Even as a former champion, there was little I could do to touch the ITC from within, even though I damn well tried. They gave me a lot of my power, fame, influence, and money ... They could easily try to take it away. Not that I wouldn't put up a serious fight, but they could make my life *very* difficult. The politics of it all made me want to scream, but

I was learning to play the game for a longer term strategy. I just had to keep reminding myself of that.

"Now, I know you all know that's pretty much a bunch of bullshit," I said, sighing and pulling my thoughts back to the present issue at hand.

Greer.

Nova raised her brows in surprise and Greer's lips twitched into a small smile.

I wanted to see a smile that reached her eyes. But I quickly squashed that thought down and any other thoughts regarding her lips.

"Special Agent Waverly?" I said, letting her take over some of the conversation.

"Nice to meet you all. You can just call me Waverly," she said with a soft smile, nodding at everyone. The woman was a pure siren by the records I had received. Her voice could trap people into spells, and she could make them confess their deepest desires and secrets, as well as make them do unspeakable acts.

Of course, there were laws and regulations prohibiting any type of activity that would cause harm to someone, their reputations or their relationships, but I had no doubt the reason she worked for the FEC was because she could legally use her gifts in her job. Not being able to use your powers, that were a part of your very being, could cause some serious emotional and mental damage if it went on for long periods of time.

And I was pretty sure there were not very many pure sirens left. They had a target on their backs for quite some time and were often manipulated to be used by the old kingdoms in intellectual warfare several thousand years ago. They were forced to go into hiding for a while until things became more civilized.

It also meant that she nearly glittered with beauty. Her black hair almost fell to her hips and her light brown skin glowed. Her eyes were bright pink, framed by long spiky lashes. She wore a standard FEC uniform that fit her like a glove, hugging her curvy frame and gliding along her generous hips and thighs. It was a black jacket with shiny silver buttons running along the left side of her neck to her hip bone. Snug straight leg black pants came down to meet her black leather combat boots.

"All right, let's just get right to the point," Lux said harshly. "Edward does not care about Greer when all this is said and done. I imagine the little speech earlier was straight from his mouth, right, Ky? So first and foremost, Special Agent Banks, your team has access to anything and everything you need to catch whoever is behind this provided by Gilmore Enterprises."

Damn. Straight.

"Yeah, he doesn't give two shits about this situation and no one else at the Trials does either, because right now it's under wraps, which means the only people legitimately invested in this are in this room," I replied.

Edward was a gigantic prick, and I knew Lux would make him pay for the way this situation was being handled. And he deserved it.

"Honestly, I would help you for the pure sport of taking Edward down," Nova said with venom in her voice, her fire eyes dancing. She seemed to have power rolling off her in waves.

I had never met Nova Zemen in person, but I had heard of her. A blood witch was not a common affinity for witches. There were said to only be a few masters of blood magic left in this world. It made my fire and explosive power seem trivial and juvenile. It had also been rumored that she had refused immortality several times. I couldn't help but wonder if that was true and what the story was behind that.

I didn't know what Nova's beef was with Edward, but it felt like a good idea to keep on her good side.

"Officially, I will comply with what the ITC has to say, but un-officially Ky has briefed me about the situation and my team will do everything we can to help. There is something not right about this and I don't just mean in the general sense, but targeting the ITC is ballsy. And dangerous, not to mention whoever did this clearly knows intimate details about your life Greer. Which means they know that you have powerful friends..." Waverly said, her voice almost dancing around the room. She nodded at Lux for the last part.

Whoever was messing with Greer Roberts could be trying to manipulate Lux as well. He had voiced that fear earlier and it had merit. I just really hoped it wasn't true, because we didn't need any more people targeting either of them.

"But this is a bit of a race against the clock. From what Ky has told me, you all have no idea why someone would do this, and until we have some leads the trial will continue and you will either have to participate or pay the cost that the trial demands," Waverly said seriously, knowing the gravity of the situation.

Nova growled and Lux looked ready to change into a beast at any moment.

I glanced over at Greer then, eyes focused and staring straight ahead like she was working out all the details in her head. She had been all anger and fury for the last meeting, so this was a definite change of pace. Even when we had chatted briefly on the roof, she had been aloof. Less anger and more sorrow, but this focus was new.

This woman was literally looking at part of her life being taken away if she lost the first round and then death if she tried to escape the contract. She didn't look angry and wild anymore. She looked calculated and cold.

It had never been confirmed, but I had always wondered if the added years granted to the top one hundred were borrowed from those who had lost them in the previous rounds. So much life would be taken away from so many participants. Not that time worked that way, but it always felt like a bloody mess for time to be taken away from so many and infinity given to those who won. Plus, blood contracts were scary as hell. And I didn't have a clue how they legitimately worked.

There was no known way to give people back years which had been taken. Just like there was no way to reverse immortality once it had been gifted. Whoever had come up with the system long ago had a sick sense of humor.

"So I have to play," Greer said.

It was the first thing she had said since we arrived.

"If you want to protect your life cycle, then yes ... Until we can find the impostor," Waverly said gently as her pink eyes softened.

"Kyra," Greer said, her head slowly turning. Her green eyes met my scarlet ones. "I need you to give me the contestant I was assigned to deliver to the ITC."

Her eyes seemed to simmer. What exactly was her plan here? Make it past the first round? Keep going until she couldn't anymore?

"Greer ... You realize that the longer you compete, the higher the risk. The first round if you lose, you either lose one-sixth of your life cycle *or* you promise that to the government in hard labor. The next round the loss is a third, then half, then two-thirds, and then five-sixths ... I know this isn't a good option now, but it will cost you the least," I said, knowing that she probably knew all this, but the further you went in the Trials, the greater the cost of losing. It was a horrible lose-lose situation.

And she was *human*.

It would be nearly impossible for her to compete with the other contestants and species. Sure, lots of humans entered because it would be one of only a few shots of immortality, but not very many did well. A lot of other species entered because it wasn't a big deal for them to lose years off the hundreds they had, whereas humans barely had a hundred if they were lucky. It was cruel but it was the way the world had been designed, and the Trials didn't help even the playing field.

In fact, it made it worse.

Much worse.

"I am well aware of all of that," she snapped. There was that snarl again. It oddly brought my fire closer to my skin. Little flames danced on my fingertips underneath the table. My body was itching for a release of *something*.

"So you are going to try and compete?" I said, drilling my eyes into hers.

"I'm going to win," she said, straightening her spine and rolling her shoulders back.

"Okay…" I said quizzically.

Win this round? Win the next? I mean, she needed time. We all did in order to get to the bottom of this, but the longer it took, the more dangerous it would be for her to lose.

"I'll pass the first round in the next few days. We need to set up a meeting with the Trial Lord and anyone else who is important enough to be involved. I have something I want to propose to them," Greer said, looking toward the witch. The witch met her gaze and seemed to understand what Greer was referring to.

"Are you going to share with the class?" I said with a bit of irritation. I was already so out of the loop with my regular job that I didn't need it here too.

Who was Greer Roberts, really? That question had been floating in my brain continuously for the past week.

"Not yet. But soon. I need to work a few things out. In the meantime, get me the contestant I'm supposed to kidnap and set up the meeting," she said, standing and stating it all matter-of-factly.

She simmered with determination, like she had figured out the whole damn puzzle.

I suddenly realized Lux had been oddly quiet during all of this. I glanced over to where he sat next to Greer. A muscle in his jaw was feathering slightly. His gold eyes burned with anger and … fear. He was scared. I knew that they were extremely close, but if Greer really was as close to his heart as he had claimed, then Lux would be losing the one person in his life who he considered family.

No power, fame, money, or anything else could save Greer now. The Trials were, after all, meant to be an equalizer in a sense. They were meant to be taken seriously and once you signed up … well, the only options were winning or losing.

"Can I talk to you for a second, Greer?" I said. "Alone?"

"Sure, why don't we go for a walk…" she said, glancing over to Nova and Lux.

"We will keep working on things here," Lux mumbled, clearly unhappy about how things were going. Nova offered a genuine smile and nodded, a new light in her eyes.

"Let's get coffee this week. I'll have Lux give me your number," Nova said.

"Great!" Greer said cheerily.

"Special Agent Waverly, you are more than welcome to stay and ask any questions you need. Please let me know if you need anything. I'll be in touch soon," I said, nodding toward the siren.

She looked over at Lux and Nova. "Okay, I'll let you know when we find something," she said and then turned to Nova to ask a few questions.

Greer grabbed Lux's hand and gave it a light squeeze. "Be back soon," she said.

She disappeared down a hallway to what I could only assume was her room and reemerged with combat boots, a thermal instead of her hoodie, a white fuzzy hat, and a light blue coat that came down to her mid thighs.

She looked a little more alive than when I walked in earlier and it made my heart warm. She was scrappy and strong, and I liked it. Everyone here seemed to have an authenticity that I didn't often get in my section of society. Titles, power, and money weren't the main factors here. Character and integrity were.

It was a nice change of pace.

"Let's go," she said, nodding toward the elevator.

I hadn't bothered to shrug off my black double-breasted coat from earlier and I quickly slipped on the black leather gloves I had stashed in my pocket, even though I didn't really need them. It was more so people didn't give me odd looks.

"What did you want to talk about?" she said without turning toward me, a bit of skepticism in her voice. Back on her guard with me.

"The Trials," I said simply.

"Okay," was all the response I got.

The elevator was slowly passing all twenty-five floors. The confined space made the scent of her hard to ignore. That vanilla with a little bit of spice. It made something stir inside me and I ignored it for the time being.

She was in way over her head with this.

But I could at least do my best to help her, for Lux's sake. I kept telling myself that. I hoped that I would soon believe it didn't have anything to do with the way Greer continued to hand my ass to me with her snippy comments.

"So let's talk about the first trial." I pulled out my phone and sent her a quick text.

Her phone dinged and she looked at me with one brow raised and opened the text.

"How'd you get my number?" she asked while opening the file.

"Really?" I said, chuckling softly. "Lux gave it to me. That's who you're supposed to kidnap and deliver to the ITC. And I'm gonna tell you how to do it," I said confidently as the elevator doors opened to the lobby. We walked silently through the large open lobby.

I gave a nod to the front desk security personnel as we walked through the glass doors.

"All right, tell me," she said, smiling as we walked into the cool January air. This one reached her eyes and it was beautiful.

A few flurries had begun to fall and they weaved their way into her shining dark red hair that now fell in waves underneath her snow-white hat.

I would help her get to the next round.

Because something told me that Greer Roberts was not going to give up so easily.

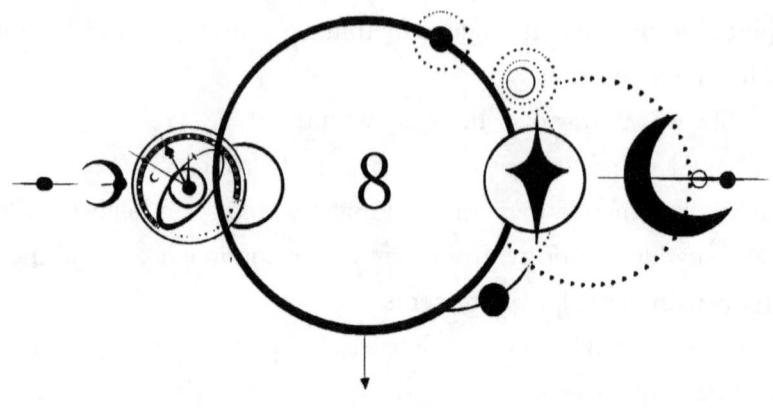

8

Greer

Kyra and I walked silently side by side. My body seemed to be in tune with his every movement, like I couldn't help but be pulled in by his center of gravity. I tried not to make it obvious that I was sneaking glances at him.

When I had been searching into his past, there were quite a few interview headlines saying the handsome Kyra Valequay, the Easterner who won the Trials ... It was gross the way headlines seem to be fixated on where he was from, as if he owed it to people to provide the answers of the other side of the world. I wondered what had drawn him to Odessa, considering it was full of ignorant ass people.

I mean, the city of Odessa was the biggest city in the Republic of the People, which is why the Immortality Trials were held here. Maybe the Trials that had been the reason. The Republic had been created hundreds of years ago around the same time as the Trials and occupied the Western Hemisphere of the world. It was meant to be a melting pot of all of the old kingdoms, species, races, and powers that occupied the world.

It seemed like that had been another lie the media had weaved considering the way Kyra was treated in interviews as either a fancy show pony or someone to be suspicious of because he grew up outside of the west.

I thought idly again how I basically knew nothing of the Eastern Hemisphere, where Kyra was from. It was just widely accepted that people didn't need to know and thus didn't ask questions. Which was weird.

I knew more about the Western Hemisphere, but not from traveling myself—just books and the internet.

There were five big cities in total in the Western Hemisphere. Odessa, the largest and the capital, smack dab in the middle of the continent. Thayer was located right above Odessa and then Kionstein to the northeast. To the south, there was Blythedale and Nicen. All of the cities were relatively the same, with varying populations. Smaller splashes of people popped up between the cities and the varying terrains. I had mostly grown up fluttering around Odessa, and that's where Lux and I had gone to university.

It was said that the Western Hemisphere, and the capital city itself, was the land that had been blessed uniquely by the old gods. If you believed in them, that is, and the stories that were told about how we all came to be.

People had fought, clawed and killed their way above one another for so long in order to achieve status, wealth and power. Some races had almost completely been extinct during the long wars of the old kingdoms. The Republic of the People had been made for *all people*. Which is why there were rules and regulations for all races of life and checks and balances for all power.

But humans still were at a bit of a disadvantage because they were born without power. Powers were hereditary. So you could get your powers if one of your parents was gifted, but it wasn't guaranteed. And if both of your parents were human, you were screwed. Like me.

And some people still had weird thoughts about keeping their power "perfect" with their children and didn't want to taint it with *human* genes. Not everyone felt that way but enough people did.

And for some fucked up reason, the Republic thought the Trials would help soothe all this discord. The Trials were meant to give *all people* a chance, but it was really more of a way for the Republic to flex its power.

Odessa was a beautiful city. It had skyscrapers, music, culture, and people of all sorts. Lux and I had decided to permanently reside here because this was where his family business was headquartered and where he felt like he could make the most impactful change.

But I couldn't help but wonder as I walked the city streets with Ambassador Kyra how he had made it here. Why had he chosen to enter the Trials? And, honestly, how the hell had he won? I knew he was a powerful warlock, but he didn't grow up in the Republic. He grew up in the Eastern Hemisphere, which I knew almost nothing about. I already doubted a lot of the government's bullshit and their story of the east was another one full of holes.

Along with the rumors of it being old and traditional, it was said the Eastern Hemisphere was full of dark magic. Danger and chaos were said to go unchecked there, but the Republic was so in love with itself it all could have been a ruse. They might just be a little sensitive to the fact that the eastern nations did not welcome Western Hemisphere citizens. In fact, none of them allowed western visitors. Travel between the nations was non-existent, which was why it was even weirder that Kyra had entered and won the Trials.

"Why did you enter the Trials, Ambassador?" I asked as we walked further and further away from my home.

Kyra had suggested we grab some coffee and find a place to get comfortable before he detailed how I was to move on to the next round of the trial.

"First of all, I refuse to answer that question until you stop calling me *Ambassador* and start calling me Ky," he said, his ruby eyes sparkling with amusement.

Damn, if those eyes didn't pull you in.

"Second, I suppose like many other people, the draw of power, wealth, and immortality were enough to suck me in," he said casually.

It wasn't that I didn't find him attractive. Because he was.

Fuck. He really was.

I kept thinking about the moment on the roof where our hands touched. Who knew hands could incite a bit of arousal?

There just was something about him that made me a bit nervous. On edge, which oddly I felt like he liked.

I took another sip of my steaming latte and squinted at him.

"I think you're lying," I said as we walked further toward the Crystal River. It wound its way through the heart of the city and was lined with parks that offered plenty of quiet, open space to talk about how I was supposed to keep my entire life cycle intact for as long as possible with the Trials.

He laughed then, a beautiful dark sound echoing from his chest. It made my toes curl a little.

"Why do you say that?" He glanced over at me while enjoying his cup of coffee.

"First off, *Ky*," I said, emphasizing his name. His lips twitched at that. "According to my research, you were powerful before the Trials. Plus, as a warlock, you already have about four hundred years to live. Not to mention you are not from the Republic. In fact, it says that your parents immigrated here from the Eastern Hemisphere when you were about fifteen. So you went through high school and college here … and it seemed like you had a promising future of becoming a lawyer ahead of you. Until you decided to enter the trial," I stated innocently.

Something about Ky didn't add up. There were bits and pieces of information missing when I had done my own research. I had done a decent amount since I last saw him, and I planned on doing much more.

I still couldn't believe the things I had read online about the conspiracy theories people weaved because he was Eastern born. It just went to show that people were suspicious of the mystery that was the other side of the world and Ky didn't owe anyone an explanation. The hypocrisy and bigotry in our society extended to so many, even a winner like Ky.

But then I had found so many other things about what he did for others and how he was involved in the community, and it made my heart squeeze a little. He had layers and I wanted to figure out where exactly the real Ky was under all of it.

"Sounds like you did quite a bit of research on me, Greer," he said.

"I wanted to know who I was dealing with," I replied.

We could now see the river up ahead, and we made our way the last few blocks to a park bench dusted with snow flurries. Ky flicked his hand and the flurries were chased away by those small flames again that he had warmed me with on the roof. The touch of his fire and his power felt again oddly intimate and sensual. I shivered not from the cold.

I laughed delighted at the magic and he gave me a wink of ruby in return. Up on the roof I had been trying for aloof, and now it didn't seem as important. Plus, it wasn't often people used their powers so flippantly, but it was nice to know that I would never freeze to death with Ky around.

I snuggled myself into the corner of the bench and faced Ky as he sat down and crossed his legs. I brought my feet up to rest on the bench so I was completely facing him.

"So fill in the blanks, Ky," I said, trying not to be distracted by the fact that his hair kept falling into his eyes.

"All of that is true…" Ky said, gazing toward the river line. There were a few people milling about, but the cold and light dusting had chased many away.

"My parents left the Eastern Hemisphere on a special visa because they wanted me to have a better life. A better chance to use my powers and get a better education," he started.

"But I was a bit resentful. I felt they used that to force me into things I didn't want to do. I wasn't super interested in becoming a lawyer, but it felt like what I had to do since my family had fought so hard for me to have something better than they had."

"They were farmers who had to work day and night. And when I was younger, I didn't really understand…" Ky swallowed and looked down at his coffee cup as if trying to figure out how to explain what had happened. I didn't mean to bring up anything uncomfortable, but I needed to know if I could trust him and I needed to know who he was.

"My mom did something similar … She wanted something for me that didn't fit. It was hard for me to deal with," I offered. "It's not easy to fulfill your parent's desires, especially if they aren't really yours."

So we did have more in common than I'd thought. It was getting harder and harder for me not to like him.

Silence filled the space and I watched him think through what he wanted to say. He studied my face, and heat blossomed in my belly. The urge to shiver was creeping up my spine again, but then he finally started talking. I almost sighed with relief.

"Precisely. It was difficult for them to understand that. And I just thought they wanted to ruin my fun as a teenager. I didn't understand that it was more than that," Ky finished, and something flashed across his face that I didn't quite know what to do with.

Pain? Disappointment? I couldn't tell.

"When I was in law school, my parents and I got into a huge fight … and I decided that I wanted to take my life into my own hands. So I entered into the Trials knowing that it would be at a great cost," Ky said, his eyes finding mine, the intensity of his gaze had that heat building up once again.

Damn.

There was more to that story, but I didn't want to push. For now, I let the silence fill the space between us until he continued on.

"And when it first started, I thought I would just try and make it the first few rounds, and then take whatever loss I could when I got beat out," Ky said quietly. "But then I realized that what I wanted was the power to help people like my parents, who felt like leaving their home country was the only option they had for a better life. I wanted to help people who were treated like less than because of things they were born with or things that were simply out of their control.

"So I made a choice, to win at any cost, and I did things to win that cost me greatly," Ky said, letting the words hang in the air.

I wondered what Ky had had to do in order to win. In order to survive the Trials. Not just physically, but emotionally. He cleared his throat and looked down. He ran his gloved hand through his dark hair and gave a crooked smile that didn't quite reach his eyes.

"Does that answer satisfy you?" he said playfully.

"For now…" I said gently, tilting my head to one side. There was more to Ky than what he had shared, but it was good enough for now. I would take my time getting through the rest. I thought I would rather enjoy it.

And I wasn't exactly laying out my life story here either, so it would do. For now.

"So why are you helping me?" I asked. This time I crossed my legs and leaned forward, getting right in his face to look into those sparkling eyes and see if I could see the truth behind them.

The fires encased in their orbs flickered as his face flashed in shock for a split second before he regained his composure.

"Because Lux is my friend. And it's the right thing to do. I'm supposed to help the contestants before, during, and after the Trials," he said, his gaze flickering from my eyes to my lips for a split second.

Interesting.

"Nothing else?" I said, challenging him with my eyes to give me something else that showed that he could be trusted.

He glanced around the park area, now covered with a fine layer of snow and leafless trees and shrubbery. There was no one else around.

"The Trials are a tradition that could use some reformation and your case brings to light some things that could enact positive change. And I would like to be a part of that," Ky said, this time fully facing me and putting an arm around the back side of the bench.

"I know what the Trials are like … and it's not something that people should have to go through in order to be…" He seemed to struggle for the right word. "Seen and heard," he finally settled on.

So even people who were a part of the Trials knew that they were archaic? Why in gods' name were we still doing this? I wanted to scream my frustration, but I kept it in check. Screaming in Ky's face wasn't exactly a way to gain his trust or his help.

Plus, from all the things I read, it seemed like the Trials had given him something over those who seemed to be determined to meet him with scorn. It seemed like for the most part he used it well, but I could only imagine the delicate balance he had to maintain in order to be the whole freaking face of the Eastern Hemisphere, which was a burden he never asked for.

"What exactly are you planning to do?" Ky said. He leaned in a bit closer so our noses were *very* close.

I leaned back a little because it felt hard to breathe when he was inches away. My heart started beating at a rather alarming rate.

"I plan to play … until we get to the bottom of this," I said casually.

"And?" Ky said, leaning back as well and arching one of his brows.

Suddenly, it felt like this conversation was like a game of cat and mouse, and I wasn't sure which role I was filling.

"And when you become aware of things, Ky, of the true nature of who powerful people are, it's difficult to become complacent," I said, choosing my words carefully.

I hadn't given a lot of thought to the Trials before, because it was easier to ignore them than try and fight them. My bubble with Lux had suddenly burst, and now I didn't really have a choice. I would have to play, and I would raise some hell while doing it.

Additionally, I was tired of sulking. I had wanted something to give me purpose and it felt like, for some reason, this fight was it. For people like my mom, other humans and even people like Ky. I was no longer content with just sitting on this. I suddenly had something bigger than myself and I wanted to engage with it. I felt like I needed to.

"Well, when you become aware, you now get a choice. You get to decide to be a part of the problem. Or you decide to be a part of the solution. And it just so happens in either situation I lose," I said seriously.

There were not very many options I could get out of this scot free. I could either sacrifice some of my life cycle or pay servitude and let the ITC continue to terrorize the people who fell victim to the trial in general. *Or* I could figure out a way to ignite a flame for change. For reformation. Because either way, I would lose some of my life. I might as well go out fighting for something bigger than myself.

I had been struggling to quell this restlessness in my life. And for some reason this cause, so to speak, had landed in my lap. I didn't really have a choice, but I was ready to make a difference.

"So I would like to be a part of the solution to do something better," I said matter-of-factly. Because Greer Roberts was no longer going to sit back on her ass and ignore it.

I was going to take a stand if it was the last thing I did, because I was really tired of being underestimated by people like the Trial Lord.

"Okay," Ky said. His ruby eyes seemed to light up with something. The small flames around us flickered out and the orbs were gone. "Let's talk about how to get you past the first trial." He offered his gloved hand as he stood.

With my coffee gone and my hand glove-free, my fingers felt frozen to the bone. I had forgotten my gloves on the way out.

But as soon as I grabbed Ky's gloved fingertips, warmth flooded into them just like before and stayed that way. I intertwined my fingers with his and he gave me a surprised smile.

"I forgot my gloves … Think I can borrow a little warmth?" I said playfully.

He peeled off his gloves and put them on my hands. His fingertips brushing my wrists and his gloves several sizes too big enveloped my pale fingers. He grabbed my hands again after adjusting the gloves and made eye contact as our fingers meshed together and I felt heat go up from my hands to my arms then across my belly.

"Better?" he said a bit huskily.

Again, there was this sense of intimacy that made my own warmth gather in my belly. I swallowed.

"Yes," I said, sounding much more composed than I felt. "Thank you. How do you … how do you make it go through my body?"

His eyes twinkled as we walked, holding hands like a normal couple. Even though we most certainly were not.

"Magic." He winked and I laughed.

His hair kept falling into his eyes and it was driving me crazy. I wanted to see every bit of his dazzling ruby eyes. But I suppose looking at his profile and ogling over his jawline and cheekbones wasn't a bad trade either.

"No shit, Sherlock," I said.

"Most of the time, it just goes to the immediate area around the skin. I'm not sure why for you it's going through your entire body," he said casually, and I nearly choked on my breath. I'd basically just admitted that I was hot for him. I almost groaned.

I cleared my throat and said instead, "Why don't you tell me about this plan of yours?"

The rest of the way, we planned how I was going to win the next trial and move on to the next round.

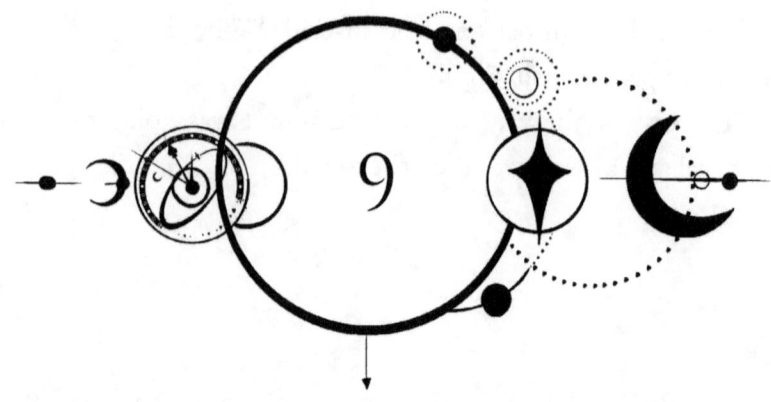

Greer

Kyra and I got back to the penthouse later than expected. Nova and Waverly had already left, and Lux was spread-eagled on the couch.

"Hiiii…" I said as I walked in with Kyra. I shrugged off my coat and slipped my boots off to reveal my bright pink socks.

"Took you long enough," Lux grumbled as he pressed mute on whatever he had been watching.

"Do you want a beer or something?" I asked both of them as I made my way into the kitchen.

"Yup," Lux said, still pouting on the couch.

"Sure, thanks…" Kyra said, a bit unsure of himself standing in the middle of the open foyer. Aww, he looked like a lost puppy. With really nice arms. And eyes I wanted to get lost in.

And I really need to get laid.

I sighed loudly and got a funny look from Lux.

I just felt lighter after talking with Ky was all. I was ready for what lay ahead. I had a plan of attack and that was more than I could say then a few hours ago. The darkness that had been looming around me for the past few weeks seemed to have some sunshine pouring through.

"Ky, you can sit down next to grumpy ass over there. He looks ready to snarl at something, so you might want to be careful," I said, grabbing three beers and popping the tops off each.

Lux stuck his tongue out at me as I handed him a beer, and Ky nodded in thanks as I handed him his. I sat next to Lux and tilted my head as I took a long sip.

"What's up?" I said.

"I called *Mr. Edward Harrington*," he said, making his voice an octave higher on the Trial Lord's name. I chuckled lightly and Kyra snorted. "The bastard basically said that there was nothing he could do within the timeline of the first trial." Lux scowled.

"So I need to pass the first trial and then he'll actually listen to what I have to say?" I said, not surprised in the least. I was pretty doubtful that after the first trial he would listen to me either.

He was stalling.

Fucking fantastic.

"Yes, and he basically refuses to listen in general because *blood contracts cannot be falsified*," Lux said, rolling his eyes.

It didn't matter if I had an airtight alibi. Whoever orchestrated this had a plan and was doing everything they could to achieve their goal, whatever that was. They were smart and probably pretty dangerous. Whatever the end goal was, it couldn't be good, at least not for me.

"I'm going to move to the next round in the trial. The day after tomorrow," I said confidently.

Lux raised his brows at me and sat up from his slouched position on the couch.

I pulled up the file on my phone and pushed it to his nose.

"This is who I have to capture in order to move on," I said carefully.

When Ky and I had been out, he had mentioned casually that when I first brought my case to him and the Trial Lord, he had looked into the contestant I had to deliver. He technically wasn't supposed to interfere in the ITC, or offer any aid to help one contestant over the other, but as a liaison and advocate for the contestants, he said the rules were gray since it was a relatively new position. Technically, he would help any contestant if they asked, but no one had ever dared to ask for this *specific type* of help. I wondered why more people didn't approach him, and then stupidly smacked myself because I knew people didn't know what to do with him. They were all afraid of something too different from what they knew.

And those feelings made people react very badly and not kindly sometimes.

"Franklin Wittenger. Age: 142. Race: Green Nymph," Lux said as he zoomed in on the picture. "This is all the information you get?" he asked, a bit shocked.

I had said the same thing when I got the file.

A picture.

Name.

Age.

Race.

The Trials really were trying to weed people out fast with this first round.

Good thing social media and Google existed, because I had found other information relatively fast and Ky had helped fill in the gaps.

"He works on the south end at the Crestwarden Bank. His break is at one o'clock. He usually takes a stroll along the south end of the river and grabs a hotdog to go at a stand close to Jorhand bridge. I'll use this," I said, holding up a clear liquid vial.

"Okay, what's that?" Lux said, squinting at the vial and taking it from my hands, rolling it between his fingers. He went to open it and I snatched it out of his hands.

"If you smell it, it will knock you out instantly," I said, laughing slightly.

I had almost done the same thing when Kyra had handed it to me.

I explained my plan to grab him and drag him to the ITC headquarters. The official rules said no one else could help me physically obtain him, so I would have to drag his ass into Lux's car myself and then he would drive us to the ITC.

"Ky, I'll call you when it gets done," I said, nodding and finishing my beer.

"Okay, I'll talk to you the day after tomorrow, then," Ky said, draining his drink and heading toward the elevator.

"See you all later," he said, waving as the elevator doors dinged shut.

"You like him," Lux said, eyeing me and sitting up a little straighter as soon as the doors had shut.

"Well, have you seen him?" I said, laughing and playfully pushing Lux as his gold eyes danced.

"Greer Roberts with a crush on Ambassador Kyra!" he squealed in a high-pitched voice.

I started roaring with laughter. "Gods, Lux, I'm twenty-four … what the hell does a crush even look like?!"

"I approve." He patted my hand and winked as he got up and gathered the empty beer bottles.

"More like he's hot and agreeing to help me … and I'm hot and desperate not to forfeit my life to the Trials. And he's nice," I said, frowning on the last part. "I don't know how I got here," I mumbled, walking over to where Lux was standing at the kitchen sink, furrowing his brow.

"This is easier … talking about my life like it's normal. Like I could hook up with some hot warlock who is also nice and forget that my life is actually on the line," I said hoarsely, swallowing hard at the end.

A knot in my belly had formed and it seemed to swallow my insides up.

"I know," Lux said, walking over to put an arm around me. His scent and presence provided a steadiness I was desperately craving.

"When I was younger, I would play the entirety of the Immortality Trials. I always was ganged up on and lost because I was human. I never made it past the first round. And I would pout and huff and puff and honestly it makes me sick. It makes me sick that I played it as a kid and I'm actually in them now. The whole thing makes me want to vomit." I said, a chill running down my spine. I looked at Lux then. There was love and compassion in his eyes. My heart squeezed and I was so thankful to have him by my side.

"All you have to do is grab that guy the day after tomorrow," he said confidently. "Then we have more time to figure this out. Which we will." Lux said, removing his arms and grabbing both my shoulders to look me in my eye.

"And by buying myself more time, this Franklin guy loses time … how messed up is that," I said, tears swimming in my eyes.

"But as a nymph, he could live to be 750 years old even with a sixth of his life cycle forfeited. Not to mention he signed up for this knowing the consequences," Lux said with resolve in his voice. "You never agreed to this," he said a little softer. "And if you lost, you would have significantly less time than that guy…" Tears were now slipping down his beautiful dark brown cheeks.

"Okay," I said, closing my eyes and exhaling long and hard. "Let's get through the next few days." I gave him a weak smile.

"Yes, we will take it day by day," Lux said, pulling me in for a hug.

I would win.

I would move on to the next round.

Hopefully everything would go according to plan.

But first I needed to have a chat with Nova.

☾

I was waiting at my favorite coffee place in the city a few blocks from my place. I had texted Nova the day before and had gotten here early to grab a spot.

I loved Roasters & Co. because it had little alcoves like booths with pillows on the bench seats and curtains you could draw closed if you wanted more privacy. I had chosen a spot in the back so I could see the front door but that was nestled far enough away from others that things could be private.

I had opted for lemon tea today, because my nerves were working on overdrive with everything that had happened in the last few days. I had decided in this moment of strength that perhaps more coffee was not the answer. I started tapping my fingers on the dark wood table and started to regret that decision when Nova walked in.

I knew very little about Nova and was curious as to why she wanted to help me so adamantly. Lux knew a lot of people and he was in the business of collecting favors, but I was having a hard time thinking that Nova would do anything for anyone else that she didn't want to do or that she didn't believe in.

She smiled and waved at me, her silver stars winking across her skin. She walked up to the counter and ordered, her eyes laughing at something the barista had said. She was tall, with long, strong arms and legs. Her pink hair and stars might have looked ridiculous on someone else, but on her it was a power move. It seemed to say I play by no one's rules but my own and I play the game of life better, so watch the fuck out.

Today, she wore all black with white boots and a pink teddy bear coat that went to her knees. She waited patiently as the barista handed over a steaming mug of what looked to be a cappuccino.

"Hey! Thanks for meeting me," I said as she slid into the seat opposite me.

"Sure, you've just made my life significantly more interesting, Greer," she said, taking a small sip of her drink before shrugging off her coat.

"I don't mean to sound ungrateful. But why are you so ready to help me?"

I trusted few people. Lux was my best friend and one of my only friends. Because most people who weren't human didn't see the need to have a human woman around. We were seen as playthings and hardly ever sought out for any type of friendship by the powerful and influential. Nova was both. I couldn't help but need to understand more of why she was here, helping me, when my experience had told me to be cautious.

People sometimes surprised me, like Arlo for example, which was one of the many reasons I stayed at the lounge, but I needed to know her reason from her own mouth.

She laughed then, a dark, twinkling sound, and her stars seemed to shudder in pleasure.

"Right to the point, I see. I appreciate that. I assume there are not many who are willing to offer their help for free to you? You have been hurt and burned before, I assume?" she said, not in an accusatory way but more like she acknowledged that this was difficult for me and that she understood.

"Yes, it's not often that powerful people help out of the goodness of their heart. Usually Lux is the driving force, but I get the feeling that there's no way you would be doing something you didn't want to do no matter how much he pushed," I said carefully.

This was not supposed to be about me, it was supposed to be about her.

Her fiery eyes seemed to flash and sizzle.

"You would be right about that. I don't do anything I don't want to do. I think we are more alike than you think, Greer. As a blood witch, I am faced with a myriad of reactions. Some fear me, hate me … want to get close because of my power, want to simply control me. I am one of the last powerful ones of my kind and I am 213 years old. I have seen the terrible and disgusting things our world has produced and the things that are accepted and normalized. I don't have many friends either." She smiled secretly like she read my thoughts earlier.

"There are few that I feel a sense of kinship or that I can truly believe their intentions to be genuine. I knew Lux's parents, in fact, and I remember seeing Lux as a small child and then again when he was a teenager. I don't normally interact with children, but he wriggled his way onto my lap and asked me about my stars. Unafraid and uninhibited.

"He said he wanted a friend. Something in his gold eyes told me he really did and maybe I did too. Most people didn't see him, I did. I knew that he struggled with his parents and their traditional values. I knew that it weighed on him. So I told him that if he needed a friend I would come and do my best. He never asked for that favor until last week. So I knew that whatever it was, was important and that the man Lux was now was someone I could get behind. I never stopped keeping tabs on him. He sparked something in me that I wanted to see through." She said everything while keeping her eyes glued to mine.

I didn't know this story. Lux had a way of crawling into people's hearts and making a forever home there. It was one of the reasons he was the absolute best male I knew. But most people didn't speak ill of his parents at all, let alone say out loud they straight up knew they were not supportive of Lux's life.

My icy walls were starting to thaw with Nova.

"Our world is broken. It was never really whole anyways, considering the way the old kingdoms treated everyone. But a large part of that is these Trials. I have been lobbying and fighting against Edward for a long time. I tried reasoning with him for many years, then tried to undermine him. I have looked for a way to truly dismantle this system for a long time, and it so happens that you provided a unique opportunity for me to try a different avenue.

"I often wonder what is the point of having great power if I can't do a damn thing to help those who truly need it. A whole system has been created so those who are vulnerable simply for being who they are suffer the consequences that society deemed their punishment long ago. It's not right … It's morally repugnant and I know Lux is one of the few people who work against the rules we are supposed to abide by. I didn't fully understand his active participation in it until he called me. Until he told me about you."

I was transfixed to the spot.

It seemed like there were indeed good and just people in the world.

And I so happened to have a best friend who actively drew them in.

I mentally kicked myself for allowing myself to stay hidden for so long. I could have been living life fully if I allowed myself. If I hadn't been so afraid of the other side of Lux's life. It would have been hard, sure. I would have had people sneer and look down at me, but I would have had the chance for something else, for relationships that were deeply fulfilling and supportive.

I didn't realize that there were people like Nova, and maybe even Kyra, who were trying to change things. I had been so wrapped up in my own world for so long that I forgot that out there, there might be people who would add to my life in ways that I never knew existed outside of Lux.

Nova smiled softly again, like she could read my thoughts as if they were plastered right on my face.

"And I so happen to believe that we should live and die. That immortality is simply another tool for those in power to stay in power and shove those they deem unworthy further into oppression. It's why I continually refuse the offer when the ITC approaches me. It infuriates them and it's kept pretty secretive, but it brings me great joy to turn them down year after year."

I laughed at this, and some of the tension I had been holding on to in my shoulders seemed to roll away.

"I would pay some serious money to see the looks on their faces whenever you refuse them," I said, smiling openly at her.

"So, Greer Roberts, I'm helping you because I sense something in you that I haven't felt for a very long time in my relatively long life … a friend who is ready to fight for what she wants and demand what she deserves. Someone who has seen trauma and hardships and made the choice to get up another day and fight," she said, taking another sip of her coffee.

"I really only decided that day that you were there that I would no longer sit idly by. I don't want you to be disappointed if I fail. I might. I have been hiding away for a long time in my comfort zone because the world has not been kind to me," I blurted. I wanted to treat her with the same honesty and transparency that she offered to me.

She tilted her head and crossed her arms, smiling.

"I know, Greer. But it only takes one moment … five seconds of deciding to be brave to make a difference. And the world has not been kind, but I don't think you will fail. And if you do, I'll help you pick up the pieces. Because it has been a long time since I have had friends who truly see me and believe in what I know to be true and right. So maybe today we both turn over a new leaf to be brave enough to ask for help, to accept it and cherish what true friends can offer," she said steadily.

It wasn't often that people spoke so openly and candidly about anything.

"I would like that very much. Not to mention, it would be nice to have a woman around instead of just Lux," I said, snorting slightly. Nova laughed and her stars blinked bright for a moment.

"Thank you, for not just helping me but for all of it. This whole thing is a shit show, but I'm grateful to have met you because of it," I said, really meaning it.

I hated when people said bad things only happen to you because you can handle it. As if the universe was testing you all the damn time for fun.

I wasn't grateful for being entered into the Trials. At all. I could die, easily.

But I could at least acknowledge that there were other things in my life that were positive. I didn't love the way I got here, and I would have chosen a different path to get to this point, but either way I was glad Nova was on it.

Nova nodded at that and placed her hand on top of mine, squeezing my fingers slightly.

"Now, let's talk about this counter contract. We are going to set a bit of a trap, so to speak, and it will at least get us some much-needed information. Edward simply won't know what he is up against," she said, smiling wickedly, and her orange eyes seemed to blaze with something new.

I was ready to take the next step.

The fire in her eyes seemed to ignite my own, so we went to work on planning my next step in this long and violent game of chess.

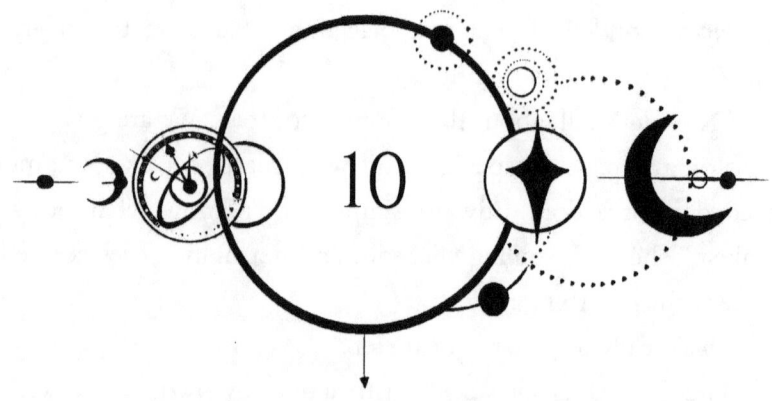

10

Greer

Remember when I said I had a nice easy plan laid out for me to win this first trial because of Ky? Well...

Everything did *not* go according to the plan.

This was not like when I was a kid. At all.

No running around the playground here and having a do over when someone lost. These stakes were much higher.

I stood in the freezing weather with snow steadily falling from the sky for about thirty minutes. Maybe he wouldn't go to his regular place today because of the weather? I checked my watch and it said *1:22 p.m.* This guy's break was only an hour and usually he was strolling the river walk at this point.

"Any sight of him?" Lux said in my ear.

He had insisted that we wear earpieces like we were the freaking secret service.

"Not yet," I grumbled, trying to look casual but feeling anything but.

My eyes scanned the river, the bridge, the park, looking for any sign of this guy. Finally, my eyes landed on him about a hundred yards out, walking toward the hot dog guy.

Gotcha.

I suddenly became engrossed in my phone as I watched him walk up to the stand, get his food, and make his way back to the bridge.

Quickly, I began walking, trying to keep my pace steady. I thumbed my switchblade in my pocket nervously. I wasn't planning on using it. It just helped bring a weird sense of comfort if things went really south.

I remembered when I was younger and was first learning how to use it, how I would sit in my bedroom before I went to sleep and pop the blade in and out, slicing a few times before settling into a rhythm.

Click. Out.

Slice right. Left. Jab.

Click. In.

I would do it walking home from school late at night when I had stayed too late at the library and missed the bus. The nervous energy that I had when I was younger seemed to push into me with a vengeance. Except I wasn't sixteen anymore. I was twenty-four, and the reality of this situation was I needed to get this over with as quickly, quietly, and as non-violently as possible.

So I used the physical presence of my blade to calm me as I walked along the river.

The man's green hued skin was covered in snowflakes, and he hustled toward the stand. He wasn't particularly large, but I was also five-four and averaged sized, so relatively that didn't mean much. He was maybe five-eight and, like, 165lbs? I definitely had a little weight on him, so that would help me some.

I could do this.

Why did this guy enter the Trials? Did he have a family?

I swore and cut those thoughts off real quick. It didn't matter. I needed to do this. I had never agreed to this, *he* had.

I was just a few steps behind him when he stopped, and I casually turned to inspect something on my phone. His emerald eyes looked at me quizzically and he pulled his black coat tight around him.

Shit.

He turned away and started walking a little bit faster to the bridge. I wrapped my hand around the potion in my other pocket so hard I'm surprised it didn't break and I started to walk faster.

He glanced back again, his emerald eyes widening in recognition as he realized what was happening and started running.

"Godsdamnit," I said as I took off after him.

He raced toward the bridge and I sprinted toward him. I was huffing and puffing, trying to catch up to him and trying not to fall on the slippery concrete.

He was almost halfway across the bridge as people were jumping out of our way.

"What's happening, G?" Lux said in my ear.

"Shut up," I growled.

I began pumping my legs faster, and I felt like I was flying and everything around me was moving in slow motion. The world seemed to still as I closed the distance between us.

I catapulted into his back and seriously misread the depth because I caught him around the back of the knees, slamming both of us into the concrete, nearly smashing my face into the ground. My knees cracked against the concrete and I yelped out.

I meant to knock fully into his back. I groaned as the hard concrete caught the rest of my body—that would probably leave a bruise.

He was frozen for a solid five seconds after getting the breath knocked out of him. I tried to pull the vial out quickly, but he was scrambling away. He slammed his foot into my face. My head snapped back, and I knew I would have a raging headache for the next day or so. I tasted blood in my mouth as I slammed back onto the ground, this time catching my hip bone with an ugly crunch.

"Shit," I said as I tried to get up and belly flop on top of him in an effort to subdue him, but failed miserably and ended up smacking both of my hip bones down on the hard, cold ground as he rolled away.

I staggered up, going for another grab with blood dripping out of my mouth. I was trying to keep him steady while he was trying to land another kick to my face and crawl away.

I wiggled the vial out of my pocket and attempted to open it.

"Get away from me!" He snarled and caught me in the abdomen, which was honestly an improvement to my face being smashed again. He pushed with both of his feet and sent me flying. I went sprawling with the wind knocked out of me and the vial I had been clutching bounced away from me a few feet to the left.

He was clawing at the slick concrete, trying to stand, and I sucked in a gasping breath that made everything hurt.

I made the split-second decision to grab the vial and then try again to knock him down.

Five seconds of bravery, Greer.

I could do this.

I shoved myself off the snow covered concrete and sent all my willpower to my legs.

I sprinted to the left. Time seemed to slow around me, and I slid low to grab the vial in my hands and pivoted on my feet to run after him again.

This time I didn't miss, as he sprinted away and I battle-screamed, launching myself right at his back and tumbling both of us to the ground with a crunch of bone. I scraped my hands in an attempt to break the fall, but we both went rolling and this time I was quicker.

I pulled my scarf up to cover my own nose and mouth and popped open the vial with my other hand and shoved it at his face before he could get up again.

He tried to squirm away and something in my belly rolled. He looked scared and embarrassed. I let those emotions slide over me and pressed the vial underneath his nostrils.

His eyes widened then went dark, and he went limp underneath the weight of me.

Breathing hard, I closed my eyes and gave myself a solid ten seconds to kill the nausea rolling in my belly.

"I'm sorry," I mumbled as I grabbed his armpits and dragged him the remaining thirty yards to the other side of the bridge. I wished I didn't have to do this, but I needed to win. He had more years than me and he had signed up willingly.

I hadn't, and I tried to use that to comfort myself.

People milled around, looking alarmed. I gritted my teeth as I pulled his body toward the end of the bridge so Lux could pick me up.

"Official Immortality Trial business," I said to a particular horrified couple walking by. Immediately they relaxed and even told me good luck.

I attempted a smile, but it came out as a disgusted sneer.

Why in gods' names was this ever considered normal?

Because it really wasn't.

Lux was laughing into my ear. "Sounds like you got him."

"Shut up!" I growled. "Meet me on the east side of the bridge, you ass."

Lux pulled up in a black sedan and rolled down the window. He went to get out of the car and I hissed, "You can't touch him, otherwise I get disqualified and it doesn't count."

I remembered Ky's words that no one could physically assist me in the kidnapping. Lux could drive the car, but he couldn't touch him.

Lux quietly raised his brows as I struggled to get this man in the back seat. Finally, I tucked his feet in and got in the front seat to a grinning Lux.

"That wasn't so bad," he said. "Except it looks like your face took a beating."

"Just drive," I huffed out, my eyes directly forward.

And he did.

I flipped down the mirror and surveyed my face. An angry indentation was already forming on my face that matched the underside of his shoe. Great. I wiped the blood dripping off my mouth and took a swig of water to try and rinse the red out of my teeth.

I looked at my palms that were covered in scratches and then winced, thinking of the bruises that would probably be on my knees and belly from his feet and the hard reality of the concrete. Something I should probably get used to, now that the trial was in full swing.

The city roared past, glassy skyscrapers and dark office buildings lining either side of the streets. People of all colors, shapes, species, and sizes roamed throughout the city and went on with their day like it was totally fine for people to kidnap other people for the sake of power.

Ugh.

We arrived at the official ITC building and I swallowed hard. I kept glancing back at Franklin, trying not to feel guilty for cutting his life off by a sixth. It would be easier if he had been a bad person or something, but he'd seemed normal when I'd looked him up. Boring, even. He hadn't even used his magic to defend against me.

He seemed terrified and angry.

Why the hell were you in the trial?

We pulled up to the building where two security guards were standing. I hopped out of the car and pointed at one. "I'm a contestant and I have my hostage," I said nonchalantly.

They looked at one another and nodded as they got the unconscious man out of the backseat in one swift motion.

"Go to the elevator and head to the tenth floor. You'll need to wait until this is verified and then you'll get your next set of instructions," one of them said in a deep voice.

I nodded and then nodded to Lux.

Let the games begin.

I walked straight to the elevator and pressed the up arrow to find the Trial Lord himself waiting for me as the doors opened.

"Hello, Miss Roberts," he said. "This way."

He had clearly been expecting me. I didn't know if that was a good or bad sign.

Probably bad, but I needed to set the second part of my plan in motion, the one Nova and I had worked on for hours the day before.

His gaze flickered to the indention on my face. The only recognition that anything was amiss.

Then I followed him and resolved myself to be brave, again.

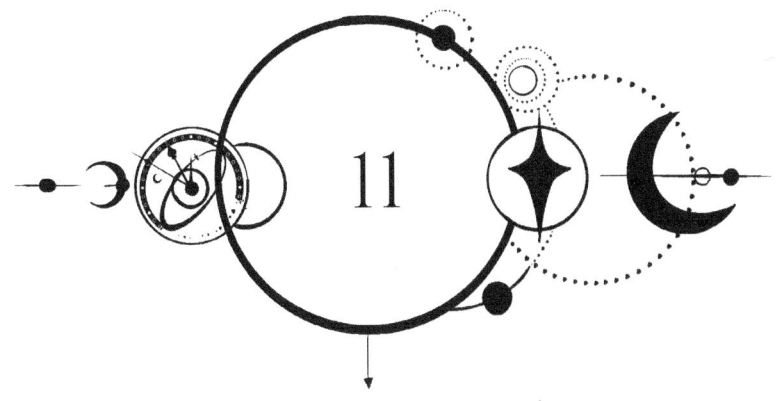

11

Greer

So you passed the first round, congratulations." Edward smiled through crooked teeth. It wasn't friendly. It felt menacing and manipulative.

"Now you'll listen," I said as I sat across from him, perched behind a large oak desk.

This was clearly his personal office. It was pretty bare, besides the large desk and two bookshelves framing either side of the room. There were no pictures or anything personal loitering around the room. In fact, the bookshelves seemed to be filled with the same style black bound book. A large window opened up behind him and two chairs were placed in front of the desk, which was where I was currently sitting.

"Now I will listen," he said.

He looked like he was enjoying the fact that I was in this position. Maybe he was behind the falsified blood contracts. Nova and I had talked about this yesterday, but we didn't get very far into that theory. We needed more information.

There were always plenty of contestants entering the Trials. The whole thing brought in an incredible amount of money to the

ITC and the government. Why create this whole ruse for someone like me? There were too many unanswered questions, and my plan today was to start to uncover some of them.

"I want to offer a counter contract," I said slowly.

After Nova and I had spent several hours getting coffee, she came back over to my place so we could loop Lux in. We had all been up late trying to come up with a ridiculously high monetary number to throw at the Trial Lord in order to get a read on him.

I don't recommend trying to put a dollar amount to your life. It isn't particularly enjoyable. I really needed to stop doing things that sent my anxiety skyrocketing, but alas, this was the reality of my life at the moment.

He sat back in his chair and brought one long fingernail to tap against his chin.

"A counter blood contract?" he said, looking intrigued.

"Yes," I said evenly. I needed to see his hand. I needed to see exactly what he was playing at, because if he was involved with whoever had falsely admitted me, it would make things exceedingly more difficult. But at least we would know what I was up against. It was hard to fight an enemy you didn't know and couldn't pinpoint.

"Now, why would I do that? See, Miss Roberts, there are a lot of contestants who try to counter the blood contract once their failure is … inevitable," he said lightly, as if he had this conversation all the time.

Which maybe he did. It wouldn't be unheard of for someone trying to work their way out of the blood contract once they figured out that they couldn't win.

I mean, I would try it even if I weren't in this position.

"There is nothing I can do if the blood matches unless the impostor comes forward and confesses and pays with their life." Edward gently folded his hands on top of his desk and somehow managed to stare down his nose at me.

Nova had told me that if he really wanted to, Edward could null and void the blood contract. But if he did that with mine, he would have to do it with all the contracts. Which I knew he wouldn't do, because then his precious trial would come crashing down. So it was pretty much a given that he wouldn't take my offer unless it was ridiculously high.

And even then, if it got out that he had accepted an offer from a human woman, it would not bode well for anyone. Including myself.

So even though I wanted him to take my offer, for this whole thing to be over as quickly as it started, there would be consequences if he accepted. And I would still need to know who actually had entered as me so we could make sure that person never did anything like that to me, or anyone else, ever again.

"The Immortality Trials must have payment for winning and losing. The Trials help lots of people reach their highest potential. It gives everyone a fair chance of winning and it gives hope," he stated like he was reading it out of the official Immortality Trials handbook.

Gross.

"So, you see, there isn't much of anything you could offer as a counter contract because I already seem to have the upper hand. I admire your dedication to this falsehood you have claimed, but you see my hands are tied."

His sickening smile reached his eyes this time.

What a prick.

"Not to mention the blood contract demands an equal or higher exchange, so unless you can offer me something like that, I am going to have to ask you to leave," he said, gesturing toward the door.

"Twenty million dollars," I said, trying to rein in my anger.

Lux, Nova, and I had talked it over and he would pay for my life.

Which was honestly really, *really* messed up.

Was my life worth twenty million?

It made me sick to put a price on my head. Lux was the one who actually came up with the number, and I just had numbly nodded my head.

I shuddered to think of how much good that money could do for the causes that Lux, Nova and Kyra supported. I didn't deserve that money, but Lux would pay it.

Nova had said that would be more than enough in the eyes of the blood contract. She said it had to be a bit inflated because if he refused, we would know for sure he wasn't going to aid me, at all. Which meant the ITC wasn't going to aid me, and Waverly could only do so much on her side without their support.

I still needed to get a better pulse on her as well, because even though Ky had brought her in, she still was employed by the ITC.

The whole politics of this made my head spin, and I was *reall-lyyy* hoping he would take the twenty million.

But then again, I didn't want him to, because I didn't need Lux literally paying for my life.

My head space continued to be a confusing place to live for many reasons.

A slow smile spread across this man's face. "What an interesting offer. But no. Money will not allow you to escape. And I imagine it isn't yours either ... but rather Luxton Gilmore's. What an interesting relationship you must have if he is willing to put so much money on the line for you..." he said in a really creepy way. "Therefore, you might want to start training for the next trial. Good day, Miss Roberts."

"Why won't you let me out for twenty million? That's more than enough to cover it and you would walk away very rich. Are you hiding something, Edward? I was falsely admitted to the Trials, and you won't accept that as truth either. Seems a bit suspicious that you won't take such a large sum of money or believe what I have to say…" I said, innocently batting my eyelashes.

"I will overlook your blatant disrespect, Ms. Roberts, in insinuating that I am up to something nefarious. If I accepted your money, I would have to accept everyone's pleas. You do not get special treatment, and until I get proof you were admitted, I am not interested in hearing you cry wolf. Very typical of a human to behave this way, if you ask me. This conversation is over," he said curtly and turned to pick up his phone.

And just like that, I was dismissed. I had literally just offered my entire life in a lump sum and he had flat out refused with no hesitation. I had tried to call him out on not believing my claims and been told I was manipulating the situation simply because I was a human looking for special treatment.

None of which was surprising exactly, but it sort of was. It was twenty million dollars, for gods' sake!

What was he protecting that he wouldn't accept that sort of offer? He was a fool to refuse such money. He could have made it so that no one would know that the deal was made.

But at least we had some sort of pulse on where he was at. It definitely seemed like he never had any intention of accepting anything that I was going to offer. My truth or my money. He was as bad as Nova said he was.

Maybe even worse.

Now we knew that I wasn't going to be able to slide out of the blood contract, we needed to move forward in preparing me for the Trials and put all our effort into the investigation.

And we could entertain the idea of whether he was involved with my admittance to the Trials, or if he was just happily watching it all from the sidelines?

There were so many unanswered questions and too little places to start.

I stormed through the building, trying to find my way back to the lobby, and realized I was a bit lost.

Shit.

All the hallways looked the same, and no one seemed to give me the time of day as people hustled about.

I didn't have the energy to deal with any more assholes today. So I took a right looking for the stairs and walked straight into Waverly.

"Oh, Special Agent," I said.

"Greer! What are you doing here? Did you make it past the first trial?" she said. Her light brown skin was a little flushed, and her dark hair was up in a high ponytail. Her beauty was almost ethereal, and her voice moved around you like a warm embrace. The power of the siren.

She was a little shorter than me, but her energy took up space.

Her pink eyes were lit in surprise.

"What happened? Your face looks like it met someone's foot…" she said, looking concerned.

"Yes, I passed but not before I got kicked in the face. It's fine, though. Actually, do you have a minute to chat?" I said, looking around at the other people here skeptically.

"Yes, of course. Let's go find an empty conference room. You sure you don't want ice or something?" she said, nodding and turning on her heel and leading me through the corridors.

"I'm good!" I said, wincing as I tried to make an overly expressive face and my nose and cheekbones practically screamed. I sighed. I would need to deal with that physical pain later.

Right now, it was time to see where Waverly Banks stood in this fight.

"What did you want to talk about, Greer?" Waverly asked as she closed the door to a small conference room. Her voice seemed to whisper across my skin. It was a sensation that I was having a hard time getting used to, but that was the gift of the siren.

The room itself was pretty plain. A table and some chairs, a large television with wires hanging from the wall.

I looked around to see if there were any obvious listening devices. Not that it really mattered. I just didn't like the idea of anyone eavesdropping.

I made myself comfortable in a chair and Waverly sat opposite of me.

"You. Why are you helping me, Waverly?" I said, not trying to sound accusatory but simply wanting to understand where she stood in this. I knew where Edward stood now; a wholly unhelpful prick who may or may not be involved in why I was here but was unwilling to let me out of my contract, even for twenty mil.

She smiled softly. "I understand you being on your guard, Greer. I know humans face things that I could never imagine." Her pink eyes seemed to be shining with empathy and understanding. "But there are not many of my kind. And even fewer places where we are welcomed and supported. The FEC uses me and I use it. It's not a perfect system per se, but I try my best to hold myself and my team to a high standard of excellence and integrity. Many people mistake me for a human until they hear me speak, and then they know … I'm not saying I know exactly how you feel because I don't. But I have had glimpses of it, and I know that is unacceptable and disconcerting, to say the least."

Her eyes took on a dreamy quality.

"Sometimes I dream of a world where people are accepted exactly as they are and there is no association of worth to power, wealth, race, species, etc., but I was always a dreamer … Lots of people think it's silly when I talk like this, but I learned a long time ago that the opinions of others only hold as much value as you give them. It can sometimes be lonely and cynical, but I would rather be alone than be surrounded by people who act as if they are owed power and privilege by simply being born. And I am hoping in your case I can actually help you. I know cases like this get pushed under the rug. I've seen it happen many times and have tried my best to offer my support through my job or off duty…" The dreamy eyes had been replaced with something a bit sinister. Her eyes seemed to say that she had done things that would not be looked upon favorably with the FEC.

"I don't think that's silly at all … This isn't supposed to be an attack by any means. I just … I don't know how to do this very well. Let other people help, when I've gotten looked over, ignored, or fucked with before … It's hard for me to accept this, you, your intentions, you know?" I was stumbling over my words.

Here was Waverly proving me wrong, just like Nova had.

There were good people out there and I just hadn't worked very hard to find them because I was afraid of what else lay in the world. I rubbed my fingertips to my temple where the headache was forming from being foot slammed earlier.

"I know you are just trying to navigate this the best way you know how … You don't need to apologize. Just know that I am here for you as a resource and a friend. It seems like you could use a few more of those and honestly I could too," she said, folding her light brown hands together in front of her.

"I've really only ever had Lux. Having you and Nova help me…" I trailed off.

"And Kyra," she said, winking.

I rolled my eyes.

"Yes, and the Ambassador is sort of a hard pill to swallow. I practically jumped down Nova's throat too. I've never had girl-friends who met me where I was at. Who just were there because they were good people and wanted a friend as opposed to some-thing else…"

"Probably not surprising since I demanded an audience with you and asked what your intentions were like a sixteen-year-old girl's dad on a first date…" I said, laughing and putting my head in my hands. I winced, forgetting the angry welt and probably bruise that was blossoming on my face.

She laughed too and it sounded like a song.

"When you're used to the world being against you, it can be hard to accept there are people who would treat you differently. I think that's valid. I've felt it in different entities … people want my power for their own gain. They want to control and manipulate me so they can do it for others. I've had many … males, especially, try to take advantage of that. But when you care about someone, it's not about control. It's about giving them space and support to be-come what they want. It's about letting them write their own story and being happy to play a part in their joy, hardships, and every-thing in between," she said, smiling fully at me.

Damn, I wasn't expecting to find friends in Nova and Waverly.

It felt nice. Warm and fuzzy.

"I think I want to get drunk with you and Nova sometime and shit on society," I said suddenly, perking up and laughing a little.

"I would like that very much. Name a time and place I'm there," she said cheerily.

"One more thing…" I said, tilting my head to the side. "How old are you?"

She smiled broadly. "If I told you I was seventy-eight, would you tell me I didn't look a day over twenty-five?" she said, winking.

I laughed again loudly and without restraint. "Which means you both could probably drink me underneath the table. Guess we'll just have to wait and see," I said, standing up and moving toward the door.

Waverly met my stride and stood next to me a few inches shorter than me in her pristine FEC uniform.

She pulled me in for a tight hug. "You have no idea what I'm capable of, Greer." She smiled and laughed wickedly as we left the room.

I felt lighter. Like pieces of my life were making a bit more sense.

That just left Kyra.

The piece of our team that didn't snuggle in like the rest. In fact, it felt like it had some jagged edges that I was interested in smoothing out with my own hands … and other things which actually made zero sense.

He built a heat in me that made me quick to anger because I didn't know what to do with all this feeling inside me. Like it wanted to bubble out and explode in a movement of breathtaking release. And I wanted to drag him down with me and into it just to see what would happen.

I shook my head and decided that would be my next obstacle.

Figure out what the hell to do with Kyra Valequay.

☾

I made my way out of the building to where Lux was sitting in his car.

"What took you so long?" he said, concern forming on his brow.

"I talked to Edward and then I ran into Waverly," I said calmly as I slid into the car. "He refused, of course," I grumbled, slouching in my seat and folding my arms across my chest.

"Asshole," Lux said, gripping the steering wheel.

"I think I'm making friends…" I said absently as we drove off.

"Are you? Look at Greer Roberts making girlfriends!" Lux said, feigning over-the-top excitement.

I laughed and shoved at his shoulder.

"I'm happy for you, G. These are good people," he said, smiling over at me.

"Maybe I should have joined you more … you know, at the rich socially elite parties," I said quietly.

"Nah, I think you still would have hated it. Plus, Nova, Waverly, and Kyra are of a different breed … Special. Like you," he said, winking.

And there was Kyra again. The piece that wasn't fitting in quite like the rest.

Later. I would deal with the weird heat in my belly that spread through my body like his power, *later.*

I fell silent and let my thoughts drift back to Edward. We all knew he would refuse, but it was at least worth a shot even though the dollar amount still made me want to vomit uncontrollably.

I had a bad feeling that whoever was behind this was playing a much bigger game than we knew. And I had no idea how we were going to find out more about who had entered me before more of my life cycle was gambled away.

The Trials could burn in hell for all I cared, but I didn't want to burn down with it. They didn't care about me. They didn't care about the other contestants. They just wanted their money and to flex their godsdamn power.

But now I had some powerful friends.

Ones who were interested in the same things.

Ones who didn't care that I was human, they didn't think me weak or pitiful. They accepted that I was capable, strong and resilient.

I wasn't going to take all this lying down.

"Lux, call Kyra. I need to get ready for the next trial," I said confidently. I needed all the help I could get.

Including from Ky.

My unsolved puzzle piece.

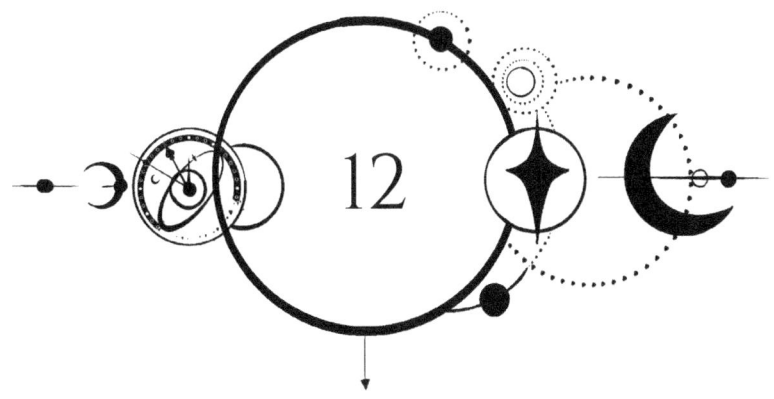

12

Kyra

Well, Greer passed the first trial. That was a good sign, and Edward had flat out refused the money offer, which told all of us that he should be investigated.

Because who the hell turned down twenty million dollars? Nova had told us that there wasn't a specification in the contract that said he couldn't void it for something of equal or greater value and Greer's life estimate was actually far less than twenty million. Not that that piece of information was helpful, but still. It was sickening enough to put a price on someone's life, but there wasn't much of a choice.

Plus, Lux had insisted the number be high because her life was important to him and because we needed to incentivize him to take it. But he didn't, which meant there was definitely something really fishy going on behind the scenes, and now we needed to get Greer ready for the second round.

How was it that just a few weeks ago I had no idea who Greer Roberts was and now I couldn't get the scent of her and that long wine-colored hair out of my head?

It was a bit invasive how often she floated into my head even though we had only spent a handful of moments together.

She basically had a death sentence hanging over her head. She was human and pretty much doomed to fail. But here I was thinking about those green eyes and moving my entire schedule around to help her and Lux through this mess.

"Earth to Ky..." Lux said from across the table, snapping his fingers in my face.

"Right, sorry," I said, straightening in my seat and looking over to where Greer sat next to Lux with an amused smile on her lips and Lux looking a little bit pissy.

The welts and bruises on her face had made a rage well inside of me that I didn't understand. Her top lip was swollen and cracked. She had said she had been kicked in the face, the stomach and her hands were scraped up. Which wasn't uncommon for the first trial, but it still made me furious that someone had done that. But they looked like true battle wounds. She looked like a true born warrior.

It was sort of sexy, which didn't make any fucking sense.

I really needed to get this under control if I thought these things were attractive. What the hell was wrong with me?

Nova was here again. It seemed as if the witch had taken a liking to Greer and the case. They had a closeness to them that didn't exist the last time I saw them together. It seemed like Greer was good at forming those "soul connections" as Lux had said.

Another pang of something hit my chest. What exactly had they shared that made them so close so quickly?

Nova was incredibly smart and had invaluable knowledge about the blood contracts and it seemed like she was now fully invested in the case. Agent Waverly was here as well, and she kept stealing glances at Nova when she thought no one was looking.

There seemed to be another relationship that had formed overnight with Greer. I had no idea where she was finding the time to connect with Nova and Waverly.

How was everyone suddenly so close to her?

Were they all drawn to her strength like I was? The fire inside her that seemed to grow with every passing day. I cringed, thinking of how embarrassing all of this sounded in my head. I really needed to get it together and stop my own stealing glances at Greer like a shy schoolboy. I forced myself back to the present and what I needed to communicate to this newly formed team for Greer.

"We need to start training you for the next trial, right away. It will be thirty days from when the thousandth contestant turns in their hostage," I said, trying to bring my focus away from Greer's swollen lips and toward the situation at hand. It was proving to be a bit of an oddly difficult task. I wanted to chase her pain away with my mouth.

Clearly, I needed to take a lover or bed someone quickly because it had been how many months? Too many to count and clearly my body was feeling the effects. I sighed and received a look from Lux like he could see straight into my head.

I cleared my throat and looked away.

"The next trial will be physical fitness, and the top 750 contestants are the ones to make it," I said, trying to work through my head how the hell she was going to get through this one.

This is where most humans fell off. Almost all other races had stronger physical abilities, or they could use magic to bolster their bodies in order to win. Not to mention she hadn't been training for this at all because she had no idea she would need to. Some people trained for *years* before they entered the Trials.

"We won't know the physical fitness test until the conclusion of the first trial, which could be any day now. We need to start preparing your body now for whatever comes your way," I said finally.

It could very well be anything. For mine, we had all gotten dropped off at the base of a mountain and got told to climb until the first 750 people made it. I had nearly died several times as exhaustion and fatigue took over and the rocks became dangerously steep. It sometimes still haunted my nightmares. It was meant to weed out the weak, but it seemed a bit unfair to anyone who had animal instincts, shifting or gifts considering it was that much easier to push your body to the limit when it was already accustomed to doing so.

"Okay, let's start in a few days," Greer said seriously.

"What about the case, Waverly?" she said, directing her attention to the siren.

"Well, we know that the impostor has to be a shifter. Realistically, they were for hire. So we find the shifter and then we can get you out of the blood contract and then we can get to the bottom of why this happened in the first place," she said confidently.

Waverly had confided in me earlier that she was really only with the FEC because it gave her full range to use her powers in a way that was safe, and she felt like she could actually help people. Plus, they offered protection … Sirens were rare, and it was something she didn't often tell people until absolutely necessary.

Magic really was a fickle thing.

"There are only a handful of powerful legitimate shifters in the city capable of duping a blood contract and I already looked into them. They all have airtight alibis for when the impostor entered you. But as far as the more criminal ones … that list is longer. The mercenaries are dangerous, and we would need to pay them some visits to check out where they were when you were being entered. I am guessing it was someone for hire and that whoever paid them is the person we want to talk to," Lux said.

I watched Greer tap her fingers on the table. "I have someone at the lounge I can connect with. They are well connected within the underbelly of the city. They usually come in on the weekend … Which I guess means it's a good thing that it's only Monday," she mused. "I'll talk to him this week."

"You're still working at the Shadow Lounge?" I said, trying to keep the shock out of my voice.

"And?" she said, narrowing her eyes and squaring her shoulders at me. There was that fiery anger sizzling in her. It practically matched my own.

"You're participating in the Trials, training, this investigation and working a full-time job…?" I said, ticking off all the things on my fingertips. "It seems like a lot of things on your plate right now," I said, trying to convey concern but coming off a bit pretentious.

"I've got it handled, thank you," she said, snarling through her words.

Why did we always end up snapping at each other?

"Okay, well, we will start at six a.m. on Thursday," I said through gritted teeth. She couldn't afford to be distracted. It would get her killed.

Her eyes nearly bulged out her head. Clearly, waking up early wasn't part of her busy schedule.

"How about nine?" she countered.

"I have a full-time job as well, Greer," I said, tilting my head to the side and flashing a grin.

"Fine, but bring some coffee," she grumbled.

Lux snickered and Waverly looked busy with her phone, leaving Nova to scowl at the whole thing.

"Mkay. Well, I'm going to get some food. Text me your takeout orders, I'm heading to the potsticker place around the corner…" Greer said, moving around the penthouse to grab her coat.

"I'll go with you," I said, and it was like the whole room stopped and everyone's eyes were on me.

"I can handle getting food on my own," Greer said, narrowing her eyes and pursing her lips while leaning over onto one hip.

"Yes, I am sure you can, but you shouldn't be out alone because of the trial. We don't know what you're up against … Plus, you're injured." I looked over at Lux, who smiled goofily at me and Nova, who had one eyebrow raised. Waverly smirked.

"I'm fine. But okay … Come on, *Ambassador,*" she said, over exaggerating the last word.

"Don't forget your gloves this time," I whispered, brushing my mouth close to her ear as she stood at the kitchen counter. She stiffened and I could have sworn she shivered.

She whipped her head around, so her mouth was dangerously close to mine.

"Didn't realize holding my hand was such an inconvenience for you, Ky," she said, her green eyes blazing. She stalked over to the elevator and I got in beside her.

The doors closed to an amused looking Nova, Waverly, and Lux.

She was pouting next to me slightly and looking straight ahead.

I stepped in front of her and put my hand on the wall beside her head. Her lips opened in a little o of surprise.

I grabbed one of her hands and interlaced my fingers through hers, and brought it to my chest.

"It wasn't an inconvenience, I just don't want you to get frostbite," I said, holding her gaze and laying a heated kiss on her gloved palm. Her eyelashes fluttered a little bit.

"Why are we always snapping at one another?" I said, letting my eyes travel along the lines of her bruises and angry red shoe marks. I stomped out the rage that consumed me when I thought of someone hurting her. Her hair was in a braid today, traveling down the beautiful curve of her back.

"It seems like everyone else in there has seen a part of Greer that I haven't. Why exactly haven't you shared that with me?" I said, tilting my head slightly and sending small waves of heat off my body as I leaned in closer to her, her hand at my heart entangled with my own and my elbow now leaning against the matte black walls of the elevator.

She swallowed and I looked at the curve of her throat.

I didn't like to play games. But I didn't know what to do with this need to be closer to her and know her. It was a bit foreign to me and I didn't want her or anyone else to get up in this as collateral damage to what was going on with her case.

Lux was a good friend.

But I had never felt a pull or push with someone before like I had with her.

Her eyes seemed to sparkle with something I didn't quite know how to name.

"You stir something in me. I can't explain it. It puts me on edge," she said a bit breathily. Now our faces were only inches apart. The elevator door opened, and she gently put her arm out and I walked back a step or two.

"And I would say I put you a bit on edge as well, Ky..." she said as she pulled away and walked out of the elevator, forcing me to follow her with this deep need for her thrumming through my veins.

We were waiting in the small cafe for our to-go order. We had said little on our ten-minute walk here after the intensity of the elevator.

The place was small, with only a handful of plastic chairs and tables, and a white counter and a menu board hanging above. When we walked in, Greer had smiled and said it didn't look like much but they had the best potstickers in the city. It smelled heavenly, and I left her inside with a small smile on her lips as she waited for our order. My assistant had called and asked about my schedule this week and I didn't want to talk about Greer in front of her to my assistant.

I told her that I would chat with her later this evening because we needed to work out Greer's training schedule. She was demanding quite a bit of my time without seeming like she actually enjoyed it. I ran my hands through my hair and sighed.

Why did every interaction with Greer leave me emotionally raw and prickly?

There would certainly be lots of time for us to figure it out with all the time we would be spending together. She just got under my skin in a way that made me want to strip myself and her bare to figure out what the hell this energy between us was.

I growled slightly, trying to keep myself together. It wasn't just attraction but something else that made me want to see what happened when we truly collided. I had a feeling we would both be reeling.

I took about thirty seconds to get this strange arousal under control and I walked in to see some male chatting her up.

She had grabbed the food and had a smile painted on that looked like the most insincere expression I had ever seen on her face. Her spine was rigid, and this guy was right up in her space.

He was taller than her and looked almost wolfish, with dark hair coming to his shoulders and wide shoulders with pale skin and brown eyes. He could be an animalia or shifter.

Something in the way he was leering was animal-like, not human.

He leaned in and smelled her, tracing a finger across her swollen lips and then the welts on her cheeks.

White hot rage roiled through me and I forced myself to stay calm. To not unleash my fire on this male.

Her face melted into horror, then anger to extreme discomfort. Her eyes flashed and she pushed him away. Her eyes connected with mine as I strolled over.

"Hi, babe … Looks like you got our food. Can I help you with something?" I said, slinging my arm around her shoulder to level my eyes with the predatory male in front of her. He smiled, showing pointed teeth, and tilted his head to the side.

"Ah the Eastern Ambassador, Kyra," he said, scoffing at me, recognizing me from the media and not taking kindly to who I was and where I was from.

"A human woman and an *Easterner*," he sneered.

I hadn't heard someone say Easterner with such disdain in a long time. It made the fire in my veins flare in response. People scoffed at me because I was from a world they knew little about. Too bad the Eastern Hemisphere was much more of a force to be reckoned with than they believed. There was a reason I had to keep the east a secret and this male was not worth my time.

I danced fire in my fingertips and let my eyes flash and darken as Greer was brimming with anger beside me.

"None of your business. You need to get away from me now. Or my boyfriend here will light your ass on fire. And while you're at it, maybe don't treat any woman, human or not, like a piece of meat, asshole. And keep that disdainful tone out of your filthy mouth when talking about the Ambassador," she spat, and I tried not to burst out laughing or get hung up on the word boyfriend, as this man sputtered and stalked out, mumbling something underneath his breath.

"I know you didn't need me … I just wanted to help," I said, retracting my arm from her and opening the door for us to leave.

Her expression softened, like she was surprised by my words, and I gently took the food out of her arms and started walking so she couldn't protest too much.

"Thank you, for saying that and doing that back there. It's nice to be taken care of sometimes. I'm sorry he was so rude to you," she said softly, pushing her hands into her coat.

I shrugged it off.

"I've been called worse, Greer. But I appreciate you saying that. Are you all right?"

Being an Ambassador kept certain things at bay, but it wasn't foolproof.

"That happens a lot … at the Shadow Lounge, and it's exhausting. I have to have armor on all the time, so to speak. Physically, mentally, and emotionally. It's hard to imagine some people aren't exactly like that guy back there, you know?" she said, sighing, and I saw the weight of it all on her shoulders flash in front of those green eyes. They filled with water and then they cleared, going back to normal.

"So thank you, for sharing that burden tonight," she said, smiling uninhibitedly at me. It was beautiful.

"Always," I said. The answer seemed to surprise her slightly and she bit her lower lip, trying not to smile even wider. It seemed like I had a better understanding of why she snapped at me. She didn't quite know where I fit in with her experiences of other powerful males.

"How about the rest of you? Are these pieces of you okay too?" I said, stopping and gently cupping her chin and brushing a thumb across her limbs trying to erase that man's touch. Her eyes went wide, and it seemed like she held her breath as I danced my fingertips across her cheeks and bruised nose.

She didn't move, though. I saw a crack in her armor here as she fluttered her eyes closed. Her dark lashes spiked across her normally pale but now slightly blue skin.

"Honestly, it hurts like a bitch," she said, laughing darkly and then wincing, pulling a hand to her belly.

"Greer," I said. She kept her eyes closed and slowly lifted the oversized sweater she was wearing to show two giant foot-sized bruises splayed across her pale ribs and belly.

I swore and she opened her eyes, and without breaking eye contact, she pulled her shirt down and took off a glove to reveal the slashes across her palms. I wanted to take it all away, the physical and emotional pain.

I reached for her hand and brushed a kiss across the scratches on her hands.

"Ky…" she said as something fizzled in her eyes.

"I'll help you be more careful," I said quietly, feeling like that this was partly my fault for not preparing her better, for throwing her into a wolf's den.

"I know how to be careful. I've been beat up worse than this," she said, her armor sliding back into place, and she took a step back, slipping her gloves back on. The moment of vulnerability was pushed aside.

"Greer—" I started, but she waved me off. What did it mean that she had been beaten up worse than this?

"Don't worry your handsome head over it, okay?" she said, walking forward. "I'm starving, so let's go."

I tried not to dwell too much on the fact that she thought I was handsome and swallowed, deciding to let go of the conversation. She could tell me on her own terms, I wouldn't push her.

"Okay, but I will be extremely disappointed if these potstickers don't live up to your raving review..." I said, trying to lighten the mood.

She laughed loudly. "Oh, don't worry, they will."

We both walked back to her place in a more comfortable silence. Some of the edginess between us seemed to be smoothing out slightly.

But I kept going back to the parts of her body that were bruised and broken from the trial and how she had acted like this wasn't the first time she had gone through this type of physical pain. And then the man at the store...

I was going to have a hard time not getting my emotions involved, because fuck if they weren't already.

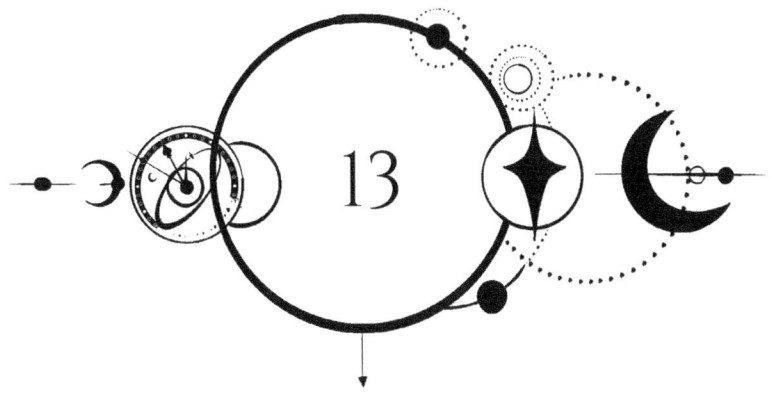

13

Greer

I'm so glad you both are here!" I practically squealed as Nova, Waverly, and I got comfortable on the couch. I had made Lux leave because I hadn't had a girls' night ... well, maybe ever. And for some reason, I felt like I needed a moment to breathe from the big bad Trials.

I had called them over the day after we had had our discussion about the next trial. Ky and I were supposed to start training the day after tomorrow, and then I was set to meet with my contact at the Shadow Lounge.

I felt like I deserved a moment to just be normal.

And normal people did happy hours on Tuesdays.

"To be honest, I haven't had a girls' night ... like really ever, maybe since I was a teenager," I confessed, looking into my glass of red wine.

Waverly was seated across from the glass coffee table separating us. She had come from work but had opted to borrow an oversized hoodie and leggings from me. They swarmed her a little bit, as she was shorter and more petite than me, but she looked cozy. She had piled her dark hair up in a topknot and snuggled into a pile of pillows while cradling her glass.

Nova had come, looking fashionable as ever in a matching sweat suit that was pink tie-dye and a cropped hoodie with high-waisted sweatpants.

"I think the last time I had genuine friends that I *wanted* to drink with was over a hundred years ago," Nova said, laughing as she tucked her long muscular legs underneath her and sat between Waverly and me.

"I guess it's lucky we all found each other, then," Waverly said, her voice oozing warmth and floating through the air, a wide smile spreading over her light brown skin.

"I wanted something normal, you know ... since things are anything but normal right now," I said, scowling and taking a big swig from my glass.

"At least you passed the first trial, which is huge. One day at a time, but I think we should halt trial talk tonight," Waverly said, finishing off her glass and reaching for the bottle to pour herself another.

"I agree. We are already living and breathing it day in and day out. Let's give ourselves a break and just enjoy tonight," Nova said.

"Okay, here's what I'm thinking. Wine, chocolate, face masks, hot tub, and gossiping..." I said, listing everything off on my fingertips and grinning broadly.

"Don't even protest because you can borrow a swimsuit, Waverly Banks, otherwise you can just hop in naked, got it?" I said, and she blushed a little while Nova laughed.

I gathered our supplies, and we all changed to go sit in the hot tub that was on our balcony, attached to the infinity pool. The stars shone in the sky and the city was lit up like a Christmas tree as we all relaxed with seaweed green face masks plastered on our faces, steam rising in the freezing weather.

Red wine and chocolate littered the sides of the blue tiled hot tub.

"Greer, those are some serious bruises and welts," Nova said, staring at me as I got up to reach for the bottle of wine.

I looked down at my body and saw the huge foot-shaped bruises that accompanied the skin on my soft belly and snaked up to my ribs. Today, they had turned a deep blue and purple. I also had matching bruises on my hips from slamming into the ground and my knees. My body looked like it had been used as someone's punching bag. Everything hurt, honestly, but I was managing.

I had already seen the welts on my cheeks today and my lip was still pretty swollen.

But I'd had the shit beaten out of me a couple times as a kid, so it's not like it was completely foreign, but it seemed like as an adult you didn't bounce back quite as fast.

"Yeah, they hurt like a motherfucker..." I said, wincing as I bent over to get the wine and pain laced through me.

"Worth it for wine," I said, pouring myself a victory glass as the warm water soothed my aching body. I took a long swing as the alcohol warmed my insides.

Nova laughed and her stars twinkled on her skin.

"I think I've got a balm to help them. I'll make it and bring it over tomorrow," she said softly, and I nodded my thanks.

"Nova," I said, looking up at the sky and seeing only a few stars there, " can you tell us about your stars?"

"I haven't been asked that in a long time..." she said, smiling softly. She looked at ease and her stars seemed to sparkle even brighter.

"I was born with them and sometimes I wake up with a new one. They respond to strong emotions. Like now they are glittering because I feel happy and at peace. I love them, actually. When people think of a blood witch, they think of darkness, evil ... and just like any magic, it can be used for bad, but it has so many ways that it can be beautiful and powerful, full of energy, life, and love. Even though the rest of the world may think I am one thing, my stars remind me that I can shine bright with love and light even in the darkest times..." she said, peeling off her gel green mask and patting her face dry with one of the gray towels I had brought out.

"Blood is powerful, but it gives us life. It is unique to each person. I can feel your blood right now thrumming through your veins, giving you life and revealing your strength. It's a life force, and I feel honored and humbled all the time to be able to connect with it and use it responsibly."

"They are beautiful, just like you and your power," Waverly said, a little tipsy, her cheeks flushing. Nova smiled broadly at her.

My heart warmed a bit at the sight of them.

My friends.

"Waverly, will you sing a song for us?" I said, knowing that sirens had voices of angels, and my liquid courage was daring me to make requests.

"Aren't you demanding tonight?" she said, laughing. Nova laughed too, and tonight we were all just regular friends, tipsy and silly, enjoying the night.

"I haven't sung for anyone in a long time ... and never just because I wanted to. I hardly ever get asked to sing simply for a song. But for you two, anything," she said, her dark hair curling slightly around her ears from the steam rising off the pool.

And she started to sing; loud, clear, and beautiful.

There once was a siren out at sea
She met a ship that set her heart free
The winds then sang, she met her lover
She learned to live up above

Soon her love for the sea did call
She had to make a choice once and for all
One day, her love chose to let her go
To return to her first love the sea once more

Her heart did break and tears were shed
But her true home laid deep in the sea bed
She sang her sad siren song for the love she lost
Never fully being able to weather the cost

Her days were spent swimming to shore
Looking to spot her love once more
Her love was always torn in two
So she spent her years, only happy in a few

Da-da-da-da-da
Da-da-da-da-da-da-da
Da-da-da-da-da-da-da-da-da-da

She sang to the stars and her pink eyes danced. The song was sweet and wrapped around us, hugging our flushed cheeks.

"Sirens used to roam the seas. A lot of songs I learned when I was younger were from my older sister. The songs of the sea were passed down through the generations of sirens. This one was one of my favorites…" she said dreamily.

"What happened to your sister?" I said, still swaying slightly to the song she had sung as if the notes lingered around us.

"We had a bit of a falling out when I was younger ... so I'm not sure exactly," she said, frowning slightly.

"I'm sorry, Waverly, I didn't mean to pry," I said, reaching out through the clear blue water and grabbing her hand, squeezing softly.

"It's okay. I haven't thought about her in so long. That song brings back happy memories of us laughing and shouting it at the top of our lungs to see who could be louder," she said, chuckling slightly. Nova offered an empathetic smile.

"Greer, we really need to ask..." Waverly said, a mischievous grin chasing away the clouds of sadness that were there moments before.

"What is going on with you and Kyra?" she said, eyes widening as she feigned innocence.

"I mean, you could cut that sexual tension with a knife," Nova said, raising an eyebrow and sipping on her wine.

I laughed and pushed myself out of the tub to sit on the edge.

"I honestly don't know. He makes my blood boil in a way that makes me sort of angry but excited. I've never really had that reaction to someone before. And I know he is a good male, but sometimes he is just so arrogant ... And he literally can never keep his hair out of his eyes, it's so distracting..." I said, pouting a little, and they both burst out laughing.

"What?!" I said, wide-eyed and feeling the alcohol swim around in my head.

"You need to sleep with him," Nova said simply, shrugging her shoulders.

Waverly's mouth dropped open. "I was going to say you should go out with him, but Nova just got straight to the point..."

"I mean, he's a good male, I can vouch for that. He has a shadowed past, but I imagine he has his reasons. I think you should see what happens," Waverly said, smiling.

"And I think you both are hot, horny and ready to go. Sometimes I can literally feel your arousal in your blood. So please do something about it," Nova said matter-of-factly.

"You can feel other people's horniness?" I said, laughing tears streaming down my face. "I am so sorry!"

"I mean, I can't say I don't like it sometimes..." She smirked and we all erupted in more laughter.

"Greeeeeerrrrrr!" someone howled from inside the penthouse, and I saw Lux stumbling through the place, hanging over a laughing and smiling Kyra.

My stomach started doing these weird flip-flops and my blood began to heat.

"See, like that, it feels nice you know?" Nova said, winking at me, and I nearly fell out of the tub as I cackled.

I hopped up and wrapped a towel around me before padding inside.

Lux was absolutely hammered in his usual ensemble of tight jeans and a trendy looking sweater. Kyra was dressed casually as well in jeans, black leather boots, and a white cable-knit sweater. His scarlet eyes were laughing, and his hair kept doing that maddening thing where it fell into his eyes.

We locked eyes, and they turned dark as he quickly scanned over my body, which I suddenly became aware was me in a towel and only a small black triangle tied bikini underneath.

I forced myself to breathe as Lux was smiling and laughing, calling my name.

"What are you yelling about?" I said, giggling, walking over to him and putting my hands on either side of Lux's face. His gold eyes were unfocused.

"I got drunk…" he slurred, smiling and grabbing my face gently in both of his large brown tattooed hands. "Your poor face, Greer."

"I know, I think everyone in our building knows now," I said, chuckling as Ky struggled to steady him with both of us holding each other's faces.

"I love you, and I really need you to not die in the Trials. Like I will die, if you die … And no more foots in faces," he said, suddenly very serious and his eyes were trying to focus but they couldn't. It was laughable, except that what he said went straight through my heart and almost killed my tipsy wine buzz.

"No dying here, babes … But we gotta get you to bed. Right, Ky?" I said, sliding into the other side of him as Kyra supported most of his weight again. I tried not to wince as my body screamed at me, but I wasn't about to let Lux face-plant on the floor.

Both of them had several inches and some pounds on me, so I was just doing my best not to get dragged down by Lux.

"Hiiiiiiiii, Waverly!!! NOVAAAAAA!!!" Lux said wildly, whipping his hands around to wave frantically. They giggled and gave a little wave.

I nearly fell over too. Kyra was clearly trying not to laugh as he was biting his bottom lip and smiling. I did the same, until we made it to Lux's room and I pushed him onto the bed.

"Take your shoes off Lux and then you can sleep, okay?" I said, moving to help him as he swatted me away and crawled underneath his navy sheets and looked at me, his gold eyes glowing.

"I know you both haven't talked about this … but the tension here," he said, wildly whipping his eyes between Kyra and me and gesturing with his fingers, "is palpable. So maybe figure that shit out." He closed his eyes and snuggled into his pillow.

My mouth dropped open and I had to cover it as I snickered and Lux began snoring slightly. Kyra closed the door behind us and doubled over laughing.

Neither one of us seemed to be embarrassed by what Lux said. I mean, he wasn't wrong, but we hadn't really talked about it either.

Ky straightened and wiped tears from his eyes.

"I'm so sorry. I couldn't hold him off any longer. He started going right in on double gin and tonics before I got there. He's been so worried about you and the Trials that I think he just needed a moment to forget..." Ky said, softening his gaze and taking a step closer to me.

I swallowed and was suddenly very aware that I was in just a towel and a small bikini.

"It's okay. It's been hard on everyone," I said, my mouth suddenly very dry and Kyra suddenly very close. How did his muscular arms end up caging me into the wall with his ruby eyes inches away from mine?

"It has..." His voice dropped a little lower as he took one of his fingertips and traced my collarbone, leaving warmth in his wake that started to move and dance across the rest of my body. Wet heat shot straight to my thighs. I bit my lower lip and Ky's eyes flickered there.

"Hi..." I whispered as his fingertips continued their feather light journey across my skin, leaving little tingles here and there, and suddenly my skin was too tight and too warm. My hand slipped away from my towel and I let it pool to the floor as I stood there in my swimsuit.

Ky took his time looking at every inch of me, and his eyes flared at the bruises on my belly, hips, and knees. He then angled his body closer to mine until they were almost touching but not quite. I wanted to crawl out of my own skin as desire shot through my body and made my lower belly quiver.

I was frozen in place. I wanted him to press into me so I could feel every muscular, beautiful part of him against me even though my body was broken and bruised. His hand started to move, gently, across all the places that were bruised, trailing my belly, and I nearly moaned. Then he was on my hips, gently brushing over the angry purple skin.

"Hi, Greer…" he said, closing the space between us as his lips gently brushed against mine, swollen and cracked. I wanted to slam my mouth to his, but I knew that would be a very bad idea right now and would probably end up with my lip reopening. I closed my eyes and arched my back as his hands continued to dance across my skin and then his lips were tracing the bruises on my belly and I nearly fell over. I laced my hands through his hair as he got on his knees and gently kissed away the hurt on my stomach. Then he moved to the dips of my hips and I thought I might shove him to the ground and crawl over him and throw my injuries to the wind. He danced his fingers lightly to my knees and kissed those too, moving his lips down the length of the soft skin of my inner thighs and sending sensations straight to my center. He groaned as I fisted his hair harder and moaned his name.

"Don't stop…" I begged, and I could feel him smiling as he continued the memorization of my skin with his lips.

No one had ever touched me so tenderly, like I was something precious to be preserved. I looked down and he was still on his knees, moving his lips across the cuts and bruises of my body and he looked up, his scarlet eyes nearly feral. I shivered from pleasure and released my hands from his hair as he stood up and kissed the scrapes that lay there too.

He was killing me with his hands and mouth and he had barely done anything.

"Ky…" I said, practically begging, and he leaned in to kiss my temples. A breathy moan escaped me.

I was losing myself in the soft and warm sensation of his hands and mouth. My whole body felt swollen and hot with need. I wanted to drag him off to my bedroom.

Curse these fucking Trials and my battered body.

"Greeeeeeerrrr!" Lux howled from his bedroom and Kyra stilled, smiling into my temple. I swore loudly and colorfully.

He laughed then, and pressed his lips gingerly to my forehead. I could get lost in his kisses.

"I think his need for you is more important than mine is right now. And I don't want to hurt you. You need to rest and heal…" he said, picking up the towel and handing it to me.

"I think I should go. For now … unless you need me for something else. I'll see you the day after tomorrow at six a.m. for training, if you're still up for it," Kyra said, smiling, and my whole body was still tingling from where he was just starting to explore my body with his mouth.

"Okay," I said, closing my eyes for a minute. And then I smiled. "Okay, Ky … I'm up for it. I'll see you the day after tomorrow." I stood on my tiptoes and placed a light kiss on his lips.

"GREEER!" Lux was howling again.

"I'm coming, Lux!" I said, laughing and rolling my eyes.

Kyra was backing toward the elevator.

"Bye," I said with a little wave and sighed loudly as Ky laughed and waved back.

"Lux, you are such a cock block," I said as I walked into his room.

He pouted and asked if I could be the big spoon because he couldn't fall asleep. Because of course I would. I just wanted a certain someone else to be my big spoon.

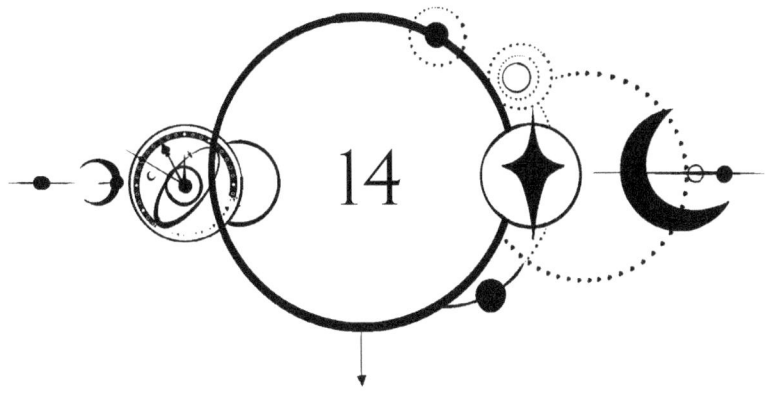

14

Kyra

It had been two days since I saw Greer in that tiny black bikini, wet, bruised, and slightly tipsy. Two days since we had done something about the sizzling heat between us.

I had thought that maybe when I had a taste of her, I wouldn't need any more. But for the past two days, I could think of absolutely nothing except her beautifully pale skin, smooth and soft as silk, and the way it responded to my touch even through the angry bruises. The swell of her breasts barely contained in that tiny scrap of fabric that I had wanted to rip off with my teeth.

Her strong, graceful legs had been on blatant display, and my biggest regret was not being able to get her backside view, where that beautiful ass was in desperate need of my admiration.

Greer's wine-colored hair had been curling around her face from the steam and was piled high on her head. I had wanted to take it down so it could fall around her shoulders and frame her green eyes and flushed cheeks.

I had wanted to do so much—had wanted to take the pain away with my touch and erase all the bad with the pleasure I could give her. But I didn't want to hurt her. And she had needed to take care of Lux, which I respected.

He had been beside himself when I'd finally arrived at the bar we were meeting at. My meeting had run late, and I had found him two double drinks in. He had poured his heart out about how he was worried about the Trials, the case, and Greer.

I was too, honestly.

There wasn't much headway in the investigation, and the second trial would be coming up soon. With each trial, the stakes were higher and higher. And each day, I seemed to be falling deeper and deeper into something with Greer.

Now here I was, at the penthouse at 6:00 a.m. sharp, ready to see her after two agonizing days away. Coffee in hand, I met a groggy-eyed Greer, who wore tight black leggings and a white thermal. Her lip looked to be pretty much back to normal, and the bruises and welts on her cheeks had gone down to a shadow of what they were before.

Her hair was braided back so the long tail hung right above the beautiful curve of her backside. I wanted to reach out and touch her, but we hadn't talked about what happened between us. Nothing had changed except we had both made a move, and somehow bringing that up at 6:00 a.m. did not seem like a good idea.

Plus, I got the feeling that Greer was not a morning person.

I had texted her last night asking if she still wanted to do this, and she said her injuries were much better due to some special balm Nova had made for her that helped the bruising and swelling go down significantly. From the progress on her face, I would say it had worked amazingly well.

Today was all about training so she could survive the Trials, not my horny desires. I was also excited to see what she would bring to the table; she had beautiful curves and muscles all over her body, but today we would see what they could actually do.

I had texted her about thirty minutes ago telling her to be ready for a run to start and then after that we would move to strength and flexibility training. She hadn't texted back. I fully accepted that she had rolled out of bed just a few moments ago, but damn did she look good a little disheveled.

She smiled grumpily and reached for the coffee I offered, taking the whole thing down in about two seconds flat. Who drank caffeine like that first thing in the morning?

"Are you going to be okay?" I said, raising one eyebrow and chuckling slightly.

"Are *you*?" she said playfully, her voice still in that sleepy, husky state.

Damn, my need for her was really going to be tested this morning. She seemed unfazed, and I told myself to breathe.

She rolled her neck a few times and bounced on the balls of her feet.

"Shall we?" I said, noticing the anticipation in her body start to build as the caffeine worked its way through her veins.

She nodded and stepped into the elevator. Neither one of us said anything as we went all the way down and made our way out into the dark, cold morning. I let the cold wash over me to shock my body into behaving. She seemed unaffected by my presence, and I wondered idly if I was overreacting to what happened a few days ago.

"You can set the pace," she said as we walked a few blocks away from her building.

Nodding, I started to pick up the pace. To her credit, she matched my strides the whole way, even though I had almost a foot on her.

Neither one of us talked much as the sun started to peek over the horizon. The city was quiet at this time. The only sounds were our feet against the pavement and the puffs of our breath. It was nice running alongside her, not having to keep up pleasantries. It was easy. Peaceful. Almost like we could forget the heaviness of the Trials and the intensity of the investigation.

I looped us through the city and checked my watch as the minutes ticked by.

We saw very few people on the street, and office buildings, apartment complexes, restaurants, and coffee shops flew by in a flurry of glass, brick, and steel. I guided us back toward the penthouse to where Lux's full-service gym awaited.

Greer noticed us heading back toward her building and looked at me with new light in her eyes. "I'll race you back," she said and took off sprinting.

Her strong, short legs pumped hard and fast as she laughed wickedly, rounding the corner and taking the last several blocks like a speed demon.

I took off, trying to catch up to her, and as I rounded the corner, I could see that she was already almost to the building.

How the fuck is she that fast?

Panting and sweating, I finally made it at a much slower pace to the entrance of the building.

"Did you time travel here?" I said, huffing as she threw a water bottle at me, courtesy of the doorman.

"Maybe you're just slow," she said, shrugging and smiling.

Her thermal had come off, revealing a cropped tank top that showed off her muscular arms and broad shoulders. She chugged down her water and I tried not to blatantly stare at her lips.

"What's next?" Greer said casually, looking as if she didn't just haul ass the last quarter of a mile.

"Let's move on to the strength and flexibility conditioning," I said as we moved toward the elevator.

"Okay, *immortal*, show me how it's done," she sneered on our way up. She was slowly coming to life, instead of the grumpy morning monster I had seen earlier. Wisely, I decided not to comment on that and instead matched her playful banter.

"Is that a challenge?" I said, moving closer to her as I reached out and tucked a stray strand of hair behind her ear. Her eyes shone bright and she licked her lips.

Godsdamnit.

She leaned in and cocked one eyebrow. Her eyes traveled along the length of my body, as if sizing me up.

There was that spike of desire going straight to my cock.

Again.

"Do your worst," she said with a twinkle in her eye. The grogginess of the morning was completely gone and was now replaced with her usual gusto and sass.

The elevator arrived on the twenty-fourth floor, Lux's personal floor where he kept all of the things he didn't want in the penthouse. He also wanted the other tenants to have access to the gym, home theater, spa, and sauna. It was completely empty this morning, and overlooked the city with its floor-to-ceiling glass windows and state-of-the-art equipment.

I chuckled. "You asked for it."

Greer Roberts wouldn't know what hit her.

15

Greer

It was cute that Ky thought he was stronger and faster than me. It was even cuter when he realized I had duped him after our strength and flexibility workout had him panting and me running circles around him.

What I hadn't told him was that in college I had worked at the student recreational facility, teaching fitness classes and leading bootcamps in order to pay rent and get groceries. I knew how to build strength, endurance, and stamina. I had been doing it even before I had arrived at college.

When you're little and human, you have to find ways to stick up for yourself and fight. Hence my obsession with keeping my switchblade on me 99 percent of the time. I refused a long time ago to go in without knowing how to pack a punch or how to properly defend myself.

I didn't let the fact that we were poor growing up stop me from getting creative and spending hours at the school library reading and watching videos on the computer on how to protect yourself. Other little kids played sports after school, while I would watch hours of videos and then recreate them with my own body.

We were finishing up some stretches when he finally collapsed on the ground and groaned, throwing one impressively muscled arm across his eyes. "Greer Roberts, you are a liar."

I studied his body soaked with sweat. At some point, he had discarded his layers from the heat of the workout and all that was left was a pair of black athletic shorts that hung low on his hips, revealing a whole masterpiece of muscles that gave way to hard abs, a chiseled chest, and beautiful arms that begged to be touched.

I had felt some of that body just a few days ago, but not nearly enough of it. The thought curled my toes, and the memory of his lips on my body started that heat in my veins again. I wanted him to do it again, wanted to see what happened when I pushed him further. I wanted to touch and be touched by him.

The balm Nova had given me had restored me to a normal human being who most definitely could have sex with a hot warlock now. And boy was I ready to pounce on Ky.

I had been thinking about it the past two days in great detail and had to relieve some of the tension myself, but in reality I didn't want to touch myself. I wanted Ky to touch me.

I needed to know what that would feel like.

My body was practically aching for it at this point.

I had struggled not to jump him as soon as I saw him this morning. I had had to keep my horny, sleepy self in check with little words and slamming my coffee just to get through the run with him.

He had a tattoo of what looked like flames and geometric shapes, creating a breathtaking image snaking up his back. It was practically daring me to touch it. The only oddity was the red crystal embedded above his heart, where red lines snaked away from the glowing stone and ran over his shoulder and down his torso.

I wasn't sure, but I believed that it was a warlock tradition. Some witches and warlocks were born with crystals pulsing power into their veins if their powers were from the elements, and other times their power grew over time without the aid of a gem. It was said to be a good indicator of strength and power.

Nova didn't have one, but blood witches were such a rarity and different from traditional elemental witches.

I wanted to run my fingers over his crystal and trace the lines running off it almost as much as I wanted to lick the sweat droplets off his neck, but somehow that seemed a bit inappropriate at the moment.

In a public place.

At my apartment gym complex.

Even if Lux did own it.

With his arm covering his eyes, I had a full view of his god-like body. I tried to clear my head of horny thoughts and focus on his comment. I was struggling to remember what he said, and instead kept getting snagged on his body and the kisses he offered the other night.

I laughed and said, "I never lied, I just let you think what you wanted…" I let my gaze travel lower to his powerful legs and the bulge in his shorts.

It didn't hurt to look, right?

Fuuuuck.

You could just add horny to the other list of problems I had going on at the moment.

Horny for one immortal in particular.

He propped himself up on his elbows and looked at me with those ruby red eyes, his dark hair slicked back with sweat. We were sitting very close, practically touching, and I wanted less space between us.

"Are you some fitness influencer on the side or something?" he teased, pushing himself up to a seated position and closing some of the distance between us.

I snorted loudly, throwing my head back. "No, definitely not. I taught bootcamps and fitness classes in college as a way to get through school. Actually, when I was younger, it was either figure out how to be strong or get the shit beat out of you. So I chose the former," I said, shrugging the last bit off.

Lots of kids got bullied in school, and being a poor, little human girl without a dad made me an easy target.

His eyes softened and he stood, offering his hand to help me up. "Well, I'm sure they got their asses handed to them just like I did today."

No pity in his words. More like understanding. I was starting to notice Kyra did that a lot. He was good at listening and offering validation, instead of just feeding you lip service or talking for the sake of it.

I grabbed onto his hand and let him hoist me up. His touch made my skin warm and tingly, like it did every time we touched. He didn't let go right away and instead tugged me in a little closer.

"How is it that you're beautiful even after ninety minutes in the gym?" he mumbled, finally releasing my hand and tucking a loose strand of hair behind my ear.

Mmm, I liked it here with him. My belly fluttered in anticipation of his touch and his lips.

I swallowed and watched his ruby eyes suddenly go dark. Desire shot straight through me, pooling right between my thighs.

I tipped my head up and tilted it to the side, trailing a finger down his chest, along those hard abs, and paused above his shorts.

"That's nice of you to say … And as you can see, I am more than recovered, for all sorts of physical activity…" I said as he closed his eyes and shivered against my touch.

I flicked my eyes around the gym, double-checking that we were alone.

"Greer," he said huskily. His body seemed to go rigid as my finger played with the waistband of his shorts. "I haven't been able to stop thinking about you in that tiny black bikini for the last two days…"

"I've wanted to jump you since you showed up at my doorstep this morning," I confessed.

He laughed loudly and gently cupped my chin and ran the other hand down my spine, still slick with sweat from our workout.

"I've wanted to taste you since the first day you stormed off in that conference room…" he said barely above a whisper.

Well, that was unexpected.

I met his eyes with my own heat and shifted my body closer to him. I wanted to feel more of him against my hands. I wanted his mouth on mine. On my body. I wanted his hands running over me and him inside me. I wanted all of it, and the other night had been just a taste. Enough to whet my appetite but not nearly enough to satisfy.

"What are you asking?" I said wickedly, trailing my fingers back up toward his jawline. A silky smile spread across my lips.

He pressed the hand that had been trailing my spine flat against my lower back and pulled me close, so his breath tickled my ear. Suddenly, my whole body was tingly from head to toe. Another rush of wet heat made its way between my thighs and every part of me ached to be closer. I clenched my thighs together, trying to relieve some pressure.

It didn't do a damn thing.

"Can I worship your mouth with my own?" he whispered into my ear, gently biting my earlobe. "Can I explore every inch of your body with my hands?"

Oh, hell.

"Can I make you come again and again?" he said, moving his mouth toward my jaw.

A groan escaped my lips and I pressed my sweaty body against his, needing to feel his body on mine.

"Yes," I breathed as he started working on the other ear, his hands making their way toward my ass.

"To what?" he said, smirking against my jaw as he got closer and closer to my mouth with those beautiful, sensual lips.

I pulled away and surprise flashed across his face.

"To all of it," I said right before I wrapped my arms around his neck and crushed his mouth to mine. The control I had before snapped as his lips moved hungrily against mine and his hands began to greedily run up and down my sides, sending shivers through my body.

He groaned in approval and I nipped at his lip. I needed more of him. More of his mouth. More of his gorgeous body. I ran my tongue along his bottom lip and opened my mouth slightly, inviting him further. He pushed his tongue in and grabbed for my braid, gently tugging as he moved his mouth down my neck, toward my breasts.

He sunk his teeth into my shoulder and I groaned. He gently tugged on my braid while the other hand started circling my hardened nipple and working its way underneath my sports bra.

I moaned loudly, breathing out his name. "Ky"

Suddenly, I knew that we weren't alone.

I gazed over to the entrance to find Lux casually leaning against the doorway, smirking.

"Don't stop on my account, please," he said, snorting as I smiled wickedly at him.

"Godsdamnit, Lux! The other night and today too. What in holy hell do you want?" I hissed.

Ky pulled away and something flashed in his ruby eyes that I couldn't quite place. Annoyance? Amusement? Arousal? All three?

Because same.

His eyes darted between mine and Lux and he laughed.

"Damn, Lux, you sure have perfect timing..." Kyra said, crossing his arms and smiling crookedly.

"Nothing, just wanted to see how things were going," he said casually, eyeing both of us up and down. Clearly enjoying that he just interrupted what could have been a *very* happy ending for me. For the second time in a row in the last seventy-two hours.

I was gonna kill him. Seriously.

And I would enjoy it.

Desire still churned in my belly and by the look of Ky's cock in his thin gym shorts, his desire was still there as well. I turned to him and gave his hands a squeeze.

"We *will* finish this later, otherwise I might spontaneously combust," I whispered with a wink and sauntered over to where Lux stood at the entrance.

I looped my arm around his waist. "It's great, but let's leave Ky to finish up on his own..."

If I didn't walk away now, I would quite literally rip Ky's clothes off and fuck him in front of Lux. My control was barely leashed and I needed a second to breathe, away from his presence, otherwise I might lose it.

With that last thought, I took my swaying hips out the door, thinking of how it only took the looming end of my life cycle to find someone who made my toes curl with just a few words.

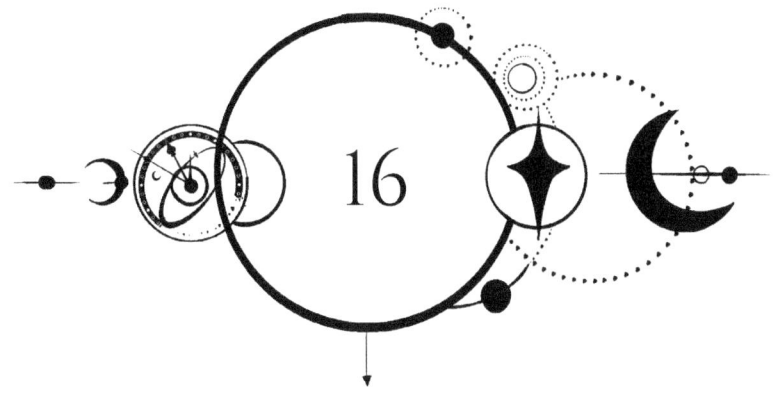

Kyra

I needed to clear my head after that session with Greer. I stepped in the shower, to let the cold water shock my body back to normal.

It honestly was probably a good thing Lux had come in, because I would have taken Greer right there on the gym floor if we hadn't been interrupted. Wincing, I realized that as far as romance goes, fucking on a gym floor was pretty much at the bottom of that list.

Not that we owed one another romance ... but I wasn't an animal. And I wanted to give her more than just sex. She deserved that and much more.

I quickly got out of the shower and tried to figure out what I was going to do about it.

This was now the second time in the last seventy-two hours that we had both given into the tension that had been swirling around us.

Greer would soon be deep in the throes of the Trials. I was supposed to be an adviser and a friend, not some horny teenager who couldn't keep his dick in his pants.

I was trying to reconcile with myself whether this was genuinely a good idea. We were adults. We were allowed to do what we both wanted, but she had a lot on her plate and I didn't want to add anything else to complicate it. I groaned, trying to figure out what the best course of action was.

How far would I let this go? How far would Greer let this go?

Not to mention I hadn't exactly been honest with her either. But then again, I had never told *anyone* why I had really done the Trials and the truth about my parents. Why I couldn't speak of the Eastern Hemisphere.

I had used the same story over and over again in post-victory interviews. I had practiced it for weeks before the Trials were over, so there would be no way anyone would discover the truth.

Especially because Eastern Hemisphere people didn't play in the Trials. I was an anomaly. It was supposed to be my hidden truth but someone else had used that information against me. To make things harder.

To punish me further.

But I had no proof, and it didn't matter if it was who I thought it was. I was powerless against him.

I had been a bug underneath a microscope post victory, and I would be damned if I let the people of the Republic and the ITC know about my home and who I was.

People wanted to know about my past. They no idea what the real rules and regulations of this world were. Only what the were fed. They were blissfully ignorant.

And I couldn't share who I was with Greer. I couldn't share it with anyone, and I didn't need people poking around. I had kept it mostly under wraps the year after I had been crowned the victor, and after that people just moved on to the next new shiny thing.

Not that any winner had as interesting a backstory as I did. In fact, they were all pretty typical, and most of them left to go drink, sleep, and party their way through the rest of their lives as winners. But that wasn't a privilege I could afford myself.

It wasn't what the gods had intended.

And Greer was more than just some woman. She was a friend. And more ... I just wasn't exactly sure what that was.

Lux was a friend too. A damn good one. But neither one of them could know every intimate detail of my life. Some things needed to be kept secret for the safety of others.

And I had bought myself some time by winning the Trials.

How much time ... Well, I wasn't exactly sure about that.

I looked down at the crystal cemented right over my heart. I had had some pain there in the last few days, which was never a good sign, but it had gone from a stabbing intensity to a dull ache.

The last time it had bothered me consistently was right before I won the Trials five years ago. Ignoring it until it went away felt like the best course of action, and honestly it was probably nothing. I resolved to deal with it later.

Sighing, I went to get dressed when my phone dinged.

> **Greer: I liked the way we ended our workout today. Maybe we can try to actually finish soon. Third time's the charm. ;)**

Fucking hell.

I looked down to see my cock getting hard all over again with thoughts of her sweaty body pressed against mine this morning. And then to that damn black bikini.

I was in serious trouble here.

> **Me: I don't think you need my help at all anymore with your workout but I like to finish what I start...**

About five minutes passed before I got another message.

> **Greer: Instead of in the gym you could come to the lounge. I'll talk to my contact and then we can finish what we started.**

I chuckled to myself and quickly shot off another text.

> **Me: Business and pleasure. I'm in. I'll be there at 8pm.**

Well damn, that was pretty straightforward. She could handle training on her own from how she handed my ass to me this morning.

It was very sexy.

But I would hold her accountable and be her gym buddy if she needed.

I was practically putty in her hands at this point. She could ask whatever she wanted and I would probably say yes. I rubbed my hands across my face and wondered what I was getting myself into with Greer.

However, I still couldn't figure out how she had moved so fast the last quarter mile. Most humans couldn't outrun any other races. It was as if she teleported to the door. Maybe she ran track or something in high school? She mentioned that she had worked at the student rec center in college, but that wouldn't exactly explain her hyper speed.

It really wasn't that important, but it nagged at me.

On the bright side, she was definitely better suited to handle the next trial than I had anticipated, which was a relief for myself and the rest of the team, I was sure. This investigation wasn't going to solve itself overnight. And I really hoped the physical trial would be something she could handle.

This was the most dangerous trial for her as a human. People would target her. See her as a weaker link and think to get her pushed out of the ranks.

I shuddered thinking about my own physical strength test and how I had seen some of the other races pick off humans and break their legs before they could make it the twenty miles up the mountain.

It was disgusting.

And I didn't do anything to stop it.

And neither did the ITC.

They removed the humans from the game and healed them, but they still had to pay with their life cycle or government servitude.

She needed to make it through this trial. Two hundred and fifty others would be cut, so she at least had a decent chance, but who knew what they would come up with this year? Something disgustingly entertaining for the viewers at home, I was sure.

But then she still had to go through the next few trials.

She would make it past the next round. She had to, and then whoever did this to her in the first place would pay.

Lux, Nova, Waverly, and I would make sure of it.

17

Greer

My guy was sitting at the corner booth drinking a gin and tonic. Just like I had expected. He was known by the name Viper. I had no idea what his real name was and honestly it didn't matter. He tipped well and he was friendly in a way most males were—creepy but manageable. And he would help me get to the bottom of my dilemma.

The lounge was decently quiet, with a steady stream of patrons coming in and out, but nothing too busy. For a Friday, it was pretty calm.

Arlo was behind the bar, charming his way through everyone as me, Maeve, and Parker wove in and out of the tables, getting drinks, flashing smiles, and collecting tips.

Kyra had come in about twenty minutes ago and was nursing a glass of red wine. He looked absolutely delicious in dark red fitted slacks, a suit jacket to match, and a black button-down underneath with the first few top buttons undone. I could see the small lines that reached away from the crystal embedded in his chiseled chest.

I tried not to lick my lips just thinking about it.

He kept his look casual with an arm draped across the back of his plush chair, and his ruby red eyes looked almost bored with a smirk on his lips. But I knew he had been watching our guy since he got in—and me, for that matter.

It made my skin tingle just thinking about his gaze. I was really struggling with control when it came to Kyra. I needed to get it together for the next hour or so.

His dark hair would occasionally fall into his eyes, where he would brush it aside with those strong, callused hands. Such a distractingly delicious gesture.

I was ready to explore what we had now started *twice* but never got to finish. It was clawing at me and making me edgy again.

I checked the time again and it was nearing 8:30 p.m. I had already told Arlo what I planned to do, and I had the other girls briefed on what I needed them to do and when.

I ran off to the bathroom quickly and checked myself out.

Tonight, I wore a skintight black dress that opened at one shoulder with black pumps. I put on some fresh dark purple lipstick and ran my fingers through my curly red hair. I needed this guy to work with me here, and I was not above using my looks to get the shit that I wanted. If he was already going to objectify me, I might as well get what I wanted out of it.

I rolled my shoulders back and headed toward his booth, very aware that Ky was watching my every move. It made me want to rip my dress off and straddle him in the booth. But I kept my eye on the prize and moved away from him.

Viper wasn't exactly a physically intimidating man, but he looked exactly like his name. He had sharp green eyes and a bald head that seemed to shine unnaturally. His skin crawled with colorful tattoos of every type of animal. But it was really his teeth that earned him the nickname. His two fangs were elongated and pointed like a snake's, and his tongue was forked and thin, which he used to down every last drop of liquid from his drink.

It was said that he was some sort of creature birthed from a demon long ago. It had taken the form of a snake and a mortal and had made a child that was … well, that was something like Viper. His fangs were said to be laced with deadly poison and his eyes and movements incredibly sharp.

I winced thinking about his fangs. It wasn't like I was planning on getting bitten, but the thought gave me chills.

His eyes flickered to mine and his lips broke into a predatory smile.

"I'll take another drink, love," he said, flicking his tongue toward his glass.

When I slid into the opposite side of his booth, surprise flashed across his eyes and he cocked his head to one side.

"Now, Greer, what do I owe the pleasure of having you sit with me this evening?" he said, hissing slightly, his empty drink momentarily forgotten.

I put on my best smile and leaned forward, putting my chin in my hand.

"Well, Viper, apparently I have made myself an enemy to someone with an unusual skill set…" I said slowly, piquing his interest.

At that exact moment, Maeve came over and placed two drinks in front of us, just like I had told her to do. Sparkling water with a lime for me, and a gin and tonic for Viper.

"That seems to be quite a predicament you're in," he said and took a sip of his new drink.

I leaned back, relaxing my posture, and took a sip of mine as well.

"I was wondering if you could help me locate them and what the cost of that would be," I said, lacing each word with sugary sweetness.

Lux had said he would cover the cost, but I wasn't trying to lose his fortune here. Sometimes, when I thought of how much money Lux truly had and how much he was willing to drop to help me, it made my stomach churn. Like twenty million for my life.

Ugh.

Even though this was a bit out of my control, I didn't want to waste his fortune.

I reached across the table to place my hand over his, and did my best not to flinch as his eyes turned absolutely feral at the touch. He flicked his tongue across his teeth.

"I need to find them quickly and quietly. And since you're one of my favorite regulars, I thought you could help me out," I said seriously, not letting my eyes leave his.

He stared at me for several moments before taking another sip and setting his glass down.

"Anything for you, Greer..." he replied, his fingertips pulsing underneath mine. I gently removed my hand to pick up my glass once again and rest my chin on my palm.

"Why don't you tell me who you're looking for," he said as he narrowed his eyes at me, his gaze roaming over my body.

I literally hate all males of all species.

Well, except for Lux.

And maybe now Kyra. I fought hard not to flick my eyes over to him.

I needed to *focus*.

"I'm looking for a shifter. A powerful one. One that can and will change into another person for the right price, and one that would be absolutely undetectable under a blood contract. And one that doesn't have an alibi," I said with steel in my voice, all the sweetness left behind.

I waved my hand and without saying a word, Arlo gracefully picked up Viper's empty glass and deposited a black folder with all the information I had on my impostor.

Viper's gaze flickered to the folder and he opened it, scanning the details. Suddenly, his face darkened and his jaw tightened.

"This could take a few days ... I'll get back to you as soon as I can. Put this on my tab. Be careful, Greer. You might not like what I find." And with that, he threw back his drink and stalked out the door.

That was ... weird.

I had the sudden urge to wash my entire body.

Is that how all back-alley deals were done?

Creepy.

I hoped he could find what I needed and that it wouldn't come at the cost of Lux's entire inheritance, even though he would pay it. I was getting really tired of spending his money for a mess that neither one of us had signed up for.

I curled my hands into fists until my long, dark nails dug into my palms. My breathing started to hitch and it felt like someone was sitting on my chest. I swallowed hard and closed my eyes. Panic started to crawl its way into my blood.

I would survive this.

Lux and I would fix this.

I wasn't going to let someone play with my life.

The Trials were something I could handle. I just needed to take it one step at a time. There was no reason to panic at this exact moment in time. I could *do* this.

This wasn't the first time my anxiety had spiraled out of control.

I had panicked a lot when I was younger, when my mom and I had to swiftly move from place to place. Or someone would come pounding on our door, demanding something we didn't have. Or when men got too close and I was emotionally drained and had to physically push them away. Or when people flung insults at me or ignored me for being human. Or when bullies had sucker punched me in the gut and there was no one to help me.

So many things built the perfect storm for this and I had to remind myself I wasn't the scared little girl anymore. I wasn't alone. I wasn't powerless like the world wanted me to believe. I could do this.

I had to remind myself I had people in my corner who were helping me.

Who would fight for me.

Lux. Waverly. Nova. Ky.

Whatever reason someone was doing this, it wouldn't matter when they were behind bars and I was out of the Trials. This would be a soon-forgotten nightmare. I just had to keep buying myself time.

No matter how much I tried to distract myself with playing around with Kyra, or having girls' nights with Waverly and Nova, or dicking around with Lux, it didn't erase the reality of my situation right now.

I was in danger. But I didn't need to let the fear incapacitate me. At least not right now. I could save that shit for later, when more of my life cycle wasn't on the line.

I would win one way or another because there was no other option.

The weight on my chest started to lessen as I counted back from 100, focusing on my inhales and exhales.

"Greer…" a deep voice said.

A hand covered my fist and sent little tendrils of warmth up my forearm. I knew it was Ky. I enjoyed the intimate touch of his power for several seconds, letting it ground me and flow through my body, chasing away tension.

My eyes flashed open and Kyra was sitting across from me with concern on his face, his ruby eyes clouding with something unreadable.

He gently uncurled my first and laced his fingers through mine. His hands felt like they melded perfectly to my own. I wondered if every time we had held hands he had thought the same thing, or if it was just me.

"Are you all right?" he said, giving my hands a squeeze.

Little jolts of electricity made their way through my palms and went straight to my groin with the pressure of his fingertips in between mine. I could enjoy this with Kyra right now. We did have some unfinished business to attend to.

He was so beautiful it hurt, with his sparkling eyes and hard jaw. His hair was doing that thing where it tried to fall into his eyes again and it made everything else fuzzy in my head when I thought about it too long.

I swallowed and tried to refocus myself on the task at hand. I needed to let him know what Viper had said.

But I kept getting distracted by Ky's hands, or hair … I clenched my jaw and forced myself to talk about what had just happened.

"He said it would take a few days. But he would get back to me," I said, willing the heaviness in my chest to dissipate. I pulled on a mask of composure and leveled my gaze at his.

"I know you're scared…" he said carefully, like I might bite.

I blinked a few times. Ky was getting better at navigating my moods and knowing what I needed to hear.

"But one step at a time," he said, squeezing my fingers once more before sitting back in his seat and releasing my hands. My palms instantly felt cold without his heat.

My body was begging for that heat. And now that the business with Viper was done, or, rather, initiated, I was going to allow myself to enjoy my *Ambassador*.

I nodded, biting my lip. "I get off in about an hour … you okay to wait for me?" I said, sliding out of the booth and standing up.

He grabbed my hand once again, that warmth crawling up my forearm, and placed a kiss on my knuckles, just a brush of his lips across my skin.

All these touches were driving my body crazy.

"Always," he said with a wicked grin.

I laughed out loud, which made his grin spread wider, and headed back to the bar, counting down the minutes until I could finally give into this need that Kyra had ignited within me.

☾

I finished up my tables at the end of the hour and slithered behind the bar to find the personal bottle of champagne I always kept back there. I just needed some bubbles to help chase away the heaviness of my life at the moment.

It was really the little things that kept my head from exploding and my tears at bay some days when I let it all overwhelm me at once.

And what better solution than champagne?

I quickly retrieved the bottle, my coat, and my purse and started to make my way toward Ky when a cold hand grabbed my arm.

I whipped around to see a young man who looked no more than eighteen staring up at me with ice-blue eyes and pale skin. He had golden hair that seemed to flicker and shine. It was as if the whole lounge had gone silent and held its breath when this man wrapped his icy fingers around my arm, seeping the chill straight to my bones.

The air in my lungs felt too cold and I found myself slowly sitting in the chair next to me.

His eyes danced with amusement as he looked around the lounge, as if time itself had frozen.

"Interesting…" he mused, flashing aggressively white teeth.

He was dressed in a navy pinstripe suit with a white button-down. He looked young, but I knew better than to judge someone on their appearance. There were races that froze the aging process at eighteen … he could be an immortal for all I knew. He had an energy that made me feel small and insignificant, as if in a single blink of an eye he could unleash something dark and powerful.

This was not looking good.

My lips felt heavy and my limbs didn't feel like my own.

"Who are you?" I said, finally finding my words.

His hand released my arm. A shudder went through me, but the lounge around us remained suspended in time and space. Ice laced through my body and my blood.

"A friend … Greer Roberts, you will have many choices ahead of you. Be wary of who to trust and who has their own interest at heart. Changes are coming. You are the key. Use that power wisely," he said with a smile that didn't quite reach his eyes. "The gods have willed it so. We've been waiting for you." His voice was almost musical.

"I don't believe in the gods and I have no power," I said slowly, trying to get my mouth to catch up with my brain.

He cocked his head to the side, like a predator examining its prey. There was something in his eyes that didn't sit right. Maybe pity? My breath threatened to come in heavy pants as I tried to control my racing heart, even though my body felt weighted down with ice.

What is wrong with me?

How was this guy so powerful?

"You should. I'll be seeing you soon," he said.

Before I could respond, it was as if the bubble that kept out the rest of the world popped with an audible crack and he was gone, leaving me wild-eyed and shuddering.

I sat shocked for a few moments.

A familiar warmth started traveling from my shoulder to the rest of my body, pulling me back to the present, and I felt Ky's hand on my shoulder.

"Gods, Greer, you're freezing … Are you okay? You look like you just collapsed in this chair from seeing a ghost," Kyra said, worry etching his features. His ruby eyes were dark with concern and his fingers were gently making circles on my shoulder.

I quivered once again, his touch chasing away the cold.

"Did you see that boy?" I said, sweeping my gaze back and forth across the lounge, wondering where he had gone. Not very many people knew how to or could teleport on a whim. He had disappeared in an instant.

"What boy?" he asked, furrowing his brows and looking around carefully.

I swallowed. "You saw me sit and then came over?" I said, trying to make sense of the whole interaction myself.

"Yes…" he said, cocking one eyebrow and waiting for me to continue.

I straightened my spine and was surprised that I held on to my bottle of champagne. I stood up, grabbing for his hand, and led him out into the cold night air.

"Do you believe in the old gods?" I said, my head still spinning from the encounter with the stranger.

"What do you mean?" he said carefully.

I didn't answer right away. I just stared at his face, trying to memorize this picture. His hair was in his eyes, and his strong hands kept making their way through his dark locks in an effort to push them out of his field of vision.

His ruby eyes held mine and he didn't seem at all surprised by my question. I pulled him deeper into the cold, eager to get away from the lounge and away from Viper and the random boy who'd shown up.

The night air was crisp against my cheeks and suddenly I found myself opening the bottle of champagne with a loud *pop*. The bottle steamed and hissed as bubbles came out. I took a long drink in front of a bemused Ky.

It danced on my tongue and warmed my belly, drawing me back to reality.

I offered the bottle to Kyra and his lips twitched up as he brushed his hand against mine, sending little tingles throughout my body, and took a long drink himself.

How was it that every touch just made me want more?

"We might need more," I said finally. I gazed out to the city streets where people were milling around and walking through the starless night, oblivious to the changes around them.

Something sinister was happening to the world.

And somehow I was in the middle of it.

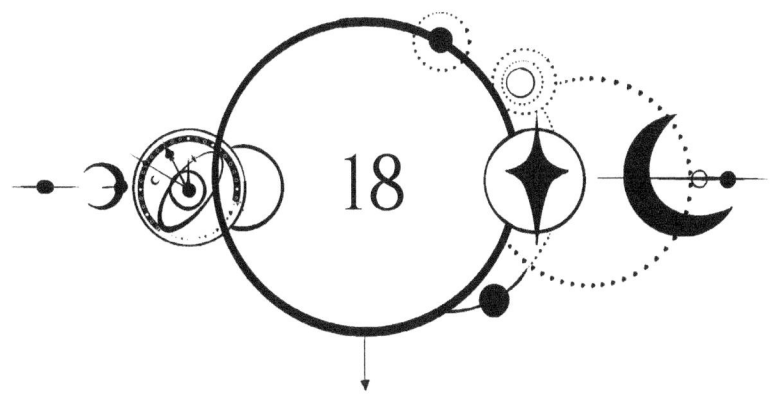

18

Greer

We ended up back at Ky's place, which was seriously nice. Not as nice as Lux's and I's place, but still nice. It practically screamed bachelor pad.

You walked into a small entryway with a large modern kitchen that had all gray cabinets and a dark marble island with enough seating for six. It opened up to a sparsely decorated living room dominated by a black sofa and two gray chairs centered around a large flat screen TV. There was a gray wood dining table with seating for ten, and a floating staircase that led up to a second floor.

Each room flowed effortlessly into the other and everything was big and open.

Not too bad for a winner of The Immortality Trials. There was little personality to the space, but it was welcoming in its own way. It was a walkup, so I assumed the second floor housed his bedroom and maybe a few others. Maybe even access to the roof.

We ended up grabbing takeout from a place close by, and I told him about my unexpected visitor.

"I don't believe in the old gods…" I said for the second time this evening.

"At all?" Ky said, lightly crossing his foot over his ankle on the dark leather couch, a flute of champagne between his long fingers.

"I mean, we get told in school that the gods were the original immortals and that they created the heavens, earth, and hell. And that eventually they wanted nothing more than to fuck around with the world they created, so they gave power to rulers and created races and species for fun. Eventually, they let their playthings run wild and they retreated back to the heavens and hell, bored of what earth had to offer. Then they let the kingdoms clean up their mess as power struggles and civil wars broke out, and their parting gift was the Immortality Trials. Which dates back thousands of years ago ... I'm supposed to believe that they are just sitting around fucking with people for fun and watching us all run around like a twisted reality TV show? It just seems like an unrealistic ideology..." I said, filling up my drink once again.

No longer was I scared of what that man-child had said in the lounge. I was a little bit irritated and pissed. Anger was easier to cling to than fear and anxiety at the moment.

"Hmm, interesting. I don't remember my history classes including the words 'fucked up'..." Kyra said thoughtfully with a serious face.

I broke out in a grin and gently shoved at his shoulder.

"Well, what did you learn? I know things were probably different in the Eastern Hemisphere..." I said, turning my head to the side.

People didn't talk about the Eastern Hemisphere. It was briefly spoken of in school how it had become independent nations and refused trade and contact with us. It was like the cousin nobody spoke about—the family didn't really keep tabs on them, besides to check in and see if they were alive.

There was little information about it online either. It was as if it was a different world, and Ky hadn't mentioned much about it, even when I had inquired about his past.

The whole thing felt like the Western Hemisphere was trying to cover something up.

"Pretty much the same thing. Gods were the original immortals. They created all other life and let it run free. They took a step back when chaos was raining, and immortality was offered as a gift to those who were worthy and the Immortality Trials were born," he said, easily reciting almost exactly what I'd said.

"Our books mention pretty much nothing about the eastern side of the world…" I said, letting my words trail off so he would continue. I was looking for any bit of information I could grab on to about his past or his home.

"We learned about you all, and your history as well as ours. But I promise the Republic is much more interesting than where I grew up…" he said with a casual wink as he stood up and walked over to get another bottle of champagne.

"Do you want another?" he called before I could inquire further.

"Yeah," I said before finishing my glass.

It felt like Ky was avoiding the topic. I didn't know what had happened there or what it was like, but I was sure he would tell me when he was ready.

My phone buzzed and it was of course from Lux. I had texted him about what happened, and we agreed to talk more on it later. I would fill Nova and Waverly in as well.

I could feel a headache brimming at the base of my neck whenever I thought too much about it all. The Trials, the investigation, my inevitable doom … It made my head spin.

Ugh. I really would peak in my twenties. I sighed loudly at that thought.

I had been living blissfully the past few days in my sexually aroused state and happiness that I finally had more than Lux for a friend.

"You okay over there?" Ky said as he came back over with another bottle, popped and ready to go.

"Oh, yeah, just thinking about … everything…" I mumbled as I grabbed the bottle and drank straight from it.

"I can get another bottle if you'd like that one to yourself," he teased, flashing his perfectly straight teeth.

I laughed and took another long drink.

"But it's so much more fun to share," I teased back, handing the bottle back to him and daring him with my eyes to abandon his glass.

He snatched the bottle from me and took a long drink, his ruby eyes never leaving mine.

I really needed to know what his hands felt like again. When we trained the other day, it was just a little taste. And the time before that had barely been a touch compared to what I wanted from him.

I wanted a release. I wanted Kyra.

He somehow made everything seem less scary. He seemed to keep the darkness of this situation at bay whenever he was around. I didn't feel like I would fall face first into the black hole that was the last few weeks when he was here. It was as if his touch of fire helped light a different way.

And his lips.

I needed to feel those again too.

Desire started to work its way through my body, and I moved to take the bottle away and set it down. Ky's gaze followed my movements, his eyes dancing. He wanted it too. I knew he did. I smiled remembering the words he had said to me in the gym.

His eyes seemed to pulse red as candles sputtered to life in random places around the room and the bulbs above dimmed.

Smooth.

I smiled broadly as I stood up in front of him, his eyes sparkling and then simmering as his gaze roamed across my body from head to toe.

"I've wanted to take off this dress all night..." I said slowly, keeping my eyes connected to his. My whole body felt like it was alight with need.

He stood and brushed his hands against my thighs with that featherlight touch and gently pulled the hem of my dress up. His hands raked over the dips of my hips, the sides of my breasts, and then my arms as he lifted my dress cleanly up and over me, discarding it to the side.

His fingers slid down the sides of my shoulders and my arms and he murmured, "Me too..."

"I believe you asked if you could make me come again and again the other day ... I assume you are a male of your word," I said huskily.

He smiled wickedly and whispered against my skin. "Oh, yes, I haven't forgotten ... don't worry." His words danced across my ear and cheek.

I stood bare in front of him except my black lace covered bra and thong.

He kept trailing his fingertips over my skin, sending little pulses throughout my body, and I knew my desire was already soaking through my panties and leaking onto my thighs.

"Greer, you're beautiful," he said, gently tracing my spine until he reached my bra clasp. He gave it a tug and pulled it away, exposing my already hard nipples and heavy breasts. My body was aching to be touched by his hands.

"That's better," he said as he brushed his lips across mine.

I greedily reached for his bottom lip in between my teeth, but he pulled away, smiling and chuckling.

"You said I could worship your body with my mouth and my hands, and I keep my promises, Greer," he said, pushing his lips to my neck, leaving little spots of heat everywhere his lips and hands touched.

"Ky," I breathed out, reaching out for him, and he tsked.

"You first..." he breathed, gently pushing my hands to my sides.

I swallowed.

I wasn't going to argue with that.

Suddenly, his tongue was working its way around my nipple as his other hand was on my other breast. I groaned and leaned into him, threading my fingers through his thick black hair. He began to suck and nibble, drawing out the pleasure on my hardened peaks almost painfully so. I was breathing hard before he continued the same thing on my other breast, and the wetness I had for him was nearly soaking my skin as I clenched my thighs together. He was destroying me with his mouth and his tongue, and he had only given attention to my breasts.

"Ky," I moaned again as every scrape of his teeth and touch of his lips made my legs grow weaker and weaker. My whole body was throbbing for him. Pleasure started to curl in my belly as his kisses began to get lower and he slowly pulled my tiny lace thong down my legs, his fingers dancing over my skin as his lips moved further down until I was standing completely naked before him.

"Mmm, Greer, you're already so wet for me..." he said, trailing his steady fingers along my inner thighs, feeling the moisture there before stopping right next to my center. I ached for him to find me there. His mouth, fingers, cock … something to release the coiling in my body.

"Breathtaking," he whispered against my skin as he took in the full view of my body and I felt like I could feel his eyes move across me. He knelt and trailed kisses across my hip bones, my thighs, and my soft lower belly. Suddenly, his thumb was over my clitoris, making small circles, and I could no longer control what was coming out of my mouth as a throaty moan escaped my lips and my head fell back.

"Ky, please," I said, begging him for more as my body began to coil and vibrate with the pleasure he gave. And then he was gone.

My eyes flashed up and I felt his hands on mine as he made me sit down on the couch, fully bared to him, and pulled my ass to the edge and got on his knees once again. He spread my knees apart and settled between them.

"I want to taste you, Greer."

He started to trail his lips against my inner thighs and then placed one finger in me, which I met with a groan.

"Mmm, so ready…" he said, smiling. He pulled it out and licked it while staring into my eyes. I nearly came right then and there.

"More," I breathed.

He smiled wickedly and bowed his head until his mouth was on me. His tongue began to move and my whole body was washed over with pleasure. He placed two fingers inside me and began to pump them in and out while his tongue lapped, swirled, and sucked on the bundle of nerves there.

It was like he had never tasted anything so delicious and he was devouring me with his mouth so he could memorize the taste of me. I closed my eyes and started squeezing my own breasts, trying to release the tension that was threatening to explode out of me. I looked down and met Ky's gaze as his eyes flickered to where I was kneading my own flesh, and he growled in response. The vibrations of his lips sent a new wave of sensation over my clitoris as he continued to move those long fingers in and out of me. I was so full of him already, but it wasn't nearly enough.

Pleasure started roaring through my body fast and hard and had my back arching and my hips moving so I was riding his tongue and his hands. I clenched my thighs around him and moved my hands to his hair, wanting to feel more of him. I moaned his name again as he continued to move his skilled mouth against me and chase me toward my climax. I felt like a fire was roaring inside me and it was threatening to overtake my entire body.

"Come for me, Greer," he purred, his lips moving against me.

Gods I wanted to.

I needed to.

My breath was coming in pants and my body started to coil until I was nearly shaking. Waves of pleasure crashed into me, sending me over the edge and moaning his name, eyes closed and head back. It rocked through me, shooting sensations through my entire core, making my toes curl and my body throb and convulse in ways I didn't even know were possible.

He continued to lick and suck as I throbbed around him and soaked his hand.

"Please," I breathed as I tightened my grip on his hair and dragged his mouth up to mine, tasting myself on him. I wanted his mouth on mine and his cock inside.

I opened my mouth for him, wanting him to fill up every part of me. Inviting him to take over this part of me just like he had with my clit. I wanted him with an intensity I couldn't explain, even after that earth shattering orgasm.

It was as if whatever semblance of control he had before snapped and he wrapped his arm around my waist and the other came to my neck, squeezing slightly. He crashed his mouth to mine and in a swift motion I was underneath him, lying flat.

He quickly pulled off his shirt and his pants and I got to see his glorious god-like body on full display, all hard muscle and beautiful olive skin. He reached into his pocket and pulled out a condom.

I shook my head, not wanting anything between us. "I'm on birth control and I get checked regularly. Do you?" I said, mentally giving myself a pat on the back for even having the brain power to think of such things when all I wanted was Ky's body inside mine.

He nodded and said, "Are you sure, Greer?"

I answered him by wrapping my hands around him and feeling the length of him as he groaned into my touch. He braced his hands on either side of me and hovered his mouth above mine. He felt so good. Hard and smooth, just aching to be put inside me. A small bead of cum leaked out of his hard cock and I swiped it with my finger and sucked it into my mouth, looking at Kyra the whole time. He twitched in my hand as his eyes went blood red.

"Inside me, now," I commanded.

He crashed his mouth to mine hungrily, devouring my lips as he pushed himself inside, filling every inch of me until the base of him was connected with my entrance and I moaned into his lips.

"You feel so good, Greer," he whispered.

I wiggled against him, wanting more friction. Needing to feel him move inside of me with a fever I couldn't explain.

"Ky," I said as he began to slowly pull himself out and then thrust fully into me again. My hips reached up every time to meet him, needing him to fill every piece of me.

All I could think and feel and see was him.

He grabbed my hip with one hand, the other hand tangled in my hair as he began to thrust himself into me, slowly at first and then quickly, pounding into me like his life depended on it.

My hips met his rhythm until his whole body was tangled with mine and I felt like my entire being was overwhelmed by him. The pleasure was building again in my lower belly and when his hand started to circle around my center once again, I was completely undone. The orgasm crashed into me without warning, and I wrapped my legs around his hips and felt myself squeeze around him. Unable to do anything but hold on as my legs shook and my body tingled with the feelings of pleasure reaching every part of me.

He groaned and thrust even harder, chasing his own release as mine washed over me again and again until he emptied himself into me. He shuddered and plastered himself against me as his orgasm raged through his body.

He breathed my name and his ruby eyes connected with mine.

I didn't have any words to say, so I kissed him again until I didn't know where I started and where Ky began.

And I realized that no one had ever touched my body like that.

Like it was the most beautiful and desirable thing in the entire world.

19

Kyra

Greer's beautiful body was tangled with mine on the couch.

Her deep red hair was spilling across my chest, half covering the stone embedded in my skin. She was running her fingers up and down my torso. The only sign that she wasn't asleep.

A smile played on my lips as I thought about all the things I could do to make her moan my name again. It made me hard again thinking about it, but I didn't want to break this moment. At least not yet. The need for her had turned into something deeper and unexpected. I didn't want to let it go.

She was without a doubt the most beautiful, extraordinary, and fearless person I had ever met.

The thought swirled in my head and shocked me as I realized I had moved into very unfamiliar territory. Before, I didn't know where this would go, and now I was a bit scared of how quickly I wanted her all to myself.

How quickly I wanted her again and how scared I was that I would lose her to the Trials.

My hand trailed down her spine and the other rested behind my neck. I tried to chase away the worries that seemed to plague my mind with the realization that Greer had pretty much taken ownership of my body and my head.

I had lied earlier. I had seen the stranger she had talked about, but I couldn't very well say that I knew him or rather of him.

It wasn't often that the messenger of the gods, Afton, made an appearance.

It wasn't necessarily the *worst* omen. But it wasn't a good one. It was a warning.

The whole place had been frozen in time when he connected with her arm, including myself. I could see and observe what was going on, but it was as if time had stopped; stillness and silence had settled over the earth except for the two of them. And I was merely watching from afar, like seeing someone through a window.

It seemed odd that this visit would be connected to Greer's falsified entry in the Trials, but how could it not? Something bigger seemed to be at play here, but I didn't exactly know what that was. It was extremely unsettling.

My phone suddenly began ringing and I groaned slightly, not wanting to disturb Greer.

She started to sit up and pull away. I wrapped my arms around her and pressed her soft skin against mine, wanting to fill her again.

"Leave it," I said, moving my hands down her body to grab that beautiful ass of hers.

"It might be important," she said, propping herself on my chest and pointing those striking green eyes rounded with blue on mine.

"I don't care," I said, starting to get hard again as my hands worked their way down her body and I sat up to connect her lips with mine.

"Okay," she mumbled as I brushed my lips against hers and gently bit her lower lip. The moan she let out made the need for her explode through me until my phone started ringing again. She smiled against my lips and pulled away as I lay defeated and ready on the couch.

I grabbed the phone off the coffee table and answered it. "This better be life or death," I snapped into my phone as Greer began to move further down my body with her lips.

"Ky, they announced the next trial!" Lux said cheerily into the phone.

Well, shit.

I swore underneath my breath. We couldn't pretend like this wasn't happening. No amount of sex or fondness for Greer would chase away the events of the world.

Greer's lips were poised right above my hard cock and she smiled wickedly up at me. The smile quickly disappeared when she saw my face. She sat back, grabbing the blanket on the back of the couch and wrapping the white fabric around her body.

I saw her slip the armor on that she used for the rest of the world. Her eyes became hard and her expression settled into something neutral. She was just starting to shed that barrier with me, and it sent a sharp pain through my gut to watch her slip it back on after she had just taken it off.

"Does Greer know?" I said, sitting up, trying to ignore my erection and the image of Greer's mouth on me. I stood up and reached for my underwear and pulled them on.

"No, she isn't answering her phone," Lux said with a little amusement. "Did I interrupt something? Maybe the reason why you both seem to be unavailable?"

I could practically see him feigning innocence with wide eyes and a neutral expression. Lux was always popping in like this. I couldn't even be mad at him, but damn if his timing wasn't too spot on.

He knew perfectly well what we were doing.

Bastard.

"She's here," I grumbled.

I put the phone down and put it on speaker.

"Lux, tell us what you found out," I said, sitting back on the couch, feeling a little empty without Greer's body tucked into mine.

"Hi, G," Lux said, practically gushing over the phone.

"Can we not?" she said grumpily to no one in particular, with a mix of irritation and amusement on her features. "What's so important, Lux?"

"The next trial has been announced. I thought you would want to know…" Lux said, all playfulness leaving his voice and stone setting in with the mention of the Trials.

"What's the trial?" Greer said, straightening her spine, practically reading my own thoughts. She started to strap on more armor, receding back to a place that kept her guarded and safe from the rest of the world. The one she used when she was scared of what lay ahead.

"It's scheduled thirty days from now. They're dropping you all in the middle of the ocean and the first seven hundred and fifty back to shore win," Lux replied, his voice annoyingly neutral.

"Great," Greer mumbled and stood up, letting the blanket fall around her as she gathered up her clothes and started to pull them on aggressively.

"Well, we can chat when you get home … no rush," Lux said. I could practically hear the wink in his voice. He hung up and I turned to see Greer already dressed and gathering her things.

"You don't have to leave, Greer," I said.

I want you to stay.

"I just need some time to think about this," she said, her lips twitching into a halfhearted smile. Her red hair was a bit wild and the look on her face was laced with anxiety.

"Can I drive you home?" I said, quickly pulling on my clothes so she didn't run out into the cold by herself.

"That's okay. I'll figure it out," she said, cocking her head to the side. In a blink of an eye, she was out the door and on the street.

The moment we had before seemed to splinter and shatter right before my eyes as I watched her make her way down the dark streets of the city.

As far as a physical trial goes, it wasn't the worst. She was strong and athletic. She could make it to the top 750 as long as she knew how to swim and they didn't throw anything too dangerous into the waters. And no one tried to drown her ... I quickly shook that last thought out of my head. The test was mostly about your ability to manipulate your body in a way to survive, not to fight things off in the water, so I was really hoping they wouldn't decide to start getting experimental this year.

Why did she practically run out of here?

I had seen that same look earlier, after she had talked to Viper and after Afton had trapped her in the weird time bubble. It was as if she was holding the whole weight of the world on her shoulders and in sharp moments of pain, it ripped through her. Like she was looking death itself in the face and trying to be brave.

Sighing, I texted her and told her to let me know when she got home.

I would help her survive this.

I had a feeling the rest of the world would need help surviving what was coming next too.

☾

We didn't talk about what happened at my place. At least not right away.

I arrived at her place the next morning to start her aquatic training.

There was no playfulness or teasing banter when we sat across from one another in her dining room. She had pulled her hair back in two long braids and was wearing a black one piece with a hoodie. Her strong legs were pulled up to her chest and she was sipping on some black coffee.

"Hey," I said softly.

Her green eyes remained unfocused, gazing mournfully at nothing.

"Where are you, Greer?" I said, leaning my forearms on the table, wishing I could just leap across the space that separated us and consume whatever grief was plaguing her thoughts.

"What?" she said, snapping her gaze to mine. There was a flash of sadness, and then indifference masked her features. The armor she wore so well was beginning to crack.

"You look distracted, like your head isn't here…" I said carefully.

"I was … I am. I keep acting like my life is separated from these trials and letting myself get sidetracked with things I shouldn't be doing." She sighed and looked into her coffee.

Was she talking about last night?

"Greer, about last night…" I started and she stood up suddenly.

"I can't do this right now, Ky. Can we just start this training? I just need some time to sort this out in my head, okay? I just … I'm not in a good headspace to have this conversation with you right now, please," she said, her eyes watering slightly.

"You don't have to do all of this alone, you know … You don't have to figure it all out. You're allowed to live your life and do this. You can do both," I said quietly, moving toward her side of the table to stand in front of her.

Her shoulders sagged and she looked at me like I couldn't possibly understand.

"But I do, actually. Have to do this alone. I could die, I could lose some of my life and only have a few years … I'm trying not to push you all away, but in the end it might be better than to let you all not become collateral damage to what my life has become … What I forgot it was this past week. And I'm a survivor. I've done what I needed to do to make it this far. And it isn't pretty. I've lost myself to grief and anger before, and it took everything in me to come back. And I don't want to drag anyone down with me…" she said quietly.

She was right. I didn't fully understand what she was saying. What other demons in her past threatened to drown her?

"Greer…" I started again and reached for her, but she turned away and it was like someone had dumped cold water on my body.

"Just give me some time, Ky. I'll figure this out and talk to you when I'm ready." She smiled sadly, walking over to the balcony and peeling off her hoodie.

She was all curves and smooth, pale skin, but the fire that I had become so accustomed to within her seemed to be barely burning. A whisper of what it had been last night and in the past week.

I followed her and opened the glass door to the balcony.

"You don't scare me, Greer Roberts. I can handle what's going on inside of your head and what's going on outside of it. Just because you could die, doesn't mean you are not worthy of love and support now…" I said, standing next to her and wanting to run my fingers along her jawline and erase the pain I saw splashed across her features.

"Yes, Ky … But just because it doesn't scare you, doesn't mean it doesn't scare me…" she said softly, and dove into the pool.

My heart ached as I watched her disappear underneath the blue water.

The next two hours I called out times, strokes, laps and she quietly followed all my instructions before slipping out of the pool to where I handed her a towel.

She patted herself off and looked up at me, seeming a little bit lighter.

"Thank you, for giving me some time and space to sort things out … I like you, Ky. More than I thought. Things are just a bit complicated in here and here," she said, tapping one long black fingernail to her temple and her heart.

I wanted her to open up to me and to show her how complicated things were in my head and my heart too, but I just wrapped my arms around her instead.

"You're gonna get wet," she squealed, then giggled as I squeezed her tighter.

I oozed warmth and the droplets evaporated from both of our skin in a steaming hiss.

"You know, I'm not that worried about it…" I said as she broke out of my grip and shoved past me.

"Same time tomorrow, Greer. I'll be here when you want to talk," I said, watching her walk into the penthouse.

"Yeah, yeah … Big bad immortal warlock trying to save the day," she said, waving me off and smiling.

Greer might have been scared of the Trials and her own demons, but I was scared of how much I wanted to wash all those fears away. How much I want to sweep her into my arms and pro-tect her from the pain of the world and herself.

☾

The next few weeks were full of me showing up in the morning and Greer swimming laps and treading water, with light banter and semi-comfortable silence. We hadn't talked about the night we slept together since that first day of training and she hadn't said much about what was plaguing her thoughts. I would sometimes catch her scowling, rubbing her temples, or her eyes would be unfocused like she had been transported elsewhere.

I wanted to push her to tell me. But she had asked for time and space.

I was trying to give it to her, even though it was killing me to be so close to her but have her be so far away. At one point, I asked if she wanted to train alone and she had smiled and said, no, she liked the company.

I didn't know what else she needed from me. I felt lost on how to make this better.

I wanted to make it better.

I just wanted her.

It was like this trial in particular had swept the joy out of Greer's life and she was just a bystander. I couldn't blame her. This would be hard. The other contestants who had heightened physical abilities or anything that gave them a water affinity would have an advantage. She would need to keep her wits about her and not give into exhaustion or fatigue.

But I didn't want her to think of me as a distraction that she needed to keep in check. I wanted her to lean on me for support and realize that I could help make her stronger.

Currently, I was sitting at her table with Lux, having a beer while Greer was at work.

"Does Greer seem distant lately?" I blurted out.

I was going crazy in my own head about this and I needed to talk to someone else who got what was going on.

Lux was one of the best people I knew. He was one of the few wealthy individuals in the city who actually cared about the less fortunate and marginalized communities in the Republic and then actually did something about it. It wasn't even limited to the building we were currently in but a lot of other programs and charities.

He cared about change and people.

He cared about humans.

Additionally, he was smart and fun as hell.

A plus side to all of this was getting to hang out with someone who wasn't just trying to use me for my money, power, or fame. Or treat me like I was an inconvenient oddity from the east. We just got to exist as Kyra and Lux.

I had gained a lot in the last few weeks and it seemed like Greer was slowly losing it all.

"Like, is there something else eating at her besides all the current situations?" Lux said, sighing. His gold eyes looked empathetic and distraught at the thought of his most beloved best friend going through the hellish ordeal that was these trials.

"Yeah," I said and took another drink of my beer.

"She'll talk when she's ready."

He placed his elbows on the table and downed his beer. He wore a tattered band tee and dark jeans that showed off his broad frame covered in dark brown skin and magically bright colored tattoo art.

Great, she had said the same thing. I didn't know why I had thought I might get another answer, but it was worth a shot.

"I know that you know what happened the night you called about the Immortality Trials ... Greer and I have barely talked or done anything else since. I just don't want to make things more complicated for her than they already are ... But I want to let her know that I can help her and I'm not just a distraction, you know?" I said, looking at my hands, unable to meet Lux's eyes.

"Why don't you actually talk to her about it? Greer is my best friend, but she's had to be strong for a really long time and she's had to do it alone for a lot of her life. Sometimes she just needs someone to tell her that you know she can do it alone, but she doesn't have to," Lux said thoughtfully, leaning back in his chair. "Not to mention she's had shit luck with males, so don't screw it up. Ky, if you really care about her, then talk to her. If it's just for fun, then don't worry about it, but get your expectations under control and communicate what you want." He looked at me, smug as hell, like he was some kind of relationship expert.

"She asked for time and space. It's been two weeks ... It's not just for fun. I want more ... from this ... us ..." I said, trying to find words for what exactly I felt.

"Keep being around and giving her the option of help. Create the opportunity for her to come to you. She will—and when she does, don't fuck it up," Lux said, keeping that smug ass expression on his face and sipping his beer.

"Well, you don't need to be such a cocky bastard about it," I mumbled, getting up to get another drink.

Lux laughed out loud. "Stop moping and maybe go meet her after work. She'll be done soon anyway. Try and talk to her then."

"What? You don't want to hang out with me anymore?" I called from the kitchen.

Lux walked over and slung an arm around my shoulder, leveling his gaze to mine.

"Somehow I get the feeling that us hanging out is already a regular thing…" he said, squeezing my shoulders and then aggressively pushing me toward the door. "Go and fix your shit."

He walked off to his bedroom, giving me a wave.

Sighing, I put on my coat and headed toward the elevator, hoping that tonight Greer would talk to me about what was going on in that beautiful head of hers.

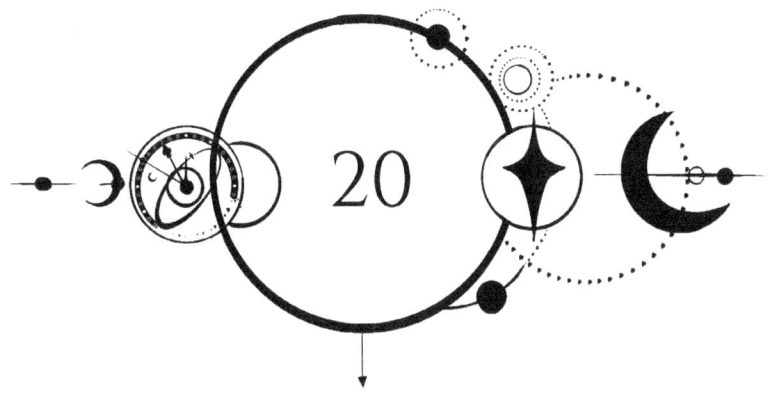

Greer

It wasn't that busy tonight. It would have been nice if it was. It wouldn't have left me so much time to stew in my own thoughts.

When I came in, Arlo had asked me what I was moping about and I had nearly burst into tears right then and there and sobbed about the heaviness that was on my chest about *everything*. The Immortality Trials, the stranger who grabbed me in the bar a couple of weeks ago, Ky, the fact that Viper hadn't gotten back to me and he hadn't been in, and me spilling my coffee this morning.

Even though that last one wasn't that big of a deal.

Instead, I had just asked him for a hug and he happily obliged, telling me, "You'll figure it out, love. You're one of the good ones," and planting a kiss on the crown of my head.

I was distancing myself from Ky, and Lux, for that matter.

I had talked to Nova and Waverly about it in our group chat a little bit, the overwhelming doom. They had been ready to rally in support, especially after I had spilled the beans on what happened between me and Ky.

Which was oddly comforting, since I had never had a girl group chat, ever, and it felt like I could just word vomit my feelings through memes and gifs and they just got it. I didn't explain all the details or thoughts swirling inside me, but it did help me get through the day.

I didn't want to talk about all the things that were going on in my head. At least not yet. I just wanted to make it through this next round and then I would lose it. I knew in my brain that I was avoiding Lux and Kyra because they both wanted to push to open the flood gates inside me because they were nosy and stubborn males.

And mostly because they cared. Like a lot.

But what I really needed was Viper to get back to me.

Ugh.

Ky and I probably needed to talk about what happened the other night. I mean, it felt magical. Truly. I hadn't had sex like that in ... well ... ever. I had actually never had sex like that in my life. The things he did with his hands and mouth made me want to tear my clothes off every time I thought about them. I didn't exactly know what that meant, but I was trying not to overthink it too much with everything else going on.

And he had been really sweet the last two weeks in training. He was giving me the time and space I had asked for. I could tell he wanted to push back but he didn't.

I also knew there were still things that he was holding back. I could feel it and I didn't want to give up pieces of myself if he couldn't do the same. Even though at the moment I was seriously avoiding him because I just couldn't have a conversation about my emotional state right now. I felt like a jenga tower one brick away from toppling over.

I really liked Ky, but I also wasn't a stranger to males. I knew that he could be bad news with his complicated past and immortal status. And even though he had been thoughtful, kind, and delicious in bed, it didn't mean I completely trusted him with all of *my secrets.*

Especially the ones that made my own skin crawl and I had only ever told Lux.

I didn't usually strip myself bare to anyone, and I was terrified that if I did I would drag him into the depths of me and cause irreparable harm to us both. So I had been holding him at arm's length the past two weeks as I spiraled in my own head.

I felt like all I did lately was train, think, work, think, sleep, think, eat, think, repeat.

I was running toward exhaustion trying to get myself under control.

And right now, I didn't necessarily need any distractions with the trial so close. What I needed was to focus on getting through it, and then I could unpack the long list of things that were currently occupying my thoughts, starting with one extremely attractive immortal.

He was more than just a distraction—I knew that in my heart —and more than just a good fuck, but I wasn't mentally and emotionally prepared for more at the moment. I wasn't expecting to *want* more, let alone have it fall into my lap.

Additionally, this was where things got really interesting for the Immortality Trials. This was where it started to become televised outside of the first announcement ceremony. Where bets and rankings and brackets would be made official. This was where I would be on display for the whole world to see. I would just be a name and a number to so many. Barely worth noticing or recognizing simply because I was human.

But it also painted a target on my back. Something I needed to be careful and mindful of.

I was really not looking forward to it.

At all.

People would literally be watching me, hoping that I would fail so they could win money.

What a terrible way to live my life.

As if I had consented to this. To any of this. I wanted to scream to let something out, but my phone interrupted my whirlwind of thoughts and emotions. I quickly pulled it out.

> **Viper: 1892 South Second Street.**
> **Your shifter is there.**

Followed with a picture and a name.

> **Viper: Emmett Dahm, no alibi and the only**
> **one dumb and arrogant enough to do the job.**

He was youngish looking, with curly brown hair and long legs and arms. He had to be at least six-foot judging by the photo, with brown eyes and pale skin. He looked like a perfectly normal, unassuming white male.

I studied the picture for a few minutes and then pocketed my phone and looked around. Arlo had already said I could leave early. I needed to see this bastard to confront him and get to the bottom of this. Then I wouldn't have to compete in the trial where I would have to swim like my life depended on it—because it actually did. I wasn't ready to kiss a third of my life cycle goodbye, because I sure as hell wasn't choosing government servitude.

I chewed my bottom lip, trying to decide what to do.

I wanted to go now.

But I wasn't going alone.

I texted our girl group chat and asked if they were busy.

Just a regular old girls' night out. Uncovering crime and shaking down bad guys. It felt like something that made sense for us, honestly. I chuckled quietly.

They both said they could meet me in twenty minutes. I checked on all my tables and told Arlo I was taking him up on his deal of leaving early.

I was going to get to the bottom of this.

Tonight.

☾

Nova showed up in glittering silver overalls, with patent leather pointed toe booties and a black long sleeve top underneath. She had simultaneously shown up looking like she was ready to kick down a door and go out to the club.

Waverly had obviously come from work and hadn't changed from her standard uniform, but honestly the girl was already beautiful, and the uniform looked like it was made specifically for the lovely swells and curves of her body.

They had both hugged me tight when they arrived.

I was more than okay with welcoming their reassuring arms and supportive energy.

I was glad I was in my black jumpsuit that I had paired with chunky black combat boots. I felt like I was ready to kick some ass. I pulled out my switchblade, ready to get some information.

"Seriously?" Nova said, eyeing my blade, laughter in her eyes. "What are you in, West Side Story?"

"Oh, fuck off," I said, giggling.

She shot me a wicked grin. Waverly pursed her lips together to keep from laughing.

Both Waverly and Nova had become so much more to me in the last few weeks. They were my people now and they had my back. I was exceptionally grateful that they were here.

Nova was clearly invested in uncovering the injustice of the Trials outside of our friendship and she was one badass powerful blood witch. She had been working behind the scenes to uncover ways people had fooled and worked around blood contracts before for the last few weeks.

Waverly had also been doing everything she could with the ITC to get them to take the investigation seriously. Even though it felt like someone was literally paying them to look the other way.

I was glad to have them on my team and I honestly wouldn't want anyone else to have my back.

"Thanks for being here," I said, pulling my coat tighter around me to keep out the cold.

Nova's dark face speckled with silver stars broke into a full smile that reached her orange-fire eyes. "Of course. You can't get rid of us now. Plus, I can't wait to ask this shifter how he managed to completely fool the blood contract, or, more importantly, who taught him how to do that."

"This is a good step for the investigation. Maybe we can end this, once and for all. And we can start having normal girls' nights that don't revolve around catching criminals!" Waverly said cheerfully.

"Now, what would be the fun in that?" Nova said, laughing. I couldn't help but join in too.

I wondered if I would ever get back to normal again.

The address that Viper had given me wasn't too far away, so we decided to walk. Plus, with Waverly here it made it more official. Whatever we found she could use in the investigation. And the Trial Lord, *Mr. Edward,* could finally get off his high horse and believe me and get me the fuck out of the Trials.

I was still seething that he hadn't taken the twenty million dollars, even though I would have felt eternally indebted to Lux. The whole thing was just asinine.

The address led us to a back alleyway, to a bright green door that had one singular lamp above it. The alley was littered with some trash, but mostly it was cloaked in darkness and the only thing out of the ordinary was the strange, aggressive color of the door.

It was quiet and isolated, though.

Probably a perfect place to hire someone to do something illegal.

Waverly stepped up and banged on the door.

"This is the FEC. I have a few questions for you," she said, her siren powers gently weaving through her words and making even me want to answer any questions she asked tonight.

We each stood there for about thirty seconds, our breath coming out in little puffs, waiting to see if anyone would come. Waverly banged on the door once more and gave out her siren command again, but no one came.

She went to try the old door handle that was covered in rust and was met with resistance.

Frowning, she took a step back.

"How are we supposed to get…" I didn't get to finish my sentence as Waverly kicked in the door in one swift motion and broke the lock.

"Like that," she said, smiling, looking rather pleased with herself.

I looked at Nova, who only smiled with a bemused look in her eyes as the stars around her temples seemed to dance with laughter.

Immediately, it opened up to a staircase that was lit up with an unfortunate fluorescent green hue. It looked like scraps of paper, dirt, and grime had been permanently cemented to the once-black stairs.

But the smell is what hit me first. It was like rotting flesh and a bitter tinge of something else.

"Something's not right," Nova said, starting toward the stairs and climbing upward, her brow furrowed and lips pursed.

Waverly and I followed suit. I attempted to close the door behind me, but Waverly had successfully smashed the lock, so it was no use.

The top of the stairs opened up into a large room with what looked like a bar several yards in front of us and then a wall off to the left and more room to the right. There was a large living room covered in misshapen and dark furniture, with that same greenish hue settling over the space and the same grime that covered the stairs.

It was like living at the bottom of a swamp.

Who the hell lives like this?

"Reveal yourself and come forward and answer the official FEC questions," Waverly said, lacing her voice with the siren's command yet again. She looked around the room as if taking mental notes of all the details, which she probably was. It didn't feel like a good sign that her commands weren't working.

It actually felt like a very, *very* bad sign.

I nervously flicked my switchblade in and out, trying to focus on moving one foot in front of the other.

There was another door at the end of the living room that opened up to a hallway, with one side leading toward a kitchen and the other leading toward what could only be bedrooms and bathrooms.

"I'll take the kitchen. You two check out those rooms," I said, making my way toward the right while Nova and Waverly headed to the three doors on the left.

The smell was wrong. It was getting stronger and filling my nose and mouth with disgust, like it would soon choke me. The kitchen was just as nasty as the rest of the place and there was still no sign of this shifter.

"Greer … You're going to want to see this," Nova called out from one of the rooms.

I quickly made my way to the sound of her voice, where Waverly was already on the phone with someone in the corner of the room.

There was a large bed and trash littering most of the floor. A computer was set up on the other side of the room, with piles of clothes and other miscellaneous things.

But the most disturbing thing was the shifter lying face up, his mouth slightly open, with jeans, a red hoodie, and tennis shoes on. His eyes were glazed over and his skin looked ashen.

"Is he dead?" I said warily, forcing myself not to gag on the smell that was now almost suffocating me.

I tried not to let panic wrack my body as the only legitimate lead I had for my case was slithering farther away from me. My freedom barely had a flicker of hope if this shifter was dead.

He wouldn't be able to confess.

He wouldn't be able to tell the truth.

I would still have to complete the Trials.

I knew in my fucking bones that this was our guy.

The smell in the room was threatening to drown me. It was like a sewer and a landfill had a baby and sprinkled rotting flesh on top and shoved it into an enclosed space.

"I don't know…" Nova said, looking confused as she leaned over the body.

"You don't know?" I repeated.

He looked pretty *fucking* dead.

"His blood isn't flowing and it's turning to rot in his body," Nova said, still sounding confused and almost in awe.

"Nova, he sounds pretty dead," I said, trying to keep my breathing under control. My heart was racing and threatening to pop outside of my chest. My ears were ringing, and spots of black were pebbling my vision.

"But he shouldn't be. His blood … is immortal. I can feel it. I can smell it underneath this filth. He shouldn't be able to die," Nova said, choosing her words carefully as she let a hand hover above this man's body. Her face looked like she was trying to figure out an impossible puzzle, as if she didn't quite have all the pieces.

"I called my team. They are on their way … I contacted Lux and Kyra as well," Waverly said, concern etching her face. She took a few steps toward me. "Greer, are you all right?"

My face was pale, and my eyes were unfocused. I needed to get out of here.

"He doesn't have a pulse, but you can't kill an immortal," Nova mumbled as she moved her hovering hands around his body.

Nova's eyes lifted and connected with mine, both of them realizing at the same time what this meant.

"You can't make a dead man confess … He was our only legitimate lead," I whispered. I felt numb and my heart dropped to my stomach.

"I need some air," I mumbled before stumbling out in the hallway and back through the rooms lined with garbage. The smell seemed to cling to my body, my throat, and coat my tongue. I tore down the stairs and out the ugly green door.

I sucked in the cold night air and looked around wildly, wishing I could just stop the world for one moment in order to lose my shit in private.

Instead, I slid down the brick wall opposite of the hideous door, where darkness hugged me and the shadows swallowed me, and pulled my knees to my chest.

The tears wouldn't come.

It wasn't sadness that threatened me but hopelessness.

A sense that I had fallen into a lightless hole that went on for eternity, with no one but myself to hear the screams that echoed through my head.

Instead, I stared at that green door until the echoes in my head faded, like everything else, into nothing.

How was I supposed to escape this nightmare if it wasn't in my dreams?

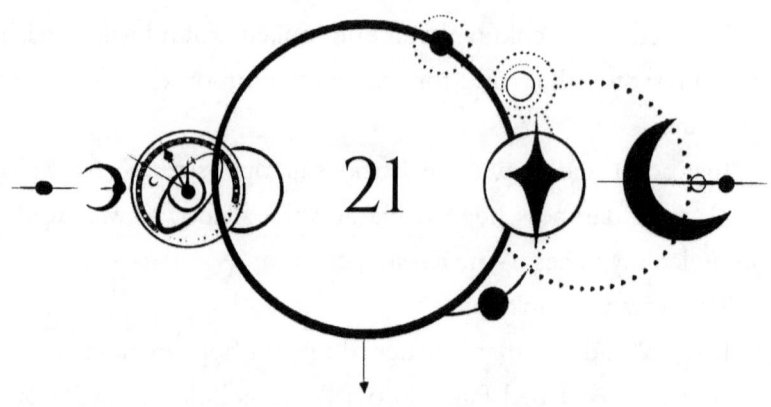

Greer

I was five when I first noticed that my mom wasn't "normal." I remember waiting for her after school and I was the last kid there. I was getting sympathetic looks from the teachers and a few moms who were hanging around on parent pickup duty. My mom was twenty-five minutes late. She was almost always late, but not this late.

I heard the other moms whispering.

She can't even be on time for her daughter.

Poor thing I hear she lives in her car.

Do you see how haggard she is? I can smell alcohol on her breath.

Disgraceful and disgusting.

I didn't know what those words meant, and I didn't dare bring it up with my mom when she finally came to pick me up ten minutes later.

The next memory I had was when I was a bit older, maybe eight.

My mom would have swings of happiness, where the sun seemed to shine brightly around her like an angel, and she laughed loudly and without restraint.

Then other times she would hardly smile with her eyes at all, and she would go through the motions of what it looked like to be happy.

Even though I was young, I was smart. I knew other moms were not like this. I would watch them with their kids and it was like I could see a dark cloud hanging over my mom.

I distinctly remember being picked on at school one day and coming home with a black eye and bloody nose because some of the other kids were talking about their parents and I had said I didn't have a dad.

They called my mom a nasty bitch.

Me a dumb human dog.

A waste of space and no wonder my dad left.

I didn't know what those words meant at the time, but they hurt.

They lit a fire in me that sent me screaming and catapulting myself onto the little faerie boy who had started the name calling in the first place. I scratched and clawed, blood-curdling screams ripping from my throat until three other kids pulled me off him and beat me senseless.

So when my mom had picked me up and cleaned up the blood, I was sent straight to bed.

I got up later wanting some water, walking to the bathroom of the dingy old apartment we were staying in at the time because my mom had worked out a special deal with the landlord. I saw my mom in the bathroom with a rainbow of pills in front of her.

She popped two or three.

She looked like a ghost, a shell of a human, and she was on the phone with someone.

"I'm getting worse, it's getting worse ... I don't know what to do for her. She deserves better." Tears streamed down her pale face and her hair was limp down her back.

I scurried away, deeply uncomfortable with how broken my mom looked.

That's when I began to spend time in the library, tucked away learning what I could about how I could keep my own monsters away, because it seemed like whatever my mom was doing wasn't working.

Throughout the years, more events like these would happen.

I would catch my mom in a state of duress with pills, booze, men, cuts, bruises, etc.

She would always try and hide it from me.

She tried so hard to play the part of a happy mom. She did her best with what she had, and I know she loved me fiercely. She told me so every chance she got and said how proud she was.

But I was ashamed of her. The brokenness. The pain she tried so hard to hide.

When I was a teenager, I was especially cruel. I was snappy, irritable, and spent less and less time around her. I thought that by distancing myself from her I wouldn't be associated with the mess of a life she had and people would see that I was above it. Better than her.

My embarrassment, guilt, and shame for her, for being human, was revved up at full force until I turned sixteen.

I was reading a book in the library, like I did most days, avoiding others because it was easier that way. I had gotten the reputation of being the human girl you didn't mess with because I would hunt you down and cut my name into your skin.

In my defense, I had only done it once to a male animalia who had tried to force himself on me outside in the soccer fields on my walk home. He had absolutely deserved it and it served my reputation well.

So I tried to stay hidden away in the library until most of the kids went home to their comfy houses and steady families. On this day, I was reading a book about a young woman and she was talking about her mental health struggle.

Depression.

Anxiety.

Suicidal thoughts.

Self-harm.

My stomach dropped and my heart clenched. I felt like I was reading about my mom. I tossed the book aside and started researching on the library computer about all of those things. At sixteen, I didn't realize that moms dealt with that. That anyone dealt with that.

Which was totally naive, but I had been so focused on surviving and keeping my own anger in check that I hadn't really given the rest of the world a thought, except that I was perpetually angry with it.

After that I tried to be kinder to my mom. Help her in any way I could.

I decided that I would in fact go and get an engineering degree because I didn't want her to hurt anymore. I wanted to take away the pain and darkness that had been eating at her for over a decade.

So I worked hard to get a scholarship, to not be a burden and not ask for too much or be anything but a smiling, happy teen.

But along the way I ended up becoming too much like my mom.

I hid away from my own feelings of loneliness and isolation.

The darkness seemed to eat at me too.

I had read that depression could be hereditary; sometimes I wondered if it was etched in my bones to feel sad and lonely. If my soul had a permanent black stain on it and neither my mom nor I had much hope of escaping. My mom had been dealing with it for years and she was still standing, so I could deal with mine.

I pretended that I wanted the engineering degree because that's how I could save myself and my mom, and because nobody else seemed to care about us anyways. As humans we were easily ignored and disposed of.

When I finally went off to college, I distanced myself again from my mom.

I got swept up in the drinking, the parties, the sex ... My new best friend Lux.

I coped in ways that I thought were normal.

Even though they weren't.

So when I got the call that my mother had committed suicide, I broke.

I blamed myself for not calling more. For not fighting for her harder. For not being there when she needed me. For selfishly thinking that I was allowed moments of joy, numbness, and ecstasy when she would never have any of it.

My own gnawing darkness fed on that guilt and shame. Growing and expanding inside me, telling me that I was indeed the reason that she died, and it was funny that I thought I had any hope of not ending up in the exact same place she did.

If my mom couldn't run away from what ran through her veins, how did I think I had any chance of escape?

Because maybe fate decided a long time ago that this was my destiny. That no matter how hard I ran from my mom, from her darkness and the one that prowled inside me … I, too, would *never* be free of it. The only way to release it would be through death by my own hand.

It was never written in the fabric of who I was to be happy.

To be carefree.

To be anything but pain, suffering, and sadness.

A burden to those around me. If I let anyone close enough, it would probably swallow them whole too. It would spread like a disease, a sickness that was so contagious any glimpse of it on me would infect someone else and cause irreparable damage.

The world wanted to treat me like a piece of trash because I had no power and my life span was short.

Therefore, the cruel path of fate had branded it on my heart when I was born that the life I was to live would only end in catastrophe and those around me would pay the price.

No one would be able to look at who I was and what I was and think that I was worthy of anything else except contempt and sadness so deep it oozed out of my pores.

But someone did.

Lux did.

He looked at what lay inside me and offered his hand.

He clawed through it, when I didn't want him too. When all I wanted was for my own pain to end just like my mom's.

But he never let me go.

He never let me surrender to my own thoughts of death. To the guilt and shame that writhed in me and created nightmares in the daytime. To the memories and ghosts that haunted me, making my throat raw from screaming and my eyes swollen shut from the tears.

He never gave up.

And I told myself that I wouldn't allow myself to get there again.

To fall so deep, hard, and fast that even Lux might not be able to pull me out again.

I didn't want him to have to continue to rescue me. I should be able to figure this out by now.

But I was reminded again of something I read when I was sixteen: that depression was something you had to deal with forever. It never went away. I would always have a kernel of it inside me, but as long as I kept it locked away without feeding it, it should have been fine.

I should have been fine.

But here I was again.

Falling into the darkness once more.

Except this time, I wasn't so sure how I was supposed to get out when so much was out of my control. When someone unbeknownst to me was trying to get me killed.

And it was laughable to think that I could start a relationship with someone like Ky right now, as if I had any business letting someone in who would inadvertently have to deal with what was inside me at one point or another. It was a lot to ask someone to make you want to live on days you wanted nothing more than to die.

Lux carried that burden, and sometimes it hurt my heart so much that I had to sit down and breathe before I had a full-fledged panic attack.

And here I was gathering more friends, like Nova and Waverly.

None of these people asked for the burden that was me. They had no idea what I was capable of, or what damage I could cause to them or myself.

The hopelessness that I chased away before was snaking its way back into every fiber of my being and I was scared.

For myself, for Ky.

Lux.

Waverly.

Nova.

But this time, it felt like death chased me.

I felt like I was running from it, desperately trying to free myself from it while it dragged me under, threatening to choke out my life.

I wanted to fight the Trials.

The person who'd pushed me into this.

The world for ever allowing the bigotry and hypocrisy that raged through the Republic.

I wanted to fight for something better, but what if it didn't matter?

What if no matter what, I was always destined to be swallowed whole, and no matter what I wanted, my fate had been sealed the moment I was born?

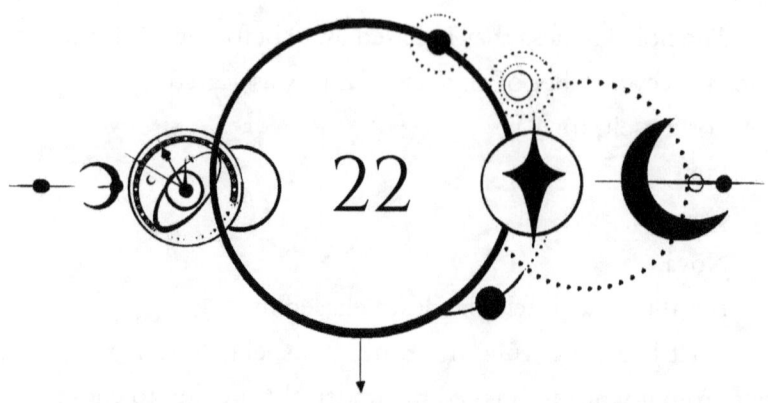

22

Kyra

W here's Greer?" I asked Arlo when I walked into the Shadow Lounge. It was relatively quiet that evening and I didn't see her wine-red hair anywhere.

There were only a few people occupying the dark cushioned chairs and couches. The booths were sparse, and Arlo seemed to be the only person working at the moment.

"She left early," Arlo said nonchalantly while filling up glasses with clear liquid.

I must have looked pretty confused because Arlo patted my hand and said, "She said she had something she needed to take care of," and then he walked away.

I pulled out my phone to texts from Waverly and Lux.

> **Waverly: Greer, Nova and I found the shifter. We think he's dead. Come to this address: 1892 South Second Street.**

I read it three times.
Shock. Worry. Rage. Fear.

All swept through my body and threatened to be released through my flames. I counted to ten and breathed through a clenched jaw. If something had happened to Greer … I couldn't even finish the thought. It made my head swim and my flames pulse at my palms.

They didn't need angry destructive Kyra. They needed calm and grounded Kyra.

I rubbed my hands over my face and tried to exhale slowly.

Is that why Greer had left? To take on the shifter?

Why hadn't she called?

I mumbled a goodbye to Arlo and he waved me off.

Lux: I'm on my way already. See you soon.

"Fuck," I said. If the shifter was dead, that would cause serious issues for the investigation.

Greer would still have to compete in the Trials, and we would need a new lead. There had to be a way for us to find out more information on him to see if he was hired. Surely someone in Lux's tech company could figure out how to hack into his accounts or something?

It was cold as I made my way out of the lounge into the city streets. I shoved my hands in my gray coat and started heading to the address since it wasn't far.

My breath was coming out in puffs. I warmed my hands with my power and let the heat radiate through me and relax my shoulders.

So much for us talking tonight.

Did they have to fight him?

Did one of them kill him?

How do you not know if someone is dead?

Waverly didn't say anything about any of them being hurt, so I assumed he was dead when they found him.

Dammit, that was not good.

I continued to walk through the cold night, barely taking note of the people around me until I saw FEC cars pulled up to an alleyway and Lux's black Audi R8 parked a little bit further down.

I picked up my pace, and the other FEC officers took one look at me and recognized me as the Ambassador. They easily let me pass through, some of them mumbling hello or looking wide-eyed and giving me a nod, or avoiding eye contact all together.

Waverly was standing amongst some of the other agents and her eyes flickered over to the opposite side of the alleyway where Lux was sitting on the ground next to an empty looking Greer. His arm was draped over her shoulder and she had curled her knees to her chest.

Lux looked grim and pissed.

Greer looked like a void.

I quickly made my way over to Waverly, her pink eyes keeping tabs on the agents coming in and out of the building and her mouth in a hard line, occasionally barking orders.

"What happened?" I practically growled.

Her voice was calm and collected. "We got here and nobody answered. So I broke down the door and we found his body upstairs. Nova said that his blood was rotting from the inside out and that underneath the smell and the filth, he had immortal blood. He isn't breathing and his heart isn't beating," she said, softening her voice on the last few words.

"How do you know he's an immortal?" I asked, albeit a little more confused—you couldn't kill an immortal.

That was the whole point of immortality. You would not die, and you could not be killed. Even if you cut off your own arm or head, it would grow back slowly and painfully, but eventually you would come back. Even if you burned someone's body and spread their ashes, they would *still* come back. Slowly and grotesquely at first, but they would come back to the way they once were.

"Because I can tell. I can sense everyone's blood and immortal blood is different from regular blood. And Waverly fact checked it to the immortal database and he's in it, even though he has a warrant out for his arrest due to criminal charges. I have never heard of a criminal having immortality, usually people just cover up immortals' transgressions, but I would guess that he got immortality after he got charged," Nova said, looking slightly annoyed.

"How did he get immortality then?" I said, questioning more and more of the facts of the investigation that didn't seem to add up. He was an illegal shapeshifter for hire who was wanted for crimes … how the hell did he get immortality? That didn't make a damn bit of sense.

"We don't know. The reason behind it says *classified*, so I would need to get someone with higher clearance than me to find out and tell me. Which is a bit odd, considering there aren't very many things I don't have access to in the FEC," Waverly said thoughtfully, chewing on her bottom lip.

She looked about as confused as I was about the whole thing.

None of this made sense.

How did this shifter get immortality?

Why was it classified?

Who would have hired him to impersonate Greer?

And why was he now dead?

And how the fuck did someone kill an immortal?

"We will wait seventy-two hours to pronounce him dead to see if he regenerates, but Nova said she felt death in his blood…" Waverly trailed off.

"This ... this is not good," I finally said.

Nova scoffed and Waverly laid a gentle hand on my arm.

"No, it's not," she said quietly.

Someone called her name from inside the building. She sighed, then headed up there, waving us off. I turned to Nova, her eyes as fiery as ever.

"How ... how do you kill an immortal? How do you sense death in blood?" I said, trying to find the right words for the millions of questions floating around in my mind.

"You don't ... At least you couldn't before," she said softly, as if the weight of this realization had finally fallen on her. If there was now a way to kill immortals that only a select few people knew ... that information would be very valuable and very dangerous to the ITC and, well, frankly, every immortal.

"Death in the blood feels like emptiness, stillness, and silence. Life in the blood feels like small vibrations, with captured energy making a humming sound to my hands and ears. This ... this felt like endless nothing. Like a void had been opened in his body and nothing but death could come out," she said, her voice hardening. A shiver ran through her body and she wrapped her dark star-studded arms around herself.

I conjured up a small fire orb and floated it over to settle close to her chest.

"Thank you," she said, smiling softly.

I said nothing and nodded.

I looked over to where Lux was sitting with Greer.

"She can pass the next trial, Kyra," Nova said, practically reading my thoughts. "Her wounds run deeper then you know ... Be careful with what you ask and what you are willing to give." She looked at me knowingly.

There were not very many people who knew what I was or what my past held. I had worked extremely hard to separate myself as far as I could from what lay behind me. She couldn't know who or what I really was.

So if it wasn't about my past, what about Greer's?

I turned away, avoiding her gaze and saying nothing, and headed toward where they were now crouched together, conjuring up a few other fire orbs and setting them around them in a half circle to create warmth.

"It's coming for me..." Greer said with her eyes closed, facing Lux, two fingers pinched the bridge of her nose. A switchblade popped in and out in her other hand, like a nervous tic.

I had no idea she carried one.

She had obviously come straight from work, her all black jumpsuit clinging to her body from her throat and her ankles. Her coat lay beside her in a crumpled heap, like she had wanted to feel the bite of the cold air.

"What's coming for you?" I said, gently extending some warmth from my own body to hers. Her shoulders seemed to relax slightly.

"All of it, just like before ... but worse," she said hoarsely and turned away from Lux and me. She stood abruptly and kept her eyes down.

She sulked over to Lux's car and ripped open the door and slammed it shut.

"I'll talk to her," Lux said, hands in his dark gray overcoat, his eyes narrowing to sweep between his car and the steady stream of activity going on around Waverly and her team.

Nova nodded over to us and headed inside, probably to help with the investigation since her blood magic could tell them if there was any blood they had missed in the apartment that didn't belong to our shifter.

"What did she mean when she said it was coming for her?" I said, pushing my hair out of my eyes and clenching my jaw.

Greer felt a million miles away, and even though I knew it might very well be in both of our best interests to not get involved with one another, I couldn't help it. I didn't give a damn about timing.

I wanted her. All of her. The good. The bad. The ugly. Greer Roberts had taken a claim to my heart and she didn't know it yet.

"It's her story to tell," he said, nodding grimly, and started toward the car.

I watched him get in and drive away.

I didn't know what scared me more … What Greer had said or what Nova had said. Either way, I was about to find out sooner rather than later.

I was tired of being left in the dark.

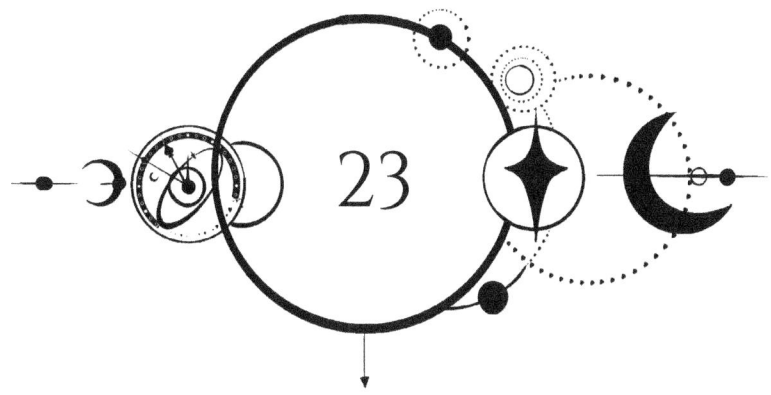

23

Greer

It had been almost a week since the shifter was officially pro-
nounced dead. The investigation had now turned into how
someone could kill an immortal and my own reality had
seemed to put on the back burner. The ITC didn't care about the
one girl who got duped into the Trials ... they were much more
concerned with how their precious resource of immortality could
be taken away and destroyed. Which wasn't surprising, since the
whole Trials were based on safety, desirability, and the luxury of
not dying.

You were practically invincible as an immortal.

However, it was now a little over a week before the second trial.
I had been swimming every day with Ky and doing things to in-
crease my breathing strength and to condition my body for the trial
ahead.

Kyra was doing his best to give me space and leave me be.

I knew that seeing me in the alley had freaked him out. I'm sure
his patience was wearing thin with me.

Maybe it would push him out in a way that could protect us
both. It was childish, really, for me to act like this, but everything

hurt too much right now. I was feeling too much too soon for him, and the rest of my life was trying to drown me.

I didn't snarl or yell at him.

Sometimes I wanted to.

But I didn't want to push him away that bad. I just wanted to feel less at the moment. And being around him was like all my nerve endings were exposed and sending signals to all parts of my body simultaneously.

I simply existed and listened and went through the motions of the regimen he had set into motion. So much different from the girl who had raced him through the city just a few weeks before.

But a lot had changed since then. I was beginning to change.

I couldn't face my own demons at the moment, let alone verbalize them out loud, and the easiest way for me to survive the next trial was to take one step at a time and work to get through each minute, each hour, and each day.

My mom had been alone, isolated, and hopeless whenever I had gone to college. And that hopelessness had swallowed her whole, leaving a broken woman behind who saw no other option except that the end to her ever-flowing stream of pain could finally be over with an overdose of prescription medication.

I had known she was struggling, but I thought me going to college, getting a nice job, and fixing our life would then fix her.

Fix us.

I thought I had more time.

I didn't realize the darkness had slowly made its way into every part of her being until it was too late. Until that fucking call tore me open and left a gaping wound to fester in the daylight.

She left no note or sign that she had thought about me in her last moments.

It was selfish to think she should have given something to me in a time where she thought that everything including my own life would be better off without her.

I had had the same thoughts shortly after.

That Lux would be better off without me. The world would probably be better off without someone like me.

But Lux wouldn't allow it. He made me heal. It was painful and uncomfortable, but I was finally okay enough at some point to live life again.

So I had worked through that hurt.

That grief.

That anger and blame.

But since this whole fucking thing had started it had snuck back in. Threatening to drag me into a space I had worked really hard to claw my way out of.

But sometimes a darkness would creep into my blood and work its way into my heart. It terrified me just like it did before.

The anxiety would crash into me, knocking me over leaving me paralyzed, while the darkness clung and crept over every inch of me filling my mouth and my vision until all I could feel and see was nothing.

And right now, I felt empty.

The nothingness seemed to cling to me like a second skin.

Lux was the only one who knew about how far I had fallen before. About how my mom's death was the catalyst for something inside me. How I was worried that the things that had haunted her would one day corner me as well, straight into death.

I had already been struggling before the whole trial mess had started; it had never gone away and now it was just heightened with everything else going on.

This emptiness, though, felt like before, like when she had died … except worse. Because this time I knew about it. And it was an internal battle of me wanting to cling to my life clawing my way through the broken thorns of my reality that threatened to drain the life right out of me. I wanted to live and fight this but something else inside me whispered that it would be easier to succumb. To die. To give in.

Some days the voice was a whisper, barely anything at all, and then other times it howled in me like it did the other night when we found the body.

The sweet serenade of it had called to me even though I knew better. I knew I didn't want it, but it tempted me in a way that made my whole body limp and my head susceptible to its whims.

I had beat it once with the help of Lux.

I could keep it at bay again.

And I knew in my head that I would have to deal with this creeping creature at the back of my mind my entire life, but I had crafted my own cage for it years ago. It seemed like the iron will that had kept it locked away for years was disintegrating between my fingertips every day that the investigation and the Trials loomed ahead.

It had cracks in it before the trial began, and now each time something went wrong, it was like one bar at a time was ripped to shreds and the aching emptiness that sat inside reached its dark tendrils out even further, taking small pieces of me every time.

How was I supposed to explain that to Kyra?

We were more than friends—but what exactly?

The sight of him made my heart ache, and every time he walked into a room, I wanted to feel his hands and lips on my skin.

We didn't owe each other anything. We barely knew one another.

At least that's what I told myself to make things easier, but it didn't seem to be working.

I couldn't easily tell him that I was terrified that the things that had broken when I was younger and in years passed were oozing like old wounds threatening to rip apart my heart right now. Even though what I really needed to do was focus on fighting for my life.

Suddenly, the door to my bedroom opened and Lux stood in my doorway.

I had been in bed for most of the day trying to sort out my own thoughts and feelings.

Ky had left hours ago after our swim practice, and I had crawled into bed after stripping down to nothing and pulling an old hoodie out of my closet and a pair of underwear that easily could have belonged to somebody's grandmother.

I was wrapped in my all-white comforter and squinted at Lux. I sniffed the air, and the smell of pancakes, bacon, and coffee began to snake its way into my room.

He was wearing a pair of gray pants that hung low on his hips and nothing else. His tattoos wrapped around his torso, arms, and hands as he stood there leaning against my doorframe with his arms crossed and his black hair, crafted in braids, was tied back.

I really felt bad for anyone Lux looked at, because how could you not immediately fall in love with this beautiful man and his clever gold eyes? His whole body was wrapped in muscle covered with dark brown skin and ink, enough to make anyone swoon.

I had always wondered why I couldn't have just fallen in love with him, instead of only feeling sisterly affection toward him. It certainly would have made some things easier.

"You need to eat," he said, twitching his lips up in a smile at me sniffing the air and sitting up.

"Are you trying to bribe me with pancakes?" I said, untangling myself from my sheets and slipping my feet into a pair of white fluffy slippers.

"Yes," he said, chuckling.

"Well, it worked," I said, shuffling past him and making my way to the kitchen where a feast lay ahead.

"I know you're worried, G," Lux said, standing at the counter with his dark brown hands braced on the white marble countertop.

I started to grab a plate and pile it high with chocolate chip pancakes, bacon, eggs, fruit and anything else I could get my hands on. I hadn't realized I was so hungry until the sweet smell of chocolate hit my nose.

"And I know it isn't just the Trials. You are not your mom, G. And you are not who you were when she died either," Lux said softly as I started to pour myself a cup of coffee.

I carefully set it down, sitting at the counter and looking up at Lux.

"What if I'm not strong enough…" I said, searching his face as if the answer was right in his gold eyes and he could tell me the secret to keeping everything at arm's length. "What if I train my body day in and day out, but in the end it doesn't matter because the biggest threat to myself is something deep inside of me that is as old as I am? What if this hopelessness was born in my heart waiting for this exact moment before swallowing me whole? I couldn't save her … And the only reason I made it out last time was because of you. I feel like I can't even save myself, even though I want to. This time it's different. It's like I know what I'm fighting, I know I want to live, but it makes me think otherwise … It sometimes swarms me in moments of weakness and I feel helpless. Hopeless…" I whispered, looking down at the pile of food on my plate. I closed my eyes and placed a hand to my forehead.

I looked up and tears started to slide down my cheeks.

"What if it doesn't matter what I want … What I choose because it's already been decided for me? What if my fate was sealed the day I was born? What if I was always destined to be *this*? Hopeless and empty … Dead by my own hands or by the world forcing me to give in to this. Going through life fighting for every single day until finally I can't take it anymore and *this* doesn't feel like an option worth living for anymore…" I had never said those words out loud.

They horrified me. They haunted me when I was younger, and they were like thorns in my side now, hitting all my tender spots.

What if I was destined to the same fate my mom had been? People didn't want to die. But what they wanted was for pain to end. For some sort of reprieve. And I knew that in my mother's final moments that was what she wanted. She didn't want to die; she wanted the pain to end and she felt like the only choice she had was death at her own hands.

What if I slipped into the place where the only option for me was death or pain? I don't think I would survive it. I felt the claws of it scrape against my mind some days, especially now when I felt vulnerable, weak, helpless and hopeless.

I felt like I was fighting an internal battle that would result in my own life or death, while the Trials loomed ahead like an external battle waiting for me. I was like its prey, falling weak to what lay inside me so it could pounce and deliver the finishing blow.

"G, it's not about strength. You will always have a choice. And when you feel like you don't, you have people in your life who are willing and ready to show you that you do. That no matter what there are other options for you. Your fate isn't decided. I don't know why someone falsely entered you into the trial, but we will find them out and make them pay. But what I do know is that you are a fighter. A survivor. And the resilience that sits in here," he said, placing a palm over my heart.

"It's what will carry you through this time. You don't need to be strong all the time … Your pain isn't your weakness but your strength. And whatever continues to come your way we will fight together. I didn't let you fall all the way before and I won't let you fall again. And this time I have more help … And so do you," he said with a softness that nearly broke my heart.

Tears were shining in his eyes as mine flowed freely down my cheeks. I reached out and wrapped my arms around his muscled abdomen and pushed my face into his hard chest.

"I love you," I said, squeezing tight.

"I love you too," he said, wrapping his arms around me and kissing the crown of my head.

I hiccuped slightly and pulled away, wiping the tears off my face and tucking my red hair behind my studded ears.

"I'll pass the next trial, we will figure out this whole shifter business, and I will keep my mental sanity in check…" I said, digging into the pancakes first and feeling the sweetness burst in my mouth. "Easy," I said, trying to sound confident but feeling anything but.

Lux started to make his own plate. "Greer Roberts isn't someone people should mess with and you're going to remind them why," he said, sliding into the seat next to mine.

I laughed out loud and a smile crept on my face. He was right. I just needed to remind everyone who they were dealing with.

Including myself.

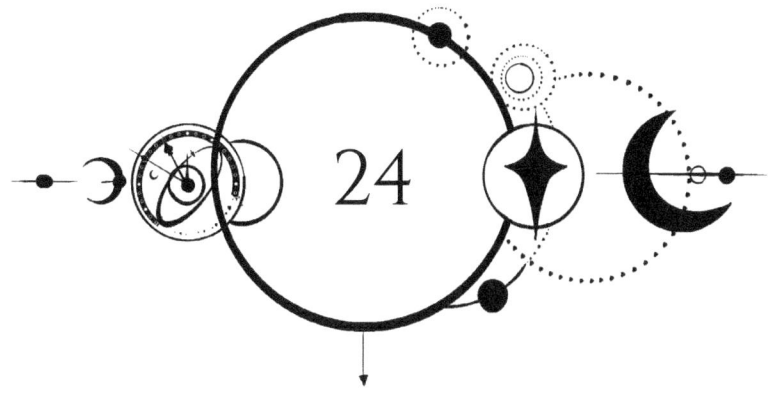

Greer

It was the night before the second trial ceremony.

Because this was the start of the televised portion of the Trials, all contestants had to participate in a ceremony where we were paraded around the city. We were shown off to the patrons and viewers at home like cattle at an auction.

From there, we would all be loaded into planes to complete the second trial, which would involve flying to the coasts and being dropped off into the middle of the ocean. How far off the coast … I had no idea. Since the trial was a test of physical strength, A.K.A. surviving and swimming, I wasn't exactly sure how many miles would fit into those categories.

Nova and Waverly had come over the night before to offer support and download any more information they had found out, which wasn't much, and for a more *normal* girls' night.

Waverly couldn't seem to track down what the classified reason was as to why the shifter had been granted immortality. It was as if the paper trail behind it had completely vanished and it had been fabricated out of thin air. Which wasn't exactly comforting.

Nova had been working with Waverly's team in order to discover how someone could have rotted an immortal's blood to the point of no return and death. She said that her best hypothesis was that someone had injected him with something even though no injection site had been found. But whatever had been injected had attacked the blood cells in the body and had turned them against one another and destroyed the cells.

The night had ended with them both wishing me luck and long hugs, as if me losing this trial didn't mean me kissing a third of my life goodbye. Instead, it was like I was simply going away to band camp or something.

Lux had asked what I wanted to do tonight before the televised Immortality Trial parade and I had told him I didn't know. I had to be at the ITC headquarters at 9:00 a.m. in order to be dressed appropriately and lined up with the rest of the contestants to be paraded around at 10:30 a.m.

So now it was 4:00 p.m. the day before the whole world would see me compete for my life, and I felt very unsure of what to do. I shouldn't do anything wild, because I would need all my strength for the day and trial to come, so drinking copious amounts of alcohol was out of the question.

It was still cold as shit even though it was now March.

Lux said he would be home around 5:00 p.m. after some meetings. He was trying to find someone within his own circle who was good enough at tech surveillance and intelligence that could start to look into the weird details behind this shifter. We were trying to see if there was something we were missing since it was still our only truly viable lead. There were too many weird details about the case that didn't add up at this point.

He wanted to get some outside perspective and expertise to help us navigate the oddities.

I had already talked with Viper and he said he would ask around but so far nothing had turned up. He said that a lot of the people for hire were on edge with the death of the shifter. I didn't tell him that he had been turned into an immortal, as I didn't think it was something he needed to know.

Nonetheless, he said a lot of them had been tight lipped because they were worried about their own jobs and scores since the shifter was well known and renowned for his work. No one wanted to be next.

4:15 p.m.

I found myself calling Ky.

I told myself it was because I craved the warmth he provided with his powers and that he was a *friend* who knew what the Trials were like, and not because I ached to be near him and feel his touch. I had pushed him away long enough.

He picked up on the first ring.

"Hi," he said carefully, like I was a rabid dog that might bite. I laughed then and tension started to release itself from my neck.

"I don't bite, Ky," I teased.

I could practically hear him smiling on the other end of the phone.

"You just haven't … reached out very much in the last few weeks outside of us training together. I wanted to give you the space you asked for … I'm happy to hear your voice though," he said.

A.K.A. I'd been very emotionally unavailable and distant the past few weeks.

Which was absolutely 100 percent true. I had been keeping my distance. But I was ready to close some of that. I wanted one normal night before more shit hit the fan. Talking with Lux had made me feel better and I felt lighter. I wanted to bask in that with Ky.

"I know, but I wanted to know if you were busy. Would you want to come over and maybe go for a walk or something, grab some food?" I said, trying to figure out what exactly I wanted to do with Ky besides pull his clothes off.

He paused for about five seconds.

"I can be over in about twenty minutes. I'll pick you up and we'll go out for a while. Maybe it will help take your mind off things … Put on something fancy and we will have a little bit of fun," he said happily through the phone.

"Okay, I'll be ready," I said, smiling into the phone like an idiot and a warmth spreading through my belly. I hung up then and flung myself off the couch, shooting a quick text off to Lux saying that I was meeting Kyra for dinner and that I would see him later.

I ran to my room to change and make myself look less … well, less like I had been in my pajamas all day. Which I had been.

I told myself I wanted to look good to make myself feel better right before the Trials, and not because a certain warlock would surely be looking deliciously handsome in one of his work suits. And certainly not because I wanted to make him wonder what the clothes would look like lying on the bedroom floor.

I chuckled to myself and started to get ready, knowing that whatever happened tonight, I was glad to spend it with Kyra.

☾

I was ready right before he got there, and I was waiting in the lobby when he pulled up in his matte black Maserati. I nearly choked on my own breath. I sometimes forgot that Kyra was ridiculously wealthy as a former immortality winner and Ambassador of the Republic, because his place was nice but modest compared to ours. Not to mention he spent a lot of his money giving back to the city.

But I guess all boys had their toys and damn if this wasn't sort of a sexy toy.

He pulled up and hopped out of the car and walked over to me. He was wearing a dark green suit that was tailored perfectly to his body with a crisp white button-down underneath with the top few buttons undone showing just a few of the lines that snaked away from the stone cemented into his skin.

He wore a black overcoat and black leather gloves. He looked like the picture of wealth.

A silver Rolex could be seen peeking out from his coat and his hair, getting quite long now, was whipped back by the wind showing off his ruby eyes and square jaw.

His full lips broke into a beautiful smile as he strode over to me, and I couldn't help but smile back.

His eyes flashed before he crushed his mouth to mine. His warmth seeped into me when I wrapped my arms around his neck to keep myself upright as his mouth hungrily devoured me. He tasted like mint and desire all rolled into one and a warm wetness went straight between my thighs.

As quickly as his lips had met mine, they were gone, and he was holding me at arm's length.

"I've wanted to do that for weeks now," he said, slightly frustrated with a half-smile. "You look beautiful, happier..." he completed as he greedily took in my outfit with his eyes sparkling.

I had opted for a black velvet dress that hugged my body with a high slit up the side. I wore a mesh long sleeve turtleneck underneath that was patterned with red velvet whorls. A collage of silver necklaces snaked down my throat, and my hair was half swept up where it fell in gentle waves down my back. I finished off the look with black pumps and a pale pink faux fur coat that went past my knees.

I smiled and rested my forehead against his.

"Thank you, you look good too," I said.

This time, I gently pressed my lips to his, taking my time and opening myself up to his tongue, trying really hard not to groan on the street right outside my apartment building.

He slid his hands around me and his warmth began to fill every part of me before the cold had even seeped in.

I smiled against his lips and he pulled away, quirking one eyebrow up.

"What?" he said, still close enough to share my breath.

"If we don't leave now, I might drag you inside," I said. "And I would really like to go out with you ..."

He laughed then, flashing his perfect smile, and grabbed my hand and led me over to the car, where he opened the door for me.

"Whatever you want, Greer," he said, smiling at me before making his way back to his side.

"Do you like surprises?" he said, sliding into the car, where the dark leather interior made things feel cozy and snug.

"I have a feeling I'll like whatever you do..." I said teasingly and winked at him.

"Good answer," he said, chuckling and pulling away from the curb as he placed his hand on my bare thigh and gave a small squeeze.

Tonight, the rest of the world could wait.

The Trials were tomorrow's problem, and tonight?

Tonight was just for me and Ky.

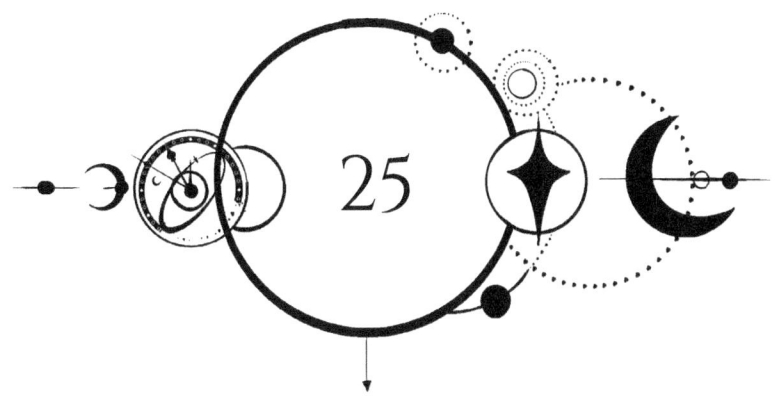

25

Greer

T hanks for dinner," I said, walking into the penthouse with Kyra trailing behind me.

I shrugged off my coat and looked around for any signs of Lux. He had said he would be out most of the evening, but I wanted to make sure.

The food had been truly amazing. I hadn't been on a real date in … well, a while. And Ky sure knew how to wine and dine.

"Of course," Ky said, slipping behind me and wrapping his arms around my waist and pulling me in close and nibbling at my ear.

"Why'd you push me away all those weeks? I wanted so badly to poke and prod you into opening up to me but I stayed away. I wanted to respect the space you had asked for. But you seemed so sad. So far gone into your own head … Tonight you seem better, lighter … Can you tell me now?" he said while working his mouth along my jawline and splaying one hand across my belly and the other wrapping around my shoulders.

My heart raced as my body started to melt against his.

"I didn't know you cared that much…" I said a little breathlessly, desire wrapping its way through every inch of my body.

"Liar," he said, moving my hair away from my neck with a brush of his fingertips and creating little bursts of sensations along my throat. I swallowed and he practically purred, pressing me deeper into him.

"Answer me, Greer," he whispered against my neck.

"I'm scared," I panted as I closed my eyes and pressed my back into him. "That I'm not strong enough to survive Trials or my own demons. I was slowly unraveling before the Trials … And I'm afraid that this is the start of me being swallowed whole by a hopelessness that is so vast and dark that I won't be able to escape. It happened before, in college when my mom OD'd, and Lux pulled me out of it, but it's still there…

"And this time," I continued, "I don't want it to consume me. But sometimes it's so seductive and everything hurts, and I feel too much and I want to feel nothing, and other times I feel nothing and I want to feel everything, and I've been battling with it for the last few weeks … I'm afraid that I won't be able to fight it off fully, that eventually it will come and take me no matter what I do. That it will scare people like you and Nova and Waverly away. That I won't be worth saving from myself. And that you will be disappointed to know that I am not as strong as I appear to be…" I mumbled, shocked by the words that tumbled out of me as Ky continued to hold on to me and move his mouth along my neck.

It was as if with each touch of his mouth and his hands, he laid waste to the emotional wall that I had built up around myself the last few weeks.

"I almost lost myself to this hopelessness before … I was so far gone I didn't want to save myself. I wanted to die. Lux fought me for me. And I can feel it coming again and I am absolutely terrified…" I said barely above a whisper.

"Greer," he mumbled against my hair.

"And this … This scares me too. Us," I whispered, fully surrendering to the emotions I had kept at bay the last few weeks. It felt like I had finally released some of the tightness that sat in my chest, all while Ky enveloped me in his warmth and I could feel his hardness against me.

But he didn't move; he just held me against him while I poured out my emotions.

He slowly let go and turned me and lifted my chin so that our eyes met. "Look at me, Greer."

I fluttered open my eyes, not realizing that I was squeezing them shut, to see the sparkling rubies of his eyes. There was a fierceness in them that made my heart swell. He wasn't scared of what I had just told him. He wasn't going to back away.

"Your light burns brighter than anything I've ever seen. Nothing will take away that brilliance. You will not fail, Greer. That light will push against the darkness and demons that are inside you and the ones that are in the world. You're allowed to hurt and ache and be scared. But you don't need to be afraid of this … Of us. Don't shut the people out who would help pull you out of those fears. You don't have to do this alone. I want all of you.

"And the parts that you are scared of that you want to hide, that you are afraid will turn me away? They won't. I want those too, and I will be right by your side and lifting you up and out of the darkness if it threatens to pull you in. We all have demons, and I won't let yours keep me away from you." He gently kissed my lips and cupped my chin.

I didn't know what to say.

No one could compare to Ky.

The way he made me feel and ache.

The way he just saw me.

I was undone by his lips and I fisted the front of his shirt in my hands and yanked him into me, almost sending us tumbling to the ground. That seemed to change the course of our kiss, because suddenly there was an intensity there that hadn't been before.

"Are you sure?" he said against my mouth.

"Yes," I said and reached for him again.

"Which door, Greer?" he whispered, pulling his mouth away with a wicked smile. He ran his hands down my arms and pulled me gently toward the hallway, where my bedroom was waiting. I nodded my head to the right and in one swift motion, he pinned me to the hall wall, crushing his lips to mine. I wasn't ready for his mouth and wrapped my arms around him as he pressed me harder into the wall. My whole body burned for him as he pulled me close and started to unzip my dress and let it fall to the floor.

He smirked and desire darkened his eyes as he found out that I wasn't wearing any underwear.

Whose idea was this, really?

Mine, obviously.

He fanned his hands against my belly as his mouth moved across my ribs, using his teeth to lift my long sleeve mesh top up toward my breasts, his teeth gently scraping my skin through the fabric. I groaned, wanting nothing between us, and finally he flung the fabric over my head with his steady hands.

"No bra, no underwear…" He chuckled softly as he gazed over my body.

I began to arch toward Ky, reaching for him, but he gently pushed my hands to my sides and wedged them behind my back so I was completely laid open for him.

"Mmm, I want to take my time with you, Greer … I've been waiting to taste you for weeks again," he mumbled against my collarbone as his hands started to skim their way over my body and knead my breasts.

"You know I couldn't stop thinking about it…" he whispered as his hands moved lower and his mouth closed around my aching nipple. "The feel of you around my hard cock … The taste of your orgasm…"

I groaned his name, and I couldn't think straight. My body was completely limp and pliable in Ky's capable hands. I closed my eyes as my breath started to come in hard pants and wet desire spread between my legs, aching and throbbing for him. He moved his mouth over to my other breast as he massaged my ass and started moving his hands to the front of my thighs.

"You're so beautiful, soft and wet…" He slipped one finger inside of me and I struggled not to fall down the wall as he explored inside me, as his finger continued to work inside me. He slipped out of me and I immediately missed the sensation of his hand, but then he moved his mouth to mine and kissed me long and deep, exploring every inch of my mouth with his tongue. He moved one hand to cup my ass and the other to the bundle of nerves that practically screamed for his hands.

I groaned into his mouth as I sucked hard on his tongue and he moved his finger gently on my clitoris, heat moving through me and pleasure rolling inside me, begging to be released. But I needed more friction. More of him. He was teasing, taking his time, and it was almost painful. With my arms behind me, I couldn't touch him and I was completely vulnerable to whatever he wanted to do.

It aroused me even more.

"Please, Ky…" I said against his lips and he smiled, trailing kisses toward my ear.

"Please, what?" he said, nibbling and biting my earlobe.

"More, please make me come…" I begged.

He laughed darkly against my neck. "Don't worry, baby … I will."

He slipped his finger back inside me and I clenched around him, shivering from the sensation of him inside. His thumb continued to make lazy circles around my clitoris, teasing me and drawing out long groans and bursts of delicious warmth that shot through my belly and down to my toes.

I moaned and grinded my hips against him, chasing my orgasm as his lips started working their way back down my body, traveling between my breasts. Just as I was about to push over the edge, he slipped his hand away and left me dripping and empty without him. I flickered my eyes toward him, surprised, and his eyes fixed on mine as he tasted the finger that was just inside me.

He closed his eyes briefly and said, "I love the way you taste, Greer. I've never had anything else like you."

Before I could get a word out, he dropped to his knees and lifted my right leg up, wrapping his hand around my thigh, keeping it securely on his shoulder as his mouth feasted on me and his other hand palmed my ass. His tongue started to swirl and tease around my center.

The only thing that was holding me up was the wall at my back, my arms still pinned behind me and Kyra at his knees. His mouth and hands held me steady as he started to suck and lick at my wetness, and the sensations of his mouth made my whole body feel like it was on fire.

He savored and ravished me like he would never be able to taste enough. That I was the most delectable thing he had ever eaten, and he was feasting on every single piece of me.

"Ky," I said, nearly breathless as my senses were overloaded with the tight tendrils of ecstasy running wild through my body. I moved against him, loving the way he met my rhythm and commanded his own.

My lower belly started to tighten; I clenched around his tongue and the waves of pleasure threatened to drown me in bliss. I continued to arch my back and moved my hips against his mouth quicker and with more urgency as I gasped for breath. I was met with a growl deep in his throat and him tightening his hand on my thigh and ass as my inner thighs locked around him.

I was racing toward the edge. I felt like I was being dragged by his mouth as he pushed me until I erupted around him and I called out his name as heat and pleasure swelled and flooded every inch of my body. Crashing into me, threatening to collapse me to the ground.

Ky released my leg and I nearly fell into him, barely able to recover from the intensity of the orgasm that was still ripping through me and his mouth was on mine again.

"Good girl, you kept your hands to yourself the whole time…" He chuckled as he massaged my wrists and his lips moved against mine. I could taste my release on his tongue and I wanted to permanently cement myself on his mouth.

It was all I could do to hold on as he lifted me up, cupping my ass and feasting on my lips like the orgasm he had just tasted was not nearly enough for his hunger for me.

I wanted to be filled by him in every way.

We crashed into my bedroom and he laid me gently down on the bed before he started undoing his own clothes. I could see his erection straining against his suit pants and I nearly came again.

I drank in every detail of him: that chiseled body, the dark red pulsating crystal and the tattoo barely peeking over his shoulders, and the hard cock that he just released from his pants.

"Ky," I said, reaching for him, and then he was on top of me with his hungry mouth and my hips arched to him.

"Please, Ky," I said, pleading with him to be inside of me so I could feel him, all of him. He groaned and pressed into me as if savoring the moment he slipped inside with a deep growl. Then his control snapped and he was pounding inside me. I wrapped my legs around him and felt completely filled as his mouth collided with mine and his hand went to work again at my sensitive center and we both raced, out of breath, to our climaxes. Again.

I exploded around him first, clawing my nails into his back and clenching my thighs against his sides. He erupted next, breathing my name and whipping his head back while his ruby red eyes flared and then simmered.

He collapsed on top of me, still filling me, and I wrapped around him, feeling the weight of him and the smoothness of his skin layered over corded muscle. He carefully slipped out of me and laid next to me and turned to face me kissing my mouth gently before pulling me to his side and burying his face in my hair.

I drew lazy circles on his chest with my fingertips and threw one leg over his so his thigh nestled in between my legs.

Ky made me feel like the most treasured and beautiful woman in the world.

And what he had said … And then what he did … I had never had someone see or hear me the way he did. No one had ever said anything like that to me and certainly not right before they devoured my entire body.

I shivered against him and snuggled closer and I felt warmth leach into my body from his as his power radiated in me.

I was at a loss for words.

So I closed my eyes and let his warmth chase away the darkness that had started to creep into my body the last few weeks. I let the sound of his breathing be a steady constant into a dreamless sleep, where for once the nightmares seemed to flutter away, too scared to come close to the light that flickered inside me.

"Goodnight, Greer ... Sweet dreams," Ky whispered as I drifted off.

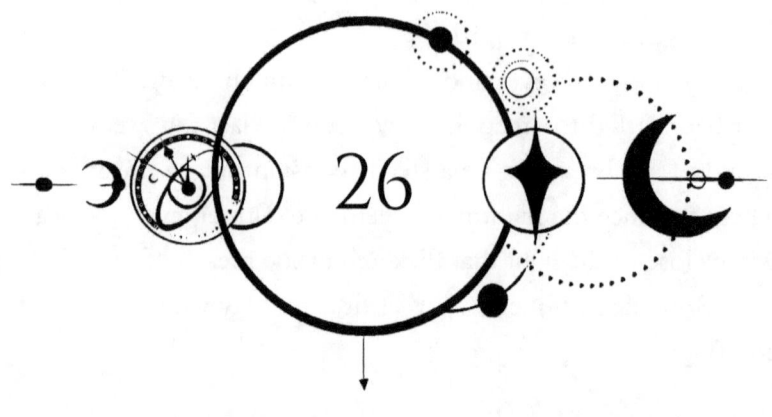

26

Greer

I woke up tangled in Ky's arms and legs. And I gave myself a full sixty seconds to stare at him. I still wasn't exactly sure what we had shared last night, but it felt like something much *more*.

I had avoided him for weeks thinking he would shrink away from everything that I had on my shoulders. But he didn't. He said he wanted to carry it with me. I smiled thinking of what he had said and then grinned even wider about what he had done.

It felt like whatever else we would face would be manageable if we did it together.

I sighed, thinking that I could have had this a bit sooner if I wasn't so stuck in my own head. It wasn't to say that everything was better now. I still felt the anxiety and depression of the Trials, the investigation, my life, but I felt like I could finally allow others to shoulder the burden. And Ky was someone that saw me and wasn't afraid. Wasn't turned off by all the baggage.

It felt good. We felt good. And I had a new energy within me.

Which was good, because today was the day of the second trial and I had to go to the ITC headquarters to get ready for the parade.

Ky would be there and give a few words during the opening ceremony as the Ambassador and a former winner. I gently released myself from him and pressed my lips to his brow. His mouth was slightly open, and his face looked so peaceful it made my heart ache.

I slipped into my bathroom and looked at myself in the mirror.

Wild red hair and sharp green eyes rimmed with blue.

I didn't feel so afraid anymore.

I would get past the next trial and everyone on screen, in the entire Republic, would know that to be human wasn't to be weak. I wouldn't let the world swallow me whole. I would tell the world my story and I would control the narrative.

I quickly finger combed my hair and tied it back in one long braid and brushed my teeth. No use in putting any makeup on … I dressed in black leggings and a black turtleneck, slipping my combat boots on and grabbing for a light coat before giving one last look to Ky snoring softly in my bed.

I smiled knowing that a small comfort would be that he would be there today. And he would be on shore when I arrived. I just had to get through the next forty-eight hours. I swallowed and took a deep breath knowing that things would be different after this.

I slipped out of my room silently and walked into the kitchen, where the clock read 8:19 a.m. I was supposed to be there at nine or face immediate disqualification.

Lux was standing in the kitchen, already ready to go. He would be watching the ITC parade from the sidelines. He would also be at the end of the finish line courtesy of Ky and his connections, not to mention everyone was interested to see who Lux would be betting for even though he wasn't betting on anyone.

The social elite loved to be nosy bitches about who everyone else was rooting for. They would think I was his human pet or plaything for sure. I rolled my eyes at the thought.

I looked at the food Lux had set out for me and a wave of nauseous rolled through me. I needed to eat in order to have appropriate fuel for the trial to come but nerves were fluttering in my belly.

I sat down without saying anything and Lux sat down next to me.

"You ready?" he said, squeezing my hand.

"Ready," I said and started to eat my breakfast sandwich in silence.

"Lux?" I said quietly, suddenly needing to ask him something, setting down my food.

"Why did you pull me out of the dark when it would have been easier to just leave me be?"

"Because I love you," he said, pulling my small pale hands into his own, large brown tattooed ones.

"Because sometimes soulmates come in the form of a best friend. And when you love someone you fight for them even when they can't fight for themselves. You have a piece of me Greer just like I have a piece of you. I was either going to crawl in that hole and die with you or pull you out. There was never any option to leave you. The easy choice would have been to surrender with you. But I knew then that the world needed someone like you to come along and shake things up..." he said, drilling his gold eyes into my own.

Tears started to well in my eyes and a few slipped out.

"Thank you. I love you," I said, squeezing his hands and leaning my forehead against his.

"I should probably wake Ky up," I whispered.

"I'm sure he'll wake up soon. Come on, I'll drive you to the headquarters and then I'll come back for his lazy ass," he said, chuckling as he got up and poured some coffee for me to go.

We both silently walked over to the elevator and I took a few deep breaths.

I would get to the next trial.

And then the one after that.

Until I won.

"You will not fail, Greer…" Lux said, wrapping an arm around me.

I nodded silently as we plummeted down to the first floor.

☾

Lux dropped me off at the headquarters a few minutes before 9:00 a.m. and as soon as I got there, it was complete and utter chaos. Participants were loitering all over and I tried to get a good look at who I would be competing against. For this trial, Ky said it wasn't as important to know your competitors because it was more important to focus on yourself and your strengths than others.

But I was desperate for more information about who and what I was up against. There were all types of species and races around. Dwarfs, shifters, witches, warlocks, animalia, fairies, nymphs, pixies, etc. I didn't know all the names of specialized species and races, but you could usually tell there was something different about them. Humans were easier to spot up close because there wasn't anything *more* about them. You couldn't feel the ooze of power that others who looked human gave off.

From the looks of it, there weren't many others who were just human. I swallowed and kept my head down, trying to keep a low profile and not draw attention to the fact that I was a young, powerless human female.

Any grounding and gusto I had held on to earlier suddenly felt very, *very* far away.

I was herded around by different people in ITC uniforms and pushed into a room with other female contestants that housed about a million stainless steel lockers. I was handed a uniform that looked like a glorified wetsuit and a key that said my name on it and my stats.

Our instructions were to find the locker with our corresponding key and dump our stuff inside. Then change into our uniform and finally someone would come around to collect us to start the parade at 10:30 a.m.

Greer Roberts. Human. 24.

I almost gagged at the sight of it. There were hundreds of others with names, stats, races, and species, everything blurring together and making my head hurt. The locker room was roaring with noises of people talking, laughing, orders being barked and someone hysterically crying.

"Are you nervous?" a small quiet voice said next to me. She looked like a small pixie, with blue hair and iridescent skin and a body the size of a twelve-year-old.

Her stats said *Andromeda Lucas. 108. Faerie/Nymph.*

I looked at her bright blue eyes and nodded.

"I wasn't anticipating the ceremony to be like this," I said, swiveling my head back and forth to the chatter in the room and the overwhelming presence of different powers crowded into a small space. People were constantly running in and out, while the white ITC uniforms weaved in and out, trying to control the herd.

"It's a lot to take in. But it will be over soon," she said, tilting her head to the side and smiling shyly. "I'm Andromeda. But you can call me Andy." She extended her small hand.

"Greer," I said, nodding to her and giving her small hand a firm shake.

"Oh, it looks like we are all lining up. Come on!" she said, practically giddy, looping her arm through mine and pulling me along with surprising strength for such a small person.

I wanted to throw up, and the scuba suit we had been given felt like it was suffocating me since it was zipped up right underneath my chin and covered every inch of my body except my head. I had pulled my hair back into a tight braid to start so it wouldn't get in my way.

We were shoved around until we had some order to us and we were in lines of twenty people wide and five deep.

We were all gathered into a long hallway with a huge metal door at the end and light leaked through the side from the outside. I could hear someone speaking on the outside. Was that Ky giving his opening remarks?

My heart ached at the thought of being in his arms merely hours before. The small faerie was to my right and a girl who looked like a half cat, half human stood on the other side. I didn't dare crane my neck to make out her name and species. Instead, I looked directly in front of me at the large metal door.

How in gods' name I had made it to the very front of the parade line was a blur. I had been dragged by Andy until all I could hear was the muffled sound of an announcer outside.

Applause erupted and the door whined as it lifted light blinding my eyes and roaring filling my ears. I lifted my hand to protect my eyes as I blinked away the spots in my eyes.

Someone in the corner of the hallway with an ITC uniform yelled "MOVE" and so we started to walk. The door had opened up to the main street of the city that snaked through downtown. It was about a three-mile walk to where helicopters waited for us to directly march into, to jet us off to the trial.

The whole thing felt archaic and like I had just signed my name over to a cult.

Thousands of people lined either side of the street as a blimp soared above us keeping time with all 1000 contestants. It contained the Game Lord and the cronies who made comments on the opening ceremony as well as Ky. I tried to look up to find those familiar ruby eyes, but the only things I could see and hear were the blinding sun and the sound of the roaring crowd on either side, which seemed to dull all other senses.

I looked over to either side of me and behind me. Some of the contestants were stone-faced, some waving and smiling, others looked smug, and some had tears slipping down their faces.

The crowd was overwhelming and the buildings surrounding us seemed to loom over me all glass, brick and concrete closing in around me.

I had never watched this part of the Immortality Trials. Or any of it, really.

I could never bring myself to do it. It was easier for me to pretend it didn't exist, and that everything was safe and sound in my little life with Lux. I mentally kicked myself for not doing so sooner and turning a blind eye to this monstrous tradition.

What a privileged little bubble I had been in.

Ky had said I just needed to keep my cool during the parade, that I shouldn't get rattled by the crowds and the chaos, but I was struggling to keep my pounding heart in check.

The blimp ahead was roaring out information about how to watch the Trials and how to place your bets. On either side of the blimp, pictures, stats, names, etc., would flash every thirty seconds or so, so everyone could see who was being offered up to this immortal sacrifice.

I felt like I was floating through time and space as I kept putting one foot in front of the other and it felt like the crowd and skyscrapers around me were coming in closer, choking off my airway.

Suddenly, a small hand slipped into mine and squeezed. I looked over to see Andromeda with a small smile on her face walking hand and hand with me.

I let her small hand ground me as I tried to control my breathing and remind myself that this was only the beginning. And that this is when the real trials would begin. It would only get worse from here.

The sound of the crowd seemed to fade away and the world seemed to pause as I closed my eyes and thought of Ky, Lux, Nova, Waverly ... I chose them. I would make it through the next seventy-two hours.

The sound of the crowd leaked back into my head and I felt my feet move to the weird anthem they supposedly always played for the Trials. We rounded a corner where more people were clapping and roaring and I could see the helicopters at the end of the parade line.

Each step felt like a death march. I could see people screaming with drinks in their hands. Laughing and pointing like we weren't actually real people. The air was thick with the smell of alcohol and sweat. The suits we were in were suffocating and I looked over to where a group of males were making derogatory gestures to our group.

My head was spinning, and the large black helicopters loomed closer.

I wanted to run. Sprint right past the transports and run until my feet couldn't move anymore. But I would be signing my own death certificate if I did that. So I continued to move and flinched when someone threw a bottle of something at us, silently cursing myself for being at the front of this gods damn parade.

Instead, I held on to the small hand in mine like my soul might escape from my palm and she was the only thing holding it there.

I was strong.

I could do this.

I trained for this.

I walked until I was strapped into the helicopter seat by delicate pixie hands and lifted into the air with 200 other contestants. I barely saw them. Barely heard them. Everything else faded away as I repeated to myself again and again that my light burned bright, brighter than anything else, and I would not fail.

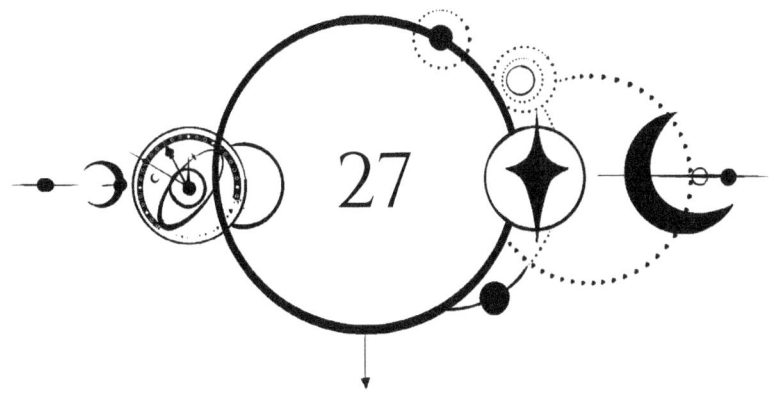

Kyra

I saw Greer disappear into her helicopter, looking empty and holding hands with a small female next to her.

Lux and I were on board a luxury plane that he had personally hired. We landed on the shore where the contestants would finish. Neither one of us had words for what was about to happen.

The helicopters would be dropping the contestants off in the next twenty minutes. It would take them a little bit longer to get to their spot on the coastline where they would have to take the fifteen-mile swim, which would take anywhere between two to four hours. So not exactly the middle of the ocean but still pretty damn far.

Right about now on board the helicopter they would be scanning each contestant for any type of device or advantage that would constitute cheating.

I shuddered thinking about how invasive some of the checks were as if I would be hiding anything inside me. But some people did. This is where the intensity of the Trials kicked up a notch. People were here to win. They would take blood and not think twice about it. Especially human blood. They would think it was their duty or their right to do so in the Trials.

A thousand people would be dropped fifteen miles off the coast and the whole Republic would watch as they swam as fast as they could to avoid the government servitude or life cycle reduction that would befall on the slowest 250 people.

Sometimes in the physical trials, if people knew they wouldn't make it, they would kill themselves to avoid the punishment. Greer's mom had committed suicide. We hadn't talked about that and I really hoped she wouldn't have to relive that trauma.

I silently cursed myself and realized I should have told her. I just didn't know how and it was too late.

In my own trial, several people realized they weren't going to make it to the top of the mountain and they had ended their own lives. It was something that still haunted my nightmares.

I hadn't told Greer about it because I didn't want to add to the fear that was already taking root, but that was before I knew about her mom. And about Greer's own experience with wanting to end her own life.

Nice, Ky.

I rubbed my eyes, trying to not to think about it now.

I had told Greer that her body would be able to make it. That would be the easy part. We had worked up to swimming for four hours at a good pace. She was already strong in her body.

What would be hard was the mental fortitude. Her mind would start to lose focus and if she wasn't paying attention, she could make a fatal mistake. Fatigue and exhaustion would play tricks on her. She needed to stay focused and only use her mind for the task at hand. Only focus on what is absolutely necessary, nothing else, is what I had told her.

I had hoped that by taking her out last night, us talking and then sleeping together would help her relax and clear her head. I didn't exactly know if I had accomplished that, since I didn't get to see her this morning.

When Lux had woken me up and said she was gone, I panicked. I had tried not to let the fear of losing her settle into my very bones, but it was buzzing there now. I was helpless to her right now.

I hated it.

My thoughts wandered back to Greer competing. When I passed the physical trial, I had come in with a mantra. Something to say over and over again with each breath I took to get me to the top of my mountain. I'd suggested she choose one to get her to the shore. She had never shared what she had chosen.

I was bouncing back and forth between trying to focus on the task at hand and last night.

Godsdamnit. I was not doing a very good job.

Last night we had shared more than just our bodies and now I was trying to stifle my own fear of losing her. I knew that she had been struggling with everything, it was completely understandable and valid. I only hoped that last night provided a moment of reprieve and my words had offered her the comfort and strength she needed.

I couldn't stand to lose her when I had just learned that my life had absolutely been dull without her in it. It made me feel like a loaded powder keg. If something happened to her in this trial, I wasn't sure how much control I could practice. So I prayed to the gods that it wouldn't come to that.

I looked around at the crowd of people around us. Waiters were weaving in and out of the sand offering champagne and hors devours. They had set up tables on the beach and tents for the rich and wealthy to get comfortable watching the live footage that would show the contestants. Bets had already started to go through the official gambling office and the thought of someone betting for or against Greer made me want to punch someone in the face.

The whole ordeal was horrifying.

There were screens all around and you could pick up your own handheld one where you could choose which contestant to watch or span the entirety of the competition.

Lux and I had settled into a couple of chairs underneath an umbrella each with a handheld screen gripped tight between our hands. I swallowed hard and looked over to see Lux sitting rigid in his seat, a muscle in his jaw feathering. Whenever anyone tried to smile or breeze by, we both gave them blank stares and they quickly scurried away from the moody Ambassador and wild shapeshifter tycoon.

The sea was relatively quiet and there were not many waves cresting the shore. It was almost beautiful.

Almost.

There were medics and official ITC employees on standby for when contestants would ring in and those who were ready to whisk away the losers.

We both had dark sunglasses on to hide our eyes. About thirty yards to our left sat the Trial Lord in his tent, laughing, drinking and looking positively cheerful. I wanted to choke him.

"The contestants will be dropped in sixty seconds," an announcer said, and people quickly found their white tents with cushy chairs, chaise lounges, and their personal screens to sit and watch. A few scrambled to grab drinks and yelled at the wait staff to bring this or that.

I looked over at Lux again and his mouth was set in a hard line.

"Come on, G," he whispered to his screen.

"Three, two, one…"

The screen counted down until it panned to all 1000 contestants being dropped into the water simultaneously with a huge splash. Some looked sort of human. Some were obviously other races, and others were things that I didn't have a name for, but it didn't matter.

I was looking for a specific redhead and no one else mattered right now.

Some were already swimming toward shore and others were getting their bearings. They quickly peeled off from the large commotion of the crowds that they had been dropped in with and started swimming. Some with grace and some without. Clearly, there were some with water affinities, but it was illegal to use your powers outside your own body for this. So even if you could control water you weren't allowed. But you could add muscle to your body or turn into a fish or mermaid if it was in your power and use that.

Lux cursed underneath his breath and I scanned the screen, looking for the panel to pop up where you could choose contestants to watch, so I could zero in on Greer.

There she was, treading water while the small woman who had been next to her in the parade floated nearby on her back. It looked like they were talking. Something looked wrong ... the small woman's body looked wrong and it wasn't moving properly.

Had she been injured in the drop?

She was so petite, so if someone had kicked her in the drop or had landed on her, she probably wouldn't be able to swim.

"Don't do it, G," Lux said gruffly. He had removed his sunglasses and his gold eyes were wide.

We both watched as Greer, who was one of the last people treading water under the drop, let the small woman grab on to her shoulders and she began to swim.

"She can't swim all that way with someone on her back..." I said, my voice barely a whisper.

No, no, no, no.

She had lost precious time to start and she had added at least another sixty to eighty pounds to her own body.

"Godsdammit, Greer," I said, slamming my tablet on the table and getting stares from some of the other patrons.

Lux looked at me, practically snarling. "I swear to gods, if she loses because she was a good fucking person, I am going to kill her."

We were both seething but not because she was helping this woman. But because she could lose. And if she lost, she would reduce her life.

I had just started to plan for Greer Roberts to be in my life for quite some time.

I looked out to the horizon and prayed to the gods she didn't believe in that she could make it to the top 750.

28

Greer

I didn't know how much time had passed since the drop.

The water was warm. The wetsuit had kept most of my body heat trapped inside. I tried to keep my head clear and think plain, simple thoughts.

When I first dropped, I had felt the scrape of nails against my wetsuit, like someone was trying to grab on to me and drag me under, but I had kicked away fiercely and apparently whatever had lurked beneath me decided I wasn't worth the time.

I was glad they hadn't broken through the suit or my skin, because I had a bad feeling that blood would attract the wrong kind of attention.

Someone else had come close to kicking me in my face during the commotion of the drop and I would be damned if I let that happen again after the last trial.

I had watched as everyone else fought or swam away from the drop. I had needed a second to compose myself as water pushed into my ears, nose, and mouth. I fought to the surface quickly and took note of my surroundings, which was when I first noticed Andromeda. Now she was like a small backpack, clinging to my shoulders as I set my pace and swam toward the shore.

I could practically hear Lux and Kyra cursing as I had told Andromeda to grab onto me. She said I should leave her. That I should go on without her. She had been crushed under a brute of male who looked like he might be half whale himself. Her leg was broken, at the least, and maybe her foot as well.

I wasn't going to leave her. I had a choice. And I was going to make the right fucking one.

So I swam with her attached to me.

I knew I had lost time in the drop. But I would make it. I had to.

I had already passed a few people who were struggling in the water or simply floating. Some made weird grabs at me and I thrashed away. I didn't know how to fight in the water, and those who simply floated by, I wasn't sure if they were alive or not. I didn't want to know. I couldn't help them now.

I couldn't allow myself to focus on anything else except the strokes of my arms and the kick of my legs.

Ky had told me to focus on my mantra. To focus only on what I needed to.

So I swam.

And swam.

I didn't know how to keep track of time in this place.

I was so focused on just moving that I let myself get lost in the waves and didn't see anything coming.

"Greer," Andromeda said, sounding a little afraid.

I started to say what when I felt the same nails, or more like claws, clamp on my ankle and pull me fiercely under and I swallowed water. Salt stung my eyes and I tried not to choke.

I looked around and realized that Andromeda was several feet above me and I was still being pulled by what looked like a mermaid, far away from Andy and back toward where I had just come from. Back toward the drop.

A scream started to escape from my throat and I clamped my mouth shut, realizing I would lose precious air that way. I focused on the mermaid's clawed hand and kicked out. She looked back at me with her bright blue eyes and greenish-looking skin and bared her teeth at me.

Her claws had sunk into my ankle, drawing red tendrils out that snaked through the water.

My blood would be like a beacon for the big, bad, and ugly.

She had turned back around, and her rainbow-colored tail was thrashing close to my side as she dragged me along.

I was running out of air and I still needed to kick back up to the surface, so I did something absolutely despicable. I sent a silent apology up to anyone who was listening and made my move.

I grabbed her feathered tail at the end and pulled hard in either direction, ripping through the soft, scaled skin. It tore too easily, and I winced as I tugged harder. She screamed and green blood erupted from the rip as she let go. Her mouth moved and I could have sworn it was a *fuck you*. I flipped her off for good measure and she swam away hissing, deciding that I wasn't worth the fight.

I looked up and realized I had black dots in my vision. I could absolutely not pass out right now, so I kicked hard and pushed my arms until I thought my lungs would explode and I burst through the surface.

I gasped for breath and looked around for Andy.

She was floating so far away, and she held up a little hand, wiggling her fingers.

"FUCK!" I screamed and started swimming toward her.

I had lost time, strength, and energy.

And now I was bleeding.

I swam over to her and noticed a few others swimming as well, but they seemed too focused on the shore ahead.

"Andy, I'm bleeding. I can still swim but I need to stop the blood," I said as she pulled herself back onto my back.

She ripped her own wetsuit in a huge feat of strength. This shit was practically indestructible and she tore it like I had the mermaid's tail. She wrapped the fabric around my ankle, securing it tight and climbing on my back again awkwardly as I tried to stay afloat.

"Swim, Greer," she said weakly, so I did.

I wondered what that mermaid had cost me.

But I emptied my head like Ky had said once again and continued to find a rhythm that pounded through my lungs and pumped my arms and legs.

I soothed over the rush of adrenaline by counting back from 100 over and over again until I couldn't count anymore. My arms became exhaustingly heavy and my legs felt like they might actually fall off. My ankle was starting to throb and ache. Andy was feeling very heavy on my back.

I needed something else besides my own thoughts.

"Why did you help me, Greer?" she whispered suddenly, giving me something else to focus on besides my exhausted and battered body.

"Because you saved me in the parade..." I said, gasping out each word.

She was silent for a while as she contemplated my answer.

I don't know exactly why we had saved each other, but I was learning to lean on people, and I wouldn't have made it through that damn parade without her. And I wouldn't leave her here. I couldn't.

"Andromeda," I choked out between breaths and strokes, needing more of a distraction. "Tell me a story."

I needed to feel my body less.

I needed to numb myself to survive this.

Something announced above us that an hour had passed and 100 people had made it to shore. Probably anyone with a fucking water affinity, like that mermaid who tried to drown me. Or anyone who could change their physical body probably had made the fifteen miles easily. A bit unfair that we had only just found out on the helicopter what the distance was to swim, seconds before the drop.

The average person would take anywhere between three to four hours to complete that.

Ugh.

"I'll tell you about the gods of old and how our earth came to be," she said quietly, and she did.

In the beginning, there were twelve gods and goddesses. They were the original immortals.

They began to create others in their own image, playing with their own gifts and the gifts of the mortal realm. They created witches, warlocks, fae, shifters, mortals, centaurs, and many other types of creatures, races, and species to color their world. Other gods were made and born, as well as demi-gods. Creatures that were half god and half something else.

They soon began to create so much life that the luxuries of the mortal realm seemed to diminish. The gods and goddess no longer wanted to reside on earth. They wanted to keep immortality for themselves and let their creations figure out their own misgivings. Eventually they left the mortal realm in chaos to return to the celestial realm, where they could slumber and observe, unaffected by the dealings of earth.

Soon they saw that their creations were destroying one another in wars, famine, disease, and hate. They offered the kingdoms of earth a gift if they could find peace so that one day the gods and goddesses would come back to rule over earth in a way that was pleasing to them, just like at the beginning of time. They would grant immortality to the mortal realm for those most worthy and loyal once again. So they gifted immortality to few and then granted the power to give immortality to the realm. They promised one day they would be back to collect those who were worthy and rule over the mortal realm once they had the key to do so. They would cleanse it of the impurities that seemed to infect humanity. It is said that they will return when the oracle's prophecy comes true:

Time lies with those pure of heart
Immortality will show how the world tears apart

The infernal, celestial, and mortal realms will collide
And many will sacrifice and cease to be alive

For the one who breaks the world anew
Will have to pay back what has always been due

I had never heard the story of how our world came to be told like that. When the hell did an oracle prophesize when the old gods and goddesses would come back? We had seers now, but I had never heard of anyone seeing the future or the past of the old gods. Not to mention, not very many people actually paid patronage to the gods anymore. It had been thousands of years since their supposed reign. There were few immortals who dated back before the kingdom wars.

It didn't matter.

Andromeda continued to tell stories of her own kind, distracting my mind and letting my body go on autopilot.

She told stories of the stars and of her life until another ding sounded. They announced that two hours had passed and 350 people had made it to shore.

Shit.

I could now see the shoreline ahead, but it was still far away. I had another hour to swim at least, maybe more. I could hear some swimmers close by and I could see a few up ahead but I had no idea where I was compared to everyone else. I didn't know how far I had to go. And I wasn't going to waste precious energy looking to either side to see where I was at compared to everyone else.

I just kept going forward.

I will not fail.

I will not fail.

I will not fail.

At some point, Andromeda had stopped telling her stories and the only sounds that filled my ears were the waves, the other swimmers, and my own breath.

My arms ached and my legs officially felt like they weighed twice their size. My lungs burned and my eyes stung. They had given us special contact lenses that were supposed to give us the ability to keep our eyes open in water, but the salt clung to my lashes and my eyes burned from the constant assault of water. I thought I may have lost one of them when the mermaid attacked, but I couldn't be sure.

I could taste the salt in my mouth as I tried to breathe the way Ky had taught me and not get water slammed down my throat.

I didn't know how many times I kept chanting my mantra in my head before a third ding sounded, claiming that three hours had passed and 650 people had made it to shore.

Fuck.

It felt so close and so far. I could now make out people on the shore.

"Swim, Greer," Andromeda whispered in my ear again, her small hands clutching my shoulders and digging in harder, as if she could will me to go faster.

"Swim," she said again.

Something raw and angry inside of me snapped at her words and I began to pump my arms and legs faster and it was as if time began to slow around me, but I sliced through the water as if unaffected.

I will not fail.

I will not fail.

I. Will. Not. Fail.

Fuck the Trials.

Fuck the bastard who got me entered into this.

And fuck the fucking Trial Lord.

The shore was so close now I could make out specific bodies and I saw others around me, exhaustion clouding their features as we all raced for shore.

Another ding said 700 people had made it.

I was about fifty meters out.

I was going to make it.

I heard splashing and yelling as someone was bulldozed over by someone else in the water. I heard a splash too close and something brushed against my injured ankle. I kicked hard, trying my best to fight through the fear of being drowned again.

I had to get to shore.

Twenty-five meters left.

Ding. Now 720 people had made it.

Fuck.

Ten meters.

Ding. 730.

Five meters.

Ding. 740.

I stood up in the water, almost falling over as my body ached and groaned with Andromeda still clinging to me like a small child. I sloshed out, begging my body to keep moving as I staggered to make it all the way.

The crowd was being kept back from where the contestants swam in, and I swore I heard my name.

I willed my body to move to the nearest ITC contestant.

An old woman with graying hair in her all-white uniform looked at me with no empathy at my mess of a body and my wild eyes.

She spoke into her handheld tablet.

"Greer Roberts. Andromeda Lucas. Safe," she said passively.

Ding. 750.

The crowd on the beach roared to life as the announcer concluded this round of the Trials was over, and my vision started to fade as I fell to my knees.

"She needs help," I choked out as I gently laid Andromeda down, her small body looking slightly broken from the waist down. She smiled up at me and gave my hand a squeeze.

"Thank you, Greer … a gift," she whispered weakly, her eyes fluttering closed.

A small jolt of electricity went through my hand. I stared down at her closed eyes and her lips moved murmuring something else I couldn't catch.

"Andromeda?" I whispered, looking at her as her hand went limp in mine.

The ITC woman said something on her tablet and two people came from the crowd to pick her up and take her to a medical tent. I looked at those still in the water. Two hundred and fifty people who were now doomed to government servitude or less life. I could see it on some of their faces and a few of them ducked under the water and didn't resurface. My stomach started to roll and I tore my gaze away from someone lying facedown in the water, stumbling to my feet and trying to move further away from the water.

Thoughts of my mom flashed in my head.

Broken and empty.

I saw her in those people. She was dead in the water. Her eyes and mouth open like she had been trying to call for help but she couldn't. Her hair once lush and beautiful was limp like seaweed and slightly green. And there was no one there to save her. Just like before.

Then I saw myself in the water, facedown. Red hair floating around me. My pale skin puffy and devoid of life. The mermaid that had tried to drag me down before seemed to clutch my body and pull me under until nothing was left of me. Little tendrils of red blood seemed to dot where my body had just occupied. Until they, too, faded away and the only evidence that I had been there was a small ripple in the blue water.

I gagged and my eyes widened as I tried to focus them and tell my head that I was alive. I was not dead. My mother was not among them. I shoved my hands over my eyes, trying to scrub the image from my brain.

The darkness within me seemed to bloom as the images of myself and my mom slammed into my head, cementing themselves in front of my eyes. It felt like it was starting to work its way through my veins and finding roots in my bones.

I whipped my head around as sound burst behind me and I looked in horror to see the large crowd screaming loudly behind me. I heard champagne bottles popping and laughter and hollering. I fell down and scrambled back on my hands and started to crawl further away from the shore as spiking panic set in.

I felt trapped. I didn't want to go further up the beach or toward the water. I didn't want to face a crowd that just sat back and watched as I fought to stay afloat for over three hours and then celebrated as people took their own lives in the water.

I looked at my leg and realized the makeshift bandage had come undone and I was leaking blood all over the soft, white sand. I felt like I could feel the mermaid's hand on my skin, and I started clawing at my wounds frantically, like I could erase the memory from my body, and ended up tearing more skin.

My hands were bloody, and my mind played tricks on me as I tried to get it off me and ended up spreading it all over my body. I looked at my own blood and started hyperventilating.

I could feel the panic flooding me, making my head swirl and my heart pound in my chest. I looked toward the water and I swear I saw not just my mom's body and mine. But Lux, Kyra, Waverly, and Nova too … I tried to scream but no sound came out.

I choked on a sob as all the emotions I had kept at bay during the swim boiled to the surface and I wanted to claw myself out of the wetsuit and rip it to shreds.

I started pawing at myself again, trying to tear through the material but not getting anywhere. I was writhing on the ground, sobbing fully now, trying to get the blood off me and my suit.

"Get off me!" I screamed, feeling the mermaid's claws again as I was pulled under.

I heard my name like a whisper at the back of my head.

I threw up salt water right next to me, my stomach twisting in pain as I continued to empty the contents of my belly on the soft sand beach.

My head started pounding and it felt like a box had been set around me. Darkness started to edge in and fill my eyes. I was still clawing at my bloody body and screaming when my ears started popping and I heard it closer this time.

"Greer!" a deep voice yelled.

I didn't fight the darkness as it winked out the last of my vision and crashed into my body, sending me sprawling on the sand.

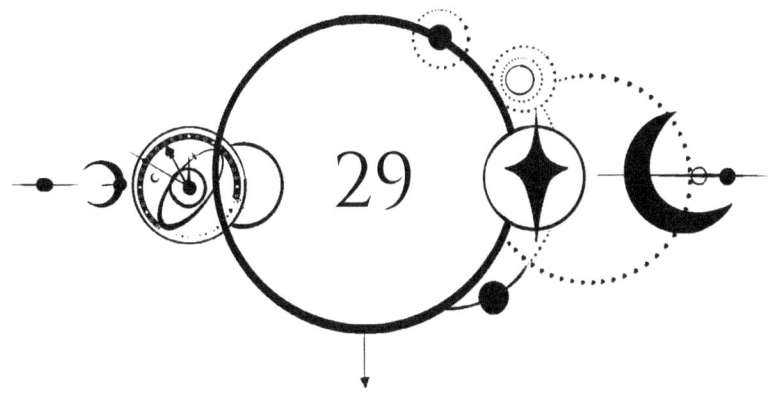

Kyra

S ir, you need to stay back," an older woman with graying hair in an ITC uniform said as Lux and I raced over to where Greer had just been throwing up, screaming, and clawing at her skin to then pass out.

"Like fucking hell I will. I'm Ambassador Kyra. Step back," I growled at her, and she simply nodded and spoke into her tablet that she needed a medic on the shore.

Lux got to her first and gently felt for her pulse and checked for her breathing.

She had blood all over her body, but the only wound that was visible was from her ankle, where five deep gashes were decorating her wetsuit. Blood oozed there and I tried not to think of the fear and rage that had erupted from me when the mermaid pulled her under.

I had shot fire out of my mouth straight into the sky with the scream that echoed out of me and sent sand exploding around me.

People stared and whispered as Lux had tried to calm me down.

My rage was not helpful now though. The only thing that mattered was getting Greer fixed up. I wanted to kill that mermaid for shredding the skin of her ankle.

I had known someone would make a grab for her. But I just wasn't ready for how it would make me feel to watch it happen without being able to do anything about it.

"She barely made it," I whispered, looking at her limp, blood-covered body sprawled on the shore. Her hair was plastered to the side of her face in a long, wet braid and she looked pale and fragile. The wetsuit clung to every inch of her body, leaving little to the imagination, but her breath was coming in steady rises and falls through her chest and belly.

"She needs to see a medic," the elderly woman said a few steps behind us.

"I have my own medical team that will look after her," I snarled again.

She looked like she wanted to argue with me, but she simply nodded and walked away.

"The instructions for the next trial will come in a few days," I said.

I swallowed hard as Lux scooped her up in his arms. I wanted to reach out and touch her. I gently kissed her pale forehead. I wanted to tell her that I was so proud of her.

That I couldn't imagine my life without her.

The paparazzi were all over the beach and I could only imagine what the tabloids would say about Lux and I and Greer. It didn't matter.

"Let's get her home. She wouldn't want to be here like this," he said quietly, cradling her in his arms. I led him around the outskirts of the crowd to where Lux's plane was waiting for us with a medic already on board.

We ducked inside and he gently laid her down on a bed that had already been prepared. A pretty young nurse who looked to be a fawn or a centaur went to check her vitals, fix her ankle, and scan her with some sort of medical device.

Lux sat down on one of the cozy leather chairs and I sat across from him and he barked that the plane leave immediately. The engine started to roar to life, and we began making our way along the runway. I looked out the window to where the contestants and patrons were celebrating. I couldn't bring my eyes to the contestants still in the water or those who had been intercepted at shore to be guided to where they would receive their punishment.

Some contestants were just floating in the clear blue water on the shoreline. I had seen some of them purposefully take water in their lungs and wait for the end. I cursed and looked away.

Maybe that made me a coward, but I couldn't watch the dead float or the survivors crumble on shore. Some begged. Some cried. Some screamed. Some did nothing. But either way it was too much. I glanced over at where Greer lay motionless and watched as the nurse continued to monitor her condition.

It would be about an hour before we landed in the city again and then maybe another hour before we would get back to the penthouse.

"I gave her a mild sedative so she can rest. She is on fluids and her vitals looked good, but I imagine she lost consciousness from shock and exhaustion," the nurse said. Her little dark horns stuck out of her mass of curly brown hair and her black nose twitched slightly.

"Thank you, Eloise," Lux said, smiling sweetly at the nurse. She nodded to him and continued to sit and monitor Greer's condition.

"What number was she?" Lux said, biting out the words.

It felt like I had held my breath the last three hours and I could finally exhale. Greer had picked up speed right before the last few numbers trailed in. I had no idea where that burst of energy had come from. It was as if exhaustion and time had no effect on her as she sliced through the water. Just like she had on our run the other day.

"Seven hundred and forty-seven, and the woman she was with was seven hundred and forty-eight," I said, remembering the number flashing up on one of the screens as we had raced to shore, where police tape had been set up to keep any of the drunk patrons from harassing the contestants right off the bat.

"Too close," Lux said, closing his eyes and leaning back. His chest was rising and falling quickly, as if he, too, was trying to catch his breath.

"Too close," I agreed, doing the same and hoping that the rest of the Trials wouldn't induce a heart attack like this one almost did.

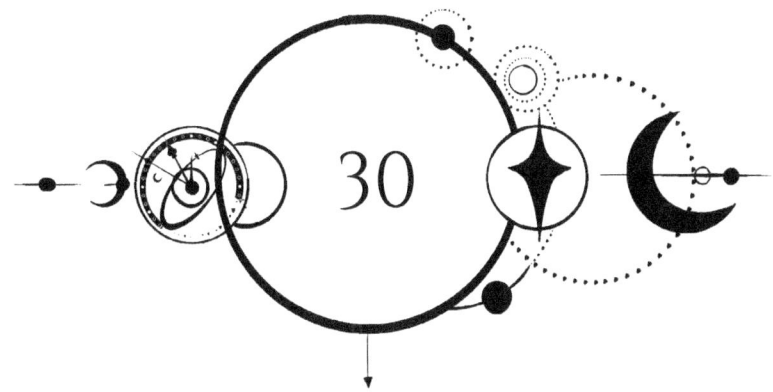

Greer

"Mom?" I said, shocked.

She was standing right in front me, looking like the pinnacle of glowing health. Her blond hair was cut to her shoulders in a bob and she had wrinkles around her blue eyes. It was always a running joke that we looked nothing alike. That my wine-red hair and her fair blond hair were at opposite ends, but she had said her grandmother had had my coloring. The same hair and the same eyes.

My heart ached at the sight of her and the softness in her smile. She was dressed like she almost always was in leggings and a T-shirt with an oversized flannel and rain boots. She stood tall and strong.

So different from the hunched shoulders and thinness I was used to. Her eyes were bright and happy, all sense of sadness and heaviness gone from her body.

I tore my gaze away from her and looked around. A black haze enveloped us like nothing besides the two of us existed. I looked down at my own glowing hands to realize that I was sitting on my knees.

"Greer, you've been given a gift," my mom said, looking down at me and coming to sit cross-legged before me.

"I don't understand," I choked out. Tears started falling down my cheeks. "Is this … real?"

"As real as it needs to be," she replied, smiling softly, almost in pity. "We don't have much time. The faerie nymph could only grant so much with her fading energy."

Andromeda?

"Greer, I need you to know that I did everything I could to protect you. In my last moments, all I thought of was you. I worked so hard to keep my own darkness at bay and not let it get its claws in you but in the end it didn't matter. It was always destined to be like this. I couldn't protect you, I'm so sorry. I wish I could have. The veil between the realms is fading and they have had thousands of years to plan for this…" she said, her tone getting serious. Her hands were gripping mine and her eyes begged me to listen.

I stared at her, my mouth agape.

"I don't understand…" I said, searching her face.

Realms?

She looked behind her, as if someone was waiting for her.

"Greer, the darkness that took me … It's in you too… I tried to fight mine as much as I could but I failed. You won't. Yours is stronger but so are you. You were made to bear the burden and live. You will survive it, I know you will. Be strong my dear," she said, pity in her eyes, as if she had waited years to tell me this.

"What?" I choked out, tears rolling down, falling onto my thighs. My body started shaking and I couldn't get enough air into my lungs.

"Win, Greer. Open yourself up to what you were meant to be. You cannot fail or it will take you too. You cannot let them take you, Greer. You cannot allow yourself to be controlled by them otherwise all will be lost and this will all be for nothing," she said, squeezing my hands, and her light started to fade.

"Mom?"

Her image started to fade and evaporate like smoke.

"Mom!" I screamed, my hands empty where hers once were. "No, no, no, no…"

I was unable to stand, as if my body was nailed to the floor. I whipped my head around, wild-eyed, and my stomach flip-flopped.

"Mom … I love you," I whispered to the nothingness.

Sobs racked my body as I wrapped my arms around myself and curled into myself, not understanding what any of this meant. Or where I was. Or what I was supposed to do.

I gasped awake, tangled in my white sheets, and sat straight up, sweating and shivering even though I was in an oversized hoodie and leggings. My hair was loose and half of it was sticking to my face as I panted.

My door slammed open and a concerned Kyra burst through the doorframe. His long legs covered the distance to my bed in a few short strides and he kneeled beside my bed.

"What's wrong?" he said, bleeding warmth into my body through his hands. His hair was disheveled, as if he had spent many hours pulling his hands through it. He had bags under his eyes, as if he hadn't slept well the past few days.

My eyes widened as I tried to remember the details of my dream with my mom. I searched his concerned face, his ruby eyes blinking rapidly and those strong brows knitting in worry.

I swallowed hard and relaxed my shoulders as his warmth made its way to every inch of my body.

"I…" I started, but I wasn't ready to share my dream just yet. I wanted to hold the memory of my mom close to my heart before I tried to decipher what her words had meant. "Um … how did I get home?" I finished.

Kyra gazed up at me and his mouth set in a hard line, as if he was trying to figure out whether or not to press further. I must have been screaming in my sleep and sobbing.

He got up and sat next to me instead and cleared his throat.

"You passed out on the beach and Lux and I brought you back here. You were screaming 'get off me,' and blood covered your body … Your ankle had some gashes but there were no other injuries," he said, taking in every inch of me as if looking for a new place of hurt. He brushed his fingertips along my forehead and tucked the wet hair behind my ear and wiped away the lingering tears with his thumb. I closed my eyes, leaning into the touch.

He was dressed in a black t-shirt, dark gray joggers, and a red athletic jacket.

Had he been here since the trial?

"I saw the people floating … um … dead in the water, and then I saw my mom, then me, then you … Lux … Nova … Waverly … I felt the mermaid on my skin and tried to claw her away and clawed at myself," I whispered, leaning further into his strong arms hugging me and his breathing steadying me. "I wanted the blood off … the death … The mermaid…"

He leaned in and placed his lips on my hair, whispering that I was safe now.

"I wanted to kill that mermaid … still do, actually…" he mumbled, and I laughed softly, the heaviness on my chest easing.

I breathed in his familiar scent and let his hands move down my back in soothing circles.

"How long have I been out?" I said carefully.

There was too much space between us, so I scooted closer to him and placed my legs across his lap, and he scooped me up. I snuggled in and let him hold me as my breath started to return to normal.

"Two days," he murmured, pressing his mouth to my forehead.

I shivered and snuggled closer.

"I was so worried…" he said, tightening his arms around me. I shut my eyes tight and let myself sink into his warmth, trying to pull myself deeper into his strong arms.

"I'm so proud of you," he said, pulling away and placing one hand underneath my chin and looking into my eyes with his beautiful rubies. He brushed his lips against mine and my whole body responded by pressing deeper into him. I wanted to get lost in the scent of him and the feel of his hands and body against my own.

I deepened the kiss and then pulled away to sit up and straddle him. His eyebrows raised in surprise.

I wrapped my legs and arms around him like a little koala and searched his eyes.

"Thank you … for believing in me. For supporting me and for being here…" I said, tracing little circles on his back with my hand and pressing my forehead to his.

"Greer…" he whispered huskily.

"Oh good, you're awake," Lux said from my open doorway. I looked over my shoulder and scooted to sit back in Ky's lap. He was also dressed casually in a fitted long sleeve and joggers. His braids were loose down his back and he too had bruise like circles underneath his golden eyes.

"Nova and Waverly are here. They have some news about the investigation…" Lux said, eyeing me over as I was cradled in Kyra's lap.

Kyra gently untangled himself from me and set me on the bed, pressing a kiss to my temple.

"Right now?" Kyra said, slightly irritated.

"We don't have to do this, G, since you just woke up. I'm sure you want some time and have some questions…" Lux said. "I can handle it and let you know. But Nova and Waverly do want to see you, they've been really worried."

I needed to know what was going on and I was more than capable of sitting down and listening to the news. Plus, I wanted to see my friends.

Ky stood up and set me down on the floor. He offered his hand, which I gladly took, intertwining my fingers with his, and Lux nodded, turning around and heading toward the dining room.

Waverly and Nova were standing around our large dining room table. It was raining outside, and the pitter-patter of the water was soft and comforting as the whole penthouse was enveloped in a yellow warmth with the gray sky opening up outside.

Both of their eyes went wide when they saw me, and I saw tears in Nova's eyes and Waverly's lip tremble as they both rushed forward and enveloped me, tearing me away from Ky's hand.

"We were so worried," Waverly said, squeezing me tight.

"You were amazing," Nova said, her arms tight around me.

I pulled away and looked at both of them and smiled. "I'm so glad to see you both," I said, holding each of their hands and giving them a squeeze.

"We don't have to do this now if you don't want to," Waverly said, her pink eyes filled with worry. Her dark hair was pulled back in a ponytail that fell in waves down her back. She was dressed in dark jeans, a fitted white sweater, and dark brown boots. Her light brown skin was practically glowing with her siren beauty and her mouth was pursed as her eyes raked over my body.

"We can table this for tomorrow. We thought you would be asleep when we got here but Lux said you just got up..." Nova said, her fire eyes framed by her beautiful long lashes and her full mouth frowning slightly, as if she blamed Lux for waking me up. She had a black leather skirt on with a gray turtleneck and fishnet tights with tall dark green velvet boots. Her stars seemed a bit dim today on her palms and temples.

I looked around at the people in the room. All of them clearly worried.

"I'm fine. I won't break into a million pieces as all of you seem to think I will," I laughed as they all looked a little taken aback.

Lux broke into a smile. "That's my girl. How about we talk first and then get some takeout from your favorite sushi place down the street?" he said, cocking his head slightly and pulling out one of the dark leather chairs around the table.

Ky had gone and gotten me a glass of water and set it down in front of me as he took the seat next to me. Waverly sat at the head of the table with Nova on her other side next to Lux.

Waverly sat tall and straight and she looked over at me, as if not trusting that I wouldn't spontaneously combust.

"Oh, for gods' sake, what is it?" I said, leaning forward.

"Two other immortals have been found dead…" she said, folding her hands in front of her.

"What?" Kyra said next to me, looking confused.

"And we know how they were killed," Nova said seriously.

"How? How are people killing immortals?" Lux said, crossing his tattooed arms over his chest.

Who was killing immortals?

And why in god's name was this connected to me being put into the damn Trials? There was clearly a reason this shifter had been killed. As soon as we got close to him as our lead, he was murdered, which was really fucking suspicious.

"A serum is being injected into them underneath their tongue. Almost undetectable as an injection site. The serum fuses with the blood cells in the body and kills them while simultaneously attacking the other blood cells in the body. It's why the blood rots, so to speak," Nova said, looking each of us in the eyes while Waverly nodded slightly.

"Your case is now a bit more serious and less well ... less about you..." Waverly said, a bit irritated.

"Of course they aren't recognizing that it's connected to your case at all, since we couldn't prove the shifter was the one who was hired to enter you in the Trials, even though he was our best and only logical lead. And I just know in my bones it was him ... I just don't know why he was granted immortality or why he was killed. Or why others are dying. But basically my time is now expected to be on this other case, and your case has been pushed further and further down the list even though I do think there is a major connection here."

This was bigger than me.

It had taken a very dark and dangerous turn. It meant that the likelihood of me being freed from the Trials was practically nonexistent now.

"Who were the immortals?" Ky said quietly. He was the only immortal in the room. I hadn't even thought about how jarring it must be for him.

Lux and Waverly could probably apply or buy their immortality with their powers or accomplishments, but the only chance I would have is if Lux bought it for me or if I won it. And I knew Nova had been offered it but had turned it down.

Lux and I had talked about the possibility of buying immortality a few times but we both had decided that we didn't like the idea of living forever. Things were meant to end. It wasn't something that either of us had really desired. Lux's parents were getting ready to make the transition to immortality right before their helicopter crash. They were over 300 years old at that point ... It had taken them a long time to build their wealth and they were ready to accept their reward.

They had already told Lux for his twenty-fifth birthday they would buy him immortality. They had an intense fight after that, which ended up with Lux shedding angry tears as he said he would not accept such a gift.

I hadn't really thought about the fact that Ky was an immortal and I wasn't. We hadn't really talked about what exactly we were doing. We hadn't put a label on us yet.

There were so many other things happening it hadn't exactly been a topic that came to the forefront of my mind.

"One of them was a former immortality winner who was a notorious partier and drug lord in the city, Nars Hughes. The other was a CEO of a major financial institute, Julio Roddero," Waverly said, looking at Ky.

"Did you know them?" I said, reaching for his hand underneath the table, my fingers intertwining with his.

He cleared his throat. "Not well, but I had spoken several times to both of them and been to a handful of events where they were as well. They weren't exactly good males … They both had shady track records, but their immortality made them untouchable. Until now," he finished, looking down as if trying to figure out what this meant.

"There was no evidence left behind on who did this and how they got a hold of a serum that could kill the immortals. My team is investigating the hit and obviously the ITC is keeping this under wraps due to the nature of the crime and in an effort to not instate panic," Waverly said, biting out the words. Clearly, she was unhappy and disappointed in how things were being handled.

"I'm going to call in a favor with a friend of mine who is a necromancer, and we are going to see if he can access the memories of the dead right before they were murdered," Nova said, her mouth twitching up slightly.

"Isn't necromancy illegal?" I asked.

It had been long ago ruled out by the Republic as an unethical practice of magic. It was a close cousin to blood magic, but infinitely darker and more disturbing. It was said that those who were blessed with necromancy were part dead themselves, a shadow of a soul.

"It is. But I don't work for the ITC so we're working around the red tape," Nova said steadily, winking at Waverly.

"I've got someone I want us to talk to at my company. She's one of the best technologists I've ever seen. Not to mention before she went straight and accepted a position at my company, she was a hacker for hire," Lux said, smirking.

He loved to hire people at his company who wouldn't normally get a chance at a steady job.

"There's a few people I could talk to at the lounge who might have connections to someone with the resources and motive to kill immortals. If we can find out who killed the shifter, then maybe we can find out if they would have hired him to impersonate me. Why someone would falsely admit me to the Immortality Trials with the intention and also the motive to kill immortals still seems to not make a damn bit of sense ... but there has to be a way this is all connected..." I said, trailing off.

My mom had said in my dream that the darkness that took her was inside me, and if I didn't win it would take me too. That she had tried to keep *them* at bay, but that I had to win and that I couldn't let myself be controlled by them.

"I ... I had a dream right before I woke up. About my mom." I glanced to Lux, whose eyes held mine steady, and I took a deep breath.

No one knew the wounds inside me like Lux did. Kyra knew some but not all.

"She said that the darkness that took her would take me too. She said if I didn't win I would be taken by it. That I couldn't allow myself to be controlled by them ... I don't know what that means but I wonder if it's somehow connected to why I was put in the Trials. I've never dreamed about my mom like that before. Like it was a message. She said she didn't have much time. That I had been gifted with this message ... It felt very real," I said, staring down at my hand intertwined with Ky's. He gave me a gentle squeeze, warming my palm.

"I thought maybe it would have something to do with my father or with her family since they all abandoned her and me. So maybe we should look into it?" I squared my shoulders and sat up tall. Lux's gaze found mine and the love that poured from them made my heart squeeze.

"Okay," he said nodding and the others gave soft smiles and encouraging eyes.

Lux's phone rang in front of him and he furrowed his brows looking confused. He quickly ignored it and I saw that it was his personal assistant. A series of dings came in as messages started pouring and then Ky's phone began buzzing next to me.

"What's happening?" I asked, starting to get scared. Both of them looked confused and started scrolling through their notifications.

"Well, it looks like you're famous, G," he said with laughter twinkling in his gold eyes.

Lux had done a pretty good job over the years of keeping the paparazzi at bay and away from us with bribes in order to protect both of our privacy. But now that I was on national TV through the Trials, I guess that power and influence could only go so far.

"Human and Immortality Trials Contestant Greer Roberts saved by tech tycoon Luxton Gilmore and Ambassador Kyra. See how these men fight for the affection of this ordinary woman in the throes of the Trials … Who will win this human heart? And how did she get these two men wrapped around her finger?" Kyra read on his phone and flashed me a photo of Lux carrying me from the beach and Ky brushing his lips across my forehead. He burst out laughing, a sound that echoed through his chest.

And then I started laughing and tears began falling down my face, and soon I was joined by Nova, Waverly, and Lux.

"I can't with the paparazzi," I said, wheezing for air and wiping the tears from my eyes.

My heart was so full with the people in this room.

"Can we eat now, please?" I whined, looking around the room at the power and love sizzling here.

"Already on it!" Lux said, and the chatter continued long into the rainy night as we formulated how we were going to get me through the next trial and who we would contact for the investigation.

I looked over at Ky; a lightness had settled over him.

He flashed a wicked smile at me, and I felt a warmth start to settle in my low belly and travel down, like his hand was trailing down my body. I nearly gasped.

Who knew his power could do that?

He winked at me and kept chatting with the rest of the group.

I sighed, realizing I just had to make it through the next trial.

One day at a time.

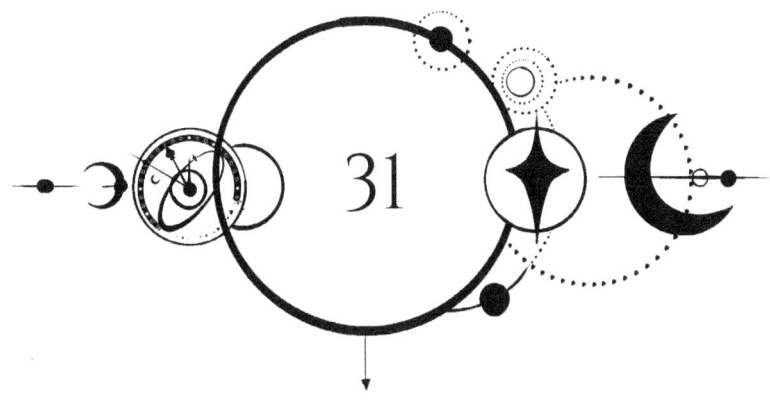

Greer

Seven hundred and fifty people were left in the trial.

The next trial would eliminate 250 more.

And more life cycles.

The next would eliminate 250 more.

Even more life would be taken away…

Until the final trial, where the top 100 would be rewarded and the winner would get immortality.

Nausea and panic would sweep into me whenever I thought about it too long. I was trying really hard to stay grounded since I had talked to Lux and Kyra.

It was working. For the most part.

So two trials down. Three to go.

The next trial would be one of wits and knowledge. They would drop each of us into a room and we would have to escape based on the clues and puzzles within the space. We would have one hour to free ourselves.

I almost laughed out loud, because in the last few years it had become something civilians would do with their friends. You would pay to get locked in a room with your friends and you would all work together to free yourself.

Except this wasn't a game. This was people's lives. The punishment for this trial was half of your life cycle or the government servitude for the same amount of time. Which was a lot for a human—and anyone else, for that matter.

I cringed, thinking of the time Lux and I had gone on a double date to one of the escape rooms. We didn't end up "escaping." Instead we laughed and giggled and kissed our dates, drinks in hand.

Things were easier then. We didn't know any better and we certainly didn't care.

My next trial was in two weeks.

The next would be a test of our "humanity".

Which was really fucking ironic considering most of the contestants weren't human. It felt like a slap to the face, but no one seemed to question it.

It was just accepted.

Then the final trial. It was always a race to the finish of some sort. Sometimes an obstacle course. Sometimes a maze. It was always a surprise that held dark twists and turns where contestants were forced to make hard decisions about how much winning really meant.

It's just another reason it was nearly impossible to win without powers. You could choose one weapon and take it into the arena and everything else was fair game.

You could use your powers if you had them, obviously. Which I didn't. And why it was basically unheard of for a human to win the entirety of the games.

We were powerless.

And I had almost died several times in the last trial and had been beaten up pretty bad in the first one. I was cutting it much too close and it would only get worse. I would only be targeted even more. At least the third trial didn't involve other people so I was safe there but the fourth and fifth would be a fight to the death.

I shivered thinking about it.

Ky and I had started weapons training this week to prepare for the final trial. I had upgraded my switchblade to a dagger, as Ky had teased me and told me I looked like I was a sixteen-year-old drug dealer or something with that "thing."

I punched him in the arm hard for that one.

My mom had given me the switchblade when I was little. I had been beaten up by some other kids at school when I was about fourteen and she had given it to me in case of emergencies. I had carried it with me ever since. In hindsight, it was an odd thing to give a fourteen-year-old, but her heart was in the right place and it had saved me more than once.

My heart clenched thinking of how my mom had tried in her own way to equip me in the best way she could because she was simply too deep in her own sorrows to protect me herself.

But the dagger felt good in my hand. Stronger. More mature.

Plus, I needed to use what made sense for me. I was small and quick. I would need to use my opponent's force against them. And this is where it was most dangerous. Bets were high for the final trial and the ITC did little to interfere with the games. People would die just like they did in the ocean. I could die. If I got there…

But that was still two trials away.

One trial at a time, Greer.

I tried to push the thought of death out of my head, but it was a bit hard considering we were presently all in the basement of a government issued mortuary waiting for Nova's friend.

Waverly had called in a favor and the place was empty.

The room was huge. You immediately stepped in and there were over thirty stainless steel tables lined side by side with about six feet in between each lining the space. Each table had its own fluorescent bulb hanging over it with a table next to it full of medical instruments. The walls on the right were lined with cold pullout drawers for the dead. And the wall lining the left had miscellaneous computers, lab stations, and machines for dissecting the deceased.

The smell was discomforting to say the least. It smelled like bleach, metal and rotting flesh. Lux and I had arrived after Waverly. She was standing in her standard FEC uniform looking a bit nervous for what was to come next.

They had prepared the three bodies for us to examine. They were laying side by side with a white sheet covering them. Lux hovered close to her, shifting his feet side to side uncomfortable with the buzzing fluorescent lights and the cold feeling of death that lingered in the air.

Neither one of us had much experience with dead bodies. Well, that is until recently, I suppose.

I stood by the door scrolling the news on my phone hugging my black jacket close. Apparently the story of Kyra, Lux and I had gone viral. So now when we left our apartment, we almost always had someone ask if we were dating, and of course the Shadow Lounge was now inundated with people who had watched the trial trying to get the latest scoop on who I was.

Arlo was thriving. He thought it was hilarious and it was great for business. I tried my best not to snap and snarl at them.

"Hey."

Kyra walked through the metal door and I looked up to see his easy smile and smoldering eyes connect with mine. He made butterflies erupt in my belly. The bags that had haunted his under eyes had disappeared and his skin had his naturally healthy olive color back. His hair was messy as always. He had come from work in dark gray slacks and a black turtleneck that hugged his muscled chest and abdomen. He was wearing a maroon knee length jacket. Immediately, my thoughts went to everything that lay underneath his stylish outfit but I tried to keep the desire in my belly in check.

"Hi," I said, smiling back at him. He walked over and kissed my forehead. This casual touching and kissing was a bit new between us. He had been like this ever since the last trial. We hadn't had the conversation about what *this, us,* was yet but I liked it. This easiness between us.

"Do I get a kiss?" Lux said, pouting slightly. Kyra chuckled next to me and started to open his mouth when Waverly next to him stood on her tippy toes and smacked loudly with her lips on his cheek. Lux looked absolutely stunned and laughter erupted from me as I doubled over, clutching my stomach.

"Feel better?" she said, winking at him, her pink eyes laughing.

He slid an arm around her and smiled down at her. "Waverly, I didn't know you had a sweet spot for me. I thought you only had eyes for Nova!" he said to a wide-eyed Waverly, her mouth slightly agape.

"Didn't think I would notice, hmmm?" he said, playfully tugging on her ponytail. She just smiled wickedly and shook her head.

"Did you tell him?" Waverly looked at me with an accusatory expression.

"No, you said you wanted to wait!" I said, laughing as a pouty Lux pushed out his bottom lip at me and Waverly grinned.

"I really hate being the last one to know," Lux said, feigning hurt.

"I didn't know … And I'm not pouting," Ky said, narrowing his red eyes at Lux and smirking.

"Yeah, yeah…" Lux said, waving his tattooed hands around like it didn't matter.

I exchanged a look with Kyra, who merely shrugged his shoulders, smiling, and slipped his hand in mine. His warmth traveled through my body.

The door swung open once again and Nova walked in with what could only be the necromancer behind her.

She smiled at Waverly first, who started to blush slightly, and Nova turned her head slightly as if not understanding her reaction. Nova looked stunning as usual. Her cropped hair was green today and her black skin sparkled with her silver stars winking. She wore black leather leggings and a white sweater today with silver booties.

The man next to her had paper white skin with short strawberry blond hair. His face was all sharp angles and he had deep red lips. Shadows seem to wink around his black eyes. One moment they would be there and the next they would be gone. He was thin, tall and dressed in all black, no coat to be seen even though it was still relatively cold out for April.

He seemed to glide through the room. He flashed a white smile at us revealing slightly pointed fangs. Shadows seemed to dance around him one moment ebbing toward him and then next flowing away. His eyes scanned the room and they stopped at Ky. A muscle in Kyra's jaw feathered as his grip on my hand tightened. Nova's friend tilted his head and a look of realization passed over his features before he turned back to Nova.

What was that about?

"Hi, sorry we're late," she said, brushing in to stand close to Waverly.

My heart swelled and I ended up smiling goofily at both of them. They had told me the last time we had had our girls' night when we were a little tipsy and I had squealed and tackled them both in a bone-crushing hug. They swore me to secrecy because they didn't want to make a big deal out of it, and I wanted to protect their privacy. So I hadn't told either of the boys which honestly I should have gotten a trophy for because I never kept things from Lux. And Ky and I were relatively new, but he had a way of making me open up emotionally that there was a good chance I could have let it slip.

Waverly narrowed her eyes at me, and Nova looked a bit confused.

"Did Greer spoil our secret?" Nova said, looking slightly annoyed and not at all surprised at me with her fire eyes.

"Why did you both assume it was me?!" I said, laughing and my eyes widening.

Waverly rolled her eyes and Nova smiled.

"Lux called us out," Waverly said, sighing, and then she slipped her hand into Nova's star-covered one.

"I'm never wrong about these things," he said, like he was a freaking love expert.

"I just didn't want to distract anyone from the investigation and the trial…" Waverly said, blushing again, which was such a Waverly response.

"You are absolutely not distracting anyone from anything. Ky distracts me all the time and it's fine. We all manage," I said, winking.

"Anyways…" I said, beaming at them. "Who's your friend?"

"Ahem … This is Sutton Hayes, my necromancer friend," Nova said, nodding to where Sutton was standing with his hands in his pocket.

"This is Lux, Waverly, Greer, and Kyra…" Nova said, nodding in each of our directions. "And these are the dead I told you about."

"Nice to meet you all," he said in a voice deep and smooth.

"The immortals…" he said carefully, walking over to each one and pulling the white sheets covering their bodies down to their collarbones.

Each face looked void of life and their eyes were all closed. I shivered. I don't think I would ever get used to looking death straight in the face.

He started chanting barely above a whisper and the shadows around his eyes darkened and the ones at his feet seemed to whisper around him. The air in the room changed, feeling heavy and staticky. There was an audible crack and Sutton snapped his fingers and all three corpses sat up.

"Fuck," Lux said and jumped back as the three corpses looked directly at Sutton with black in their eyes. The white clothes falling to their laps.

I gasped at the sight and Waverly chewed on her bottom lips as Nova leveled her gaze with Sutton nodding for him to continue.

I tightened my hold on Ky's hand. His whole body was tensed beside me. His expression was unreadable and his jaw set.

"Tell us about how you died," Sutton said, making eye contact with each one of them and folding his long white fingers together in front of his chest.

"It is not to be told," they said in unison with a voice that was old and young at the same time, and one but many. Like something echoed through them. Like death itself was speaking from all the lips of the deceased.

I furrowed my brows and Sutton looked intrigued.

"Were you injected with a serum?" he said, pursing his dark red lips.

"Yes," they answered in unison.

"By the same person?"

"Yes."

It was like watching a creepy puppet show. Everyone in the room seemed to be holding their breath.

"But you cannot tell me who…" he said, walking in front of them, pacing back and forth.

"No."

"Were they mortal?" he asked, narrowing his eyes.

I had a feeling this was not the first time he had done this.

"No."

"Did you know them?" he said, tilting his head slightly.

Silence.

"Does anyone in this room know them?"

They all blinked in response.

"Is there anything else you would like me to ask Nova?" he said while still examining the three dead men who sat upright in front of us.

"I think that's all for now," she said carefully, frowning slightly.

With another snap of his delicate fingers, Sutton had gently put all of them back to rest and went to cover them up with the white sheets.

"They aren't themselves. Whatever was in that serum stripped them of their immortality and their humanity and individualization. Something also protects the secret after death. Which is a bit un-usual. Most powers and creatures cannot extend the life of their spells after death. Only those who deal in death itself or with hell magic can find potency after life…" he said, squinting and tapping one long index to his angled cheekbone.

"Which means that whoever killed them has placed a spell or curse for after death as well. But those who deal with that cursed magic are often good at staying in the shadows. Not to mention that if it was an immortal … I would guess that it was sent by the god of hell himself, Riordan," he said thoughtfully.

"What?" Ky choked out, looking horrified.

"You can't be serious?" Lux said, looking even more stunned than he had earlier when Waverly planted a kiss on him.

"The old gods don't exist … right?" I said, scrunching up my nose.

"Oh, they exist, Greer. They just aren't very active … At least, that's what I believed until now," Sutton said, his black eyes pushing into the very depth of my soul. "And you should do more to brush up on your history in regard to the old ways. It's not the only bit of cursed magic emanating in this room. Are you not versed in the ways of dark magic, Kyra?" he said, looking Kyra up and down as if trying to figure him out.

Kyra's whole body reacted like someone had punched him in the gut and he gasped out loud, releasing my hand.

"What?" I blurted out, looking between an indifferent Sutton and a shocked Ky. Sutton just said the old gods existed like he was telling me his schedule for the day and in the same breath said that Ky had dark magic.

Ky, who was one of the most generous and philanthropic individuals in the city, used cursed magic?

"Who told you that?" Kyra said, straightening his spine and clenching his jaw. His hands balled into fists beside him.

"You can calm yourself, Ambassador. No one. Like calls to like. I am a cursed being myself, and I can see that the stone in your chest isn't an average warlock crystal. My eyes detect the curse wrapping itself around your heart," he said, sighing as if he had just been talking about the weather.

"Kyra?" I said, looking at him confused. I didn't understand. Cursed?

Waverly's eyebrows had shot up and Nova pursed her lips. Lux looked intrigued.

I felt an uneasiness in my stomach. I gently touched Kyra's arm and he slowly pulled his sad ruby eyes to meet mine. His shoulders hunched forward, and he blew out an exhale.

"What Sutton said is true … The stone in my chest is cursed by hell itself," he said heavily, each word biting out. His eyes searched my face as if waiting for me to say something.

I swallowed and met them with my own and willed the words from his mouth to not be true because a curse from hell sounded like a pretty big deal to me. And felt really bad.

Like a guarantee for bad and evil shit to pop up at any waking moment.

"Why don't we meet you all back at the penthouse?" Lux said, clearing his throat.

Waverly passed by pressing a keycard into my hand. "I'll lock the doors behind me. You can use this to get out," she said, squeezing my hand reassuringly and giving a skeptical look at Ky.

Sutton nodded toward us and they all shuffled out, leaving me with Ky and the smell of death.

"I don't understand…" I finally said after a few moments. It was weird to think that I felt so close to him and still knew so little about his past.

Ky ran his hands through his hair and looked down at the ground. Then up toward the three bodies who were currently keeping us company.

"I was adopted. My parents found me outside of their town after they were told they couldn't conceive a child. They thought I was a gift from the gods. They still acknowledge the old gods and goddesses where I'm from.

"Like any warlock," he continued, "I was born with the stone. But the stone was black. The gems are supposed to be colored. Black is … unheard of. A bad omen. So they took me to a witch doctor. She said that I had been cursed by the god of hell himself and that they should have left me where they found me. They refused to let go of me, since they had wanted and tried for a child for many years before.

"They tried for a long time to find someone who could tell them more about what the curse meant. How they could reverse it. What it meant. That's part of the reason they moved here. They wanted to find answers.

"When I was going through law school, I found someone who was exceptionally versed in cursed and forbidden magic. They said that there was a chance I could overpower the curse by entering the Immortality Trials and having power given to me outside of the cursed stone. So when I won, my stone turned red. I was granted greater power that derived from me, not the cursed stone, and it changed the color of the stone."

At some point, he had taken both of my hands in his and started rubbing his thumbs across my knuckles as I listened. My throat was dry and my tongue felt heavy in my mouth.

"You don't know any more about the curse?" I said, swallowing.

He searched my eyes as if he could will me to believe.

"I don't know much except that it gave me exceptional power. The fire I wield can be very … dangerous. It only increased through the Trials whenever I won, and I was granted the additional power of explosion through touch." His hands were still in mine.

I looked down at his hands. The power that simmered beneath the surface. I thought about all the times he had bled warmth into me. How he had cared for and loved me and others.

A curse didn't change who he was. It simply was.

But his power was dangerous if wielded inappropriately.

"Okay. Is there anything else you want to tell me?" I said, squeezing his hands, and he seemed to relax his shoulders.

"No, that's it ... I still look for answers, but it's been fruitless," he said softly.

I released his hands and lifted them to his sharp olive jaw, trailing my fingertips from his ear to his mouth. He stiffened under my touch, as if holding his breath.

"Thank you for sharing that with me..." I whispered, stepping closer to brush my lips across his.

He pulled me in close by wrapping his arms around me.

"Thank you for understanding," he mumbled into my hair.

My head rested right next to the cursed stone in his heart.

His phone began ringing, splintering the moment.

"You should answer that, and we should leave this behind..." I said, waving my hand toward the dead bodies and wrinkling my nose.

He chuckled and opened the door for me and fished his phone out of his pocket. He scowled and swore underneath his breath and answered it before I could ask what was wrong.

The heavy metal door slammed behind us and we stepped out into the dimly lit corridor.

"Sir," Ky said, rolling his shoulders back.

He listened for a moment.

"Right now?" he said strangely.

He gave a few nods and fluttered his eyes closed, his long lashes brushing against his cheek.

"We'll be there shortly." His voice was rough, and then he hung up.

"Who was that?"

I had a bad feeling about this.

Like worse than finding out your new kinda-boyfriend had a cursed stone from hell in his chest.

"It's the President of the Republic. He wants to see *us*. Immediately." Kyra said, running a hand across his mouth and jaw.

While my jaw practically dropped to the floor.

"What?"

The President of the Republic was the highest-ranking government official. He was one of the original immortals from back in the old kingdom days and was said to be a gruff man. He always granted the winner of the Immortality Trials their immortality and power at the end, in a grossly overdone ceremony. How he even knew I existed was beyond me, let alone why he needed to see myself and Kyra.

"I don't know. But this isn't good," he said, looking slightly fearful. "Greer, he isn't a kind man. He tolerates humans at best. I don't know what this is about but … please let me do most of the talking." He pleaded with his eyes.

"Okay," I said.

Kyra grabbed my hand and tugged me through the maze of the government building as we worked our way toward another one.

We hopped into his car and I shot off a text to Lux, Nova, and Waverly, letting them know what had happened.

I looked out the window at the buildings, people, and cars we passed by while Ky drove. His hand was resting on my thigh, oozing his heat into me. I covered his hand with mine and smiled over at him as he winked at me. My life looked very different than it had a couple of months ago. And it seemed like things were only getting weirder.

And more dangerous.

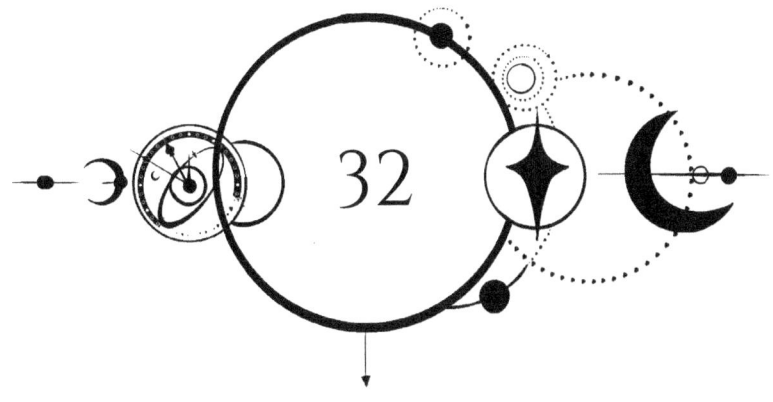

32

Kyra

Greer was holding her composure remarkably well despite the fact that we were about to meet President Adonia of the Republic.

Once arriving at the building, we were guided into a small waiting area. Greer sat up tall, stunning as usual in her skintight maroon dress, thigh-high black boots, and long light gray jacket. Gold and silver flickered around her neck, wrists, and ears. Her hair was swept back into a high ponytail that hit her mid back, looking like a dark red waterfall.

I tried not to stare but her blue-rimmed green eyes caught mine, and she smiled at me wickedly.

She had been surprisingly composed when Sutton had outed my curse.

That bastard.

Did it ever occur to the necromancer that people didn't appreciate their skeletons being forcibly dragged out of the closet in front of friends and loved ones?

I swallowed, thinking of how my feelings for Greer only seemed to grow and grow. I couldn't keep myself from touching her and wanting to know every single thing that was going on in her head. Which was dangerous, considering the position I was in.

The curse wasn't supposed to affect other people unless I gave away its secrets. I couldn't tell her, or anyone else for that matter, or else my inferno would kill them.

I had tried once.

To speak the words of my curse out loud. I was alone and in the woods, far from others. I had blurted it out hurriedly and fire so hot it burned blue ripped from my throat and destroyed the circle of trees around me.

Nothing ever grew there again. I checked every year.

I detested lying to her. But I couldn't very well tell her. I would rather die than kill her with my own hands.

But winning the Trials and becoming an immortal myself had granted a sort of relief, or freedom, that I at least couldn't be killed by the curse and that my power source was no longer just from the curse itself.

The stone had tried to stop me from entering the Trials as it rejected the idea of new power, but there was nothing in the rules of my curse that said I couldn't enter. Instead, the damn thing had caused such delirious pain in my chest that I had nearly passed out several times during the Trials. I had to resort to extreme measures to keep the pain under control so I could win and find a way to be free of it.

I nervously tapped my fingers on my thigh while I contemplated all that had happened in the last twenty-four hours.

I didn't know why the President wanted to see us. I knew he didn't particularly like me. I had spoken out against a lot of his policies and the hypocrisy that ran rampant through the Republic's government system. But I had never met with him alone, let alone with a civilian.

We had, of course, met before at government functions, parties, and at my victor ceremony when I won the Trials. But he had simply put his hand on my chest, gave me the incantation of immortality and power in front of the millions watching, and then congratulated me by shaking my hand amongst a crowd of people posing for the photo op. Then he had left.

He had been the President for several hundreds of years, and every president who presided over the Republic was given the gift of bestowing immortality. It was some seriously secret stuff that only few were entrusted with.

But President Adonia wasn't someone you just casually saw. Even Edward, the ITC Trial Lord, seemed to cower when he was near. Which wasn't encouraging.

My powers were vast. I could protect Greer, but the power of the President wasn't very forthcoming. He exuded strength and aggression. But the specifics of what his brutish form could do were not detailed anywhere, at least anywhere that I had access too.

A young female with green scales covering the majority of her body came over to us and interrupted my spiraling thoughts. "President Adonia will see you now."

I nodded and Greer got up beside me, standing tall, and flashed a smile at the woman, who led us down a hallway to large metal double doors. She nodded at them and they opened together, revealing President Adonia standing at an oak desk several yards away, with two chairs facing him and two couches facing one another closer to the door, behind him was a floor-to-ceiling window overlooking the city. The room was massive, with a small bar at one end, a large conference table, lots of bookshelves, a large TV, and a smaller, more intimate, lounging and sitting area. Everything screamed hyper-masculine, with wood and metal touches here and there.

Which made sense, since he was notorious for being a condescending misogynistic prick who rarely thought of the race divide between humans and everyone else. If I hadn't won, I was sure my smart ass would have been even higher on his shit list.

But there was the arrogant son of a bitch himself, standing well over seven feet tall and nearly three feet wide, with shoulders and arms that looked as though he could crush someone's head like a grape.

He wore an all black suit and his skin was an odd, sickly gray color. Small spikes pebbled the sides of his neck and could be seen throughout his salt-and-pepper hair. His eyes were bright green, and when he smiled, his mouth had rows of pointed teeth that made the smile look menacing instead of friendly.

His powers were said to be immeasurable strength and force, along with the power to grant immortality, which each president inherited from the previous one.

"Welcome, Ambassador Kyra and Greer Roberts," he said, his pointed teeth flashing.

I glanced over to Greer, who had planted a sugary sweet smile on her face.

"The pleasure is ours, Mr. President," Greer said sweetly with a bright smile on her face. I didn't even know why I had told her I could handle it, because clearly she was fine. I was the one who needed to find a semblance of control.

"President Adonia," I said, nodding.

He gestured to the seats in front of him and we sat down while he made his way to sit in his large black chair that oddly resembled a throne.

Nice.

"Edward tells me your investigation has become a bit complex," he said, placing his large forearms on his desk and leaning forward. His green eyes flickered between Greer and me.

"Yes, it seems like we've uncovered something quite intriguing, with Ms. Roberts caught up in the middle," I said dryly.

"How are you fairing, *Greer*? I understand your investigation is filed under the guise that you were falsely entered into the Trials. Seems convenient that the shifter who was your lead suspect is dead. As well as some other immortals … How odd that you would stumble upon something like that, when your case is so trivial in nature." He spoke carefully, his sinister eyes glued to Greer's, looking for an ounce of an emotional reaction.

Where was he going with this?

She didn't flinch or cower away. The only reaction was a blink.

"Do you want to become an immortal, Ms. Roberts?" he said, leaning back. His large gray hands ended in long, sharp claws. They gently scratched the leather and looked like they could slice someone open in the blink of an eye.

"It has never been a priority of mine," Greer said coolly, leveling her green eyes to his.

"Interesting … What do you think of immortals? Such as myself or Ambassador Kyra?" he said, gesturing to me with his long claws.

I clenched my jaw, my fire humming in response to my irritation.

What exactly was this meeting about?

"I tend to judge people based on their character. Not how many years they are given … What do you think of humans, Mr. President?" she said, tilting her head to the side and smiling sweetly.

President Adonia chuckled at that, a disturbing low and sinister sound. A pointed way to avoid her question.

"Why exactly are we here?" I said, clipping my words, trying to pull his attention away from Greer. His eyes flickered to mine like I was simply a minor inconvenience.

"Greer Roberts's investigation is troublesome. And since you, *Ambassador Kyra*, have seemed to have taken a special interest in this particular case. I wanted to remind both of you that since you are both involved with the Immortality Trials, which is highly publicized, it is of the utmost importance that this investigation remains confidential for the safety and security of our nation … I would hate for anything to happen to either of you, or your friends—Luxton, Waverly, and Nova, was it? Especially now that more resources are needed to investigate a case with real evidence, since we now have three dead immortals," he said, flashing his many rows of teeth.

Greer stiffened beside me. He acted like all of this was her fault. As if she asked for this to happen. And he was threatening us to keep our mouths shut or else our friends would pay the consequences.

I growled low in my throat.

First, Greer had been falsely admitted to the Trials.

Then, Edward had blatantly refused her twenty million for the counter contract and patronized her while ignoring her case.

Afton had visited Greer.

Our lead suspect, who was a wanted criminal and an immortal, had shown up dead.

Then, other immortals had been murdered.

Now, the President was threatening us?

What in the actual hell was happening here?

I was determined to get the bottom of it, but I couldn't pull it all together. There were still too many missing pieces and parts that didn't add up.

The President's words pulled me from my swirling thoughts.

"I would hate for anything to happen to those friends of yours who seem to be offering an unusual amount of aid to Special Agent Waverly and her team. It seems a bit odd for a blood witch and shifter to throw in their support for a human…" he said, clicking his nails on his desk.

I narrowed my eyes at him and opened my mouth to speak when Greer stood abruptly and slammed her hands on the desk, leaning toward the President. Amusement flickered in his eyes as he watched the anger roll off her. It was as if time stood still for a millisecond; the air seemed to crackle from the tension pouring off her.

"Mr. President, I can assure you that the security of *our nation* is a genuine concern of mine. Considering that you all allowed an impostor to enter me into the Trials, I can guarantee that my intentions of finding and prosecuting the individual responsible are rooted in the safety and security concerns of everyone in the Republic. Even humans. Now, if you'll excuse me, I have to go prepare for my next trial," she said in a controlled snarl, and swiftly turned on her heel and walked toward the door.

Adonia raised his brows as if the outburst simply delighted him.

"I suggest you find a way to control your pet, Ambassador. No one likes a bitch that bites," he said smugly, dragging his claws across his desk.

Fire burst at my fingertips and Greer whipped around, her hand on the door. "Let it go, Ky. We're leaving," she said, staring directly at the President, daring him to say more.

I stood and gripped the back of the chairs we were sitting in, and let my heat course through them.

"You better be careful, Mr. President. Immortals are dying. I would hate to see who's next..." I said as the chairs in front of me sizzled and fell to ash.

He stood abruptly, anger flashing in his eyes, and snarled at me, his claws extending out an inch. "Did you just threaten me, boy?" he growled.

"Merely an observation." I flashed a smile, letting fire dance at my fingertips. The urge to send my power out to blow up everything in his office swirled around in my head as anger clouded my eyes. I stalked out.

Greer was already headed toward the waiting room. I heard the President throw what I could only assume was his desk across his tidy office with a roar as I quickly followed her.

"Are you going to survive that as an Ambassador?" Greer said, concern falling over her features as she nodded toward the sound of wood splintering and breaking behind the large metal doors.

"I'm an immortal," I said with a wicked grin. "Plus, it would have been worth it." I winked at her, wrapping my arm around her strong shoulders.

"The others are probably worried. And I can't wait to see the look on Lux's face when we tell him we pissed off the President..." I said, inhaling the sweet scent of her.

She laughed loud and bright, some of the concern falling away from her features.

We walked into the elevator, past a secretary who looked pretty indifferent to the rampage currently going on down the hall.

Greer pulled me close. I placed my hands on the sides of her head and looked down into those intoxicatingly bright eyes. There were only a few inches between those beautiful lips and mine.

"He may not like a bitch that bites ... but I think you do," she said against my mouth and gently bit my bottom lip.

I groaned in response, pressing myself against her, and I could feel her laugh.

"Bite me, please … anytime, really…I'm yours," I said, and could feel her laugh again.

"Yes, you are," she said, placing a gentle kiss on my lips.

I was falling for Greer Roberts.

And I really hoped it wouldn't explode in my face.

Literally.

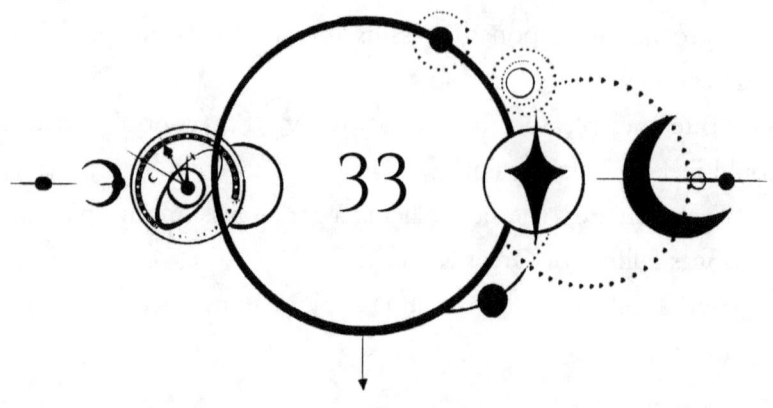

33

Greer

The next two weeks blurred by as we tried to navigate the President's attempt at scaring the shit out of me, the investigation—which apparently now included a lot of time spent with Sutton despite Kyra's grumblings—dissecting my dream with Nova, training with Kyra, and my job at the Shadow Lounge.

I had tried to contact Andromeda about my dream, but the ITC had weird rules about contestants outside of the Trials communicating without previously knowing one another. I didn't want to risk losing more of my life cycle in order to harass her about my dream. I knew she was okay. And that would have to do for now.

But I couldn't shake off the dream with my mother and how she had confirmed my worst fear of falling victim to what caused her to take her own life. The anxiety and darkness tended to creep up on me when I stopped moving, so I tried to keep in a constant blur of motion.

So here I was, the day before my third trial, meeting Lux at his downtown office to talk to some technologist about tracking down the money trail that inevitably had to exist for the suspected dead shifter who *most likely* posed as me.

I didn't even know what to think of my life currently. It didn't feel real. I felt like at any point in time someone might jump out and say, "Jokes on you!"

I knew that would never happen, but a girl could dream.

Once again, I was uncovering more than I thought just to get out of these stupid trials.

There had been some good to come out of it: Kyra. Waverly. Nova.

But why it had to happen at the risk of my life cycle and others, I wasn't really sure.

Sighing, I opened the door to the lobby entrance and nodded at the receptionist and walked over to the elevator with my own key-card. Everything was cool, modern, silver, and white in Lux's office. He liked things clean, organized, and up-to-date.

I pressed his floor number and whooshed up to where the elevator opened up to a huge open floor plan with couches, long conference tables, and cubicles artfully arranged around the expansive floor. I smiled and said hi to people as I walked by; most of them knew who I was because I used to frequently visit Lux for lunch before the whole Immortality Trial mess.

I walked into a frosted glass office where Lux sat with his computer and a smattering of papers on the long white table.

"Hiii…" I said.

Lux looked up and flashed his killer smile.

"Be still, my heart. You should charge for those," I said, fanning my eyes dramatically, and he sneered.

"I'll start charging for mine as soon as you start charging for those hair flips you do to get people to do what *you* want." He threw his head back, laughing, and I couldn't help but join in. It felt good to laugh, especially with Lux.

"Where's the technologist?" I said, looking around.

"She's coming," he said, glancing at his computer.

I had told Lux earlier that I didn't necessarily need to meet with whoever he found, but he had insisted that I be involved since it was my life on the line and this could break the case.

Which I couldn't argue with. I just had a lot of things on my plate at the moment.

I plopped down next to him and drummed my fingers on the table, trying not to let my thoughts run wild.

A lithe female entered a few moments later, carrying her laptop. Glasses were perched on her small yellow beak and her hair cascaded around her in white curls. I could see small pink and yellow wings poking out behind her back. Her whole body was pink, and she was wearing black joggers and a cropped hoodie that showed off her pink belly, with white high-top Converse.

They were extremely casual at Lux's offices and she looked comfy as hell.

"Hi, I'm Greer," I said, standing up and shaking her hand.

I had stopped trying to guess people's races and species a long time ago. If they wanted to share they could, but if they didn't it was no big deal. It was honestly more abnormal for a human to be here than anybody else.

"Hi, I'm Merrit!" she said in a light voice.

She sat next to Lux, who closed his laptop and folded his hands over his computer.

"What did you find, Merrit?" he said, settling into his chair and leaning back. His gold eyes were attentive as ever, and he was dressed casually in jeans and some designer tee.

"I looked into the complete accounts, data security, and history of Emmett Dahm," she said in her airy voice.

She flipped her laptop around so we could see.

"The last deposit made to his account was for five million dollars, and the bank note and wire were encrypted, so it took me a while to decode where it came from." She looked nervously between Lux and me.

"That sounds like money for a serious job. Like what he would have done if he impersonated someone in the Trials..." Lux said idly.

"Um, the name on the account that it was transferred from was Ezekial Gilmore," she said quietly.

"My dad? Well, this is ... unexpected," Lux said, shocked.

"I don't understand..." I said slowly, reaching over to grab Lux's hand, wrapping my fingers protectively around his. The wounds of his parents went deep. They had hated the way Lux lived his life because he didn't make power and wealth the center of it. He lived and loved freely, with no concern for the Gilmore line or their business. They had openly disagreed with and denounced him for being who he was his whole life.

And they were also very dead.

Merrit looked at our hands and made a small chirping sound. "I thought that was a bit odd. Considering the death of your parents was confirmed a few years ago," she said. "So then I began digging into the accounts and realized they were indeed offshore accounts of your father's that were always encrypted and not included in any of their will paperwork..."

Lux gripped my fingers tighter and leaned forward, his jaw set.

"Keep going, Merrit. I gave you access to everything so you could find an answer for us." His whole body seemed tense.

She nodded and continued on. "I looked at the will and business transfer that happened at their deaths, and none of it included this particular account. However, I found more encrypted files that took me quite some time to decode and get through. They were linked to a special project that had both of your parents' names on it. I thought this project might have pulled funds from this offshore account, because the expense report associated with it had an extensive list of costs associated and detailed for the project," she said, suddenly getting a bit nervous again.

Her beady eyes flickered between us as she clicked on her laptop a few more times and pulled up a file labeled *Immortalem Mortem*.

"Immortal Death," I whispered, secretly thanking the Latin elective I took in college.

"It's, um…" Merrit started and looked at Lux's attempted indifference again but the emotions in his eyes betrayed him and a muscle in his jaw twitched.

"Keep going, Merrit," I said gently, nodding.

"It contains research, trial reports, and description for a serum called Immortalem Mortem," she said hurriedly. "And there's a video that I think you should watch, Lux."

She moved her small fingers across the board until a screen popped up, showing Lux's dad, who had the same eyes, hair color, and skin as Lux. But instead of braids, a nose piercing, and tattoos, his dad's hair was cropped close to his scalp, and wrinkles lined his mouth and eyes. He wore a button-up shirt with a red tie loosened around his neck, and it appeared he was sitting in what used to be his office. The room was dark. A glass of what I could only presume was scotch was in his hands, and he was sweating.

"Play it," Lux said through gritted teeth.

Merritt made another small chirping sound as she pressed play and Ezekial came to life.

"Luxton, I assume you will be the one to find this," his dad said. His eyes had dark circles underneath them. "I don't know if you'll need this. But your mom and I have created a serum that renders immortals dead. Truly dead." He wiped his hands across his face and looked back and forth as if something behind the camera might jump out at him.

Lux's mouth was set in a tight line.

"We were commissioned to do this … We don't know who, only that it's extremely classified information and whoever it is, is extremely powerful. And they are dangerous. They paid us an impossible price. This video might not be necessary, but if something happens to us, we have things in place that will destroy the formula for the Immortal Death Serum. We should have never taken on this project, but it's too late for that now," he said, and suddenly a loud crash interrupted from behind him.

He swore underneath his breath and quickly tapped on the screen and the video ended.

"When was this filmed?" Lux said in barely a whisper.

It felt like the air in the room had been sucked out.

Lux's parents had created the serum years ago, and it was just now killing immortals? How was that possible … Why was this just now discovered and why was the serum just now being used?

And what the hell did it have to do with me?

"A few hours before their death in the helicopter accident," Merritt said, her wings fluttering a bit behind her.

"Why is this encrypted file just now being found?" I said quizzically.

"They were buried, encrypted, and filed in a way that nobody would have ever found them. But Luxton asked me to be thorough and comb through everything. I created an algorithm and AI program that could scan the files and flag anything to do with accounts, encryption, and other oddities. It took quite a long time. If you were doing it manually, it could have taken months or even a year. I believe the instructions for Lux were probably going to be left by his parents in a way that Lux could find, but they never got the chance..." Merrit said, swallowing slightly, and her wings fluttered again from nervous energy.

"Lux..." I said, turning toward him and squeezing his hand again.

His eyes looked like his mind was a million miles away.

"I always thought the helicopter accident was a little too neat … I just wanted it to all be over, so when they investigated it and said they didn't find any foul play, I didn't push further. But someone killed them for that formula … I don't know why that's connected to you now, G, but we're gonna fucking found out," he said.

He turned to Merrit. "Merrit, you know what the stakes are for this. Be careful. Let me know if you run into any trouble or find anything else. Keep digging further to see what other details you can dig up. We need to know who commissioned my parents to do the formula and who would have had access to them during that time. And keep looking into that offshore account, because we need to know who is operating it," he said, rambling off commands.

"I'll tell you if I find anything else." She nodded and stood to leave.

"Thank you, Merrit." Lux said.

"I saw what you did for that woman," she said quietly to me. "I hope you win, Greer." She lifted the edges of her beak in a smile, then hurried out.

"I don't understand..." I said, the words tumbling out. "First, I get falsely entered in the Trials, then our lead suspect was murdered, and other immortals start dying … and suddenly our lead suspect was paid by someone operating an old account of your parents, who apparently made a serum that kills immortals years ago? And then the President threatened us? And Edward is just, well, a prick who doesn't believe a damn thing I say? What sort of tangled mess is this? How the hell did all this happen? What does it mean?"

My head was reeling. Absolutely nothing was making sense.

"I need you to not worry about this, G." Lux took both of my hands in his and locked me into his gaze. "I need you to focus on tomorrow, okay? Can you do that for me? I will figure this out. I always do," he said seriously.

Lux just found out his parents were probably murdered because they created the death serum that had killed three immortals to date, and he was worrying about me.

"Sure," I said, squeezing his hands and then wrapping my arms around him.

His chin rested on the top of my head, and I wondered again how I got here. And I hoped that I could solve the riddles and puzzles of the room tomorrow.

I mean, how hard could it be?

I had a degree in engineering, for gods' sake. I could escape a fucking room.

☾

I took the long way home to clear my head. It was still a bit chilly out, but you could feel spring coming slowly.

I needed a moment to gather my thoughts and wrap my head around what was going on. It was all connected, but how? I felt like I had some of the puzzle pieces, but others were missing, and I didn't even know what the hell the puzzle looked like.

I couldn't make sense of how the death of Lux's parents was somehow connected to me being falsely admitted to the Trials. It made my head hurt and made me feel like a pawn in someone's game—except I didn't know who my opponents were, and I didn't know the rules. I felt like I was sinking into a dark hole with no clear way out, and I had to slam down the anxiety before it wrapped itself around my heart and squeezed too hard.

I turned the corner to our building and found the stranger from the bar with the ice grip and boyish looks leaning against my building as if he was waiting for me. I had forgotten about this part of my life.

Add it to the list of things that didn't make a damn bit of sense.

"Hi, Greer," he said in his musical tilt. He was wearing the same thing he was when I last saw him, and he was showered with an ethereal glow and that strange ripple of power.

"You didn't tell me your name last time…" I said slowly, stopping to stand in front of him.

This wasn't good. I could not handle any more weird or bizarre things happening to me.

People were walking on the other side of the street and in and out of my building, but no one paid me or this stranger any mind.

"Afton," he said, ice eyes twinkling as if he was delighted I'd finally asked his name.

"A word of advice for tomorrow … Remember who you are, Greer," he said, as if he was telling me a secret.

I snorted. "Thanks."

I slowly walked away, but then that ice grip found its way to my wrist again, and it was like walls slammed down around us, suspending time and space.

Again.

The air was pulled out of me and my body went cold.

I wondered if this was what death felt like. A suffocation of your own lungs as the rest of the world stood idly by and death took you in the form of a glowing boy.

"Greer Roberts, your story is unraveling quickly now. You must make it to the victors' circle." He looked around us as if just now noticing his power of touch caused the whole world to pause.

"Good luck," he said. His grip disappeared and my ears popped. I fell to the ground as the air crashed back into my lungs and the noise of the world slammed into my head.

I was getting really fucking tired of that guy.

I gasped, pulling air back into my lungs.

I received some quizzical looks as I got up, mulling over what *Afton* had said. I could feel a headache snaking its way to my temples as I headed up to the penthouse and tried to figure out if this guy was helping or hurting me.

I guess I would see tomorrow at the trial if his advice held true.

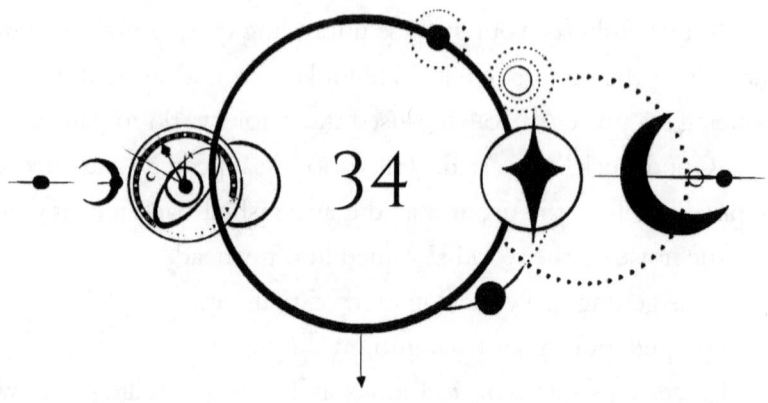

34

Greer

I arrived the next morning to the same building we had congregated for the parade. Except today, it wasn't chaotic. It was oddly quiet and calm, like the world was holding its breath for this trial.

I walked through the glass doors into the lobby and a dwarf met me there, smiling tightly and guiding me toward the elevator. I tried to control my breathing and not psych myself out. I had arrived at nine a.m. and the trial was to begin at eleven.

I was too busy trying to breathe that I didn't realize we had arrived on our floor until I was being pushed out. I silently cursed myself for not paying better attention to what floor we were on. I didn't know why, but it felt important in case I needed to run screaming from this trial.

Long beige hallways broke out in front of me and toward both of my sides, with unassuming black doors lining the walls. It felt like a creepy hotel or something. Everything was neutral and devoid of any personality or life.

The dwarf walked down the corridor to the right. He barely said anything as he flashed a keycard at a scanner near a door that had no obvious marking to differentiate it from the other bajillion black doors, and pushed me inside, slamming the door behind me.

"Fucking thanks, asshole…" I grumbled to myself.

A TV was in the middle of the room. It dropped down from the ceiling. There was a plastic table and chair directly under it and a door directly across from the one I got shoved through. The TV began speaking in a robotic voice as words rolled across the screen.

"The next trial will begin in an hour and forty-three minutes. Please put on the new uniform you have been provided, and someone will be along shortly to check that you are fit to compete. Good luck."

The new outfit was a full black catsuit made of a weird soft sweater material. It was lying on the table along with a pair of standard-issue military black boots. I stripped off my leggings and oversized hoodie to slip into my sweater suit.

I wondered why we needed this for just an escape room.

Uneasiness spread in my belly as I tried not to think too hard about what the outfit meant. Everything in the trial was extremely intentional, so I couldn't help but wonder what this was about.

I sat down in the plastic chair and three seconds later the dwarf was back, barging into my room with his grumpy face and pursed lips.

"I could have been naked, you know," I said irritably, and he didn't respond to that.

Instead, he commanded me to stand, turn, bend, etc., until he finally pulled out a pen-sized object that was thin, white, and gave off a faint blue glow. He hovered it over my entire body and the thing blinked green when he finished. He gave a satisfied smirk and pulled out a water bottle and protein bar, handing them to me. He swiftly turned on his heels and left.

"Thanks…" I said halfheartedly.

The timer on the TV screen read an hour and thirty-three minutes. Great. I had that much time to sit here and stew while people at home and at watch parties began to eat, drink, and be oh so merry.

I slumped into the plastic chair and leaned my head back, closing my eyes. I was exhausted from … well, everything. I had been working my regular hours, staying up late with Ky, doing our training in the morning, staying up-to-date on the investigation with Waverly and Nova, trying to figure out the connection of Lux's parents to our suspect … I was starting to feel run ragged.

I didn't even know what my life would look like once the trial ended, or if I lost. The thought had goosebumps exploding on my skin. Losing wasn't an option.

One day at a time would be great.

One hour at a time would be better.

I tried to count back from 100 to ease my brain, and it worked a little too well.

I dozed off in my sweater suit, telling myself I was simply resting my eyes.

"You have five minutes until the trial begins. Good luck!" a voice sounded.

I groaned and lifted my head, my neck aching.

"Oh, shit!" I said, scrambling out of the chair, breathing heavily as I tried to shake off the fogginess of my impromptu nap.

I felt like a truck had run over me. The nap didn't help at all. In fact, I felt confused, sweaty, and even more sleep deprived.

I looked at the water and protein bar sitting in front of me and nearly shoved the whole bar in my mouth. I chased it by guzzling down the water bottle and rubbing at my eyes ferociously.

I could do this.

I looked back at the clock and it said less than two minutes.

"Please step up to the door." The door that was directly across from the door I had come in. It glowed a faint blue color.

I forced my feet to move and stepped up. The minutes ticked by until the countdown began.

"Three, two, one … Begin," the cold electronic voice said.

The door swung open to reveal a completely black room, and I stepped in as the door slammed shut behind me.

I was suddenly very afraid. Why was it pitch black?

I had no idea that things were about to get much, much worse.

The third trial had always been an escape room.

I don't know why I was surprised when it wasn't.

I don't know why I was surprised when they changed the rules, since the Trials were always made to make us suffer for the pleasure of others.

I don't know why I was surprised by anything anymore, really.

I was in a black box. A TV lowered itself from the ceiling, the only light in the space.

"You must face the fear that haunts your head and your heart. You have sixty minutes to overcome it. Good luck," the robotic voice said, and the TV flickered off.

I was in complete blackness once again. I couldn't even tell where I had come in from.

I tried not to panic.

But what the hell did that mean? My worst fear? How would they know that?

"Greer," a voice said from behind me. A voice I knew. It was my mom's again. Except it wasn't. It was … different.

"Sweetie," she said, and I slowly turned. This was the mother I knew better. Her body showed the wears and tears of the years around her eyes, mouth, and the way her shoulders hunched in.

"I killed myself because of you. And the same thing that ate at me will eat at you too…" she said, pity and blame in her eyes.

I was cemented to the floor. It was my mom, but it wasn't. The words coming out of her mouth were not hers.

They were not.

"She's right, you know," Lux said. I whipped my head behind me. He was standing tall, his arms crossed, looking down at me.

"You're a burden … And you're too weak to fight what inherently lays inside of you. Of course a human would be consumed by the anxiety and depression that sits in their bones … It's nature's way of taking care of those who don't belong," he sneered. "I hate having you in my own home. You're like a stray cat that just won't leave. No matter what I do, you always stick around. It's pathetic. I wish you would disappear from my life. I should have let you kill yourself back in college."

Each word was a knife to my heart, and my knees were weak.

This was not happening

I slumped to the floor as Lux and my mother closed in.

"This is not real, this is not real, this is not real…" I whispered, looking anywhere but them, but the room was so dark I could barely see my own hands. It was as if all the light had been sucked into their bodies and the darkness clawed at mine.

My greatest fear was what was inside me.

And this trial was exploiting it so painfully I felt like my heart had been ripped in two.

"You couldn't even get a real job … You take advantage of everything I've given you. I should have kicked you out of my life years ago. You add nothing to my life," Lux said angrily, closing in, his gold eyes simmering as I curled into myself on the floor and started shivering.

Lux looked like Lux. It felt too real in the way his hair was tied back and the tattoos swirled around his brown hands. But he couldn't be here.

He wasn't here, right?

"Do you think I actually care for you? You're nothing but a piece of ass. You have zero value to me and society. You can't even afford your own life, you pathetic *human* girl. I only comforted you so I could use you … Your demons are disgusting. No one could possibly love you with the mess inside of you. It's society taking out the human trash, if you ask me," another voice sneered, and the pit in my stomach threatened to swallow me whole.

Ky was standing above me now too. A look of disgust on his beautiful face.

I nearly vomited on the floor as his ruby eyes shot daggers into me.

"Someone impersonated you at the Trials, Ms. Roberts, so that there would be one less useless mortal on this earth. Especially someone as insignificant as you … You are nothing without Luxton and Kyra. You killed your mother and that ugliness inside you is reflected on the outside. It's repulsive." The Trial Lord materialized behind my mom. A new face to validate the fears that clawed at my throat day in and day out.

That I had killed my mother. I had left her to die. And that the same thing that took her was waiting to take me too. The darkness that infected her mind and her body would one day convince me that my only reprieve was death. That I would not have the power, the strength, to beat it back, and it would drag me under and kill me slowly and painfully. Like it had almost done before.

"Disgusting creature … of course she would be infected from the inside out," Nova said, her fire eyes showing only disdain. Her silver stars were still.

I whimpered and curled further into myself on the floor.

My head whirled, and my eyes started swimming with tears. They rolled down my cheeks and my lip trembled. The people I cared for the most hated me. They saw the deepest and darkest parts of me and they wanted to run. They wanted me gone.

I wanted me gone.

The slimy claws of the emotional void I was when my mom died started to wrap themselves around my legs and arms, slithering to my throat. It felt like something was choking me, wrapping its hands around my neck and squeezing the life out of me.

"It's your fault the immortals died. It's probably your fault that my parents died too. This whole mess revolves around you and we would all be better off if you were dead," Lux jeered at me.

"You're lucky we tolerate you. You're just a dumb slut who can't do anything more than spread your legs," Ky said, hurling each word at me.

I choked on the little air that was still in my lungs. The sobs wracked my entire body as a numbness and coldness clung to every inch of me.

"No, no, no, no, no…" I whispered, hugging deeper into myself.

"Look at her groveling on the floor. She is wasting everyone's time, energy, and resources. She surrounds herself with powerful people so she doesn't have to do shit. A weak, insignificant human," Waverly spat at me.

"Just someone's little bitch. She can't find her purpose because she has none. The world would be a better place without you, Greer Roberts," said the President of the Republic.

And every person from my childhood. Neighbor. Classmate. Friend. Enemy.

They all began to materialize in the darkness, leering and chanting and calling out all the things I had never dared said aloud. They threw them at me like rocks and daggers, each word slicing deep into my heart and bleeding me to my very bones.

I was a broken human, and the world would be better off if I wasn't in it. I would be better off, because at least the pain in my heart would stop. It would cease to exist, just like me.

I didn't know how long I lay there shivering and empty, unable to move or do anything but pull further and further into myself. The tears had stopped after they had poured out in waves, and I no longer had anything to feel except the trauma around me.

It felt like hours I was pelted with the hate and disgust of every single person I had ever been in contact with.

I closed my eyes and told myself again.

"This is not real…" I said as the people got closer and closer. Their laughs and jeers wrapped around me and filled my body, my lungs and my brain.

I needed to get out of here. I started crawling on the floor, only to be met with the faces of my friends and family laughing at me. Verbally assaulting me and spitting on me.

I started to hyperventilate.

I couldn't think or hear anything.

"I'm afraid," I whispered, the sound lost in the sea of people around me.

It only takes a moment, five seconds of bravery … Nova's words found me here.

"But I am not weak," I said, closing my eyes and pressing my fingers to my them.

I just needed five seconds to be brave. That's all I needed to get through this. I clenched my jaw.

For some fucked up reason, I was here.

In this space, fighting for my life, and fighting for something more than myself. I told myself I would no longer sit idly by because of the disgusting nature that was the Trials. I would no longer turn a blind eye to the convenience of my life with Lux.

I wasn't fighting for just me. I was fighting for a world where this bullshit didn't need to happen for people to prove their worthiness. A world where the luxury of immortality wasn't necessary. A place where the rich and powerful didn't control everyone else. Where people were free of the oppression of the government and punishment of the Trials, and didn't have to hurt themselves or others for a shot at a better life.

I was fighting for something that I no longer had the privilege to ignore, and I didn't want to. I was fighting for a better world, for everyone. But I couldn't do that if I didn't make it to the next trial. I needed to show everyone, including myself, that I was willing to do what it takes to fight against a world that never gave me a chance to win.

"I will not fail," I said a little louder.

I needed to end this, not just for me. But for everyone else. Everyone else who felt like the only choice they had was no choice at all. That the end of their pain could only be found in death. That society had never taken another look at the poor, mortal, and weak and let them suffer, practically handing them to death itself.

I used that anger.

I let it consume me.

Heat my belly. My bones. My head.

Time seemed to stop as I pushed to my feet and everyone around me froze. These were not the people who loved and cared about me. This was an illusion. One meant to reflect the one within my own psyche. But I would no longer let it have power over me. I would no longer be afraid of what was inside.

Suddenly, Ky's face came to mind and his words wrapped around me.

Your light burns brighter than anything I've ever seen. Nothing will take away that brilliance. You will not fail, Greer.

"No," I said, looking around at the frozen faces.

"NO!" I screamed, and the illusion cracked like broken glass. The faces of those around me seemed to shatter into a million pieces until they were nothing more than dust floating around in the darkness.

"I am not broken. I am not useless. I am human. And I will not fail," I said, steel working its way into my words as I hurled my anger at the room and the chorus of people around me.

Sound, light, and nausea all crammed into my body in an instant.

I screamed and fell to the floor again, and I was in an ordinary room. Just four beige painted walls and a TV screen above me.

"Greer Roberts. Passed," the electronic voice said as a door opened behind me and I dragged myself through it. I wondered how much time had passed.

I felt like I had been emotionally wrung out. Exhaustion threatened my eyes and body.

But the Trials had other ideas.

☾

I stepped into another room, and a new screen lowered from the ceiling.

"Congratulations contestant. The next trial starts now."

I stood there with my jaw on the floor. I couldn't participate in another trial right now. I swallowed hard and listened to the cold voice that gave me goosebumps.

"Our esteemed donors have requested we up the ante for the Immortality Trials, and we are excited to offer you this new challenge to test your humanity. Change your clothes and start the next trial. We have taken something important from you. You will find it suspended underneath the Blood Bridge. If you take something that does not belong to you, you will be automatically disqualified. You are only allowed to touch and retrieve what is yours. Once you retrieve it, you will bring it back to the headquarters.

"The first 250 people to do this will move on to the final round. Begin in haste, contestant. Good luck!"

A pile of new clothes, another water bottle, and an additional protein bar lay on the table that I had pretty much napped on.

I stripped off the weird black sweater suit they had forced us in and pulled on the new clothes, which resembled a leather jumpsuit, with the same combat boots.

My head was reeling as I was trying to understand why in the hell the fourth trial was happening *right now.*

How had they known what my worst fear would be in the third trial? That was the most intimate detail of who I was, on display for the whole world to see. How would they have accessed that?

I tried to push the third trial away in my mind to be dealt with later. I couldn't give up now. I had to pull myself together and make it through.

And why was there pressure to make the Trials more than they already were? Who was pulling the strings here? How could they change the rules so quickly and ruthlessly? I groaned in frustration.

Too many questions and not enough answers. I tried to rein myself back into what was happening presently.

It felt like I had been in there for hours, but I knew it had to have been less than an hour. Time was not a luxury I had right now. I needed to move, *now*. The Blood Bridge was all the way across town from the escape room arena. I had no idea how many other contestants were already released from their rooms.

I flung open the door and saw some others do the same. Everyone had a wild, feral look in their eyes like they were out for blood.

Two females sprinted through the corridors and collided with fists, snarls, claws, and blood. I swallowed and looked around to see several other contestants emerging from their rooms to the expansive hallways. I took off at a run as several others did. I wasn't paying enough attention to the other contestants, and it cost me.

Someone slammed me into the hallway wall from the left with the force of a semi-truck, and I cried out in pain as the impact left stars dancing in my eyes. My head landed with a loud crack against the wall and I slid to the floor.

"Stay down, human," they snarled.

My vision faded in and out for a moment before I could figure out how the hell I was supposed to get up.

I gasped and felt blood trickle down my forehead as I tried to stand and stumble down the hall. I lifted my hand to my forehead and pulled it away with a sticky mess of red.

"Shit," I muttered as more doors slammed open.

I shook my head, trying to clear my head, but it made it much worse.

I growled and shoved the pain down, starting to run toward the nearest exit and avoid others at all costs, ducking and avoiding fists, legs, and brushes of power against my back that breathed magic.

I slammed into the emergency exit doors first with several others behind me, nearly falling as we were all pushed into another hallway. I felt hands shove at my back, and I dug my heels down and pushed back so as not to go careening toward the ground.

"You're strong for a human…" someone whispered in my ear as I felt a giant wave of force into my back trying to shove me down.

"Fuck!" I snarled as I lost my footing and was brought to my knees. They cracked against the floor.

Laughter followed and I shot up, running toward the door for the stairs.

I heard the footsteps of more pounding toward the exit door that led to the hallway to the stairs. I burst through the door where it opened to a set of stairs and saw a female straight up fly up and over the stairs and land the ten stories below at the bottom, look up, wink and disappear out a door at the bottom.

Well, *fuck*.

Someone else behind me slammed into my shoulder and nearly sent me toppling down the stairs.

"Focus, Greer," I growled. This was where people were out for blood.

Human blood.

My blood.

I needed to be more careful.

I hammered down the stairs two at a time, trying not to fall flat on my face. My legs burned and my lungs were crying out, but I couldn't stop as hundreds of contestants started plowing down the stairs behind me.

If I got caught up in the horde, I would die.

I tried not to let that fear slither into my body as I crashed into the heavy metal door at the bottom and I was shoved out onto the quiet streets. It was as if they had cleared out the city for this.

I could see other contestants coming out through a door further down—another exit, I was sure. Grunts and screams could be heard from there as they exploded out of the building. People would die in this trial at the hands of others.

The stakes were too high.

I would *not* be one of them.

My heart rate started picking up speed once again and anxiety laced its way along my spine. My fingers flexed. I desperately wished I had my switchblade or my dagger. Anything that would make me feel less exposed and vulnerable.

Some started using their powers right away, flying, running, transforming, levitating. And I just stood there, looking around for literally any form of transportation I could use. Frozen in place.

The world seemed to slow as I heard the thunder of footsteps, the clash of bodies, bones breaking, and screams.

I tried to focus on what was right in front of me.

I will not fail.

There were some cars on the streets, a few bicycles, and a motorbike. I tore over to the motorbike and silently sent up a prayer to the neighbor in my trailer park days with my mom who had shown me how to steal a bike and a car "just in case." I looked around frantically for some sort of object I could use to cut the wires and came short.

Damnit.

Now would be a great time for some claws or gnashing teeth.

A steady stream of males and females were racing toward the bridge now. Fights were breaking out; some lay motionless in the streets and others were covered in blood.

My heart sank. I would have no way to make it through the other contestants safely if I didn't have some sort of transportation. The bike was my easiest and best option. I needed to figure out a way to get it moving, and fast. I had already lost time.

A loud pop sounded and Afton stood beside me. His hand in mine.

"Holy gods," I said, gasping for breath as I backed into the bike.

Who the fuck was this guy?

"Try this," he said with a wink. The world paused for one millisecond, and then he disappeared.

I felt like I got whiplash as the air found its way back into my lungs and stars danced in my vision.

I would not pass out right now.

My heart beat a million miles a minute, but I wouldn't give into my fear. I had to get to that bridge. I would think about Afton later.

He had placed a small razor blade in my hand. I blinked at it for a solid five seconds, then I got to work. I quickly cut the wires and shorted the circuits, and the engine revved to life. I kept looking around and over my shoulder frantically, waiting for someone to attack, but no one did.

I tried to calm my shaking hands as I shoved the razor blade into my boot. I hopped on the bike and revved the engine and tore off toward the bridge. Passing some screaming contestants and a few obscene gestures.

The hell that was this trial seemed to finally have an end in sight —if I could make it—but this is where the real danger was. People were out for blood. They had entered survival mode, and I would be an easy target.

The wind ripped through my hair as I sped to the bridge and shook the thoughts of danger out of my head. I needed to focus on what I could do now, in this moment. I was no good for anything if I was dead.

I felt a slam of energy into my front and I screamed as the motorbike buckled underneath me and I swerved wide, trying to gain control. I leveled out and tasted blood, realizing I had bit down on my tongue, hard.

"Damnit," I said, trying to contain my anger.

I whipped my head around to see who had thrown their power at me and couldn't tell. It didn't matter. I just needed to keep going.

I took a deep breath and zeroed in on the task at hand.

What exactly was taken from me?

I was about to find out.

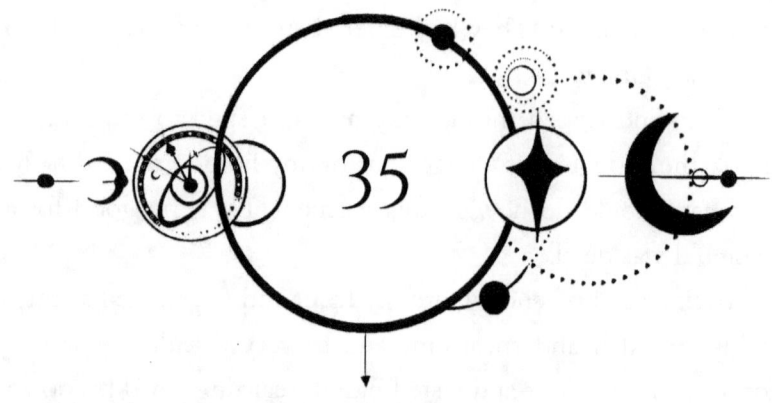

35

Greer

The wind was relentless against my skin as I pushed through the streets on the bike.

I could see some people in the air, running alongside me, and in my side-view mirror, racing for the bridge. I felt a surge of power nick my back and I pushed the bike harder. I would not be knocked off. I didn't even swivel my head to see who or what it was. I only pushed forward.

Another surge of power slammed into my side and sent me in a hairpin turn.

"Shit!" I screamed as I banked to the right and nearly became parallel to the ground. I shoved my foot out and smelled burning rubber as I fought to stay upright and pushed out, revving the gas harder.

I screamed and swore loudly as blood still leaked down my forehead. Some of it had gotten into my eyelashes, and my body was starting to feel like a rag doll from when I had been slammed into the wall, the ground, and nearly down the stairs.

I clenched my jaw and pushed the bike harder, more aware of those around me looking for a way to knock other contestants out.

344

Was this allowed?

Could they really change the Trials at the drop of the dime?

Of course they could. They wanted to put on a show.

And we were the entertainment.

I really needed to stop being surprised by these types of things.

I turned the final corner to where the Blood Bridge stood tall and proud in its dark, rusting glory and swore loudly.

The bridge spanned the river that ran through the heart of the city. The water was still and calm, albeit freezing I was sure. Hanging above the water were people.

People suspended in webbing, about thirty feet above the water and fifty feet below the bridge. A small crowd of contestants stood in awe as the bodies gently swung in the chilly afternoon breeze. An eerie stillness that settled over us as we gazed at the monstrosity that was the fourth trial.

One of those bodies was mine.

But which one? Who had they taken?

It looked like I was one of the first thirty or so people there, and there clearly wasn't an obvious way to get them out of their odd webbing sack. The calm was giving way to sticky tension and in the blink of an eye, another fight broke out. I didn't have time or power to step in and help. All I could do was look away.

I slammed on the brakes and tore off running, silently thanking Afton for the razor blade that was now tucked safely in my boot. A few contestants had peeled off and were searching for something sharp to cut their person down. But in order to do that, you had to scale underneath the bridge, cut your friend loose, and dive in after them?

The solution wasn't exactly clear for someone with zero powers.

Not to mention, I didn't know how you could tell who the hell was in each sticky webbed sack.

I groaned in frustration as those with flying affinities flew through the throng of bodies. The first body fell with a splash into the water, followed by a second splash as the contestant dove in after them.

A few people were shooting their powers at the webs that belonged to their friends, seeing if they could cut them down first and then catch up to them in the water. No one was scaling the bridge yet.

I looked around at the chaos of the crowd of contestants and realized I needed to get away from them quickly if I wanted to make it to the final trial. Dread crawled along my skin. I would have no other option but to climb the damn thing and cut my person loose.

Some people were standing on the bridge, some in the water and on the shore below, while others were standing in the surrounding area, trying to shoot their shot.

I took a deep breath and walked to stand on the bridge and swung my leg over the metal bar. Someone behind me gasped and another chuckled.

"Stupid human girl. There's no way you can win this one…" a voice said.

"She won't make it," another chimed in.

"Humans are always at a disadvantage," added another voice.

"Why did she even enter?"

The remarks kept coming as I stood on the wrong side of the railing and looked down at the stilling water below and the hanging bodies. I swallowed.

I could do this.

I had climbed plenty of rocks before. I could climb a bridge.

I maneuvered my body down the railing, past the metal scaffolding and to the metal bars that crisscrossed one another and connected with a parallel bar that all the bodies seemed to be hanging from. I moved my feet down the metal rims and slid down the diagonal scaffolding, keeping my breath steady.

I looked down at the bodies. I couldn't tell who anyone was and there were a lot of them. I eased myself off the metal and down onto the bars that ran parallel to the river. The bars connected on the outside of the structure, but on the inside they ran parallel to one another with several feet between them, which meant I would need to stick to the outside and scale the bridge from there.

Fuck.

I heard another splash below as a body was cut loose.

Who would they take?

Splash.

Kyra would be watching.

Which meant it had to be Lux.

I looked out through the metal rims to the hundreds of bodies suspended in the air.

"Lux!" I screamed, scanning the bodies to see any sort of reaction. No sounds had come from the people who were hanging, and I had to believe the ITC had done it on purpose so that we had to figure it out ourselves.

I felt a brush of energy and magic against my ribs. I clung to the bars, swerving my body behind the metal. I would not be taken out by another contestant. Not now. Not ever.

Another splash.

Shit.

"LUXXXX!" I bellowed again, looking for his long, black braided hair—and that's when I saw it. A swish of a snow tiger's tail sticking out of the back of a hanging web sack fifty feet ahead of me.

"LUXXXXXX!" I yelled again, and it flickered in response. I maneuvered myself to the outside of the metal bridge again and tried not to think about how if I fell, I wouldn't have enough time to swim to shore and try again.

I had one shot to get to Lux and then cut him loose.

Carefully, I started to move across the outer side of the bridge. The wind felt like it had paused, and the rest of the world seemed to fade away as I zeroed in on that snow tiger's tail, slid my toes across the bottom, and gripped the cold metal of the bridge.

My gaze traveled down, and it was a mistake. I was about half-way there, and my right foot slipped. I clung to the metal with my hands as my body slammed into the unforgiving steel. Tears threatened to fall, but I regained my footing and continued on, inch by inch, to that tail.

Sweat was dripping down my back and I was breathing hard, my forearms practically screaming when I found myself right above him. I could see the top of his head, and the tail had gone still.

I crouched down and felt the webbing beneath me. Carefully, I took the razor blade out of my boot and began sawing at the spider silk.

"Good luck, sweetheart," said a gravelly voice behind me. I whipped my head to the side and sliced my hand simultaneously, looking for whoever said that.

Blood pooled across my palm. "Shit," I cursed.

Blinking my eyes, I didn't realize he was behind me until it was too late.

A boot slammed into my shoulder blades as the same voice said, "This isn't for you, girl." I plunged forward, slamming my nose into the cold steel before I began to fall. I desperately hugged the beam, the razor blade cutting into my clenched fist and my feet dangling.

Black clouded my vision, and I wondered if I had a concussion from the force of the kick. My breath barely rasped out.

A splash sounded below, and I could only assume it was from the contestant who had tried to kill me.

I couldn't swing my legs back up to the beam; everything hurt too much. My adrenaline was dwindling. My arms were screaming and my nose was pouring blood. The razor blade felt like it was now permanently embedded into my skin, and the spider silk holding Lux was now about a foot away.

I sent up a silent prayer to whoever was listening and swung my legs and hips in the direction of Lux's long silken rope.

And then I let go.

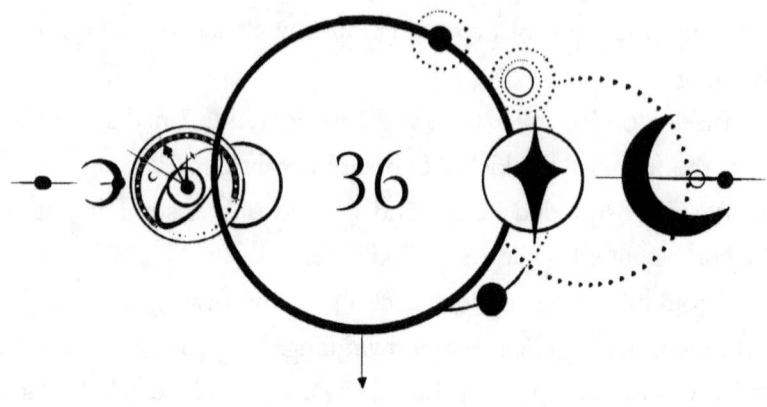

36

Kyra

I watched in horror as some brute of a male slammed his foot into Greer and she toppled off the metal beam underneath the bridge.

She was hanging on by arms alone and blood was everywhere.

I could tell her emotions were fried from the surprise they'd pulled in the escape room. It was the most disgusting and horrible thing I had ever seen.

Watching her horrors and worst fears play on screen for millions to see was a new level of brutality I didn't know existed. And the fact that I showed up and the thing that was me but wasn't me said those things to her made me want to strangle the entire ITC right then and there.

I didn't understand how they could possibly know all those things about her. How they could have found out such intimate details of her mind. Or who was calling the shots with all the trial changes. The trials were built on traditions of thousands of years. Why were things being changed now? It was unsettling, to say the least.

And poor Greer had been pounded with power over and over again as she had raced to get to Lux. I scrubbed my hands over my face and through my hair in frustration.

And here I was at a watch party for the whole godsdamned thing.

I looked around helplessly at the raging party around me of rich patrons and ITC employees. Someone cheered and people laughed and gasped as Greer hung on for her life. She seemed to be the chosen piece of entertainment. I wondered if the President had done this on purpose just to spite us and remind us who really had the power here.

I clenched my fists and walked over to the table housing the tablets for individual screening and stalked over to the edge of the roof past the official tent where the President himself was clapping the Trial Lord on the back and congratulating him on making the ITC of this year absolutely unforgettable with the quick turn of events involving the collision of the third and fourth trial.

The rich and wealthy smiled, laughed, and gawked at the contestants and I snatched a flute of champagne from a passing tray and downed it in one sip. I hoped the burning in my throat would calm the fire and explosive energy that tingled underneath my fingertips.

The viewing party was on the rooftop of the ITC headquarters. They had turned it into an incredibly luxurious bar and screening area. It made me want to light the whole thing on fire.

I worked my way to a quiet corner with a tablet and sunk into one of the chaise lounges, focusing the screen on Greer.

We didn't even have time to prepare properly for this one. Not that it would have helped, because the fourth one was always a wild card. You never knew what they were going to throw at you and this one was no exception.

I had watched in agony as Greer had swung her leg over the railing and shimmied her way down to the bridge and then worked her way over to Lux. I had no idea how or when they had taken him, but I sure as hell knew he had put in a fight and that made the corners of my mouth twitch.

She was swinging her legs and hips on the screen, and then she let go.

My heart stopped as she sailed through the sky several feet and wrapped her body around the silken thread that held Lux up, then started to slide down until she was literally on top of him.

She looked down as if she was talking to him and pulled something away from her hands and her whole palm exploded in blood. It started to leak onto the thread as she sawed back and forth with a four-inch razor blade.

Her face was already covered in red from several injuries, like it had been in the first trial. She was being targeted by others. My stomach was in knots at the sight of her bloody, bruised, and beaten.

Several other bodies splashed into the river and were accompanied by their companions, who dragged them out of the water.

Finally, only a small bit of thread held them together and Greer slid her body down so she was wrapped around Lux. In one big push of effort, she took a big swing and sliced the last bit of thread so that they plummeted into the water.

A large splash ensued, and I stared at the spot where they had disappeared into the blackness.

My stomach knotted up as I waited for them to resurface.

I vaguely heard someone say that the webs dissolved in the water, but the ITC had done something to render the other person without powers, or make them "mortal," during this trial so they could not use their powers to help the contestants. How Lux had then kept his tail was a mystery to me. He probably convinced them he always had it.

I scanned the water, waiting.

Watching.

Until Greer's red hair crested the water and Lux's dark hair bobbed up.

They clung to each other and swam for the shore where others were pulling themselves up.

I looked at the stats on the screen and saw that twenty-five had already completed the fourth trial. Some were still stuck in trial three, and some were already disqualified from both.

I swallowed and watched as they kicked and swam to shore, where Greer stood and nearly fell from what looked like dizziness. Lux caught her.

She shook her head and grabbed his hand and started running the shoreline up to the steps that zigzagged back and forth up against the stone wall that encapsulated the river.

They ran across the park to the motorbike that she had stolen.

I had never seen anyone hot-wire a bike before. I was constantly amazed by the things that Greer Roberts did. But I swore I saw Afton next to her for a millisecond when she first rounded on the bike. I don't know where she got the weapon either.

Too many things happened at once and all I wanted was for her and Lux to be safe.

She fumbled with some wires and then swung her leg around as the engine whirred to life and Lux hopped on the back, wrapping himself around her, and she took off.

They were headed toward us.

They would meet an ITC employee downstairs in the lobby to be counted as complete. With the tablet in hand, I weaved my way through the party, eager to meet them both down at the bottom floor and get the hell out of this party.

"Leaving so soon, Ambassador?" said the cool voice of the president behind me.

"I would like to congratulate *my girlfriend* downstairs, Mr. President," I said coolly, slowly spinning to face him as his eyes danced with amusement and he flashed his rows of teeth.

I would love nothing more than to unleash my fire power on the entirety of this rooftop soiree right now. But I kept the anger and rage at bay.

"Tell her a job well done, for a human," he said and nodded, turning away before I could get a word out.

I flickered my eye over to the tent that was his and where an abundance of alcohol and food lay for him and a small explosion erupted, sending meat, fruit and cheese everywhere. The crowd screamed, and I chuckled as I disappeared through the chaos and found my way to the elevator, where I let the doors slide close as I smirked at the befuddled President.

I looked down at my screen and saw that Greer was nearly here. The blood was still covering her face and her hands, but the look in her eyes told me she wouldn't stop until she got here. She was now also sopping wet, but she looked fearless.

I arrived at the bottom floor to see that some of the contestants were being checked in and bracelets were being removed from their friends, evidently the way they had rendered them powerless.

There were people everywhere, and I looked down to realize that Greer and Lux were now rounding the final corner of the street to our building, but something was wrong.

Greer looked frantic and was trying to break on the bike, but they were not slowing down.

They were coming too fast. It was like someone had short-circuited the wiring. Possibly someone with the power of electricity had tampered with the bike when she was saving Lux.

I cursed. I should have kept an eye on the bike, even though I couldn't do a damn thing about it. I almost made something else explode, but I knew that would be wholly unhelpful in this situation.

I couldn't help them. If I so much as even stepped outside she could be disqualified for cheating, so I ran to the glass doors and pressed myself against them as Lux and Greer roared down the street and they flung themselves off right in front of the glass door. I watched behind the glass as they skidded to a stop and the motorbike crashed about 100 yards down and exploded, causing everyone inside to panic and screams cascaded around me.

I flicked my hand toward where flames danced around the bike and they immediately winked out. Greer and Lux were piled together, beaten and bloody right outside the door.

"Get up, Greer," I whispered behind the glass.

Greer lifted her eyes to meet mine through the glass and I could tell she was in too much pain. The day was catching up to her and she didn't have much fight left.

Her nose looked wrong and there was blood seeping from her hairline and a little at the corner of her mouth. She now had fresh scraps against her cheek from flinging herself off the bike. I didn't even know what the rest of her body would look like underneath the contestant uniform.

Lux pushed himself off the ground and they both reached for the door handles and pulled them open.

The inside of the building seemed to still as they limped right past me, leaving a trail of trickling blood to the nearest ITC agent and Greer said, "Greer Roberts."

The ITC agent nodded and unhooked Lux's bracelet. Lux rubbed his wrist.

"Greer Roberts, trial four complete," she said, and I shoved my way to her and Lux.

Greer smiled and it was as if that simple action sent the full heaviness of the day crashing into her.

She swayed and stumbled back. I reached out, hooking my arms underneath her as we sank to the floor. I looked at Lux to see the damage he had endured, but it was minor cuts and bruises. He squatted down next to us, his eyes full of concern.

"We need a medic!" I said to no one in particular as I lowered her to the ground.

Her nose was broken badly; it needed to be reset. Blood was trickling slowly out of her nostrils and a black eye was forming.

She closed her eyes. "My nose..." she rasped out. "Needs to be reset"

"I know," I said, gently holding her head in my lap.

"Someone's coming," I said, looking around as we started to draw a crowd and I heard the door open to more contestants coming in.

She reached a bloody hand up to her face, "G, don't..." Lux said and then with a crack she reset her own nose and screamed, her mouth a bloody mess, her teeth red.

The whole room went silent, a few cameras flashed, and a group of medics rushed forward as Greer's body spasmed in pain.

"Third time's the charm," she said, smiling through blood-soaked teeth and half-lidded eyes looking at Lux.

I looked at her dumbfounded, and Lux broke into a grin.

"We can take it from here, Ambassador. Mr. Gilmore," one of them said, but I couldn't hear or see anything except Greer's screams and her mangled face and hands.

They lifted her up on a gurney and started to roll her away as she groaned out and fluttered her swollen eyes open.

"I'm pretty sure I have a concussion," she said to no one in particular as Lux and I followed the medics.

"Family only," one of them said.

Lux and I looked at each other with our mouths open as the medic went through the swinging doors and left both of us to stand there, each covered in her blood and stone-faced.

"I am fucking family," Lux grumbled beside me and I felt his pain. I wanted to be by her side. In fact, I never wanted to leave it and I hadn't even told her that. We hadn't even talked about being exclusive or anything like that.

Too much of life right now was getting in the way and I could lose her without even telling her how I felt. I needed to do that. As soon as possible, before it was too late.

"Are you okay?" I said, turning to Lux.

"Fine," he grumbled.

"What did she mean by third time's the charm?" I said, trying to work through the details of everything that just happened.

"She's broken her nose three times and reset it herself," Lux said, pride in his eyes.

"You're kidding, right?" I said, looking at him like he was insane.

But he just chuckled and said, "I fucking hate these trials."

"Me too," I said, placing a hand on his shoulder. "Me too."

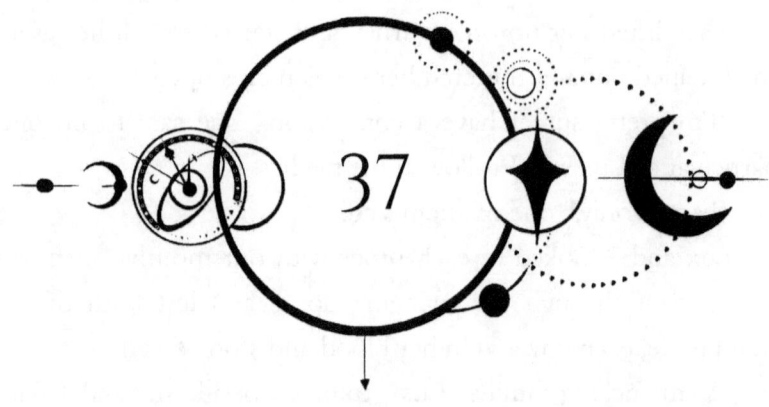

37

Greer

T he last human left in the Trials ... Did you see the way she reset her nose at the headquarters? I didn't even know that was possible..." a voice boomed, chuckling.

"Or the fact that this time the Ambassador was the one who held on to her while her other boyfriend Luxton Gilmore just stood there after being rescued?" a female voice commented.

"More on the most interesting mortal left in the Immortality Trials, Greer Roberts, when we come back. And her standing in the ITC and betting houses, stay tuned," the male announcer said.

The voices flowed into my pounding head and I tried to recap the events of the last two trials.

I had been emotionally ripped apart and the raw edges of it could still be felt in my chest. The immense pain I had when I had reset my broken nose still echoed on my face and I felt the flutters of a concussion wrack my brain.

I groaned as every part of my body ached and screamed to be left alone. My tongue was heavy in my mouth and I cracked open my eyes to see Waverly dozing off in a chair next to me and myself lying in a hospital bed connected to an IV.

"Waverly…" I wheezed out, and she whipped up from her position, her dark hair flying around her beautiful brown skin in her typical FEC uniform.

"Greer! Oh my god, you're awake," she exclaimed. Her eyes were taking me in like I had just sprouted horns and then tears started to form in her eyes.

"Water?" I said a little more clearly.

She swallowed and hurriedly wiped her eyes and grabbed a pitcher and a cup from the table next to my bed. She quickly handed me the cup and watched me swallow it and filled it up twice more before I could work to sit myself up in bed.

"Lux, Kyra, and Nova have all been here to see when you might wake up. I'll let them know that you're awake now," she said, swiping her phone from her pocket and frowning at it.

"What's wrong?" I said, settling into a seated position and trying to rearrange my body in the least painful way possible. I touched my nose gently with my fingertips and winced. I was almost sure I had a black eye … or two. I let my fingers touch my hairline and felt stitches there.

Perfect. I was back to being a well worked on punching bag.

"I have five missed calls from work," she said, pursing her lips. "I left my phone on silent because I didn't want the ringer to wake you…" Her pink eyes looked disturbed.

"Call them back. It might be about the case," I said, sounding like myself again. I gave her a half-smile that made me wince.

"I'll be right here," I said, trying to tell her with my eyes that it was okay to go find out whatever the hell was going on with the case.

"I'll be right back!" She ducked out of my hospital room.

I turned up the TV volume to listen to what the media was saying about my performance in the last trial. Even though someone had literally tried to kill me or at least make me lose by kicking me off the bridge.

And someone had tried to knock me off the bike, two or three times? I furrowed my brows, trying to remember, and it hurt my recovering nose. Then the image of Lux and I speeding toward the headquarters without the use of the brakes flashed in front of me and I realized I was losing track of how many times people had tried to kill me.

I sighed.

At least there was only one more trial.

I hadn't really thought much about what it would mean when it was over. At least, not really. And what it would mean to lose? Or win?

I had only been thinking about getting through the next day. And what if I never found out who entered me? What if we never found out how the deaths of the immortals and Lux's parents all connected back to the ITC? And what about Afton? What the hell did he mean by my story was unraveling quickly?

I had been living hour by hour and using the injustice of the Trials to fuel my fire, but I didn't actually have a plan for when this was over. I wanted to be out of this first and then I could think more clearly of a plan and how we could get rid of the Trials once and for all. How I could bring the person who started this mess to justice and how we could catch the immortality killer.

But it was nearly impossible to think about until I was free from it.

I didn't know if that made me a coward or not.

And I hadn't really shared my idea of ending the Trials once and for all to anyone. At least, not in a way that implied I was serious and committed 100% to the cause of it. I didn't have all the answers of how to make things better for everyone, but I knew the Trials would never be a part of a better world.

I briefly thought of what Kyra would think. I knew he didn't like the Trials, but I hadn't explicitly told him I wanted them to burn in hell. We also needed to talk about us … The list seemed to grow in my head as I thought through my feelings for him and my stomach started to flip-flop at the idea of laying myself bare for him.

I shook my head and immediately regretted it as stars danced in my eyes and the announcers on the TV sucked me back in as they continued to speak about the anomaly that was *Greer Roberts*.

It was weird to hear me talked about like I wasn't a real person fighting for my life. As if my greatest desire in the world was simply to compete and win the Trials as no mortal had done before. Like immortality, power, and wealth were the ultimate prize. And maybe it would be for other people, but it wouldn't be for me. I never wanted any of this.

I hadn't given much thought to actually being immortal. It seemed impossible that I would come in first anyway, so it was a moot point.

I rolled my eyes at my supposed love life and love triangle with two rich, powerful and attractive males. It made me want to throw the remote at the screen.

I had barely stayed alive and won thus far, and they were talking about my life like it was some movie. I shuddered to think of how my life could have ended at any singular point in time.

I could have not captured my hostage … I could have easily not made it to shore. I could have given into the fear. I could have fallen off that bridge. But I didn't.

I will not fail.

Waverly came back in, looking really pissed off. Her short body was rigid and agitated and she had fire in her pink eyes. No … not fire. Rage.

"What happened?" I said.

Did someone else die?

Oh gods, did Kyra die?

Maybe the President of the Republic was killed, wouldn't that be good news?

I smiled at myself with the last one.

"I've been kicked off the case … And put on an extended leave..." she said slowly, as if not believing the words that came out of her mouth.

"What?" I practically shouted, sitting up straighter and then wincing again and settling back into my bed.

"I was told that I was suspended for acting without integrity and unethically by allowing consultants like Nova and Lux on the case for you and clearly I wasn't putting all my effort into catching the immortal killer because I was *distracted* with your case, so they suspended me." Her hands balled up into fists.

"I'm sorry, Waverly. Is that … normal?" I asked tentatively.

"No, I think we were close to something. Something that the FEC and the ITC don't want us all knowing," she said thoughtfully as she came to sit on the bed, facing me.

"I think they are afraid of what we stumbled upon..." she said, looking out the window that showed the sun and the city.

I swallowed and closed my eyes. "I don't understand," I whispered.

Waverly waited for me to continue.

"I don't understand why I am a part of this. What could they possibly want from me? What could they possibly gain?" I said, exhausted by the entirety of it.

I didn't know what would happen next.

The last trial was different from the others. We would be ranked by how we finished, and glory, power, and fame would be given accordingly.

Out of the 250 to compete, only the top 100 would receive rewards. The others would receive punishments by life cycles and government servitude. But the top 100 would be granted extra years and wealth depending on how they finished. Only the winner would be granted full immortality.

Again my thoughts wandered to the nonexistent plan I had for after this.

Who am I when this damn thing is done?

Did they think I would go on with my life and pretend it didn't happen? Date Ky like two normal beings? Live with Lux in our cushy penthouse? Hang out with Waverly and Nova like we didn't speak to the living dead together?

None of that seemed imaginable.

There was no going back to normal. Especially if the games continued to go on. They were destroying people's lives and families, acting like because you had to voluntarily participate it made it okay, when in reality as a society we had allowed something like this to continue. To hurt. To let the powerful and rich stay that way and push their own selfish agendas.

I wouldn't let them continue to get away with this. The decision to end the Trials burned deeper into my heart. I let it heat my core and the anger engulf my body.

Save it for after the final trial, Greer.

Waverly's hand found mine and she gave it a gentle squeeze.

Both my palms had been shredded when I had clung to the spider silk web and the steel beams in the last trial while trying to hold on to the razor blade Afton gave me. They really got scraped up when I had flung myself off the bike too. My poor mortal body was really taking one for the team here.

My thoughts got snagged on my magical *friend* though.

Afton.

What the hell was I supposed to do with him? I still didn't know who he was or what he wanted. I just knew that he had helped me in his cryptic way and had power that felt ancient and overwhelming. I hadn't told anyone except Ky. And I had only told him about the first visit, not all the others. It felt like such a small thing in the midst of so much chaos, but maybe it wasn't.

"I don't know, Greer. I don't know what they are after. But this isn't over. We are not giving up. Lux has resources and I have people on the inside I trust," she said, smiling at me and weaving a soothing undertone into her words using her siren gift.

"You just need to focus on getting better and the last trial. You're the last human left..." she said, her voice taking on a sad tinge.

I never looked to see how many humans had entered this round. It wasn't something I thought I could handle. My heart already felt like it was being torn in about eight different ways, and I couldn't bring myself to continue to add scrapes and bruises to it.

"When's the next trial?" I said, trying to hold my voice steady.

"Thirty days. It's the maze this time ... but with added ... obstacles," she said. It seemed like she was at a loss for words.

Anything new and inventive for the Trials was a bad sign. Like the escape room turned fear fighting and the fourth trial popping up immediately after the third.

Why were they throwing curve balls into the great tradition of the Trials?

Was that also connected to the other events that were happening?

My head hurt the more I thought about it. Too many oddities were occurring. I just didn't know what the thread was that connected it all.

"The trials have never been this spontaneous. They are always calculated and cruel, but these 'new' pieces don't make sense. Why would they be rushing the timeline of the Trials? Why did they suddenly change the third trial? I feel like we are missing something. It's right there but I can't see it or grab it, but I *know* it's there," I said, shuddering.

Waverly nodded and gazed out the window thoughtfully. "Something is shifting out there, and I can't help but feel like all of this is only the beginning," she said quietly.

Thirty days until the next trial.

Thirty days until my fate would be sealed, one way or another.

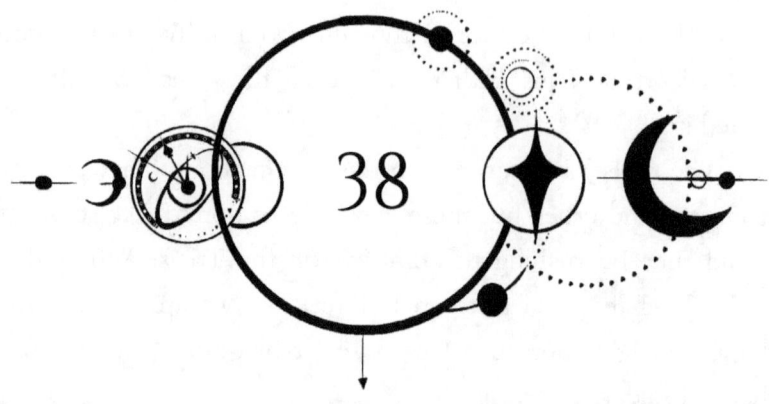

38

Kyra

We were all gathered again at Greer and Lux's penthouse.

It seemed to be quite the regular thing since Lux had called me that one afternoon to meet. Greer was tucked in beside me with a blanket wrapped around her. Her face was still a little bruised from the last trial, but they had cleared her to leave the hospital this morning. Nova had given her another tin of her special balm and at this point she should just stockpile it since after every trial she seemed to need it over her entire body.

How she didn't have an irreversible concussion either was a miracle in itself since that male had slammed her against the steel beam. Or when the motorbike brakes failed and she leaped off it with Lux.

The memory of it all made my body tense and my fire tingle beneath my palms. I wanted to choke and give matching injuries to anyone who took a swing at Greer. But tonight things seemed lighter. The last trial was in three weeks. Greer's birthday was a little over a week away and Lux and I were already planning a surprise for her that would hopefully take her mind off the last trial for a night or two.

I didn't know what would happen after the trial. It seemed a bit odd that whoever entered Greer in the trial hadn't made another move toward her. There were a lot of strange things going on that seemed to be connected but the one behind it all still eluded us. It didn't make much sense why Greer might be a part of it either. If they wanted to enter someone in the trial, why would they have picked her?

She was doing remarkably well for having absolutely zero powers or enhanced physical abilities or prolonged preparation for the Trials at all. Nearly every trial had been designed to test the body's limits and strengths, and unfortunately she was inherently at a disadvantage being completely mortal. But she was holding her own.

It made me smile to think of how fearless she had been and how hopefully after this last trial some sort of normalcy would return for her. For us. And whoever had entered her in the trial would stay the fuck away.

I still hadn't told her how I felt though. I was struggling to find the right time where we were alone and she wasn't recovering from injuries. What if she didn't feel the same way? I tried to push it to the back of my mind and remind myself that there were more pressing matters at hand, like the last trial.

Which was a bit concerning because everyone would be ranked on how fast they finished. The last trial would be a maze this time. Which was dangerous in itself, not to mention if you ran into other contestants, which you undoubtedly would, someone would not be walking away.

I shuddered thinking of how my final trial had been me roaring toward the finish line, flames blazing with little regard to others' safety. I had badly burned many contestants. Thankfully, I hadn't killed anyone, but I was so consumed by the need to have some sort of freedom from the cursed stone in my chest that I was completely blinded by winning.

After I won, I had promised to use my newfound power, influence, and wealth to help others, instead of using the fire and explosive power within me to cause irreparable harm like I had to some of those contestants that day. Like I had been cursed to do.

I turned my attention to the room in front of me as Greer laughed loudly and freely next to me while reaching for another slice of pepperoni and jalapeño pizza. There were pizza boxes strewn around the glass table and empty beer bottles littering close by.

Greer's laugh nearly undid me. She had a calmness and lightness to her that I didn't often get glimpses of. Her smile tonight was bright, and her green eyes lined with blue were clear and joyful.

She had demons that haunted her that she rarely touched on. I had gotten a deeper glimpse of them while she had gone through the fear room in the third trial. But again she had done away with them with extraordinary speed. Some of the contestants never made it out and had to be dragged out whimpering and broken.

I didn't understand why the trial had taken such a dark turn. It wasn't supposed to be anything but the regular escape room. It had been that way for years. But then again, the fourth trial wasn't supposed to be slammed against the third one. Odd things were happening behind the scenes of the Trials this year and I was anxious to have Greer out of them.

But I could explore those thoughts later. The scent of Greer wrapped around me, vanilla with a little bit of spice, made a warmness spread through me. She snuggled her body closer to mine while talking to Nova.

Sutton had gotten an invite tonight, which bothered me a little. The bastard still hadn't apologized for outing my curse. But Lux and him seemed to be sharing glances and flirty banter, so I swallowed my pride. It wasn't a bad thing to have a necromancer close, but preferably one who didn't drag my skeletons out of the closet. Especially because my skeletons could kill.

Nova and Waverly sat next to one another, fingers intertwined despite the fact that Waverly had been fired, or rather suspended, a few days ago from the FEC. Another strange event ... There were too many swirling around Greer as the epicenter that it made me nervous in a bone deep way that I couldn't exactly explain.

"Why are you scowling?" Greer said, pushing away from me slightly and pinning me with her gaze.

"I'm not scowling," I said, trying to relax my eyebrows.

She furrowed her brows in a dramatic way and pouted her lips. "This was the face you were making," she said through her teeth, and I burst out laughing.

"You're right, sorry. Just lost in thought is all. About, well ... everything, honestly," I said, sighing a little.

"But I'm happy to be here with you. Sorry I was a million miles away," I said, leaning in close and brushing my lips against hers and pulling her practically in my lap. She made a little squeaking sound that no one else seemed to notice but me. It made desire shoot straight to my groin as she adjusted her finely shaped ass right on top of me.

Her eyes went wide and then they burned with something else and a wicked smile played on her lips. And she leaned in so her breath tickled my ear and her mouth moved against it, making my whole body go rigid.

"Stay with me tonight," she purred and nipped my ear lobe. I growled deep in my throat and swallowed hard.

"You should be resting…" I said carefully as her body seemed to melt into mine and the rest of the room disappeared.

"Well, just be gentle…" she said, winking at me and moving her fingers to play with the hair at the nape of my neck. My cock started to harden even more. This woman would be the death of me.

"You know as much as I love the sexual tension that you two are giving off, I'm going to politely tell you to get a room…" Lux said, smirking at us with an arm now lazily over the back of the couch very close to Sutton.

"It was just starting to get good." Nova chuckled darkly, and Waverly snorted while Sutton simply observed with a small smile twitching on his lips.

"Don't have to tell me twice … Nothing like a near death experience to get you going," Greer said wickedly, hopping off me and dragging me toward the hall.

"Does no one else think this isn't a good idea? You got discharged … Today!" I exclaimed as she dragged me down toward her room and I got a flash of us in the hallway the other day with her against the wall.

"Good luck with that argument!" Lux called from behind me as Greer slammed the door shut, her eyes looking hungry.

I prowled toward her and pinned her against the doorway with my hips, and pulled her arms up and over her body.

"I'll take extra care with you tonight," I said, gliding my lips across her jaw, careful of the tenderness of her broken nose.

She started to melt her beautiful body against mine and in one swift motion I picked her up and laid her down on the bed and to her protest plastered myself against her, my erection pressing into her perfectly sculpted ass.

"You will lie here, Greer, and let me do the work," I said into her ear and moved my mouth down her neck to her collarbone. I worked one hand over her heavy swollen breast, teasing the nipple, and the other hand moved to slide underneath her leggings.

"Just relax and enjoy," I said darkly as I drew lazy circles around her clitoris.

"Do your worst," she breathed, and I pressed harder against her back and drove her toward ecstasy with my mouth and hands until her body was a puddle next to me and her eyes became heavy and finally she rested.

I wrapped myself around her careful of the battered and bruised parts of her still healing and let myself be filled with the scent of her and sex until sleep took me too.

39

Greer

I t had been almost a week since I was discharged from the hospital, which meant that there were only two weeks until the last trial and my birthday was tomorrow.

Today, I was spending it with Kyra training since the last trial would be basically a free-for-all for other contestants to go after one another to finish before others and there was a 100 percent chance I would be targeted, because the news had been relentless about me being the only human in the last trial and I would be a "easy" target to eliminate.

And I had been targeted before.

Again.

And again.

Fucking great.

So here I was on a surprisingly warm and sunny afternoon with spring in the air on my rooftop patio trying to use the dagger I had been working with since the second trial to use it as an extension of my arm. It didn't feel the same as my switchblade, but it was a better option and I was used to the weight of it in my hand and strapped to my thigh now.

I was fast, agile, and had good reflexes, but people would underestimate me. I would let them get close and then use their own arrogance against them. Plus, it wouldn't slow me down and no automatic, electric, or gunpowder weapons were allowed, so my options were limited. But people would use their powers. The last trial was always an all-out brawl to the end and I was becoming a very visible target.

Sweat dripped down my arms and my back as Ky would move in and attack. I would try and pin him down and he would give pointers on what I could do better. My body was already strong and I was scrappy, but I had never been trained to fight to the death or like my life depended on it.

Which it literally did.

I had had my fair share of back-alley brawls with creepy men and bullies throughout the years, but nothing like this.

"Don't hold back this time with your dagger, Greer," Kyra said, breathing heavily, his dark hair sticking to his forehead. He had discarded his shirt a while ago and looking at him made me want to throw my body against his until I was full of everything Ky.

But there would be plenty of time for that after I survived the last trial.

I twirled the dagger in my hand. I had only nicked and cut myself a few billion times before I got to the point of being able to handle it the way I did now. It fit against my blisters perfectly and felt natural in my fingertips.

"Are you not going to use a weapon?" I said when Kyra squared toward me with nothing in his hands.

"I don't need to," he said wickedly as fire danced on his fingertips.

Right.

My eyes widened as I thought about those flames licking my skin and burning to the bone.

"I won't hurt you, Greer. I'll be careful, and this is just to help you fight against someone who relies on their power," he said in a hard voice.

I could see desire in his eyes too, probably because I was in a sports bra and leggings, wet from wiggling around with him on the ground. But there was something else in it. He was scared. For me. For me to fight someone like him in the Trials.

I nodded and set my jaw and bent my knees, dancing on my toes.

Kyra lunged at me and heat rippled off him, but it was like he was moving in slow motion. I easily sidestepped him and turned and slid my foot across his back leg and he tumbled forward. The world and my head were spinning a bit.

Was he moving that slowly on purpose?

He growled and was on his feet in an instant and he shot a plume of flame at my belly and again it came at me as if it was moving through syrup. I exhaled and ran toward the flames and Kyra's eyes widened in fear as I slid beneath the heat and took out his feet beneath him and he landed, barely catching himself with his hands before he slammed his face into the ground.

Why was he holding back?

The air around us seemed suspended. He launched himself up and went to grab for my wrist with the knife, but I was faster. I blocked his hand and wrapped my arm around his neck and slammed my body against his and threw us to the ground. My other hand with my weapon pointed at his belly.

"Why are you holding back, Kyra?" I teased as he held up his hands in a sign of surrender.

I felt like my whole body was buzzing and zapping with energy and there were bubbles in my blood. I rolled away from him and stood, and he looked up at me quizzically.

"Greer, how did you do that?" he said carefully, looking at me like I had grown wings or something.

"You slowed it all down for me, that's how. Stop doing that," I said, playfully pushing his shoulders.

"No, I didn't..." he said, tilting his head at me. "You moved faster than almost anything I've ever seen before."

"No. You were slow..." I said, the buzzing in my body and ears starting to fade away.

"What do you mean I was slow?" he said, cupping my chin and looking deep into my heart with those ruby eyes suddenly filled with awe and wonder.

"It was like you were moving in slow motion, and when you shot fire at me, it was like it was coming through syrup. And then I knew what your last move was before it landed..." I said, trailing off, realizing that none of that made sense exactly.

"Do you remember the first time we ran together?" he said quietly, still searching my face and moving his hands down my arms, leaving goosebumps in his path.

"Yes." I swallowed.

"Was I slow the last thirty or so yards to your apartment building?" he slipped his hand into mine and led me to one of the chaise lounges that was sitting on the deck. I sat dumbly.

"Yes."

"What happened in the second trial when you pushed the last hundred yards or so? Was everything else slow then?" he asked gently.

"Yes..."

"Greer..." he trailed off.

"How long was I in the third trial?" I blurted. It had felt like an eternity. I still couldn't believe I had made it out in time to save Lux and pass the fourth trial.

"Maybe ten minutes?" Kyra said, crouching in front of me scowling.

"It felt like hours, that I was in there…" I said carefully. "And when Afton grabbed me, time basically stopped.." I said, scrunching up my nose and closing my eyes, not sure how to make sense of this.

"Afton?" Ky said neutrally.

"Yeah, the, uh, guy with the icy grip from the bar, he's visited a few other times…" I said, still in a daze.

"Greer…" Kyra said, looking at me with something I couldn't quite place in his eyes.

"What the fuck?" I blurted, standing abruptly and pacing back and forth before he could say anything else. Ky recovered and sat where I had been moments ago and placed his elbows on his thighs and looked thoughtfully at me.

"I think you have powers," he said, testing the words out as if they might scare me.

"Both my parents were human … How could I have powers?" I was shocked. Powers didn't just manifest randomly. They were in your blood.

"But you don't know very much about your dad," Kyra said, looking at me intently with those scarlet eyes.

"I know he was human," I said, stopping and looking at him.

"Okay," he said simply, not pushing the idea.

"Why would I just now be experiencing these … things?" I said, struggling for the word I was looking for, waving my hands frantically in front of me.

"I don't know … Usually powers manifest fairly quickly and at the latest during puberty," Kyra said softly, watching me carefully like I might spontaneously combust.

"Stop looking at me like I'm about to break," I snapped.

One eyebrow raised and he chuckled softly. "I'm sorry, I just know that this must be shocking," he said and then leaned back on his hands and smiled.

"Greer, this is a good thing! This can help you." He said the last bit gently.

He truly believed it, and he was trying to reassure me.

Except what was I? What exactly were my powers? I was super fast and super slow? And I had a few weeks before the last trial. Whereas other people had been training with their power for years.

Was I still a human? I groaned because even though, yes, this was helpful you could just slap my ever-evolving identity crisis to my list of things to work through on my to-do list.

"But what am I?" I said, looking at my hands and flipping them over like I was seeing my small pale blistered hands for the first time ever.

Kyra got up and interlaced his fingers with mine, and I looked up at him.

"Powers are typically instinctual. So it seems like they might have been aiding you this whole time without you knowing it. Normally, as a child you would have gone and sought a tutor or teacher for your powers—usually a relative or your parents, since it's normally hereditary. But since this is uncharted territory and the Trials are so close, I would say that the best bet is to let it guide you. Don't question it and let it be the extension of you it needs to be…" Kyra said with a kindness in his voice.

He knew this was another layer that was helpful yet incredibly disruptive.

"What happens after the trial?" I said, sliding my sweaty body against his and his arms wrapped around me and rested his chin on top of my head.

"What do you want to happen?" he said quietly.

"I want things to be less chaotic..." I said. Without murders, crimes, and fighting for my life. A world where the Immortality Trials didn't exist.

"Will you be there?" I said, suddenly pushing away from him and studying his features. I still had a lot of unanswered questions about Kyra. But I knew that with time I would tear down my walls to let him in and he would do the same.

"Be where?" he said, barely audible.

"At the end ... waiting for me," I said, holding my breath. I didn't know why this felt important, but I needed to hear his answer.

"I would wait at the ends of the earth for you, Greer," he said in that deep voice that wrapped around me and stroked every part of my exposed skin.

"Kyra..." I said, wanting to tell him the words that had been on my heart for the past few days.

I love you.

How was that even possible? How had he become such an essential piece of my life and what the fuck was I supposed to do with that after the Trials? He was an immortal. And an Ambassador for the Trials I wanted to end. And I was... well, I didn't know what I was exactly anymore.

His ruby red eyes flashed then, and they blazed with something I didn't know. Understanding? Lust? Care?

"I love you, Greer," he said and watched my face as I broke into a huge goofy grin and shoved him hard.

"I was going to say it first!" I said, trying my best to pout but I couldn't stop smiling. He loved me too.

He laughed and wrapped his arms around me and kissed me hard. He claimed my mouth with his and I opened myself to him.

"Say it," he said against my mouth, smiling in the same goofy way I was, and we pressed our foreheads together, my lips feeling empty without his.

"I love you, Kyra," I said, pulling away to look into his eyes and recognizing the gaze he held. The fire and sparkle that made his eyes shine like 1000 polished rubies was love. For me. And that would be enough for now. We could figure out the rest of this mess later.

"That means you're my boyfriend, right…?" I said, lifting one brow. Ky laughed loudly.

"Yes, it means I am yours and you are mine," he replied.

"Just checking since we haven't talked about labels," I said, snuggling my body to his.

"Say it again," he said, smiling broadly and walking us over to the chaise lounge.

"I love you…" I said as I pushed him down into the chair before he had the chance to do the same to me. I pulled off my sports bra and discarded my leggings. Then I removed his shorts where his cock sprung free, already hard.

"I love you," I said as I pushed him back and slithered on top of him, grazing my teeth across his chest as he moved his hands up and down my thighs. I grabbed his hands and pressed them to my breasts.

"Tell me, Kyra," I said as his hands played with my nipples and I glued my gaze to his and I reached down and slipped a finger inside myself and then another and his eyes went dark as he watched me pleasure myself.

"I love you, Greer," he said huskily and moved his hands away from my breasts, where I pinned them on either side of him.

"Again," I said, wrapping my hands now wet with my own desire around his cock and moving them up and down as he groaned and breathed it out again.

"I love you," he said, tensing his body and digging his hands in the lounger.

I replaced my hands with my mouth and licked at the head and tasted myself on him and pressed my lips up and down the length of him.

His eyes were hungrily on me and the desire in my body threatened to explode if I didn't have more of him filling me and touching me, but I wanted to see his eyes as I took him in my mouth. I wanted him to know that he was mine and I was his.

He growled and reached for me and I moved quickly like I had when we had been fighting. His hands moved slowly toward me and I was on top of him, sliding onto his hard cock where I was wet and throbbing and hot for him and time snapped back to normal.

His eyes widened in surprise as I slammed on top of the full length of him and we both cried out. He dragged my mouth to his and my body felt too tight, too coiled, and I started to move, grinding myself against him. He reached down to circle my clitoris, and I nearly was unmade right then and there.

He teased me as I moved on him and my hands were against his chest, scraping against his crystal. I locked my gaze with his wanting to look into those rubies all the way through my orgasm and it crashed into me and I began to breathe his name and his mouth was there swallowing my scream, holding my body against his as he sat up and flipped me over with my orgasm ripping through me. He pounded into me as I chased another and another until he exploded in me and collapsed on top of me, whispering "I love you, I love you, I love you," over and over again.

I didn't think I would ever get tired of hearing it.

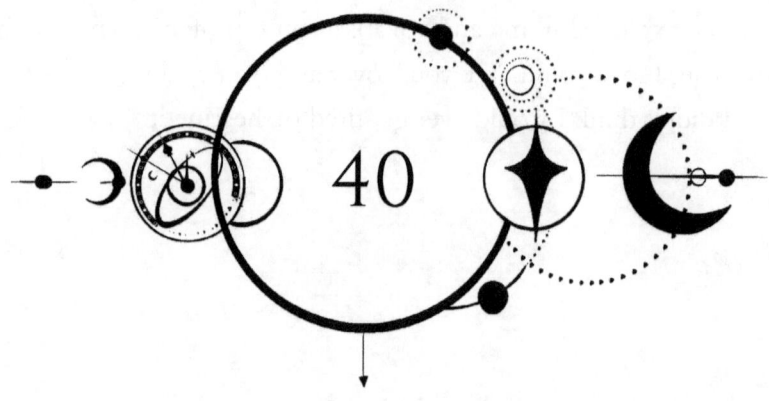

40

Greer

I was snuggled in Kyra's arms.
I had discovered I had powers.
I had told Kyra I loved him.

And he had said it back.

Oddly, the first part of my day had faded away to us having sex on almost every surface in the penthouse. I texted Lux and told him to be busy for most of the day because I was making love and he responded with an emoji of shock, heart eyes, and a wink, saying he would leave the place to us.

Tomorrow was my birthday and things felt brighter. Lighter. Maybe twenty-five-year-old Greer would feel better settled. Less fearful that the demons of her past would catch her vulnerable and deliver the final blow. More ready to take on the world and fight for necessary changes.

The last of the Trials was a few weeks away.

And I knew these boys had planned something special for my birthday and I was excited. I was allowed to find a small semblance of joy and peace among this hellish ordeal of my life where so much felt out of my control.

I knew there were a lot of things to sort through. I still didn't know why I was even put into the Trials. It felt like that was the final piece that I was waiting for and when would it come? Would it be when the ceremony was done? When the last trial and contestant got ranked and was dealt their winnings?

But tonight I didn't want to think about those things.

Tonight, I wanted to drift off into sleep with Ky's arms around me and feel safe and comfortable next to the man I loved.

So I welcomed sleep with open arms that night and let my dreams swirl around me and take me.

"Greer..." my mother's voice said.

She had found me again. The version of Mom that looked lovely and light and happy. The one that made my heart clench and my eyes water with happy tears. The version of my mom I had always wished for her.

Her hand was against my cheek and I leaned in and I felt tears slip down my cheeks.

"It's almost time," she said, a bit of sadness in her voice.

"Time for what, Mom?" I asked lightly. Tonight, I didn't want to know why she was here. I just wanted this gift. This vision of her imprinted in my head and my heart like the perfect twenty-fifth birthday present.

"I am forbidden to tell you all that I know." She looked conflicted, like she had so much to say and little time and energy to do so.

"By who?" I wondered.

"You will know very soon, my love," she said, moving to wrap her arms around me. She smelled like sunshine and rain. I held on tight.

"I am sorry I couldn't protect you from this. When the time comes, do not be afraid. What you have feared all your life is an illusion. Clear away the smoke, Greer. The power within you will feel like you are drowning like you are being burned alive," she said softly, like she was telling me a bedtime story.

I looked at her, horrified. What power? The new power I found out about today?

"But it won't... Your body will adjust. Keep your wits and your strength," she said, touching her palm to my heart and I held her hand there, feeling the warmth of her.

"It's almost time..." she said again, looking sad.

"Mom, I love you..." I said, not knowing what else to say. I had a million questions and I somehow knew she wouldn't be able to answer.

"Will I see you again?" I said, a sob hitching in my throat. I wanted answers. I wanted her. I didn't want this power or this torture she spoke of if only it meant that she would be alive again.

"I don't know darling," she said with a sad smile and her form started to evaporate.

"Mom!" I screamed as she floated away.

"I love you, my brave girl," she whispered. "Keep the world safe."

I scrambled to the space she just occupied, but it was just me and darkness like before. The only source of light was myself and my mom who was now gone.

My whole body felt like it was getting ready to run. I had nerves firing through my fingertips and toes. I tried to understand and replay our conversation.

I never got answers from the last time I saw her. And this was all I had left of her.

I didn't know what was real anymore.

I was lost.

And the darkness started to move in and claw at me until my light was snuffed out and I fell into the dark embrace of the silence and stillness around me.

"Don't scream, Ms. Roberts," a familiar voice said as I woke up to hand over my mouth and a dark figure looming above me.

I went to thrash my arms and legs, only to realize that they were immobilized. What was wrong with my body? Why couldn't I move anything? I realized that even if I wanted to scream, I couldn't. Nothing was working right.

My eyes moved too slowly, and fear wrapped itself around my heart like a vise. There were several dark figures in the room, but my eyes weren't working properly. Things were moving in a kaleidoscope of colors and bodies. Shapes would form, then splinter away and form again.

"The next trial starts in ten hours, *Greer.*" The voice was very close now. My eyes went wide and wild. I knew that voice. The voice of the President.

Why was he in my room? Who were the other all black figures in my room with hidden faces and eyes? Where was Ky? Where was Lux?!

"What an interesting surprise to find the *Ambassador* naked in your bed, hmmm? Give the man some pants, please," he said nonchalantly.

I heard a crash, and someone swore. None of my senses were working right. Did they drug me? I felt myself being lifted like I was nothing, and I knew we were moving out of my room.

"Ambassador, if you don't stop interfering with official trial business, Ms. Roberts will be disqualified ... Same goes to you, Mr. Gilmore," he drawled.

The trial wasn't for another few weeks, right? I didn't understand what was happening. Why was I being kidnapped?

My head was spinning and I couldn't keep my eyes focused and my mouth wouldn't work. My tongue was heavy and dry in my mouth.

"What the hell is this, Adonia?" I heard Kyra spit out, as if each word pained him. Had he been drugged too? Was I still dreaming?

I wanted my mom back … I moaned and I heard a growl.

"What did you give her?" Lux said, half snarling, as if he was lost somewhere between himself and one of his animal forms.

"It's harmless, really. It will wear off shortly. Don't test me or I will disqualify her and that would certainly mess with everyone's plans," he said haughtily. I felt my body swinging and moving again. It was brighter here but my eyes still wouldn't focus, and I kept closing them only to struggle to peek out of them again.

The fear that clutched my chest now had my whole body in a vise. My muscles wanted to move; they were buzzing, ready to explode the minute I could form words and full sentences and thoughts.

"Why they insisted on moving the timeline up is beyond me. It's been a royal pain in my ass, but you know how they are, don't you, Kyra? Wouldn't want to burn any bridges where they are concerned … Plus, if she wins, none of this will matter. Many before her have not, but they seem to think she might be the champion after all..." he said absentmindedly. I could practically hear the smirk in his voice, like he was delighted to tell them what they clearly didn't know.

"Who?" Kyra and Lux growled at the same time.

Why weren't they helping me? What was wrong?

Help. I tried to form in my mouth.

Please. I tried again but nothing came out, and I groaned deep in my throat again.

I don't understand.

"Your father, Kyra and his friends of course…" he said snarkily and I heard the elevator doors shut as Kyra cursed and Lux roared.

"Oh, and happy birthday, Ms. Roberts. We shall see if you make it to your next one," he said, his hot breath on my ear.

Happy birthday to me.

Then everything went black.

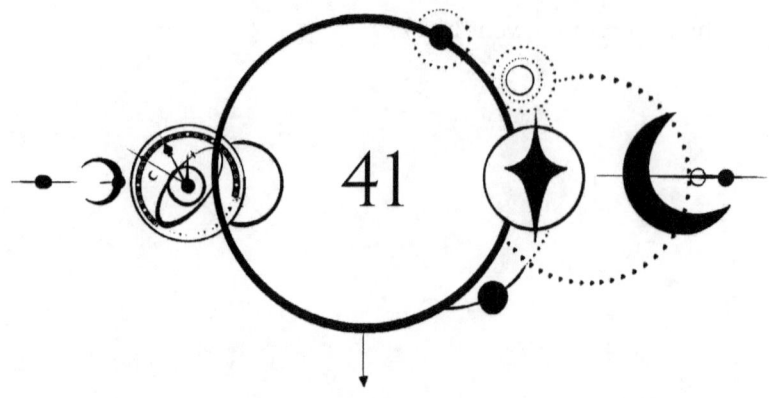

41

Kyra

It took a full hour after they had come in and snatched Greer for Lux and me to regain our normal state of consciousness and being. We both continued to go in and out of the drug-induced hallucinations until we both ended up on the floor panting and Lux was first to regain his motor skills. He shifted into his snow tiger and pounced on me as my body started to fire neurons regularly.

"What is going on, Kyra?" he snarled. His voice and eyes were the same, but it felt odd and incomprehensible coming from a giant tiger with snapping jaws and claws at my face.

"I … can … explain …" I said, trying to push his ginormous paws off my chest. He hopped off and hissed at me, his golden eyes daring me to try anything stupid as he circled around me like a hunter with its prey.

"Godsdamnit, Lux, put the cat away," I said, feeling my body jump alive all at once as fire danced along my fingertips as I pushed myself to standing. I flicked my wrist to let the fire wink out and sat at the countertop.

Why had the trial been moved up?

What had he meant when he said my father?

The stone in my chest pulsed and throbbed and then shone brightly.

I clutched my hand over it and stumbled out of the chair to the ground.

This was not good.

Lux had changed back into his normal broad, dark brown skin body covered with tattoos, and he looked down at me with fury and disdain in his eyes.

"Get Sutton, Waverly, and Nova here … hurry," I said. He had questions in his eyes, ones I couldn't answer yet.

"Lux, please! I love her. But I can't tell you what I am on my own…" I chose the words carefully as not to enact the curse that pulsed through my heart. I wasn't going to kill Lux, but I had to find a way to explain.

What did my dad want with Greer? What did any of them want with her? What was the piece of this puzzle that I was missing that made it all fit together?

A searing pain went through my chest and I knew things were going to get bad.

Very bad. *Very quickly.*

Lux hadn't moved. He looked at me like he was going to argue and shift some more, until he swore and grabbed his phone aggressively and stormed off.

I looked down. A black line had made its way into the heart of my bright red crystal.

Shit. Shit. *SHIT.*

"They're on their way," Lux growled as he came in again snapping.

"You better have a damn good story, Kyra … Or I will tear you to pieces despite loving her or not," he snarled in my face and then offered his hand and I nodded, grabbing it.

This was going to be a long night.

I looked at the clock and saw it was close to two a.m., and my heart fell to my stomach.

Happy twenty-fifth birthday, Greer.

I prayed that it wouldn't be her last.

☾

They arrived thirty minutes later. They all looked pissed as hell. I'm sure Lux had texted them what had happened. We had been sitting in uncomfortable silence waiting for them, as I was too afraid to say anything in case I decimated the whole penthouse. Lux had drilled me with questions for the first few minutes, but then I told him I couldn't answer without the others and he had snarled and growled. I was honestly surprised he didn't break anything. Then he had shifted into his lion form and stalked around the penthouse, roaring every once in a while.

"What's going on?" Nova hissed, walking through the elevator absolutely seething and she shot death glares at me. Waverly looked ready to claw my eyeballs out and Sutton a little delighted.

Bastard.

"He wouldn't talk to me until you got here…" Lux growled. "They're here, so talk."

Anger poured off him in waves and his eyes looked ready to kill. I didn't know how to circumvent the curse's locks and restrictions, but I had an idea that Sutton did.

"I'm going to guess this has something to do with the cursed object you have in your heart, Ambassador," Sutton practically purred. Everyone in the room swiveled to look at him.

"I'm guessing it's preventing you from speaking freely without consequences … I can feel it changing..." he said with a wicked smile.

The shadows around his eyes danced and they reached out to me, covering my eyes and pressing into my nose and mouth as if they were scraping against my conscience. I nearly choked and passed out, but they were out as fast as they were in.

"I cannot tell you what it is, but it has vises around his mouth and his head … But it surely has to do with his father and the identity of him. So there is no way for him to speak freely about it without injuring him or us in the process, I imagine," Sutton said, inclining his head to his side.

He tapped a finger on his chin and looked at Nova.

"There's a spell that I can use to see his memories," Nova said, closing her eyes as if searching her mind for it, and her fire eyes flared open.

I nearly sagged with relief. My blood was singing. My fire was itching to lash out at the first sound of me breaking the damn rules of the curse that had kept chains around me for my entire life. I was straining against them. The crystal embedded in my chest was aching and I lifted my shirt up to see that another jagged black crack had ripped through the red.

I met Lux's eyes.

"That … doesn't look good," he said, swallowing. Understanding seeped into his eyes and the edge of his anger seemed to be melting.

"This was never supposed to hurt her or anyone. Except me. I don't … I don't exactly know what's happening," I said, my tongue heavy in my mouth, trying to keep my flames locked down in case I said something that would betray me.

Waverly grabbed my hand and looked into my eyes with her bright pink eyes.

"Are your feelings for Greer real? Speak the truth," she sang in her siren voice.

"Yes, I love her," I said before I even realized what was coming out of my mouth. I wanted to give her the answer. I had *needed* to. The power of the siren song was strong.

She nodded.

My body seized up and in horror I realized she might make me say the curse out loud and doom them all, and I clenched my jaw.

"I won't ask you for more, Kyra," she said with understanding in her eyes. Lux seemed to relax even further, and the tension that had built in the room seemed to ease. I looked over at the clock and it was a little after 2:30 a.m.

"We have to hurry. Adonia said the next trail starts at—ten? Eleven?" I said, nerves firing in my belly. The sooner they knew, the sooner we could figure out what the hell my father had to do with this and why Greer was a pawn in his game.

"We need to tell her not to win," I said.

"Whatever Adonia knows, it can't be good for her and for her to be someone's champion, especially my father's ... It can't be good, in fact I think it's deadly," I said, suddenly very frightened for what Greer was about to step into.

For what we were all inadvertently involved in. Was this planned from the start? So many things still didn't make sense.

Yesterday had been perfect. Today was her birthday. Today was supposed to be perfect. Then we could have gone on to find many perfect days in the future.

"I need your blood to sift through the memories and a large black cauldron, boiling water, and a few other things that I need to get from my place…" Nova said, mentally checking all the things off her list.

"I'll take you there," Lux said, nodding and walking over to their outdoor rooftop.

"Why are we going this way?" she said quizzically as we all walked over to where Lux was sliding open the door.

"Because we're going to fly. There isn't much need for this form anymore, but it's the one of my family … It's the quickest animal I have," he said quietly and almost painfully, as if it hurt him to shift.

"But for Greer, we need to know who his dad is and what it has to do with her…" He turned his head and stepped outside and began to change. His long braids became spikes down his back and his clothing disappeared as scales covered his body and he grew a long, armored tail. He fell to the ground as his body grew and grew and grew. With golden scales the color of his eyes covered his body, he grew to the size of two SUVs. Claws poked out nearly the length of his arms and wings the color of midnight splayed open. A hiss of steam came out of his mouth.

"It's my family's symbol," he said without opening the giant dragon's mouth that was once Lux. I stood with my mouth open. I wasn't the only one with secrets. Nova looked fearless as she stepped up and Lux lowered one beautiful wing down and she grabbed the leather of him and pulled herself up.

She laughed wickedly. "Luxton Gilmore, I am glad to be your friend. Never in my hundreds of years have I seen the likes of you. Let's go."

"Hold on tight." He chuckled without opening his mouth and he flapped his great wings and took to the sky, soaring toward Nova's place.

"I need a drink," Sutton said suddenly, and Waverly looked absolutely dazzled.

"We will find the solution, Kyra. Together. We will get Greer back," she said, linking her arm through mine back into the penthouse where we waited the twenty minutes for them to get back.

☾

They returned shortly and Lux landed right where he transformed and he shrunk back down to the man I knew as my friend, back in his clothes with a devilish smile on his face. "You weren't expecting that, were you?" he said, laughing and clapping a hand on my back.

"It somehow makes me feel better about what you are all about to find out…" I said, laughing too, feeling some of the weight move off my chest.

"We'll see about that," he said with less edge than before.

Nova had brought all of her things and began to set them up on the dining room table. She dumped water and some random things from jars into the large flat cauldron.

"All right, Ky, boil the water," she said, and I nodded, stepping up and letting the heat erupt from hands into fire as the water danced and bubbled beneath my palms. I released the flames to hug close to the cauldron and stepped back.

She pulled out a dagger the size of my forearm and cut herself first on her palm, squeezing it over the boiling mixture, and it hissed.

"Your turn," she said, handing it to me and I sliced my hand. I dropped my blood into the boiling water, and it hissed and swirled and turned red as Nova began to chant in a language I didn't know and didn't understand. The water stilled and I saw in it the memory that had damned me for so long.

I was ten years old when I was first visited by my biological father. He found me playing in a creek near my house and swooped in and watched for a while until I saw him and I was startled. I was so young it made my heart hurt thinking of how naive and vulnerable I was to him and this world.

"Who are you?" ten-year-old me said as I was surprised by the stranger sitting in the grass merely a few feet from me.

"I am your father..." he said in a booming voice. The form he had chosen was similar to how my adoptive father had looked. Tall, olive skin, kind eyes, short black hair and an easy smile. But he was more. He almost shined, like his hair and skin were dusted with glitter and it was impossible to look at him for too long because your eyes and body would just hurt. He stood almost seven feet tall and was built with hard muscle. Power practically ran off him and his smile was feral.

"No, you're not," I squealed stubbornly. "I'm not supposed to talk to strangers..." I said, crossing my little arms across my chest and squaring up to him.

He laughed loud and openly. "Making me proud already! Such fearlessness," he said, and he shifted to sitting next to me so my little body was eye to eye with his bottomless red eyes. My adoptive dad didn't have eyes like that. No one I knew did. Just me and this man did.

"Haven't you noticed you're different, my boy? Perhaps the black stone in your heart?" he said carefully, tapping the stone. Heat erupted from it, running down my body, and flames popped out of my small hands.

"I am here to tell you what you are, but you must never speak of it until I come and fetch you once again. I want you to learn the ways of this mortal realm so we can rule it together. I want you to grow strong so that the rest of

the gods and goddesses can't reach you and corrupt you away from me," he said, his red eyes flashing.

"If you speak of it … You will destroy every living thing around you in a small radius. Do you understand?" he said gently, like he was telling me the time of day.

"You must tell no one you saw me, or that you are my son … I will come visit you every year on this day until I am ready to have you come rule by my side. Okay?" he said, and I wanted to do what he said. His words wrapped around me and settled on me like cobwebs.

"Okay," I said, completely mesmerized, and the webs turned to chains and locked themselves around my body, my head, my mouth, and my heart, and then they disappeared. A searing pain flashed so quick that I thought I had imagined it and then only warmth.

"Come, my boy! Let me tell you what power you hold as the only son of Riordan, the God of Hell. You are my prince, my boy and you will one day rule. The stone in your heart will always lead me to you and it is the source of your power. You cannot die unless someone removes it. You cannot live without it…" he said, and his words started to fade.

The memory swam in the water and it flashed forward to the year I had entered the Immortality Trial and won. It was the night of my victory he came to visit.

"How dare you corrupt the stone that I gave you? You ungrateful bastard! I will allow you this temper tantrum. I will come for you sooner than you wish, and I will make you see what you were always meant to be, and I will make it so you come begging to me! You are a Prince of Hell and when this realm is reclaimed by the gods, you will rule as I have!" He roared and I roared, shooting flames at him as if I could do any damage.

"I don't want to be the Prince of Hell. I am my own man and I refuse to be doomed to the infernal realm with you where you torture and wreak havoc on those around you. I am a good man! I will help the mortal realm NEVER fall into the clutches of you and the other gods and goddesses who are selfish and *without any integrity or honor! You created this world and left it alone for centuries. Leave it be and rid me of the curse that is you!" I was unhinged, yelling and screaming and shooting flames as we snarled at each other and destroyed everything in our paths.*

He had not visited me since. I was afraid for the day I would see him again and he would drag me to the infernal realm against my will.

The blood dissipated in the pool and I looked at it like it had ripped my soul out and laid it bare, because it did.

The fire that had heated the cauldron winked out, and everyone slowly looked toward me with more questions than answers in their eyes.

"I have not heard from him since. That was the year I won the Trials. Greer, as only the love of my life won't interest my father and the others enough to interfere. Something else is happening that I don't understand, but either way she is in danger and if she wins and becomes immortal … I have a very, very bad feeling about it," I said, swallowing.

"Okay, your majesty," Lux said, looking sort of relieved.

"Oh, fuck off," I said, burying my face in my hands as the others laughed.

"So you have a shitty father … so did I," Lux said seriously, looking at me.

My mouth dropped open. "You accept me? And this? Just like that?" I said.

"Just like that," Waverly said, squeezing my hand.

"The cauldron doesn't lie … We all have things that haunt us. I knew you had something in you the first time I met you, but you have proved time and time again to be a good man. Don't make us regret it," Nova said.

It was probably the nicest thing she had ever said to me.

I didn't know what to say or what to feel. I had kept that secret for years. No one knew. And the most important person in my life was at risk because of it. But these people around me acknowledged that I was my own man. Despite having a god as a father.

"We need to warn her before she competes. She can't win. She needs to stay as far away from them as possible," I said, glancing up at them, suddenly feeling lighter.

"The gods and goddesses are not kind," Sutton said seriously.

I nodded.

"Greer's been visited by Afton, the messenger of the gods … He was cryptic. She didn't understand what he was saying, but this is not a good sign," I said gravely.

Nova swore. "Why didn't you say anything? Why didn't she say anything?" She hissed.

"I didn't know how … And she doesn't know he is the messenger of the gods. She told me she doesn't believe in the old gods and I couldn't very well tell her about all of this without hurting her..." I trailed off.

"It doesn't matter unless we can get Greer anyways. So let's go get our girl," Lux said with a vicious smile.

"How?" I said. They would have the contestants locked down tight until the last possible second for the final round.

"I've got a plan," he said, rage hungry in his eyes. "Here's what we are going to do…"

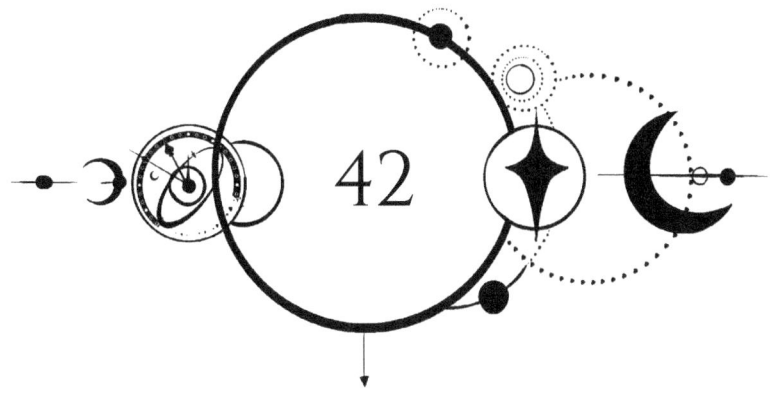

42

Kyra

I was not the biggest fan of this plan. But it was the only one we had.

We had two hours before the trial began. They had just announced on TV that *"Surprise!"* the trial was today, and they were starting soon, so everyone got ready to watch the finale because this was gonna be a good one.

I had access to the contestants so I would find Greer and warn her before the trial started to not come in first place. Whatever was being planned seemed to be connected to the fact that she would be the winner. That would at least give us some time to figure out why the hell my dad and the other gods and goddesses had to do with it.

They were not benevolent. They were selfish, childish and ruthless and they did not care for anything that did not serve them.

During the trial, Nova and Waverly would accompany me to the watch party, which I was forced to be a part of as the Ambassador of the Trials and a past winner. They would use her siren song to get information out of the President's staff and if she could get alone with him, then the President himself.

Lux and Sutton would meet us there, and Lux would play the role of CEO tech tycoon with an interest in the trial, while keeping his eyes and ears open to anything amongst the other wealthy and government patrons.

Hopefully, the trial would last long enough that they could accomplish that task. When the trial ended, I would be there at the ceremony helping crown the victor and I would have Lux come with me as a creature small enough to fit in my pocket. He would transform into something fearsome if things started to go awry.

Basically, we needed to protect Greer, get in, and get out before anything could happen.

So here I was racing through the halls of the headquarters to get any information I could before I headed to find her and figure out why the fuck I hadn't been informed of this change and why I was so in the dark about what was happening.

I nearly slammed into Edward, the Trial Lord, as I rounded the corner.

"Ambassador." He smiled, showing off his pointed teeth.

"Trial Lord," I said coldly. "Funny how I wasn't told there would be a change in the Trials and I seem to have been left off the communication about the details of this final trial," I said, testing him.

"It was only revealed to the highest level of the trial staff," he said snarkily. I wanted to strangle him right then and there.

"Why don't I accompany you to the final trial place then, hmmm?" I said, suddenly seeing a nice little in to my plan. He scrunched up his face and huffed.

I started herding him toward the way I came. "The games can't start without you, so let's move along..." I said. He stumbled forward and began mumbling grumpily underneath his breath as I followed him out to where his car was waiting for him and I easily slid in.

"Why do you insist on coming with me?" he said once he was seated in the car and he had yelled at the driver to step on it. Another car followed in front and behind, his security, I was sure, and staff.

"I thought we could have a nice little chat..." I said, searching his eyes for some semblance of knowledge.

"Do you know my father?" I said, casually crossing my legs and looking out as the city vroomed by. The old dwarf never liked me. Most like him didn't. I was uncontrollable. Young. Brash. An outsider in their eyes, but I was so much more.

And I wanted to genuinely help people, including humans.

He stiffened next to me. Which meant he was probably in on whatever my father had done to these trials. How many of them knew my father and were letting him pull the strings? What could he have said to them to change the course of the Trials so drastically? They were immortals ... they couldn't be killed unless he was the one who had the serum of death.

Which would explain why they were afraid. He was the God of Hell and could kill them and damn them for eternity, but why all the charades? What was Greer to him as a mortal with some power she had yet to identify?

It made my head hurt. I didn't have the whole picture, but the pieces were starting to make more sense.

"Hmm, thought as much. I would like a word with Greer Roberts before she competes. On order of dear old Dad..." I said, pushing as much ice into my voice as possible.

His head whipped toward me and I knew I had him.

He swallowed hard and said, "As he wishes." and we drove in silence the rest of the way until a large arena came into view. I knew this trial was a maze of a different kind of proportion.

We drove into an underground garage and he got out of the sleek black car and the rest of his staff hopped out and he barked an order for them to take me to contestant Greer Roberts's holding cell immediately.

I looked at my watch; there was an hour until the event started.

Someone stepped up and led me through the underground hallways teeming with ITC staff and buzzing with energy. I tried to catch snippets of conversation, but my head was reeling. My dad had orchestrated this whole thing for Greer. I needed to know why and how was I going to tell her that without it seeming like I was involved?

Did that mean he would ensure she would live?

Why was he offering any kind of protection?

She had survived the Trials with the odds stacked against her.

I sighed and I couldn't tell her who my dad was either, because the curse had not been lifted. The others knew because of the spell, so I would just have to tell her to not place first. Which would have been a feat in itself, but somehow I knew if my father could rig the rest of the Trials, he would do it for her. But why?

What was I missing?

"Here you are, Ambassador," the staff member said. "I will wait here as the Trial Lord said you are to speak with her for no longer than five minutes, as the trial starts very soon. I will then lead you to the watch party with all the other guests of honor." I nodded as I stood in front of a steel metal door and it slid open to where Greer was standing in a leather suit, covered from head to toe, and her dagger strapped to her thigh.

Her wine-red hair was pulled up and back into a high ponytail and her mouth was set in a hard line. The room was relatively bare except for a bed, a built-in closet which must have held her change of clothes, a bathroom off to one side and a built-in alcove that was glowing with a glass panel in front of it.

"Happy birthday, beautiful," I said in awe of her and her strength.

"Ky!" she exclaimed and threw her arms around me and I inhaled the scent of her. Vanilla and a little spice. I wanted to stand here all day with her wrapped up in me. Her body melted to mine. But we only had five minutes.

"We don't have much time," I said, not wanting to pull away but knowing this might save her life.

"You can't win," I said with all the force I could muster. She looked confused.

"Why?" she said, suspicious.

I sighed. I didn't know how I was going to explain this.

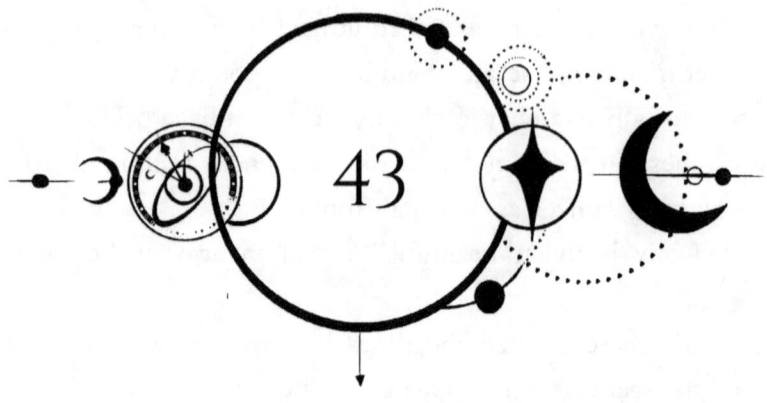

Greer

I was confused. Why wouldn't I try to win? I mean, I didn't necessarily think I was going to get first place, but I should at least try, right?

"What's wrong, Kyra?" I said, searching his eyes. The last I saw him was when we were all arms and legs, snuggled together naked. Then I had been ripped out of bed for this new trial on my birthday of all days.

"I can't exactly explain, but I think if you win, you will be in danger. Just promise you'll come in second or something." His eyes were frantic, and he bit his lip. I had never seen him this anxiety ridden before.

"Okay," I said, trusting him. I couldn't imagine I would have any luck coming in first anyways. I just needed to finish in the top one hundred, and then I wouldn't have any of my life cycle taken away.

His whole body seemed to relax, and he gathered me up in a hug. "I love you, birthday girl," he said, laying kisses on my forehead, my nose, my eyes, cheeks, and then my mouth. His kisses left hot, tingly sensations all over.

"I'll explain after this is done. I'll be waiting for you at the ceremony," he said and gave me one last squeeze. "Good luck. You will not fail," he whispered and then he was gone.

Out the same metal door he came in.

He gave one last look back before it slammed shut and I was stuck in there.

Alone. My body ached from whatever drug they gave me, and I didn't know what to do to pass the time until the trial started.

I twirled my dagger around and did jumping jacks in place. I stretched. I was a bundle of nerves waiting for this to be over. It felt like the rest of my life could begin after this damn thing.

A monitor dropped from the ceiling and an electronic voice rang out as the words appeared on the screen. "You will have two hours to complete the maze. The top one hundred contestants will be ranked on how quickly they find the center. Once you touch the button in the center, you will have won. Those who do not make it will receive their retribution and those in the top one hundred will be rewarded. You are allowed your powers and your weapon. Get to the center at all costs. Good luck. Please step into your alcove to be delivered to your spot in the maze," and the message looped on the screen as the glass door whooshed open.

I stepped into the blue hazy light and closed my eyes as I was funneled through a tunnel where I stood in my little glass cage at the beginning of my spot in the maze. Words flowed across the glass and that same voice echoed in my small glass chamber. I could only see cold black walls around and darkness. Smoke snaked its way on the ground, and I swallowed.

The last trial was supposed to be ruthless. You didn't know what you might find in here. It was made to try and make sure only a one hundred people could make it to the finish line—and not without a fight.

I tried to focus on the words that floated across the screen. There was a countdown from five minutes until the game started. Kyra had told me not to win, which was fine. I was just trying to survive. But what would happen if I was the winner?

He seemed unnerved and anxiety ridden like I'd never seen him before. I wonder if they found something out about who had duped me into this wretched thing.

I exhaled slowly and watched the numbers go down.

"Three, two, one … Begin."

The glass case around me opened. I stepped into the dark with the walls arching high above me and connecting in a midnight black ceiling that seemed to suck in all sound and light. Small lights embedded in the floor flickered on and small twinkling lights began to shimmer on the walls and the ceiling like I was living in the night sky. Ahead of me was a long corridor that split two ways. The smoke around me started to hiss and coil, wrapping itself around me. I swallowed.

Now or never.

I walked down the corridor and made my first decision within the maze and grabbed my dagger from its sheath, ready for whatever was to come. I took two steps to the right corridor and was slammed in the head with an invisible force. I cried out.

"Greer," a woman's voice said.

I didn't recognize it.

"I am so sorry, child," she said, her voice pouring sadness and sorrow.

I was in that black void again where I had seen my mother. Like a box of darkness, and the source of light this time was a woman with my wine-red hair trailing down to the ground, my green eyes with the odd rimming of blue looking right at me. She looked like me but more. Sharper. More in focus.

She was over six feet tall, glowing with high cheekbones, pale skin, and a white dress that seemed to hang off her muscular frame, perfectly accentuating her curves. The golden crown on her head sparkled with diamonds and black sapphires.

She was beautiful and powerful. I could feel it, but she had bruises and blood dripping off her wrists and ankles, and a purplish mark on her throat.

I wondered what had happened to her.

How someone who seemed to ooze beauty and power could have such visible trauma and abuse.

"Why does this keep happening?" I said, choking as the pain in my head throbbed and I looked at my own hands glowing as well.

"Why do I keep getting sent to this place?" I said, searching her eyes.

"Who are you? Who am I?" I said on my knees in the leather suit I had been given at the Trials.

"Greer, I am Xael. The fallen goddess of time," she said with sadness pouring into her eyes as she came closer and sank to her knees in front of me.

Her beauty had cracks. Red-rimmed eyes, bruises like bags underneath her eyes, dry lips.

"We don't have much time. I can only hold time for so long with you. Listen, child, you must know these things before you are taken.

"When the world was made, the gods and goddesses created all sorts of life. Including humans. But humans were made to be the weakest, made to be used and abused by the other races. They all decided together that humans would be the race that would serve the others. But they didn't anticipate all their creations fighting for power, magic, resources. They grew tired of their playthings and decided to leave.

"I begged them to protect the humans. I knew humans would suffer the most without our intervention. I begged them to stay with you on earth, but the rest were too powerful—they wouldn't allow me to stay. I was one of the few sympathizers. I saw that there was great love, value and creation in your race.

"I was scared that humans would not make it without any help, so I prepared a spell to share my power with you. The power of time. The others found me out and punished me before my spell was complete and laced my spell, which should have given you all additional life, to curse you with death.

"My punishment was to become mortal myself, fitting since I loved you all so much. To be stripped of magic and force to live one life cycle.

"It was meant to be a great insult. The worst that they could do to me...

"But I fought as they stripped away my power and my time. I still tried to save you all.

"I wanted to share my power with you all ... Instead, I doomed you all and myself.

"As I was sending out my power, they fractured and disrupted my magic. Instead of giving you all the gift of time, they cursed it. I tried to contain it but I couldn't. I limited the spread so not all mortals were affected, but enough were.

"Those who were affected would be driven mad by the power of time within them over the years. It would drive them so mad that they would take their own lives. This is what happened to your mother.

"I battled with them as my spell, and their curse intertwined.

"I made it so that one day, one would rise against the curse protected from them until their twenty-fifth birthday and fully be able to embrace the power of my spell and take away the darkness from others so no one else would suffer.

"But the gods and goddesses continued to add darkness to the spell.

"They created the Immortality Trials to be presented as a gift to the world, but instead it would be a part of my curse. They took some of my time power to be used for the winner. If the humans infected with my power didn't end their life at their own hands, they would be irrevocably drawn to the Trials so their life would be snuffed out by others. They would crave the immortality I had been stripped of and risk their lives for it.

"The one who would be able to withstand and hold my powers would be different. They would be able to win.

"But they would also have to become immortal to do so. They would have to gain what I had lost. Either way, they would need to fight in the Trials as they would make it so the world would not give them immortality otherwise. They would need to compete, otherwise the power of time would not be able to be fully accepted; it would kill them too. It would keep killing until it could be accepted. A terrible curse that was supposed to save you all and be shared among your race, but ended with the deaths of many.

"But without my power, the original gods and goddesses would only be able to award few and far between with the power of immortality. Their precious races would live and die like most things should.

"So they would need the one who could hold my power. One they would call the timewraith.

"You, Greer Roberts.

"They are coming for you. They entered you in this trial because for some reason, you were not drawn to it even though you are the one who can contain and control it. You have the ability to be their savior or their destroyer.

"Do not let them control you. They will try. I have offered my protection and my magic as the spell and curse to save you.

"There are few who will help you amongst the original immortals. Find them in the Eastern Hemisphere. Protect yourself, your people, and your power.

"I have so much more to tell you, but the time is now, Greer. Go. You must win or die by the powers thrashing inside of you. The cage I tried to create to keep the powerful curse and my magic at bay only lasts so long. Yours is breaking down as it has done with every mortal before you. They will break the barrier once you win and become immortal. It will be excruciating. I never meant for anyone to hold it all … I am sorry again, my child. Go, you will not fail.

"For it is your destiny to fight for a new world, a new beginning."

Tears were streaming down her face and her hands were on my cheeks.

I couldn't fully understand what she was saying. It didn't make sense. My head started throbbing again, and I screamed as her image fractured and my head felt like it exploded into a million pieces.

I was alone once again.

I was exactly where I had been when I started the trial.

I wondered how long I had been out.

What had just happened?

Was that real?

What the hell was the power of time?

I had just found out I had some power, but the power of time seemed to be a bit of a stretch. What did that even mean? I really wished I knew more about the origin of the world and the original gods and goddesses.

My thoughts were swirling around my head, making me dizzy, but I told myself I could push forward. I had to get out of the maze. My head ached and my body hurt like I had run a bunch of marathons.

Xael had told me to win.

Ky had told me not to.

Things would make more sense once I got out of here. I could talk to Kyra and dissect what had just happened with my friends. I could do this. I just needed to get *out*.

I didn't know what to think, so I began to walk and breathe. One step at a time.

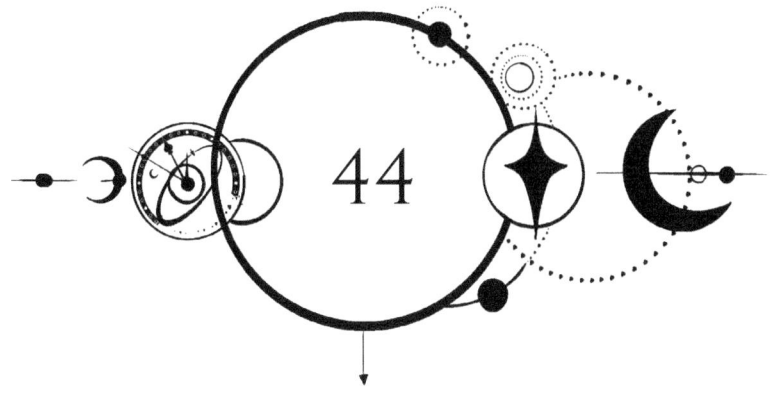

44

Greer

I was seriously lost.

I didn't know how long I had been in here, but I was completely and utterly *lost*.

I hadn't run into anything *yet*. A single soul or being. Which should have made me happy, but it made me more scared. What exactly was in this maze? What would finally find its way to me when my guard was down?

I felt like I had walked around in circles, but I had no markers to identify where I had been and where I should be going.

I wondered if I was dreaming again because it felt so similar to where I was with my mom and what had happened with Xael.

After anxiety and adrenaline had slammed into my veins for what felt like twenty minutes after I had recovered from the vision, I began to calm down and realize that the smoke around me was no longer moving.

Everything felt calm. Paused.

The lights twinkled only every few minutes, and I was moving through the space like normal.

The power I had only discovered yesterday was the only explanation for this.

Right?

Was this what Xael meant by the power of time? I could suspend things for minutes ... hours?

I didn't have any other way to explain this, but if things around me were slowing down, how could I keep track of how much time had passed.

It felt like I had already been in here several hours and I didn't feel any closer to understanding how the hell I was supposed to make it to the center of this damn maze. I wondered if I would be stuck here forever.

Greer...

I whipped my head up and looked around. There was no one. Where had it come from?

Was I about to be slammed into another dark room dream with someone else saying vague, scary, and nonsensical things?

Greer...

I followed the voice as if my body was not my own. I made twists and turns in this maddening place. The voice kept calling me and guiding me through and that's when I started to run into things for the first time since being in here.

I would walk right by contestants who seemed to be frozen in place mid stride. I walked up on two contestants mid fight. One had a sword sticking into the ribs of another; the blood didn't move, but it was leaking out like a splash of paint on a canvas.

I found another contestant dead already, eyes vacant.

Another was sitting on the ground in the fetal position.

Another broken, bloody and mid crawl.

I shuddered and wondered what it was they saw. What they felt ... that had driven them to this. Why had they entered the trial in the first place? I wrapped my hands around my arms as I moved quietly and silently through them. I gripped the dagger between my palms like it was the only thing pulling me into the presence.

I continued to skirt around miscellaneous contestants and kept moving toward the lull of this voice. It wrapped around me like silk and hugged me close. It sounded like Kyra's voice. My entire body felt called to it. Like I was no longer in control of what was happening to my feet.

I didn't care what else was going on. I just wanted out. I wanted to be held by Ky and have him stroke my hair and tell me my nightmares were all over.

I wouldn't have to keep fighting so hard anymore.

I passed a few traps where I would step onto something, and slowly, like moving through molasses, something would shoot out or the floor would give away. I saw what I thought were monsters covered in oily black skin, razor-sharp teeth and claws protruding out. Some covered in blood … I imagined the contestant I had seen crawling had been attacked by these.

It was disgusting and sad that so many were trapped with physical and emotional monsters running rampant.

I began to run as the voice beckoned me forward.

I wanted to be done.

My body was starting to feel lighter. I wondered if the vision I had had at the start was even real?

You are almost there, birthday girl.

Definitely Kyra's voice. My love. He was safe. That's why my body was magnetized to it.

You don't need to be afraid.

My heart swelled, and I was sprinting, trying to get to the end of this. I didn't know how much time had passed—or hadn't passed, for that matter—but I was sure I wouldn't be the first one.

I just wanted to be done. I didn't want to hurt anyone on the way out. I wanted these stupid trials to be a part of my past, and I wanted them to end for myself and for everybody else.

Nobody wanted to be captured in the night.

Nobody wanted to have to fight for their life.

The Immortality Trial was a weapon used against the people. It was absolutely unnecessary. People were supposed to live and die. That's life.

My whole body thrummed and felt foreign as I pushed hard into my legs.

I was running and my feet were pounding the ground following the sweet call of Kyra's voice and tears fell down from my eyes.

I wanted this to end.

I wanted it all to stop.

I wanted Kyra.

My friends.

My birthday.

My mom.

I burst out of the corridor and into a huge circle shaped room with hundreds of corridors entering into it and saw in the middle the large black button that meant the end. It sparkled like a diamond and was set upon a pedestal that was shining bright with the same twinkling lights that had kept me company though the entirety of the maze. There was a countdown hanging from the ceiling with a countdown. It had 1:48:43 on it.

I shook my head and looked again at the bright numbers counting down. That didn't seem right. It seemed to be stuck on that number. Maybe it was broken. I felt like I was floating, and everything felt warm and fuzzy. I needed to press that button.

Press it, beautiful…

"Didn't you tell me not to be the first?" I said, confusion filling my head as Kyra's voice urged and seduced me toward the button. Why had Kyra told me not to press it again? I couldn't exactly remember. I'm sure it wasn't important. I smiled to myself. I loved him. And he loved me and we would be immortal together forever.

The beautiful broken woman in my dream told me to win. I felt her urge and desperation for me to make it.

But Kyra had told me not.

What had I been so angry with before? I touched my cheeks and felt tears. I couldn't remember why I had been crying.

Everything felt fuzzy in my head.

Was I happy or sad?

Who was I trying to please here?

I think I wanted to win. I wanted to be immortal.

The smoke around me started to move at a normal speed and I walked up to the button, looking at it with hungry eyes. The clock became unstuck and started counting down at a normal space.

I licked my lips and tried really hard to remember why I shouldn't be first. It felt important. But it was my birthday! I should be able to do what I wanted on my birthday. I battled with myself as my body wanted to touch it and my head kept getting stuck on something I couldn't quite grasp, like it was just more smoke through my fingers.

That's right, birthday girl. It's yours.

I looked at the clock and realized fifteen minutes had passed with me just staring at this infernal button.

Then I heard someone coming and jealous and rage smashed into my body, nearly knocking me over.

MINE.

Take it, birthday girl.

So I slammed my hand on the button and a voice boomed.

"Our winner! Greer Roberts!"

I had been in here for hours? Right?

How did I win?

But I was happy! Ky and I would be together forever. I smiled silly to myself and giggled.

Plus, this Xael woman had said I would be powerful, right?

I couldn't even comprehend why I had thought the Trials were bad. They were good! It meant that Kyra and I would be together forever.

A glass box popped out of the ground a foot away from me and I stepped in and it slammed closed as others started running and snarling hate and rage in their eyes to the button. I was sucked into the ground where everything went black and I was slammed back into my normal state of consciousness with such a velocity that if I hadn't been in the small glass container, I would have flown across the room.

I wasn't supposed to win. I remembered Kyra's anxiety-filled warning and face only an hour before. Why had I felt different in the maze? What had happened to me there?

What was that dream earlier?

What was going to happen *now*?

I swallowed and tried to make sense of the strange euphoria I felt before and jealousy of others taking the victory. My head started to ache again, and my body radiated pain, causing small muscle spasms as I gasped for air. As if all these feelings had been at bay momentarily before and they came knocking into me acutely and aggressively all at once.

My head felt fractured from all the things that were going on.

Was I dying?

A new gas was dispensed in my moving glass chamber and I choked on it and coughed until I slipped again.

I drowsily wondered if twenty-five would be my last and final birthday before I slumped in my cage and lost all awareness.

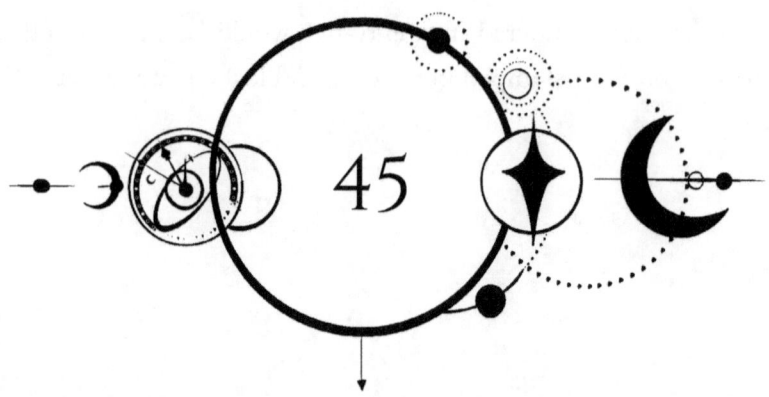

45

Kyra

Waverly, Nova, and I stared, our mouths open as Greer slammed her hand on the button.

It happened too fast.

Too fast.

We didn't have enough time. Lux wasn't here yet with Sutton.

Greer had looked delirious at the button when she got there, and she had moved like no one I had ever seen through the maze. She had covered so much space so quickly it was hard to keep track of where she was.

She had stared at the button for so long that I didn't know if she would press it. The crowd was going wild in here as she had rounded on the button in less than fifteen minutes and stared at this in a daze for just as long. But as soon as someone else had rounded on her minutes later, she had snarled and pounded the button.

"I thought you told her not to win," Nova hissed.

"I did…" I said and realized that among everything else that happened, I had never told them about Greer's new powers.

"Fuck. FUCK!" I said, my eyes blazing as everyone around us erupted in a crazed celebration. No one had ever finished the last trial that fast.

The people were going wild as other contestants started to pour in.

"New plan," I growled. "Find Lux and Sutton and we get to Greer, now!"

I didn't think her newfound powers would manifest like that, so quickly and so powerfully. I don't know how long she had actually been in the maze, but she flew through it at hyper speed.

Lux and Sutton appeared in front of us as we tried to shove and navigate through the champagne popping and screaming, crying and cursing, as people's bets exploded or crashed and burned.

"*What was that?*" Lux said, almost hysterical.

"She said she wouldn't win," I snarled to no one in particular. I grabbed Lux by his collar and looked wildly into his eyes.

"She discovered yesterday she had powers. We were training and we didn't know what they were. She can slow down others around her or speed up? She said in the third trial she had been in there for hours even though the timer had said she did it in about ten minutes," I said as Lux started to dig claws into my shoulders.

His face fell and more tumbled out. "There was so much that happened yesterday I forgot to mention it … We didn't know what it was or a name for it or how to use it. We were planning on looking into it the next day because we were supposed to have more time before this last trial," I practically screamed above the roar of the crowd and I scanned it to see if I could find the President or the Trial Lord but there was too much chaos.

Nova swore loudly and looked at all of us. Her eyes glowed. We all went rigid, as if we were soldiers being commanded. My arms dropped away from Lux and his nails tore away from my shoulders and jerkily we followed her. Sutton and Waverly seemed to move normally as we followed her in a line to one of the private bathrooms and she screamed at everyone to get out and slammed the door. She released the hold on Lux and me. We both looked at her in bewilderment.

"What was *that?*!" I gasped. All my nerves were on edge, and I was *this* close to lighting something on fire.

"Blood body control," she said, fire dancing in her eyes. "I don't like to do it because I don't like taking away free will, but what you just said about Greer is that she can manipulate *time,"* she hissed out.

"And?" Lux said, looking at her like she might bite him. Nobody liked to have their limbs moved without their consent.

"It's impossible," Sutton said. "The timewraith is folklore … She can't be," he said, not seeming so confident.

"What the fuck is a timewraith?" I said, looking frantically between them.

"It's stuff of legends…" Waverly said tentatively, but she herself was something of a legend. Not very many pure sirens were left.

"So she's a witch?" Lux said, rubbing his forehead.

"No, she's mortal but more … It was said that at the beginning of the mortal realm there was a fallen goddess, Xael. The goddess of time. She loved humans and tried to share her power with them, but instead cursed them, and then was stripped of her own power. Someone is supposed to come again and be able to hold her powers of time once more. Supposedly they can manipulate the perception of time. So they can essentially speed up or slow down time. It is said Xael's blood was the original way immortality was achieved for the gods and goddesses that if you drink the blood of her or the promised timewraith then you could be granted extra time.

They can also take away time by drinking someone else's blood … But they cannot kill immortals with their gift. It is also said that if trained probably they can jump through time…" Nova said. Fear was starting to cloud her features.

"Jump time?" Waverly asked.

"Skip time and look into the past or future."

"That's what my dad wants…" I said slowly, putting the pieces together.

"But why? Gods are already immortal. Why would they need her and why would they put her in the Trials?" Lux said.

"And how does everyone know this except us?" he snarled.

"We all have lived far longer than you, Lux…" Nova said, steadying him with her gaze.

"Her mortal body would need to be prepared, so to speak … If I remember the curse correctly," Sutton said, his shadows dancing.

"Like a lamb for slaughter?" Lux said, his mouth agape.

"The winner gets granted exceptional power and immortality. It's never been done on a mortal before so if she somehow has the power of time locked within her body ready to be embraced, she would need to fight to stay alive through it and if she were immortal, it would guarantee her survival through the fusion of power in her cells…" Nova continued.

"But it would be extremely painful," she finished, looking at us as pure terror overtook the crowd of us in the room.

"How could that have lived within her?" I said. She had talked about her darkness swallowing her whole before. Was the beast that she caged the power clawing to get out, but it had somehow been caged so it wouldn't kill her.

"Today's her twenty-fifth birthday…" I said slowly, waiting for things to fall into their place. "I wonder if whatever barrier or time limit was within her would only last a certain amount of time."

"She talked about being swallowed whole before. By the darkness that lies inside her that took her mom. But what if it's really her power that is clawing to get out? And the confines of that box are deteriorating and today it knew it would soon be free, so it's clawing its way out. It knows what's going to happen." Lux said, hardly believing the words out of his mouth.

"The timewraith is said to have ancient and old power that is compounded from all of time and life itself from the original goddess. It is possible it is forcing her toward survival … Or something else is," Nova said thoughtfully.

"There was a prophecy long ago," Waverly said with a far-off look. "It was said that the gods and goddesses would reclaim the mortal realm in their image once again once they had enough time and reclaimed what was once theirs. I don't remember the exact wording, but what if they didn't need enough time, but they were waiting for the timewraith? It would guarantee their victory over all in the mortal realm if they had her. And now that a serum is out that can take away immortality, they would practically be untouchable. What if they were waiting for Greer?" she said hurriedly.

"So Greer is about to go through a painful metamorphosis without knowing it and the gods are going to try and take her and then overtake the mortal realm?" Lux said angrily. He turned and slammed his fist into the bathroom wall.

"My dad did say he would claim this realm again. But I didn't think it would be so soon. We have to get to her. If they take her to the celestial realm, or the infernal one, I don't know how we will access her. They will rip her apart and use her. Not to mention the transformation she will go through will apparently rip her to pieces on a cellular level. Then we will deal with the gods," I said, trying to sort it all out through my brain.

How had they known it would be Greer?

Everything was starting to make sense in a horribly dark and twisted way.

"We can't go in blindly," Waverly said. Always calm and collected.

"We need to pretend nothing is wrong so we can get access to her. They will have her in tight security until she gets paraded on stage where *you* need to be Kyra, with Lux hiding on your person. I will siren sing us past the security into the vicinity so we are close if you can't get to her in time," she said, barking orders.

"We have to get her right after the President grants her immortality. She will most likely die without the power if the cage that has held the eternity of time at bay explodes at once inside her before she gets immortality," Nova said.

"She will be most vulnerable then and that is most likely when your father or another one of the gods will try and take her," Sutton said.

"All right," I said. My heart was beating wildly in my chest.

Just yesterday I had made love to Greer and thought about the life we could build together. Now I was worried she would be ripped to pieces by the element of time itself.

I looked at my watch. The entire trial was almost over, and the award ceremony would be in about forty-five minutes. "Lux, we need to go, get small and get in my pocket," I said. He looked at me like he was about to fall apart.

"Ky, I can't…" he said, clearing his throat and sucking in air. "I can't lose her. She's my best friend. She's my only family. I love her," he said, his gold eyes molten.

"I know. Me too," I said, fire dancing on my fingertips. "Always together, Lux." I offered my hand, and he pulled me into a crushing hug.

"Together," he said before he shifted and transformed into a tiny lizard and slipped into my pocket.

"Good luck," Nova said and gave me a grimace.

"Be careful," I said to the three of them.

We all nodded and headed out of the bathroom, where chaos was resuming as contestants were ranked and people celebrated.

I saw the President and the Trial Lord heading toward the elevator. I jogged over to it and stopped it with my hand.

"Heading to the ceremony, Mr. President, Edward?" I said, nodding to each.

The President sighed. "Yes, let's go crown your mortal girl-friend the winner…"

Did he not know the power she held? Probably better that way. I was guessing my father hadn't exactly been forthcoming with that information.

So we rode down the elevator together in silence to where the winner would be crowned.

Lux moved in my pocket and I glanced down.

What a fucking mess we were in.

I just hoped we could get to Greer before it was too late.

We had no plan B.

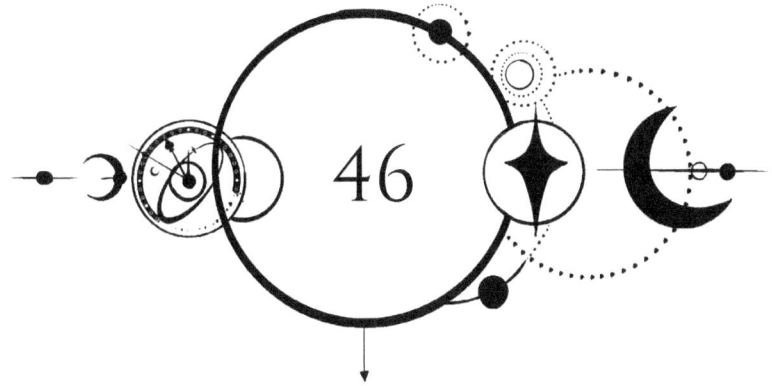

46

Greer

My head hurt. Everything hurt. My body felt too tight, like pressure was building from within, ready to explode out. I felt a tiny prick in my arm and lightning strikes in my blood. I felt like I could finally breathe again.

I gasped for air and my eyes flew open. I was between two guards being escorted through a dark hallway and my mouth felt dry as the desert.

Did I really win? Why wasn't I supposed to win?

I didn't feel good about what was about to happen.

I thought I would feel relief with that button.

I only felt dread.

I was being marched to a platform in a wide open space, and the guards surrounding me herded me toward the center. My eyes hurt. The light from the fluorescents in the hallway was too much. Like it was drilling into my brain.

I still had my dagger strapped to my thigh, and I was in the same leather outfit I had had on before.

"We're ready," a voice said, but I couldn't tell who was around me because they all were covered head to toe in gear. I felt small and feeble next to them like one shove and I would break into a million pieces. Like I was ready to evaporate at any given moment—that would at least alleviate the pressure building in my bones.

We rose and rose and rose until sunlight burst around me. The roar was deafening.

I couldn't see. I was blinded for a second and then the spots danced away, and I was surrounded by thousands of people around the circular platform going wild.

On the platform, the President was smiling in front of a podium. Ky was standing off to the side, looking grim faced and worried. There were others in robes that looked like high school graduation robes, standing about looking pleased.

It felt like something was clawing to get out of me. I looked down at my belly, expecting a gaping wound, but nothing was there.

My ears were ringing. The President walked over to me with a glowing orb in his hand.

"Congratulations to our winner! Ms. Greer Roberts, the first ever mortal to be crowned the victor!" he boomed out. His shark-like teeth flashed a smile, and his gaze took in every inch of my body.

I wanted to throw up on him but instead I smiled sweetly.

I didn't think I was much of a mortal anymore.

"The gift of immortality and power is gifted to you on this victorious day," he held out the glowing ball of light for everyone to see and a hush fell over the crowd. He turned to me. He held one shoulder in his clawed hand and I tried not to wince. I looked at Ky. He tensed and gave me a little nod.

"I grant you, Ms. Roberts, the gift of forever and the power of the gods." He smiled again and slammed the ball of light right at my heart, and then—nothing.

I felt nothing.

Absolutely nothing.

The crowd went wild as he raised my hand in his. I smiled at the crowd in disbelief and then I was ushered back to the stage I'd floated in on. I whooshed back down again.

Was that it?

I didn't feel any different.

I looked at my hands and determined that I looked the same.

The tension in my body was still building to an excruciating pain. I was struggling to walk properly, and I *felt* too much.

My brain felt like it was moving too slow, words were not coming to my mouth very easily.

A second stage lowered down.

Kyra and the President were on it, with some others. I could hear them announcing the others who ranked in the top one hundred.

"Ms. Roberts, this way please," The President said, and the parade of people walked with him, including Kyra. I tried to turn my head to look at him. To say that something was wrong with me. With this. But words were still hard in my mouth.

"Don't worry, you can speak with your Ambassador shortly," he said, sneering down at me.

We opened up to a room that looked like a hospital. It had white tiled walls and there was a table angled for standing in the middle of the room. Random medical instruments were strewn around. People in lab coats were waiting and we all get ushered in.

What is this?

What is happening?

I wanted to scream the words, but my body was no longer mine. Everything felt foreign. Wrong.

I started to panic and frantically look around. Suddenly, Kyra was next to me and his hand was in mine. He wouldn't find me with his eyes. Instead, he looked straight at the President. Waiting.

The President made a great show of taking off his jacket and rolling up his sleeves as the Trial Lord, Edward, slinked in next to him.

"Immortality has never been given to a human," he said as he rolled up his sleeves. The guards dispersed to the outskirts of the room, leaving a few of the government officials to stand close to Ky and me.

"Fundamentally, your cells will be ripped apart and made new," he said, smiling sinisterly at me.

Was he actually enjoying this?

Maybe the process would alleviate the searing sensation across my skin and in my blood.

"It will be painful, but you did win after all … We couldn't have you screaming in front of the crowd now, could we?" he said and nodded at Kyra.

"Greer, you will not die. Do you understand? You have to accept the immortality, otherwise you will die. Your power will consume you," he whispered seriously as he pulled me into a hug.

What were the words coming out of his mouth?

"The power you have is time. The cage inside you that has kept it locked away is deteriorating. It will kill you unless you become immortal. I love you," he said and then guided me over to the standing table and strapped me in with metal cuffs on my wrists and ankles.

The power of time … Just like Xael had said. Did Kyra know something I didn't? Why hadn't he told me?

Why was I the only one who seemed to be completely and utterly lost?

I didn't know what was going on. My brain still felt like it was two steps behind. Like it was doing all it could to process all the information and hold my body together and it was too much.

A new orb appeared in the President's hand. It felt different. It was giving off power and something ancient.

I swallowed and whispered out barely audible, "I love you, Ky." Tears welled in his eyes.

The President sneered. "Let go of the dramatics. She will be fine, I'm sure."

The Trial Lord bristled next to him. "Get it done," he said in a clipped tone.

The President raised his hand and slammed the ball of light into my chest. I gasped, writhing in excruciating pain as the power ripped through me and every bone of mine felt like it broke then mended and then was broken again.

A blinding light engulfed me, and I felt two people on either side like they were keeping the two sides of my body from ripping apart.

I looked to the right through screams and it was my mom. Smiling. Holding my hand.

"Not much longer, Greer. You can do this sweetie," she whispered, and I felt the love, hope, fear, and sadness she had endured all at once. It sliced through me, cutting deep and settling in my bones with a seething heat. Marking its place in my body, forever.

On the left was the other woman again, Xael.

"I am so sorry, my child. I was only trying to help you. I cannot protect you from this pain or the next as time itself settles into your bones. Fight, Greer. You will not fail. The world needs you," she said, her hands wrapping around mine and sending soothing comfort through me.

It did little, as I felt the heat of a thousand suns burn me from the inside out and I howled in pain like every piece of me was being peeled off and then put back together again.

I screamed and threw my head back and thrashed side to side until I could no longer feel my body and I lay there limp twitching waiting to be rebuilt and then an overwhelming pressure began to build in my body once more like a balloon ready to pop and it felt like I exploded into a million pieces. I was put back together again. I convulsed once more and then I felt stronger. My muscles twitched, shooting pain, and then it slowed, ebbed. Until everything settled around me. I felt different.

More aware.

I snapped my eyes open.

I felt reborn.

Ky searched my face, and the President looked smug.

"See, a few moments of pain for eternal life?" He shrugged on his jacket, nodding to those around him, and they shuffled out until it was just the President, me, and Kyra.

"You will have a visitor shortly," he said, nodding his head to us, and then left. Kyra breathed a sigh of relief and suddenly Lux was there helping Kyra unstrap me from the standing table and holding my face in his.

"G, we need to leave. Things have gotten bad. We gotta get you outta here before the prison fully deteriorates," he said as I stepped forward, free of the shackles.

Prison? What was he talking about?

Kyra dragged me to him and crushed his lips to mine.

The door suddenly burst open and there was Nova, Waverly, and Sutton, looking panicked and scared.

"How long do we have?" Lux asked.

"We don't know … ten minutes?" Nova said, and she began to chant around us. Sutton's shadows started to swirl, and fire licked at Kyra's fingers.

"What's going on? What does everyone know that I don't?" I said, my voice rising higher, and then there was a crack like thunder and electricity filled the air.

Afton suddenly appeared in front of me. And I looked at the others to see if they could see him. They all looked past him, except Ky.

"Time to go, Greer," he said with a sinister smile, and he wrapped his hand around my arm.

Kyra whipped his arm out and growled, "You will not take her."

"Ah, yes, your father wishes you to come as well," he said, looking curiously at Kyra. "Time is of the essence."

Then there was a pop and I felt like my body was being pulled apart and back together again, and we were out of the room. Suddenly, I was strapped to another hospital bed in a large room that could only be described as some sort of throne room, but I couldn't move my head side to side because every inch of me was tethered to the bed.

I looked at the dome ceiling and gothic-like structure as black metal and silver steel wrapped around the ceiling, creating gruesome images of death in the worst ways possible. I tried to see anything more, but my forehead and neck were strapped down.

Words were hard again.

Why was none of my body working the way it was supposed to at any given time?

Kyra started screaming my name, and Afton hovered above me. He winked.

Then a beautiful woman smiled above me. She was glowing. She was the most beautiful woman I had ever seen with dark brown skin that glittered like a thousand suns and her eyes were beautiful pools of blue like a crystal-clear ocean. He black hair tumbled in waves around her, and when she smiled, I felt myself melt.

"Ah, our timewraith is ready…" she said melodically. She tsked softly. "Xael's spirit found you, I see … at the beginning of the last trial. Don't believe her lies. She was a useless goddess who was foolish and ignorant,"

That word again.

Timewraith.

She had said Xael … so she was real?

My head was fracturing again. Struggling to come to terms with what was happening to me. What people were saying. Who I was. Where I was.

"Your body will fight as time in its pure element is fused to every part of your being. We have prepared your body and mind and now it is your will that must propel you through. You will either come out whole or broken. I hope it is whole … You are no use to us if you are broken." She smiled and I melted some more at her touch. She placed her hands on my temples and whispered something soft and beautiful to me. Her touch was nice and warm. It made me feel beautiful, whole, and happy.

"The cage is now fully open, Xael could not protect you forever, little wraith…" she whispered.

I heard Kyra start screaming, and I couldn't imagine why with this magnificent woman in front of me. Didn't he feel the warmth that she gave? The security of her presence? And then something creaked open inside me. Small and tentative at first.

Then it exploded.

I thought I knew pain.

I did not.

My screams ripped through my throat and the darkness that always threatened to swallow me whole devoured every fiber of my being. Again. And again. And again.

After that, I only knew pain.

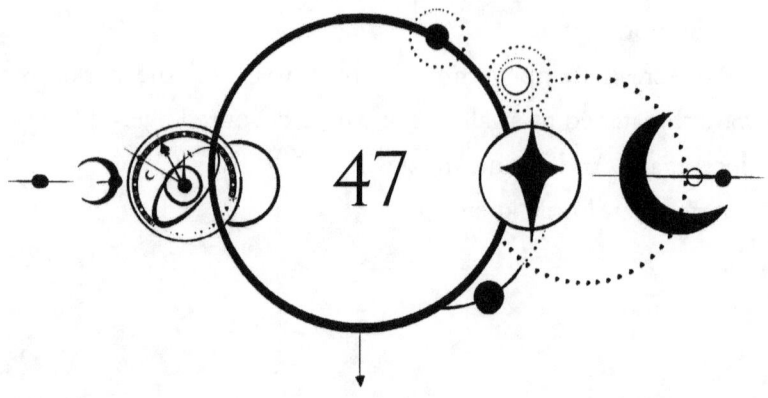

47

Kyra

How many times would I watch Greer be ripped apart? She writhed and hollered. Tears streamed down her face and her eyes would volley between opening in wild agony and shutting them so hard her whole face would scrunch up. Her body would shake, convulse and spasm and then lie so eerily still I thought my heart would stop.

Back arched and teeth bared, she would scream like her whole body was on fire and clutch the sheet beneath her, shredding it with her fingernails.

Energy, light, darkness would surge around her in whispers of smoke and be sucked back in, then violently pushed out again.

Sometimes there were sparks like lighting, and claps of thunder mixed with her cries.

Parts of her would expand and shimmer and become multidimensional, barely understood by my eyes, and then crack and snap like broken glass. Then she would look whole again to have the whole process repeated.

Over.

And over.

And over again.

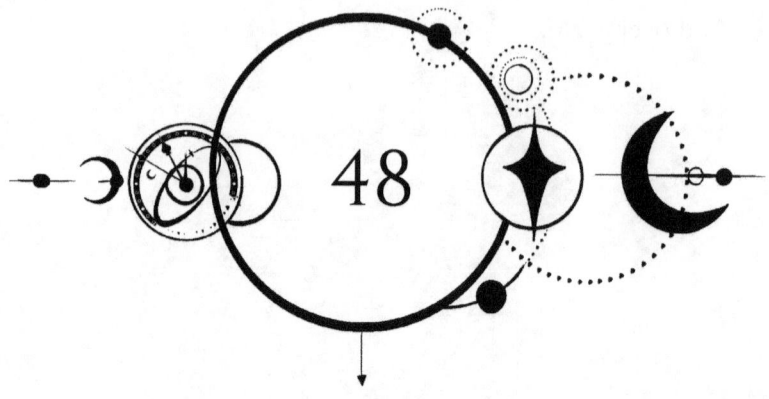

48

Greer

The darkness clawed and scraped at my mind.

My bones.

My soul.

Its claws dug deep and shredded my insides and then cradled the bits and pieces it had created and put them together with my own blood, sweat, and tears.

Only to do it again.

Each time expanding and breaking new parts and sewing them together like a makeshift doll, until my body was able to bend instead of break and welcome the caress of the beast within with open arms.

I sometimes would see flashes of my mother.

Lux.

My friends.

And Kyra.

Time seemed to stop and stand still, then blaze forth too fast that nausea would consume me.

I would wake in and out of pain induced sleep to see Kyra weeping over me.

Was he crying over my ruined body?

Of the shreds of skin and broken bones that I had become?

Was I sentenced to a special kind of hell?

I would try and reach for him, to tell him I was still here, that I wasn't dead yet.

But I couldn't.

Maybe it would be better if I died.

Maybe it would be better if the pain stopped.

If I could only rest.

And be free.

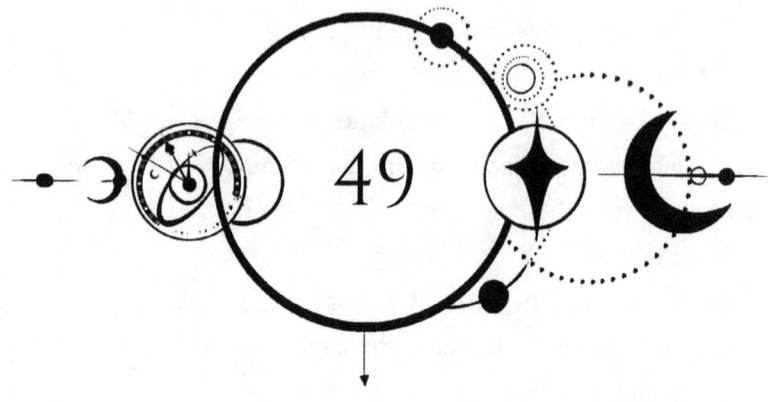

49

Kyra

Greer had been in and out of pain, waking up in delusions
with screams and jumbled words on her mouth for days
now.

I started to panic.

We had first landed in the throne room of my father and the
gods and goddesses present had watched in mild amusement and
indifference as Cerena, the goddess of nature itself, had unlocked
the prison that held Greer's powers at bay.

The throne room was exactly as expected.

Dark, moody, large cauldrons and fire bowls surrounded the
outside perimeter of the huge room. A large black metal throne sat
against the far wall with red glass stretching tall and broad behind
it, reflecting images of death. On either side of the throne were
smaller seats for honored guests, I supposed, as they had tables in
front of them with harsh gray stone and metal accents.

For the event of Greer and myself, there were plush black velvet couches sitting around where some of the gods and goddesses
were lazily drinking and picking at food that had been placed out. It

all screamed death, power, and masculinity with steel, stone, black metal, and fire.

Greer had been automatically strapped to a slab of stone like a sacrifice, with plush black silk cushions underneath her to separate her from the cold, hard stone. Her entire body had been strapped down so she could only look up. I could feel her fear. Her confusion was palpable.

I had been shoved to my knees mere feet away from her by my father, who stood tall and dark in his god form. Fire rippled off him in a dance of blue and red, coating his arms, legs, and the top of his hair. He was huge and broad with the fire dancing around his stone-gray skin and his scarlet eyes seemed to pierce through the room.

He held me down with his power as I screamed and thrashed to get to her and eventually I was subdued. They had tried to pull me away from her, but I had hollered and argued with them to let me stay by her side.

I tried calling my fire, my explosive power to me but it failed me, and my father had laughed in my face.

I had watched her be torn apart in that room for hours, unable to do a damn thing.

My father seemed to think it was quite amusing that I had fallen in love with the timewraith. But he had granted us a room where Greer was currently laying with her body restrained on black silk sheets in a monstrosity of a bed, her hair damp and matted to her forehead and her lips moving in something incoherent. They had moved her here after getting bored of her screams in the throne room.

I refused to leave her side as her powers coursed through Greer's new immortal body and manipulated it to the point of perfect execution and power.

It was absolutely revolting to watch as her powers turned her inside out and shoved itself into every part of her.

I had stayed by her side and demanded fresh clothes, damp towels for her fevers, wool blankets for her chills, water and food and anything else I could think of to help her body adjust quickly to all of time thrusting itself into her.

I had wrapped her in my arms and talked to her about the future plans I had and wept when her pale face had grown so ashen and her breath so shallow I thought I for sure had lost her.

I didn't know how much time had passed with us being here. It moved differently in the infernal and celestial realms. I had no way to contact the others in the mortal realm, and I refused to leave without Greer.

So after what felt like weeks, I sought out my father.

I took one last look at Greer spread-eagled on the bed in her restraints with one of my T-shirts on and my heart clenched. She was still. Her breathing was normal as of now, and she hadn't screamed since yesterday. But sometimes her breath would come in and out rapidly, then extreme stillness.

I wanted some damn answers.

I reached the door and flung it open to the throne room. The rooms, space, time, matter … it all worked very differently in the infernal and celestial realm.

"How much longer?" I demanded as I stormed into the throne room where my father and the goddess of the heavens and light, Phayre stood. The room was plain today. Just the throne and a table in the middle of the room with a few chairs, fireplaces lining the walls instead of cauldrons of flames.

Her blond hair flowed down to the ground, and she stood in a long white gown fit for a queen, with gold flecks and tattoos of constellations dotting her arms and her neck. A golden tiara was placed across her white as snow forehead, and her eyes looked like a clear blue sky with perfectly painted pink lips.

"Your son is quite taken with our wraith, Riordan. So interesting that he is here with our new pet," she purred, looking me up and down with her intense gaze.

I blinked at her, ignoring her comment, and turned my attention back to my father.

"How much longer will she suffer?" I snarled.

"One really cannot say … I assume soon. Then we will see if she survived the transformation," he said, shrugging his broad shoulders.

He took on the image of my adopted father today. He often did this when I was around to make me more "comfortable" but all it made me was angry and nauseous.

"Can you excuse us, dear Phayre? My son hasn't been taught proper manners..." he said, patting her hand and flashing a smile at her.

She nodded, and in an instant she was gone. Winked out of the room.

"Then what?" I demanded. "She is her own person, and I will not allow you to use her or harm her in any way," I said as fire licked my hands and my feet. The power flowed easily into me this time. I wondered before how it had been muted.

The anger at seeing the woman I loved tortured started to eat at my control.

I wanted this fight with my dad.

"You know, son … In the infernal realm, you can speak freely of your curse. In fact, I will allow you to speak of it freely in all realms now." He snapped his fingers and smiled slowly. I felt invisible chains on my body and my heart fall away.

"Stop throwing your temper tantrum. See, I rewarded you." He looked genuinely pleased with himself.

I wanted to light his dark hair on fire right now. But at least now I would have the chance to explain to Greer what I could never say before.

"Am I supposed to say thank you?" I roared and then I started laughing darkly.

"Thank you, *Father,* for the fucking curse I never wanted and for kidnapping and holding the women I love hostage," I snarled and stalked toward him with fire snaking up my arms and legs.

My father simply looked amused in his all black suit.

I wanted to wipe that look off his face.

"Son, all of this was predestined and prophesied long ago. This has been in place for thousands of years before either of you were born … I did what I needed to do and I don't regret it," he said confidently, waving off my anger.

Then he cocked an eyebrow.

"Looks like someone got out of their restraints," he said, gazing past me toward where Greer was standing underneath the black stone arch of the room, looking toward me with steel in her eyes. A heavy black door had materialized and disappeared right behind her as she had stepped through.

"Greer," I said, moving toward her and holding her face in my hands and kissing her forehead lightly.

She went rigid underneath my touch.

"We need to leave," she whispered hurriedly, panic hitching in her voice.

Except we couldn't.

I knew there was no way for us to leave right now—my father would never allow it.

I didn't know how to leave either. The only place I had been was wherever the door to our room led us, which was either the throne room or the bathroom.

"You can't, dear…" my dad said in a sickeningly sweet voice. "You just got here!" He laughed joyously.

"Where are we?" Greer asked, crossing her arms over her chest and standing straight, then she reached for my hand. I intertwined my fingers in hers.

"Welcome to Hell, my dear. And I am the King. King Riordan of the Underworld and you have become our new favorite pet. You've already met my son, Kyra," he said wickedly. "We have been waiting for you for quite some time."

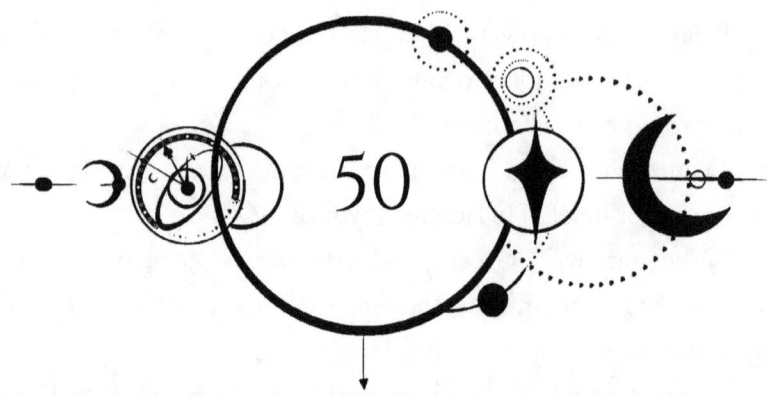

50

Greer

My mouth hung wide open when the King of Hell himself just told me that I was in hell. With him. And Kyra. And Kyra was his son ...

My heart cracked and started to break in two. He had lied to me. About his parents. About his past. Probably about loving me. It slammed into my chest and my gut like a ton of bricks.

I snatched my hand away and backed away. Kyra looked hurt and concerned. I couldn't look at those eyes. My heart was ripping apart.

I was truly alone here with no help, no allies.

Suddenly, the room filled with others I didn't recognize, and I turned to run. Kyra reached for me, but I couldn't be here. I needed to be anywhere but here. Iron manacles were slapped to my wrists and feet in a flash, a collar strapped around my throat.

I remembered how Xael had looked. Bloody, broken, and cracked with what I could only imagine was similar treatment.

I was slammed to my knees as the iron reached up from the floor and vaulted me down.

Kyra fell down next to me with irons as well. He snarled and blazed fire with his hands but the iron did not burn or melt. He howled in pain as it heated and singed his skin, transferring the magic to his own body.

I was frozen. I didn't know who to believe. What to trust and what Kyra was anymore.

"What do you want?" I said, frantically looking at the people around me as they all glowed and oozed power, strength, and legacy.

A woman stepped forward with flowing blond hair and deep sky-blue eyes.

"Hmmm … You look just like her," she said, trailing her fingertips across my jaw, and I snapped at them with my teeth. She laughed, delighted, and forcibly grabbed my chin and pressed into my skin hard enough to leave bruises.

"You belong to us, little wraith. The power of time flows through your veins, your bones, and every fiber of your being. You will help us reclaim the mortal realm in our image once more. With you … We are unstoppable, the prophecy has said as much. And now we can give and take away time at will. You will be the key to our success. Only the worthy and loyal will stand with us and you will drink the blood of those who dare to fight against us.

We are ready to claim what has always been ours. The gods and goddesses will rule once more and we need you, timewraith, to do so. Xael betrayed us, for mortals … She wanted to share her power with all of you. Instead, she doomed you. We made sure of it. But she was a clever wretch. She knew we wouldn't be able to reclaim the mortal realm without her power, so she doomed another mortal. But instead of saving you she pushed you right into our hands.

You are ours, timewraith, and you will pay for the sins of Xael, and your worthless mortal brothers and sisters, by being the one who brings them to their knees," she said lovingly, as if she was telling me a bedtime story or praising me for doing something well. "You survived the Trials and tribulations we have gifted you. Your mother's death, your weak body, your vulnerable mind, your pathetic heart, your fears, your own morality ... You have now been rewarded with great power and strength because of us.

Xael was never strong enough to oppose all of us and we knew we would need to break her descendant the way we broke her."

The punches to the gut kept coming and coming, and with each word, I felt a slash of pain in my heart and across my body that left gnashing wounds that would fester and infect with hatred and anguish.

I didn't want to be a part of this.

I refused to be used and manipulated.

I didn't sign up for this.

I scanned the faces around me. Some had more human-like forms others didn't. Some were blurry and switching rapidly, like light reflected in water. But they all had hunger, power and arrogance in their eyes.

I looked into the depths of my being and realized I was different.

The darkness within was now a part of me as much as my skin or hair was. It enhanced me. It built me. It called to me.

I looked down at my hands and remembered I had paused time by Afton simply touching me. Without thinking, I reached for Kyra and my manacles snapped my hand back. I cursed. He betrayed me. My body called to him, but he had used me. He had *lied* to me.

"Tsk, tsk, you will learn..." the woman said.

"Because in this world, timewraith, you only answer to us. Xael had to be put down, but we will keep you and use you and groom you to be one of us..." she said, smiling at me, the new pet.

"My son played a nice role in this…" the King of Hell said, looking at Kyra, who was struggling to keep his focus through the burns on his hands and feet.

I gaped at him, terror racing through my veins.

I cracked open fully at those words. So Kyra had used me. It was the most fatal blow of it all.

"No," I whispered, finally finding words. Kyra was gritting his teeth and defeat lay in his eyes.

Panic filled my lungs and choked out my words. Maybe if I denied it, it wouldn't be real. Maybe this was a joke. Maybe my heart wasn't being crushed and ripped apart in this new body of mine.

But the stabs in my heart and punches to my belly of being betrayed by the man I love was worse than anything physical I had just endured, and I saw the truth in his eyes.

"Greer, I can explain…" Kyra pleaded, and I felt the power beneath my new skin sizzle and snap.

"You lied to me! And used me!" I screamed, shaking my chains as tears tumbled out of my eyes.

"I didn't know about any of this!" he exclaimed, tears rolling down his face.

"The Prince of Hell himself was kept in the dark?" I said, almost laughing. I should have believed in the gods before.

I should have believed that this nightmare was something I would never wake up from.

I could feel the world around me like a sixth sense, the seconds ticking by.

"Yes!" Kyra exclaimed, and it looked like he really believed it.

But he had not denied that he was the prince. That he was the son of the gods and goddesses planning to take over the mortal realm and destroy those who were not worthy.

As if I could trust anything he said after he had kept such a se-cret. The ocean of emotions that had been kept at bay since I start-ed the trial were bubbling up, charged by the release of my powers and the new sense of immortality, and I wanted to let it go. I want-ed to drown in the betrayal, the tears, the pain, all of it.

"You pretended to love me?"

It was selfish and feebly unimportant in the face of the mortal world ending at my own hands, but I had to ask.

"I *still* love you, Greer!" Kyra practically screamed, but it was too late. Love wasn't enough to overcome such a betrayal.

I yelled and the world around me stood still. A large pop and stillness filled the space. Silence filled except for my screams. Time had frozen with the gods and goddesses looking at me. Kyra looked defeated and dejected in chains beside me.

I couldn't trust anyone.

I didn't know what to do.

So I let the wave crash over me and drown me until I circled up on the floor, shackled in iron, and wept.

Wept for hours, for days…

I wasn't sure.

Time eluded me and froze until I could come out stronger.

Until my body no longer shook with sobs and trembled in grief.

Until I could lie still and my will turned to steel.

I let it flood me again and again until I was stronger.

And I knew because immortality ran through their veins, they saw me weep. They could not manipulate time, but they observed. I let them see the broken girl who had lost her mother, who had suf-fered heartbreak, who had been stripped of her humanity and bro-ken to pieces, who had been taken advantage of and was naive enough to think she could run from what I always knew lay inside.

I grieved that version of myself, and the one who loved Kyra, and built up my own steel cage. I fortified it with my anger and my sorrow. I was the one who held the key this time. My tears made it stronger until I had nothing else to give.

But it would be the last time.

I would no longer shed tears for the girl I was. There was only space for the girl that was created.

So I would play their game. Until I could escape.

Hell and the gods could kiss my fucking ass. Because they made a mistake … I would be no one's pet. I would not be controlled. I would become a weapon of my own creation.

And I would no longer be weak and overtaken.

The mortal realm was mine.

I would get back to my world, and damn the gods once and for all.

ACKNOWLEDGMENTS

Wow, this has been an incredible journey. There are so many people who made this possible.

Thank you to my beta readers: Cushman, Regan, and Rachael. I was scared shitless to send the first draft to you, and I appreciate your patience and kindness with the messiness of the story at the beginning.

Regan, you rule for being my sister and always letting me spill the beans on the whole story to you so I could get it out of my face.

I absolutely need to thank my parents for being an incredible support system and providing me with all I needed on this journey. For all the hours where I needed to be holed up writing, and you checked if I had food and sunlight. I love you so much.

My amazing friends, you know who you are for championing me to follow this dream.

Thank you to my amazing editor, Emily, who provided the polishing and validation that I needed through this process.

Thank you to my formatter Jordyn, you made this a beautiful visual work of art.

Thank you to my sweet little girl, Brúlee, who snuggled up with me on the couch and provided the best puppy support.

Thank you to my partner, Logan, who pushed me to do the damn thing and never stopped believing that I would be published.

Thank you to all my followers and fellow authors on booktok. You all literally saved my life so many times when I had no idea what I was doing. You helped me on the days that overwhelm threatened to collapse my dream.

Thank you to my booktok fairy godmother, Sydney for answering all my questions.

Thank you to the random precious author friend that I met at a Halloween party who told me I should just self-publish and then I did.

And finally for those of you who will read this story. I am grateful to each and every one of you. I can't believe that I get to share my story with you.

AUTHOR'S NOTES

This story fell into my head during a time where I was so unsure of who I was and the purpose I had in this life. I felt untethered and ungrounded. But then I began to put pen to paper as I unwrapped this beautiful story that had come in a perfect package for my soul.

During this time, I struggled with depression, my own "coming out" story at the age of twenty-four, finding my purpose, and so much more. I needed to give myself permission to heal through creativity. Something I had denied myself for quite some time. This book represents so much of that journey.

I have been in love with reading for as long as I can remember, and I never dreamed that I would write something like some of my favorite authors.

I am excited to see where this journey takes me, and I am so incredibly proud and honored to share my first book with you all.

And a message for those who are feeling like they don't know where they fit into life. You have everything you need within you. Be brave. Listen to yourself and trust that you will find your way.

You will not fail.

If you want to stay updated on all the new book things you can see my updated shenanigans here:

TikTok & Instagram: @madisonnicolebooks

Website: www.madisonnicolebooks.com

If you want to share your thoughts and feelings about "The Immortality Trials" please share a review or send an email to info@madisonnicolebooks.com. I welcome all feedback and would love to hear from you!

About the Author

Madison Nicole is a 26-year-old new author who currently lives in Kansas City, Missouri where she teaches yoga and group fitness full time. You can catch Madi playing video games, reading fantasy romance books and practicing aerial arts when she is not writing or working her day job. Her favorite indulgences include iced coffee, tequila and dark chocolate. She is excited to continue to explore her writing career and bring more fun stories your way!